Praise for *The Bride o*

With amazingly vivid description and her signature humor, Michelle Griep delivers another action-packed tale set in Victorian London. In *The Bride of Blackfriars Lane*, Jackson and Kit face nonstop danger as they unravel conflicting clues to solve several mysteries. . .including how to rescue their own romance when the obstacles between them mount.

—Julie Klassen, author of *Shadows of Swanford Abbey*

Suspense, mystery, romance, and a frolicking good story! Ms. Griep displays her true talent with a tale that spins a web of intrigue on the streets of historic London that will keep you guessing at every turn. Add to that a host of fascinating characters, along with well-researched historical detail, and you will feel as though you walked the streets of London in 1885. A fun love story and an endearing end complete this masterpiece you won't want to miss.

—MaryLu Tyndall, author of the
Legacy of the King's Pirates Series

Filled with romance, mystery, and the spirit of adventure, *The Bride of Blackfriars Lane* is a page-turning jaunt through the streets of Victorian London. A story not to be missed!

—Mimi Matthews, *USA Today* bestselling
author of *The Siren of Sussex*

Witty and adventurous, this is Griep at her best! The banter between the main characters has continued in this second installment of the Blackfriars Lane series, but the stakes are higher and the danger greater. I kept flipping pages late into the night, desperate for the resolution, yet wondering, as the danger mounted, how the characters could possibly pull it off. A top storyteller brings readers a clever, suspenseful, thoroughly engrossing adventure of a book.

—Joanna Davidson Politano, author of *A Midnight Dance*
and other historical mysteries

Kit and Jackson are up to their old shenanigans in *The Bride of Blackfriars Lane*, only this time, the price they pay for risking it all may be their love! I almost couldn't keep up with the action packed into this book. I was never so happy to keep turning pages. Could NOT put this one down!

—Elizabeth Ludwig, *USA Today* bestselling author and speaker

Michelle Griep has done it again! Hold on to your bowlers for a rip-roaring adventure from the first page to the last. Between Kit and Jackson, there is enough wit, grit, and charm to keep readers dashing through alleys, rag piles, Reptiliums, docks, and more right alongside this explosive duo. And yet behind the action, depth of character and timeless insight anchor *The Bride of Blackfriars Lane* firmly in the heart.

—Jocelyn Green, Christy Award-winning
author of *Drawn by the Current*

With heart-pounding suspense and a dash of romance, Michelle Griep once again dazzles with *The Bride of Blackfriars Lane*. Not only did Jackson and Kit pull me into their heart-pounding adventure, they taught me the power of trusting an unknown past to an all-powerful God.

—Tara Johnson, author of *All Through the Night*,
Where Dandelions Bloom, and *Engraved on the Heart*

Griep has launched herself to the top of my favorite authors list! This adventurous tale had me grinning, on the edge-of-my-seat, and yelling at the characters as I stayed up entirely too late because I simply couldn't put it down. I will eagerly await her next book, but until then Kit and Jackson's enchanting story will stick with me for a long time.

—Kimberley Woodhouse, bestselling and award-winning author of
A Deep Divide, Ever Constant, Bridge of Gold, and many others.

Kit and Jackson are back, and the sparks are still flying! As their wedding nears, however, all seems to conspire against them—just one more thing to see to, one more decision to make, one last question about their commitment. Will either of them make it to the church on time? As usual, Griep does not disappoint!

—Shannon McNear, 2014 RITA® finalist, 2021 SELAH winner,
and author of *Elinor* and *Mary* (Daughters of the Lost Colony)

THE BRIDE OF BLACKFRIARS LANE

MICHELLE GRIEP

BARBOUR
PUBLISHING

Print ISBN 978-1-63609-268-3

Adobe Digital Edition (.epub) 978-1-63609-270-6

Cover Design: Kirk DuPonce, DogEared Design

Published in association with the Books & Such Literary Management, 52 Mission Circle, Suite 122, PMB 170, Santa Rosa, CA 95409-5370, www.booksandsuch.com.

Published by Barbour Publishing, Inc., 1810 Barbour Drive, Uhrichsville, Ohio 44683, www.barbourbooks.com

Our mission is to inspire the world with the life-changing message of the Bible.

Printed in the United States of America.

Dedication

Hats off to
Julie Klassen and Erica Vetsch,
my two historical partners-in-crime.
And as always,
to the One who redeems me
from crimes of my own making.

Chapter One

London 1885

September afternoons were meant for soft whispers and stolen kisses, not ash and soot and the gangrenous eye of a ruthless taskmaster. Yet here he was. Somehow cajoled into hours of sweat and toil by the blue-eyed beguiler next to him. Sighing, Jackson Forge jammed the shovel into the hill of waste and hefted out another great heap of black dust and refuse. Kit Turner could talk a bandy-legged pirate into donning a white robe and joining a cathedral choir, such was her silver tongue—just one of the many reasons he admired the fiery woman. Who would have guessed the streetwise imp he'd once thought a thief would soon be his bride?

With half a grin, Jackson dumped his load into the wooden-framed sieve Kit held out, his eyes lingering on her. Even in a ragged blue gown and threadbare shawl, more coal-smudged than fresh-faced, she was a raven-haired beauty.

He leaned on his shovel. "We've found nothing but rags, bones, and oyster shells. Aren't you ready to call it quits?"

She rested the sieve against her hip, a jaunty tilt to her head. "I am no quitter, sir, or I'd have given up on a certain raw recruit of a constable last spring."

He tossed back his shoulders. "You mean the constable who is now an inspector?"

"The very same."

His grin grew. "So, you *do* love me, then."

She glanced over her shoulder at the hillwoman—the supervisor who'd been nipping at them all day—then edged a step closer. "I'd love you more if you'd stop harping about my so-called misbegotten scheme of working incognito in a dust yard."

"Ahh, but you see, my love, I am no quitter either." He winked. "Still, as I said and will continue to say, we'll gain better evidence on the stolen goods if we give Sir Culpepper's staff another round of interviews. Someone will crack under pressure, I am sure of it."

"A waste of time, my sweet. We already have solid evidence. When we were at Skaggs's, you saw as well as I did the black dust inside the bottom of the stolen candlesticks. That could only have gotten there if they had been hidden in a pile such as this." She swept her free hand towards the head-high mound of rubbish in front of them.

"Maybe." He scratched his jaw, probably adding a good amount of grime to his face, but so be it. "I still say questioning the staff would have sent someone skittish and given away the guilty thief."

"And *I* still say the true thief isn't the chambermaid or the hall boy who disposed of the stolen goods via the dustbin. They are but small fish. Granted, we could net the minnow who no doubt was coerced into compliance, yet it's the carp who ought to be landed and gutted. Would you not agree, dearest?"

He gripped his shovel all the tighter. She had him there, and the little vixen knew it. Silver tongue, indeed.

"So"—her lips curled into an indicting smile—"the gentleman concedes, does he?"

"The gentleman concedes to nothing but wishing he could steal away to that corner over there"—he tipped his head at a shadowy cleft between a row of barrels—"and kiss that smug grin off your face."

She arched a brow. "I'd like to see you try, sir."

"Oh, would you, now?" He lunged towards her.

"Jackson, no!" she whisper-screamed. "You'll get us dismissed."

"A triumph upon triumph." With a waggle of his eyebrows, he jammed the shovel into the pile—and the tip clinked against something metal.

Instantly, they dropped in unison to dig through the mess, a race to see who would come out the victor. His fingers bumped into something hard, and after more scratching, he pulled out a very dirty and now slightly dented gravy boat. He brushed away the soil then blew off the bottom. Squinting, he examined the hallmark stamped into the metal. A crown, designating it a Sheffield piece—an exact match to the dessert stand they'd already recovered from the pawnbroker along with the candlesticks. This belonged to Sir Culpepper, all right.

"Well?" Kit asked.

Lowering it, he nodded.

"I knew it! I told you I was on to something." She shoved back a rogue hank of hair from her eyes. "Sometimes it takes a swindler to catch one."

His brows rose. "Admitting to thievery, are you?"

"The only thing I admit to is loving a certain greasy-faced dust picker, who I'd very much like to—" Her nose bunched, all rabbity and quite adorable as she sniffed. "Never mind. You need a bath, sir." She stood, wiping her palms on her apron. "Now, shall we see where that bait leads?"

"Kipes! Found a beauty, did ye?"

They both turned their heads at the approach of a stringy-haired old man, more gristle than meat. He elbowed Jackson in the ribs. "Tucked me away a silver napkin ring jes' last week. Best hide yours a'fore that lot sees it." He jutted his jaw at the hillwoman and the foreman, who huddled in conversation across the filthy courtyard. "Sackett slips plenty away these days and that's fer certain."

Even though there was no danger of the sun glinting off such tarnished metal, Jackson angled a bit, effectively blocking the gravy boat from their line of sight. "How often are things like this found?"

"Used ta be hardly ever." The old fellow shifted his shovel from one hand to the other. "But there's been a real boom in pretties since the first o' the month."

Kit arched a brow at Jackson. "Which would be when that housemaid was hired."

Jackson nodded. If—as Kit suggested—that maid had been pilfering items and tossing them in the dustbin, who was collecting them here and hawking them to Skaggs? Clearly not the ancient duffer in front of him. Perhaps one of the other pickers? But they'd have no sway over a housemaid to coerce her to partake in such a deed.

He rubbed the back of his neck, working out the knot from so much shoveling. It had to be someone higher up at Dedfield's Dust Yard—either a relative of the maid or someone who'd blackmailed her into disposing the Culpeppers' valuables.

He faced the old man. "You said you saw Sackett taking something?"

"What's good enough fer that goose is good enough fer this gander." He wagged his finger at Jackson and Kit. "But ye din't hear nothin' from me, aye?"

"Not one blowsy babble." Kit grinned.

"Back to work, ye sloggin' luggards! Yer paid to sift dust, not flap yer tongues." Hillwoman billowed across the yard, a storm cloud in a pewter-grey apron.

The old man skittered away on surprisingly nimble legs, and before Jackson could tuck the gravy boat beneath his coat, Kit snatched it from his grasp and held it out to the woman.

"There are buckets for bones, rags, rocks, and glass, but where is the bucket for a plum gimcrack like this?" she asked sweetly.

Jackson gaped. There were times he loved this woman so much, it ached to the marrow. Other times—like this—he'd like nothing better than to grab her shoulders and shake some sense into her. What was she about?

Hillwoman shot out her meaty hand without batting an eyelash. "Sackett will be wantin' that, missy. Give it to me."

"What, and let you collect the prize penny for turnin' over this gem?" Clutching the gravy boat to her chest, Kit narrowed her eyes at the woman. "Unless yer keeping this fer yerself, and maybe have been doing so these past few weeks. A little side business, eh? Bypassing the foreman and fillin' yer own pocket?"

"Yer fired, missy." The woman's jaw sharpened to a flinty edge. "Now, gimme the piece."

Jackson sighed. Kit's recklessness would ruin this whole operation. He stepped next to her and donned his most contrite smile—though with the amount of grime on his face, he doubted the effect would hold much sway. "Our pardon, madam. I fear the value of this piece has quite bedazzled my friend here. The lady and I have no idea how common it is to find treasures such as this nor where to put them when found."

"Well, well. . .ain't you a butter-mouthed gent? Hmph. Don't look it." The woman's upper lip curled. "But to set ye straight, 'tis right rare to find such trinkets, 'ceptin' for the last fortnight. But that's no never mind. Whenever treasures are found, I take 'em to Sackett, as I'm told." Her gaze skewered Kit. "My prize penny is my job, something ye'll be doin' without. Now hand over that dainty and leave yer man with the pretty words behind. He can stay, but I'm done with ye."

"There a problem here, Betty?"

They all turned towards the bass voice thundering at their backs. The foreman, Mr. Sackett, advanced, his yellowed teeth peeking through a thick gap where his lips didn't quite meet. Either the man had been walloped a good one by a sledgehammer to the side of the head, permanently knocking his jaw off center, or he was a perpetual mouth-breather.

"Aye, there be a problem." Hillwoman pointed a fleshy finger at Kit. "This kipper here's snagged a silver and won't hand it over."

"I'll deal with her. Better you should get that mess o' bones cleaned up where the broken cart dumped a load." He hitched his thumb over his shoulder. "Take a few men off barrel rolling to see it done—be quick. Dedfield's due any minute."

With a last accusing look at Kit, the hillwoman dipped her head. "Aye, Mr. Sackett."

She scurried away as the foreman shoved his open palm towards Kit. "Everything in the piles belongs to Dedfield, so give me that bauble now or I'll see ye arrested for thievery."

Without even slipping her a glance, Jackson knew Kit bristled like a cornered hedgehog. The foreman would get nowhere with threats, and in fact would only froth her up all the more. Jackson stepped beside her, breathing out a low "Steady on" for her ears, then said louder to the foreman, "If the owner is on his way to the yard right now, ought not the lady give the item directly to him? After all, as you've rightly indicated, this is Dedfield's yard."

"That ain't no lady, and I din't ask you," Sackett barked, turning on him like a mad dog. "Back to work!"

Kit's chest puffed out as she inched in front of Jackson. She planted her feet in a fighting stance. He hid a smile. Did the spirited little imp really think to protect him?

"Whyn't ye show me where the pile is, Mr. Sackett?" She held up the gravy boat. "I'll gladly leave this lovely there, safe and sound."

Jackson frowned. Why did she keep flashing that piece of silver so boldly? What plan could she possibly have in that head of hers?

"I've not the time for this." Sackett made a swipe for her arm.

Kit pivoted, keeping the gravy boat just out of his reach. "Yer in a hurry to get your paws on this gem. I wonder why. Don't want Mr. Dedfield to know about such finds? Been kipin' a side piece now and then, have ye?" Her chin lifted, almost imperceptibly, but enough that were the man smart, he'd start backing off. "Or is it ye've not just been shovin' away pieces but knittin' together the whole operation? Perhaps, sir," her tone changed, all hint of street slang disappearing, "it is I who ought to see you arrested for thievery."

"Ye snipin' little gutter rat!" he roared. "Gimme that!"

"Mr. Sackett." Jackson flashed the foreman a smile, but it did nothing to loosen the deep sneer baring even more of the man's teeth. "I suggest we talk this over with Mr. Dedfield when he arrives and find out if your records of the past two weeks match what we've been told has been uncovered in these piles."

"What would ye know about business that ain't any o' yers? Ye just started today—and ye just finished." His arm shot out like an arrow from a crossbow, one beefy finger dead-aimed on the front gate. "Go!"

"Gladly, right after we have a discussion with the owner." Reaching inside his coat, Jackson retrieved his inspector badge—which really ought to be on his hat, but if he'd learned anything at all from Kit, improvisation and theatrics were sometimes key. "I think Mr. Dedfield might be interested to know what's going on in his yard, and you're the one who's going to tell him."

By now, a semi-ring of pile pickers gawked at them. Sackett's dark eyes skimmed the workers, and one by one, they backed away. He lowered his voice to a murderous tone, the black gleam in his eyes no less deadly as he speared Kit and Jackson with a lethal stare. "You have no idea what yer dealin' with, mates."

Kit didn't waver. Not a bit. "Then enlighten us, Mr. Sackett."

"As the lady says." Jackson advanced a step. "Why don't you tell us exactly—"

Sackett sprang, planting his hands in Jackson's chest. Jackson flew backwards and crashed into the rubbish pile. An avalanche of black dust fell on his head. Sputtering for air, he fought to breathe while shoving to his feet. Grit coated his eyes, his lungs, the world, but it didn't hinder his hearing.

Metal cracked against bone.

Sackett howled.

Curses rained.

Kit let out a cry.

By the time he rubbed the last of the grime from his eyes, Kit lay on the ground cradling her wrist and Sackett's heels kicked up gravel, the gravy boat now in his hands.

"Kit!" Jackson reached for her.

"I'm fine," she huffed. "Get him!"

As much as he'd like to sweep her up in his arms and see for himself she really was fine, he turned and sprinted. He'd not hear the end of it if he let Sackett get away from her or from the chief. Swiping up a broken chunk of brick, he winged it at the foreman's head—and missed.

Sackett kept running.

So did Jackson.

"Here!" The old man held out a sieve as he flew by.

Grabbing it, he flung the round disc, this time catching Sackett in the back. The man stumbled, slowing just enough for Jackson to snatch a nearby basket of rags and bowl it like the wild chuck of a nine-pin ball. The basket hit the bend of his knees, buckling Sackett's legs. Arms flailing, he teetered in a crazed dance to remain upright. . . which he would have if not for the bones strewn all over the dirt from the broken cart. His feet slipped. Sackett tipped.

Jackson tore ahead and tackled the big man, riding him to the ground. An instant before landing, though, Sackett twisted and caught him in the gut with a sharp elbow.

Grunting, Jackson scrambled for a better hold. Boxing was a gentleman's sport, one he much preferred to this wrestling match. If he could just land a good one! Fisting his hand, he struck.

The blow glanced off the back of Sackett's rock-hard head. With a roar, he flipped, his other elbow swinging hard and smashing Jackson's nose.

Hot blood trickled over his lips. Hotter blood boiled in his veins. "Give it up, man! Hand over that gravy boat."

With a great spew of curses and burst of brute strength, Sackett rolled, pulling Jackson along with him. Not good. Now the ugly lout was on top—and the man outweighed him by at least three stone.

The foreman's dark eyes burned like embers. "Ye should've let me go when ye had the chance, mate."

Sackett raised an arm the size of a beam, and before Jackson could wrench away, the solid metal gravy boat plummeted towards his head.

Chapter Two

There were two things Kit couldn't abide. No, three. A slicer of a hangnail. The sharp yip of a Yorkshire terrier. And most of all, she could not—*would* not—stand for any harm inflicted on someone she cared about. Especially not the man she loved more than life.

Ignoring her aching wrist, she snatched up a bucket of slop water, greasy with fat and reeking of decay, and pitched the foul liquid full into the face of the foreman.

Mr. Sackett spluttered, just enough to knock his swing off-kilter. The gravy boat slammed into Jackson's cheek instead of his temple. Flesh split, but at least his skull remained whole.

In a flash, Jackson grasped a discarded knuckle bone the size of a small melon and struck back. The foreman's head snapped sideways. Jackson wrenched the other direction, breaking free of the man's hold. Both staggered to their feet, Sackett spitting curses, Jackson spitting blood. Dropping to a crouch, they crept in a slow death circle.

"Give it up, Sackett." Jackson hefted his knuckle bone.

The foreman wielded the gravy boat. "Not to the likes o' you."

A chain of whispers passed from worker to worker, catching Kit's ear.

"*Dedfield's on his way.*"

"*He's gonna pop a cork, he is!*"

"*Give this lot some space. Don't wanna get lit when the sparks start a'flyin'.*"

For an instant, Mr. Sackett froze.

Then he pivoted and sprang out the gate.

Jackson sprinted after him. So did Kit, flying through the entrance just in time to see Jackson fling the bone towards the foreman. A sickening thud followed. Mr. Sackett wobbled on drunken steps, then face-planted onto the cobbles, still as a statue.

Kit grinned at her bloody-nosed, blue-eyed hero. "You did it!"

He grinned back, swiping away blood from his upper lip. "I always get my man, eventually."

"And for such a confession, sir," a voice boomed behind them, "I shall have you arrested posthaste."

They turned in unison to face a pockmarked fellow sporting bushy red muttonchops that were so outrageously large, his eyes, nose, and mouth were naught but pinholes. Save for his devil-may-care facial hair, the rest of him was straight-lined business, from the tips of his Italian leather shoes to the bespoke cut of his immaculate black suit. In one hand, he carried a walking stick with an ivory head. In the other, a brief bag.

Mr. Dedfield. The owner of the dust yard.

She'd bet on it.

Kit hitched her thumb over her shoulder at the sprawled foreman. "The real criminal is already apprehended, Mr. Dedfield. Or at least he will be." She blinked innocently up at Jackson. "You can manage the rest, hmm?"

"Manage the rest of what?" Mr. Dedfield rapped the tip of his cane against the pavement. "What is going on here? Why is my foreman laid out like a Turkish doormat?"

"Inspector Jackson Forge, sir, at your service." Jackson palmed his badge in front of the man's face. "I regret to inform you that your foreman, Mr. Sackett, had a bit of a side business running beneath your nose."

"What do you mean?" Though the words were dressed in the trappings of a question, the man's tone implied it was a you'd-better-explain-yourself-this-instant sort of demand.

Jackson patted Kit on the back. "My partner here will elaborate while I secure the perpetrator."

He trotted off, leaving her alone with the suddenly slack-jawed businessman.

Mr. Dedfield turned disbelieving eyes on her. "Do not tell me you are in service to the constabulary?"

"Pish! They haven't intelligence enough to hire a woman." She flashed a smile, the jest entirely on him. If he—or men like him—knew of her under-the-table relationship with the police, there would be public outrage. "But I am sure you can see the need for Mr. Forge to partner with a woman as part of his disguise. Makes for a more believable front, as shown by our work here. Your trusted employee—Mr. Sackett—had quite the dodge going with an associate in service at a household in the West End. This associate—likely a housemaid—tossed valuables into the dustbin, and they ended up here, where your foreman sold the items off-market for his gain."

Mr. Dedfield shook his head, a whiff of a breeze ruffling the red curls of his chops. "I can hardly believe such a tale."

"Here is the evidence." Jackson trotted up, holding out the gravy boat. "Sackett was making off with this piece I uncovered in one of your piles."

"Is that so?" Mr. Dedfield's small eyes widened. "Well, well. Good work, Inspector Forge. Bring the man to my office if you will." He turned on his heel.

Kit cocked her head. He didn't think to enact his own sort of justice. . .did he?

Jackson frowned at the man's retreating back. "I will take Mr. Sackett to the station as is customary, Mr. Dedfield."

The walking stick hit hard on the cobbles as the man wheeled about. His face was a mask, cold as steel and just as hard. "There is nothing customary about robbing my property. This is an internal matter, and I have my own ways of meting out justice. I assure you Mr. Sackett will pay for his crime."

Kit pursed her lips. While she was no admirer of the rough-and-tumble foreman, neither did she wish to see his corpse at the dead house, and judging by the sharp glint in Mr. Dedfield's eyes, that's exactly the fate Sackett would suffer. "This is a matter of law, sir, not of vengeance."

He sneered at her as if she were no more than a splotch of manure on his shoe. "If the guilty party is punished," he said through clenched teeth, "then no matter who delivers the penalty, the rule of law has been served."

"The rule of law *will* be served in front of a magistrate." Jackson's tone left no room for debate. "If you like, I shall get word to you of the date and time of Sackett's hearing. Until then, good day." He dipped his head.

A flush spread like a bruise over Mr. Dedfield's face, nearly matching the deep red of his whiskers. Had the man never before been told no?

"Good day, Inspector Forge." Jackson's name lingered like a threat while Mr. Dedfield's gaze drifted to her. "And good day to you as well, Miss. . . ?"

"Turner." She lifted her chin, refusing to be cowed by the imperious look in his eyes.

Without another word, Mr. Dedfield disappeared through the dust yard gate. Behind them, a groan ground out roughly.

"Sounds like Mr. Sackett is finished with his nap." Jackson glanced at her sideways. "Shall we escort him to his new home in a cozy little cell?"

"I'll leave him to you."

"Oh?" He tucked a hank of loose hair behind her ear, his touch warm and welcome. "Have you another pressing engagement?"

"I do." She grinned. "With a tub of water and a bar of soap." Lifting to her toes, she kissed him soundly, then spun away and sauntered down the street. The lure of a bath beat out a trek to the station, no contest. She wouldn't really get to spend time with Jackson anyway after he locked up Mr. Sackett, not with the mound of paperwork he'd have to fill out—and she didn't relish hovering around his makeshift office beneath the station stairwell while he did so. Besides, she'd spend plenty of time with him tomorrow when his family arrived in London. After all she'd heard from Jackson of his father and brother, she looked forward to meeting them.

Once in Blackfriars, she swung down Carter Lane. This part of town was as badly in need of a good scrubbing as she was, so she blended right in—and not just because of her coating of coal dust. This was home, this neighbourhood of mismatched boards and broken glass. Every narrow-throated alley and shadowy nook was as familiar as the tiny mole on her forearm. But before she finished the route to Mistress Mayhew's Boarding and School of Deportment, she paused in front of a freshly whitewashed door with a placard swinging over it.

"Soup kitchen," she read aloud, a smile curving her lips. Amazing how letters were more than just shapes to her now, thanks to Jackson. He'd gifted her many things over the past six months, but reading was one of the best presents of all.

Bypassing the front door, she rounded the corner of the building and scooted down a shoulder-wide passageway smelling of cooked cabbage. She shoved open the back door to the soup kitchen she'd purchased nigh on a month ago now.

Inside, an array of children, ranging from infant to on the cusp of womanhood, all busied themselves with various tasks. Those who were able looked up and greeted her with a hearty, "Good day, Miss Kit!"

"Good day, ladies. Is Mrs. Martha—?"

"I thought I heard your voice." A brown-headed woman in a patched apron swept through the dining room door, a baby on her hip. "Always good to see you, miss."

"Afternoon, Martha." Kit smiled at her friend. "How are things faring today?"

Martha's gaze skimmed over her, brows slightly rising. "Better than whatever ye've been up to, by the looks of it. We just finished filling sixty empty bellies, so I'd say tha's a good day, aye?" In a swift yet gentle movement, she handed off her babe to one of the older girls. "Mind Hazel for me, will you, Alice? There's a dear." She directed the others with as much finesse. "Finish that pot, Jane. After that, please help Mary with slicing up the rest o' the bread to hand out for dinner. Harriet, see to the leftover cheese and, oh, Anna, could you recount the spoons? I fear old man Murray might've made off with another." Finally, she turned to Kit. "Take a cup of tea, miss?"

She shook her head. "I won't keep you, Martha. I was just on my way home and wanted to make sure you're not wearing yourself too thin. It wasn't that long ago you were nearly at death's door."

"Thanks to you, miss, and to God, that's no longer the case. But, well. . ." She tipped her head towards the dining room. "Might I have a word a'fore ye leave?"

Odd, that. Martha was one to pull up a stool in the midst of dish-washing and clamor, not secret away. "I always have time for a word with you, my friend."

She followed Martha into the empty public space, smaller than a taproom, with trestle tables and hacked-together benches hunkering shoulder to shoulder. It wasn't much, but even so, gratefulness welled in Kit's heart. God had provided this, and as surely as five loaves had fed five thousand, she prayed the same miracle would be accomplished here.

Kit studied her friend as she sank onto a bench opposite her. Faint shadows hung in half moons beneath her eyes, yet her gaze was clear and good colour pinked her cheeks. Not ill, but not sleeping well, either. "What's on your mind, Martha?"

"It's Frankie, miss. I fear for my boy."

Kit tapped the table with her fingernail. The lad was resilient, a former member of her team, one who never missed a day due to—no. Oh no! She sucked in a breath. "Is he ill?"

"If only it were something a dose o' castor might fix." A wistful sigh deflated the woman. "But I suspicion 'tis worse. He's hidin' some-thing, miss. I knows it. 'Course he won't confide in me, the skully little whip, but there's more to his disappearing acts than the pretty excuses he paints. He's scarcer than ever of late. Out till all hours. Nippin' off before sunrise."

"You think he's fallen in with a bad crowd?"

"I pray not." Tears instantly welled in Martha's eyes. "Yet with his sneakin' about and crafty tales that don't quite add up, I can't help but wonder. I mean no disrespect to you, miss, but since ye've disbanded yer crew, Frankie's been adrift. I don't blame him thinkin' kitchen work is fer girls, 'specially when he's had a taste o' adventure when he worked fer you. But would ye…I mean…I know ye're about to be married and all—and to a fine man, if I do say—but could ye maybe find something to busy my boy's hands to keep him from bandying about with ne'er-do-wells and cutthroats?"

Martha's voice broke then, along with Kit's heart. She grabbed Martha's hands across the table. "Don't worry, my friend. Wedding or not, I'll uncover what Frankie's been up to, and if it smacks of anything nefarious, I'll put a stop to it. You have my word. But don't fret so. How much trouble can a nine-year-old get into?"

With a last squeeze of Martha's fingers, she pulled away and bit her lip. Thinking back on her own childhood, she knew the answer to her question—and she didn't like it. Not at all.

Chapter Three

Public venue or private club, it didn't matter in which gymnasium Jackson bared his knuckles, they all smelled the same. The distinct reek of sweat and blood at M Division's Bermondsey Street Station was no different. If anything, the noxious twang was even more pungent. And why not? This was where the front forces of London's bravest kept in shape to manhandle toughs bent on breaking the law. Lowlife bruisers like Sackett. Hang the man for wasting his entire morning! And hang—

Oof!

Jackson's head snapped sideways. He staggered.

Across from him, Officer Charles Baggett bounced on his toes, a knowing gleam in his eyes. "You're a bit preoccupied this afternoon. Thinking of a certain skirt, no doubt?"

"Quite the opposite." Turning aside, he spit, then carefully tested his jaw before putting his hands back up. "I keep going over the story from the ugly mug I hauled in yesterday."

"Sackett?"

"The very one." This time Jackson dodged Baggett's left hook. "I can't get him to crack. Even after hours of interrogation, he continues blaming the dust yard owner."

"Maybe he has reason."

"He does—to wriggle out of the consequence of being snagged red-handed." He ducked another of his friend's swipes.

Baggett cracked his neck, eyes narrowing. "How do you know

Dedfield's not the puppet master?"

"He returned only recently from the continent, was gone for three weeks—the entire time the thievery in the Culpepper household took place. There's no way he's tied to the missing Culpepper items. No, Sackett is the culprit, looking for a way out."

Once again Jackson's blood ran hot, and he drove Baggett back with a series of jabs. "That's the trouble with humanity nowadays." *Swing.* "Personal responsibility is a thing of the past." *Feint.* "No one fesses up to their own guilt, just passes it on."

He lunged, landing a killer uppercut to Baggett's chin. His friend flew backwards, landing on the mat with a *whump.*

"Sorry, old man." Jackson reached for his arm and helped him up. "You all right?"

Baggett shook off the blow, his gaze a bit glassy. "I'm fine, but do me a favour?"

Jackson flexed his aching fingers. "Anything."

"Next time we spar, put your mind on your soon-to-be bride instead of some jake you locked up. It'll be less dangerous for me."

He snorted. Sage advice. As usual.

"Forge!" A roly-poly sergeant advanced, the brass buttons of his uniform straining to remain in their assigned holes. The man was a walking weapon, in danger of putting someone's eye out should one of those buttons pop loose. "There's a gent askin' after ye." He tipped his head at the black-suited fashion plate standing near the door. "And don't go dripping all over my floor, boys."

In unison, Jackson and Baggett caught the towels flying through the air.

The sergeant continued to grumble as he passed them, hardly taking a breath as he started down the back stairs.

After scrubbing his face and chest, Jackson elbowed his friend. "I'll let you win next time."

Baggett rolled his eyes. "Don't be so sure it wasn't I who allowed you the victory today. Off with you. I've got better things to attend, and by the looks of it, so do you."

Jackson slung the towel around his shoulders and stepped off the mat. Behind him, Baggett's footsteps trotted towards the same stairway the sergeant had used. Unwinding his thick hand-wraps, Jackson studied the approaching man.

The fellow's stride was strong, the slope of his nose even stronger. He clutched a silk top hat in one hand, and in the other, a pair of gloves. A dangling gold watch chain glinted in a patch of sunlight from the window, as did the pearl buttons on his waistcoat. He appeared to be middling of years. Thirty-five. Forty, perhaps. Hard to tell, but one thing was sure—this was no *gent*, as the sergeant had indicated. This was a pillar of money. Prestige. Power. In more ways than one, Jackson felt naked in his presence. What on earth was a bigwig doing in a damp-walled police gymnasium?

Jackson stopped near a line of pegs laden with his clothes and finished pulling off his hand bindings. "I'm Jackson Forge. How can I be of service to you, sir?"

"To the point, eh, Forge? I like that. Very much." A few steps away, the man planted his leather shoes—so shiny they reflected the hem of his trousers. "I am Charles Gordon-Lennox, the Earl of March."

Hounds a'fire! Jackson's breath caught. What would an earl want with the likes of him?

Conscious of the man-stench wafting from his sweaty body, Jackson retreated a step. "Your servant, my lord, one who begs your pardon for such a slovenly appearance. I'm afraid you've caught me at a rather inopportune moment."

"On the contrary, man. You were in fine form. The way you took down your opponent is exactly what I'd hoped to witness when I inquired after your practice schedule. I'm only sorry I missed the bulk of the fight."

What did this polished earl know of fisticuffs? Did he wish to learn some moves himself? Hire out for a particular skirmish? Sponsor a new champion? Perhaps, but Jackson was hardly a career boxer. Or maybe the topic of boxing was just a ruse, an excuse for the earl to meet with him here.

But why?

Mind whirring, Jackson cast the towel and wraps into a basket on the floor. "Am I under investigation, my lord?"

The man chuckled. "Scrutinization, more like."

"To what end?"

"A purely selfish one."

Odd. Brow raised, Jackson reached for his shirt. "Do you mind?"

"Have at it." Gordon-Lennox cut his hand through the air, the fingers of his gloves fluttering until he tucked them into his hat. "Your name was brought to my attention by my steward, who happened to while away an evening at a pub in Haywards Heath. Your crime-stopping abilities are the talk of that town, which is part of my constituency in the House of Lords. So, I checked into you. I must say, I am impressed with your strong sense of justice and keen eye for spotting trouble. Not to mention your quick thinking and. . .em. . . sometimes unorthodox ways of keeping the streets of London safe. You're a man who takes calculated risks, a critical thinker tempered by swift and needed action—a rare trait."

Jackson shrugged into one sleeve then the other. The man had done a lot of research into his life, and he wasn't sure he liked it. "While I appreciate your regard, what your steward overheard was no doubt tittle-tattle from my father and a certain Mr. Thicket."

"No matter how the information is spread, I like to know what's going on in the villages I represent. And in light of such reports of your impeccable service, I should like to offer you a job."

Now that was remarkable. There were other upstanding officers in service to the crown. Besides, did the earl not already possess an army of servants? Jackson met the man's gaze as he worked his shirt buttons. "As you well know, my lord, I am already employed."

"Hear me out." With a flick of his fingers, Gordon-Lennox ejected a piece of towel lint from his sleeve.

Egad! Was that from him? Heat rising to his ears, Jackson retrieved his waistcoat, hoping the earl wouldn't indict him for such an affront.

But the man didn't seem to mind. He merely straightened the cuff of his sleeve. "Next month I embark on a diplomatic expedition to Africa. While I hate to leave my wife and daughter behind, duty calls. Nevertheless, I have promised my family that I shall return unscathed from my adventure, and that's where you fit in."

Jackson stifled a wince, as much from the throbbing in his fingers as the direction of this conversation. Tending to a spoiled aristocrat was not his idea of a good time. "How so, my lord?"

The earl squared his shoulders. "I propose to hire you as my personal bodyguard, a position that—should you succeed in keeping me safe—will secure your future monetarily."

"I am honoured." Truly, he was, and extra coin would come in handy for him and Kit. Still, the man had said nothing about his new wife accompanying him on this venture. He straightened his sleeves, tugging down the cuff while daring to ask, "Would you also arrange for my bride to travel along with me?"

"The notorious Miss Turner?" The earl clicked his tongue. "I suspected her name might come up in this conversation."

Suddenly on edge, Jackson carefully donned his brown silk cravat. Earl or not, if the man said anything untoward about Kit, it was better to have the fabric around his own neck than strangling a peer of the realm's.

"Unfortunately, Mr. Forge, there is no place for a woman on this venture, not even one as reputably self-sufficient as Miss Turner." The earl shrugged. "I will be leaving behind my own wife, so I understand your hesitation, especially in light of your upcoming nuptials. But this expedition should not hinder your wedding plans in any way. By all means, go ahead and marry the woman. Bed her. Then leave her. It's only for a year. And when you return, you should find your wife's heart has grown all the fonder for you—and your bank account."

The earl removed a crisp slip of paper from his pocket and held it out.

Jackson opened the small note, and there, written in precise black ink, was a sum that could choke a horse. Maybe two. Blinking, he sucked in air between his teeth. One thousand pounds. *One thousand!* He rubbed his jaw to keep the thing from unhinging. What was he to say to this?

Nothing. He couldn't. His throat was completely clogged.

Thankfully, the earl filled in the void. "That sum is payable on my safe return to England. I think you realize that with such a windfall, you could leave the city and settle in the country amidst fresh air, where you and that new bride of yours might raise a whole flock of offspring. I don't think I need to tell you, Forge, that opportunities like this don't come along often."

For a moment, Jackson gave in to a vision of Kit in a blue gown and white apron, hair flying in the wind as she chased about a gaggle of geese and little boys who looked just like him. She bounced a babe on one hip, a girl, laughing, with eyes as brilliant a sapphire as her mother's. In this dream, Kit wouldn't have to hunt down dangerous criminals anymore. There'd be no chance of her getting stabbed or shot or chucked into the river with her hands tied—risks she would face every day if she continued helping him keep the streets of London safe.

But.

To be away from her for so long? Lord only knew what trouble the woman would be up to without his watchful eye keeping her in check. And what of his own heart? How was he to live with only half of that organ? The earl may as well ask him to quit breathing for a year.

With a last look at the possibility penned in black, he offered back the paper. "I appreciate your proposal, my lord, more than you will ever know. Yet I would rather live in police housing with the woman I love than to live without her."

"Turning down a small fortune for a woman, are you?" The earl's gaze fixed on the paper, yet he didn't take it. "My, my, Mr. Forge. You are quite the loyal man."

His hand didn't waver. "Fiercely so, I'm afraid."

"Another reason why I sought you out." The man pulled one more paper from his pocket, this one stiff, small. A calling card. He pressed it into Jackson's fingers without withdrawing his offer. "Should you change your mind, you may find me here, but not for much longer. Once I sail, my proposition goes along with me. Good day, Mr. Forge."

With that, the man clapped on his top hat and pivoted.

"Good day, my lord."

Jackson glanced at the card. Number Seven, Grosvenor Square, Mayfair. Of course. The richest neighbourhood in all of London.

He tucked the papers into his pocket. If he did accept Gordon-Lennox's offer, he would have the means to purchase a private residence to share with his new bride. Far better than the Clarkes Buildings, a squalid row of police barracks that housed married officers. He and Kit could have a home of their own. Some land. Raise children. A worthy goal. A happy one. He could fight crime as well in the country as he could in the city. Blowing out a sigh, he reached for his suit coat. The earl was right. An opportunity like this would not come around again.

Had he made the right choice?

Decisions. Decisions. Aggravating little devils. How was a girl to know which hem finishing was perfect for a wedding day? Honiton lace or a crocheted lappet? And what about stockings? A contrasting yellow—mustard, perhaps—would add a splash of colour, but a matching hue might be more appropriate. Kit frowned. Since when did she care about being appropriate? Was that what it meant to be a bride? A wife? Would she forevermore fuss about her appearance, or was this an anomaly? She puffed a stray piece of hair away from her lips. Times like these, she dearly missed having a mother to ask about all the mysteries of womanhood.

Kneeling at her feet, the white-haired Mrs. Gilman peered up, a few pins poking from the corner of her lips. The seamstress was quite squinty, neat little puckers forming at the corners of her eyes. A hazard of the job, more than likely.

"It is not too late to change your mind, Miss Turner." The pins in the woman's mouth moved but didn't fall out. "You may still go with a nice white overskirt and bolero. White is, after all, the preference of most brides nowadays."

Kit snorted. On the streets, such a colour wouldn't last an hour. Hah! It wouldn't last five minutes. The striped blue veloutine she'd chosen would serve her far better in the long run. And after all the trouble of standing still for this fitting, she was more determined than ever to wear her new gown for events other than a simple "I do."

"Thank you, Mrs. Gilman, but I remain confident in the shade I have chosen."

The woman chirruped like a ruffled peahen, yet thankfully said no more until she pushed in the last pin. "There." The seamstress studied her work, her lips as rippled as the wrinkles by her eyes. "Is that the length you spoke of?"

Kit glanced at her profile in the floor-length mirror. The bottom of her skirt hovered just above her scuffed ankle-boots, making a few of her decisions suddenly apparent. No lace trim for her, and a visit to the shoe seller was in order. She smoothed her hand along the cool silk of her skirt. "Perfect."

"Very good." Mrs. Gilman hoisted herself up by a nearby chair, adding under her breath, "But indecent, if you ask me."

Kit opened her mouth in defense, then as quickly pressed her lips shut. The woman was right. Such a length was fit for strumpets, not for a respectable bride. But she'd never be able to chase brigands in a cobble-length gown, and Jackson—God bless him—loved her despite her lack of convention. He probably wouldn't even notice where her hem landed.

The tall case clock out in the reception room began chiming, and the more bongs Kit counted, the quicker her pulse. Six o'clock? Goodness! "Are you finished, Mrs. Gilman? I must run."

She straightened the fabric at Kit's shoulders, a frown stitching her brow. "A lady never runs."

Kit smirked. "Whatever gave you the impression I am a lady?"

"You somehow caught a man, didn't you?"

"That I did." She grinned.

Stepping back, Mrs. Gilman eyed her from bodice to hem. "Well then, he must be a very special sort of man."

Special didn't begin to define her soon-to-be husband. Jackson was. . .how to describe such a handsome contradiction? A bit green in some respects—a lot, actually—but a more pragmatic mind she'd not encountered. There was a humbleness about him, a softness of heart, yet the swagger of his stride exuded confidence and strength. He could take a beating or dish one out. And most paradoxical of all, he loved her. No, more than that. He *treasured* her. Her! A street brat who ought never to have turned his head in the first place.

"My groom is unlike any other," she murmured, surrendering to the memory of his embrace and passionate kiss when they'd parted ways earlier that day.

Mrs. Gilman's scissors snipped, causing the fitting room to come sharply back into focus. Shadows gathered outside the window as the sun made its final performance for the day.

"But you didn't answer my question, madam." She curved her lips into a placating smile. "Are you finished?"

"For now. Once I sew those seams, one more session should suffice for the final touches."

Kit allowed the woman to help her undress, which took some careful maneuverings to keep from undoing any of the pinned nips and tucks. No doubt Jackson wouldn't take such precautions when removing this gown on their wedding night. Instantly her cheeks heated. Whew! What a scandalous thought. And once again she couldn't help but long for her mother. What did she know of men and their needs, what should or shouldn't happen on a first night together, other than what she'd heard on the streets?

"You look a bit flushed, Miss Turner. Shall I open the window?" Mrs. Gilman draped the blue silk over her arm.

"No need. My street clothes are much less warm."

"Speaking of which, can you manage the rest yourself? I am afraid if I don't hang this immediately, the pins might fall out and we shall have to do this all over again."

Pah! She'd rather chase a skip-footed roustabout bent on escape than schedule another two-hour torture session. "Please, see to your task. I am fully capable of dressing myself, and what's more, I shall see myself out the door when I am finished. Thank you."

"Very well. Good evening." Mrs. Gilman swept from the room, leaving behind the scent of lavender and a whispered "La! Such a singular woman."

Kit chuckled to herself as she scooted to the room divider where her worn woolen skirt draped over the top. Mrs. Gilman was the singularity, shut away with naught but thread and needle for companions, save for the silly-headed gigglers who came in for new gowns every time another dinner party—

Dinner!

She snatched her brown skirt and hastily yanked it up to her waist. Even now Jackson would be sitting down with his father and brother at the George Inn, and she should be too. As she fumbled with the buttons on her bodice, she glanced out at the darkening streets. Lamps already glowed on their posts. People scurried home before dark fell in earnest, and a rougher element crept out from the crevices they'd been sleeping in all day, which reminded her to tuck her boot blade into the hidden sheath in her shoe. If Mrs. Gilman had spied that little dandy, a round or two of smelling salts would've been in order.

Reaching for her bonnet on a hook near the window, she paused. Across the street, at the mouth of a narrow passage, several boys squatted in a circle. Boys who should be home helping their mothers instead of scheming some no-good tricks, for what else could they be up to? Well. She'd put a stop to that nonsense.

Kit grabbed her hat as she dashed out of Mrs. Gilman's shop. Though she skimmed the cobbles on quiet feet, she had barely made it halfway across the road when one of the young ruffians in a ragged flat cap lifted his face and spotted her.

"Hawk!" he cried.

Hawk? Her? She'd used the slang many times to warn her crew members when a bobby appeared, but never had she been labeled as such.

The boy shot to his feet and tore down the passageway. Four other lads followed, the last of which made her breath catch. No. It couldn't be. She ran after the smallest boy's coattails before shadows swallowed him. A thick swath of black hair hung over the lad's collar, a lad who could be no more than nine years old.

Frankie?

Without further thought, she sprinted ahead. Even if it weren't Martha's boy, she'd not let the little pipsters get away.

Chapter Four

Did life get any better than the last savory mouthful of a steak and kidney pie? Surprisingly, it did. Jackson set down his fork. After several months of not seeing his family, time in his father's and brother's presence filled a hollow in his heart he hadn't realized was so empty. Who'd have thought something as mundane as catching up on business with his father in the warmth of the George Inn's public room would be such a blessing? Even grinning at the antics of his older brother, whose mind was that of a four-year-old, held its charm. Indeed, the evening was nearly perfection, with just one little thing missing.

Kit.

Jackson shoved away his plate, worry and annoyance chasing each other like a hound after its tail. One minute he was ready to bust out of here and check the hospitals to make sure she was all right. The next, his hands clenched into fists, for more than likely, the little scamp was still trying to root out the Culpepper servant responsible for pitching the stolen goods into the dustbin...which would do her no good. He'd already heard from the superintendent that the housemaid had fled the man's employ and, no doubt, the city as well.

Next to him, Father wagged a finger at James, who was about to pick up his dish and lick it, then turned to him with a raised brow. "Perhaps you gave your bride the wrong date?"

Jackson shook his head. "I reminded her just this morning. She was looking forward to meeting you and James."

His father leaned back in his chair as a server removed their plates. "Is she frequently tardy?"

"No. Especially not for a meal. She has quite the hearty appetite."
She did. For food. For life. For him, if the kiss they'd shared earlier was
any indication. Kit Turner was a passionate woman in all the things
she loved, and he missed having her at his side. For the hundredth
time, his gaze drifted past the other diners towards the door.

A brown skirt paused on the threshold. Jackson shot to his feet
and flagged her down. "Here she is at last."

Father rose. Not James. He busied himself with folding and
refolding his napkin.

"To your feet, Brother," Jackson said. "You're about to meet your
future sister-in-law."

As Kit approached, three things became clear, and Jackson wasn't
entirely sure he was happy about any of them. Her hair had slipped
its pins in a most beguiling way, drawing the stares of other men. The
bottom of her skirt was caked with mud, which drew an equal amount
of attention from the women in the room. And beneath the aroma of
Kit's rose-scented soap, there was a faint sulfurish tang. Gunpowder,
perhaps? Or maybe she'd been running through sewers again. Either
way, what the deuce had she been up to?

And—more importantly—what would Father think of this
woman he was about to marry?

"Forgive me, gentlemen." She flashed a brilliant smile. "I am sorry
I'm late."

"Darling." Jackson kissed her on the cheek and whispered for her
alone, "All is well, I trust?"

"Just got a bit sidetracked," she said under her breath.

So, she *had* been involved in some tomfoolery, but no time for
questions now. He pulled her closer with a touch to the small of her
back. "Father, Brother, allow me to introduce my bride, Miss Kather-
ine Turner, or Kit, as she prefers. Kit, my father, Mr. Alfred Forge, and
my brother, James."

Father pressed a kiss to her hand. "Pleased to meet you, my dear. I
am honoured to gain a daughter."

Kit smiled. "The honour is all mine, sir. Jackson speaks so highly
of you."

Following his father's lead, James took her other hand and planted a loud smooch. "Pretty lady."

"Thank you." She laughed. "You, James, are as sweet spoken and handsome as your brother."

And that was it. Right there. One of the reasons why Jackson loved this woman more than any other. How many ladies would not only brave such a breach of etiquette but do so with kind words and a beguiling grin?

"Shall we?" Jackson pulled out the chair next to him and seated Kit, then waved over the server. "A slice of kidney pie, hot mash, and a cider for the lady. Oh, and refills for the rest of us, I think."

"Aye sir." The girl dipped a bob then scurried off.

Kit's merry laughter once again rang out as he sat. Was Father already telling jokes as only a father might? He looked from the guilty party to her. "I am afraid I missed the jest."

"You didn't tell me your father owned such a droll sense of humour. I rather like it."

James scooted his chair closer to her. "I like you, lady."

"My, my, aren't you the charmer?" She arched a brow at Jackson. "You'd better keep an eye on your brother. I just might leave you and go for him instead."

"Jackson would be devastated." Father leaned forward in his chair. "He is quite smitten, my dear. To the point of distraction, I'm afraid. He can hardly function for want of keeping his mind on anything other than you."

Heat rose up his neck. According to his father, he was no better than a lovesick schoolboy. "Father, really, must you—"

"Naturally he must." Kit flipped back her hair like a saucy pony, the curve to her lips just as playful. "If your father cannot embarrass you, who can?"

Hah! This from the woman who'd countless times done the very same to him? Good thing his drink wasn't yet refilled, or he'd snort it all over the table.

He reached for her hand and this time allowed his own lips to linger on her soft skin before gazing up at her. "You've managed the task of discomfiting me quite nicely, my love. Several times, I might add."

"Oh?" His father rapped the table. "It seems there's a story or two

I've not yet heard."

Kit angled her head. "Did Jackson never tell you of the first time we met?"

"Ha ha! He did not. But it should make for a good conversation."

No. It wouldn't. Which was why he'd not yet revealed to his father even half of his history with Kit, nor of Kit's own jaded past.

Before he could change the subject, Kit barreled ahead. "Allow me to enlighten you. The first time I laid eyes on your son, I picked him out of the crowd as a—"

Jackson squeezed her leg beneath the table. If Father discovered she'd singled him out as a mark to be swindled, what would he think of her? Thunderation! Tonight might prove to be as exhausting in protecting her reputation as bodily defending her out on the streets.

Kit glanced at him sideways before finishing her answer. "Em, now that I think on it, I suppose it's not all that exciting of a tale. Suffice it to say he caught my eye on Blackfriars Lane."

"And you, mine." Jackson winked at her.

Conversation lulled as the server set a plate and mug in front of Kit, then refilled each of their glasses in turn.

"Mmm." Closing her eyes, Kit inhaled deeply over her plate, then smiled as she picked up her fork. "I am famished. Do you mind?"

"By all means," his father said. "We've already eaten."

"Once again, my apologies." She took a bite before continuing. "But there is good reason for my late arrival. The wedding gown fitting was brutal. Two hours. Two! Had I known a marriage ceremony would be such a bother, I'd have skipped the whole thing. And if that weren't enough to detain me, once I left the shop, I ended up chasing some boys who were bent on trouble."

"Bad boys hurt lady?" James clenched his napkin, the skin stretching white over his knuckles. Did he fear for Kit? Or was he, perhaps, remembering his own brutal beating all those years ago?

"Be at peace, Brother." Jackson patted his brother's hand. "My bride is well able to defend herself."

"Even so. . ." Father sank back in his chair, his faded brown eyes studying him as if he were a watch cog to be fixed. "I look forward to the day when you and your new bride settle down in Haywards Heath, away from these brutish streets. Until then, at least tending a hearth and home will keep your wife out of harm's way."

As always, his father's wisdom struck home—but this time even deeper with the thought of the funds he could gain should he take up Gordon-Lennox on his offer. With only a year's worth of service, he could keep Kit safe in a country home for the rest of her life.

Kit laughed. "That's very kind of you, sir, but I have no intention of hiding out in a house and giving up my lifestyle just because I'm married. I have a soup kitchen to manage and, well, other things to attend."

His father's bushy white eyebrows drew into a line. "Once you are married, you will find those other things shall fade in importance. As a wife, it will be your duty to care for Jackson—a task that should require all your time and attention."

"I don't know about that." She eyed Jackson. "Your son appears fully capable of caring for himself."

"That I am." Jackson smirked. He'd not be a browbeaten loafer told what to do, where to go, and when to do so. He tweaked Kit's cheek with a mock pinch. "But are you not looking forward to baking cakes and gossiping at the market with the other wives?"

"Me? Bake?" She reared back in her chair. "Are you sure you asked the right woman to be your wife?"

"I asked the only woman I love, the only woman I will *ever* love."

"Well." A slow smile curved her lips. "You can be as charming as your brother."

"Speaking of which," Father cut in, "James, you may go retrieve your gift now."

James straightened to a ramrod. "Present for lady?"

"Yes."

He shot out of his chair so fast it wobbled on two legs before banging back to the floor. Jackson was of half a mind to dash after him and make sure he didn't crash into the server carrying food, but if Father was content to allow James such a freedom, who was he to play nursemaid?

"James made a little something in the workshop before we left home. It's not much, my dear, so don't set your expectations too high." Father smiled at Kit. "But it comes from his heart."

"Those are the best kinds of gifts." She dabbed her mouth and tabled her napkin. "Why, when I ran my crew at the Grouse and Gristle, I often had the men deliver—"

Jackson cleared his throat. Loud. Drowning out her words and earning him a cross look from a woman at a nearby table. The less Father knew, the better.

Kit thwacked him on the back several times. "Are you all right?"

"Fine, fine. Must've swallowed wrong." He coughed once more for emphasis. "Why don't you tell my father about—"

"A crew, you say?" Father folded his arms, suddenly all ears. "What sort?"

Kit grinned. "The best sort."

Good girl! Jackson exhaled, relieved that bullet had been dodged. As long as Father didn't ask any more questions, they would be fine. He opened his mouth to thwart any further conversation on the matter.

But Kit beat him to the punch. "I'm astonished Jackson didn't tell you, for it is quite the tale. When we first met, I had ten fellows on my crew, give or take, and we'd—"

Jackson swung out his elbow, tipping his mug.

And sending a river of cider towards Kit's lap.

Kit shoved back her chair. Fast. But not fast enough. A cider waterfall doused the bottom of her gown and her shoes. Not that it ruined anything. In fact, the liquid cleaned off some of the dried mud she'd earned while chasing those boys, whom she'd never snagged. Still, if she didn't know better, she'd swear Jackson had knocked over his mug on purpose.

"Clumsy me!" He mopped the mess with such a relish and look of contrition that her doubt faded. He peered up at her as he worked, his adorable flop of hair hanging over his eye like a puppy's ear. "Forgive me?"

Nearby, diners craned their necks, keen on the spectacle.

Kit smoothed her skirt. So much for a quiet family dinner. "There is nothing to forgive, love. No harm done."

Across from her, his father shook his head. "Even as a lad, Jackson always was one to spill his milk."

"Evidently I've not outgrown the habit." Jackson flashed her a smile just as his brother returned.

James plopped into his chair and pushed a small brown box across the tabletop towards her. "For you, lady."

"Thank you." She removed the lid. Inside, a golden watch brooch nestled atop a swath of green velvet. Picking it up, she admired the way lamplight gleamed along the curlicues at the top. Feminine, yet not too fancy. How thoughtful! She'd never owned a watch before, and this one appeared to be a beauty. The glass face dangled from a gold link and. . .hold on. She squinted. The hands didn't move, and one of them was bent. Well. Telling the time would be quite a trick with this one.

Even so, she pinned the brooch on her bodice, unwilling to disappoint the man-boy who'd suffered so much in life. "It is lovely, James."

Eagerly, he leaned forward, shoving back a swath of hair as dark as Jackson's and revealing the purple scar snaking over the right side of his face. "Lady likes?"

"Lady loves." And she did. But so much more than the gift. Her heart swelled at the larger-than-life grin spreading across James's face and the hearty "Well done" directed to her from Jackson's father. These were good people. The best. Perhaps God was making up for the many years she'd spent without a family of her own.

On a whim, she turned to Jackson. "Could we not take part of the day tomorrow to show your father and brother around town?"

He rubbed his jaw, the faraway look in his eyes reading some kind of invisible schedule. "A morning stop at the station for me is unavoidable, and I have just a few last questions for Mr. Dedfield, but after that. . ." He dropped his hand. "Yes, I don't see why not. Father, will that suit?"

"I'm afraid I must decline. I have a meeting at the watchmakers' guildhall that's likely to take all day, but I am sure James would enjoy an outing."

"Perfect." She angled in her seat, facing Jackson's brother. "Would you like to visit the zoo tomorrow, my new brother? I hear there is a baby elephant."

The whites of his eyes grew at an alarming rate. He shot to his feet, his chair clattering over backwards and hitting the floor with a resounding *thwack.* "El-e-fant!"

Once again, heads craned, with a few ugly whispers added of "I never!" and "How vulgar."

Jackson's father immediately righted the chair then reached for James's arm. "Calm yourself, Son. Take your seat."

James merely bounced on his toes, gazing at the ceiling and chanting, "El-e-fant. El-e-fant."

"In light of such future excitement, I think it best if James gets a full night sleep, and the sooner he retires, the better." Jackson's father dipped his head at them. "With that, I bid you both adieu."

"Good night, Father," Jackson said, rising along with Kit. "We'll call for James after breakfast, if that fits your schedule."

"Indeed. And dinner is on me, so no need to square things away. Good night, my new daughter." Jackson's father kissed her cheek. "Welcome to the family."

"Thank you. I am happy to be part of it."

James waved at her as his father once again reached for his arm. "Night, lady."

"Good night, James." She smiled.

"Until tomorrow, Jackson." His father guided James through the maze of tables.

Jackson turned to her. "Would you like a pudding, or are you quite full?"

"Quite." She pressed a hand to her belly.

He stepped scandalously near and whispered in her ear. "Then how about I see you home?"

She caught her breath for want of air, loving and hating that this man had such a bodily effect on her. The first—and only—man to ever do so. She stepped away and tossed a look over her shoulder. "I suppose I could allow you to tag along."

Outside the George Inn, the warm September night was a mistress, calling seductively to lovers. For a while, they walked silently hand in hand, allowing the soothing *clip-clop* of horses pulling cabs to fill the void. This was one of the things she loved best about Jackson, that they were friends first and foremost, neither feeling the need to fill in blank spaces with trite words or meaningless banter.

It wasn't until they turned onto Carter Lane that Jackson spoke. "I am pleased you find my family to your liking."

"I am pleased to have a family at long last."

"Oh?" He squeezed her hand. "Is there trouble with your father I should know about?"

"No, nothing of the sort. I simply mean that now I shall have two fathers and a brother." She swung their arms back and forth, heady with the idea. "For a girl brought up as an orphan, that's quite a boon."

"Yes, which reminds me. . .perhaps you could keep that part of your history to yourself?"

"What do you mean?" She glanced up at him.

He did not return her gaze. "I, uh, I've not actually spoken to my father of your past. Truth be told, I've not really told him much of anything about you."

Her stomach twisted, and she doubted very much it was the kidney pie and mash. "Are you ashamed of me?"

"Nothing of the sort!" Horror ran in ripples across his face. He reached for her, his hands warm on her arms. "I would never think ill of you, my love. I merely wish everyone to think the best of you."

She cocked her head. "And your father wouldn't?"

"No, it's not that, it's just. . ." A sigh ripped out of him, and his hands fell away. "My father has a habit of speaking freely amongst his friends, and one of them in particular cannot keep anything to himself. I would not have you be the talk of Haywards Heath."

Was that all he was worried about? Some barbs of gossip and slanted looks? Pish! She'd dealt with much worse in her time. "I don't mind."

"I do." His jaw clenched hard and sharp.

Her heart softened, until a worm of a question burrowed up from not only his comment but the wishes his father had made plain during dinner. "This village of yours, Haywards Heath. . . You are not thinking of trundling us out of London, are you?"

Even in the night shadows, she could see something move behind his eyes. A hint of anguish, perhaps. Some unnamed torment. Whatever the mystery, it was definitely something he was keeping from her.

"Jackson, are you seriously considering making our home elsewhere?"

"Would that be such a bad thing? Think of it." His gaze roved from one of her eyes to the other. "Wide, open spaces. Fresh country air. Raising our children in a land of milk and honey instead of muck and squalor."

There was no argument against that, especially not with a stench starting to billow in on a cloud of river fog. Living in the country did hold a certain charm, one she'd only ever dreamed about. Bleating sheep. Rolling hills. Dipping into a pond alone with her husband with no one to hear them for miles around.

She shook her head, casting aside the vision. "But what would become of the soup kitchen, the people of Blackfriars, Martha and—" At the mention of her friend, the freckle-nosed image of Frankie popped into her mind. The little scoundrel! She'd question the boy tomorrow about his doings with that group of street brats. "There is work for me to do here."

With one bent knuckle, Jackson tipped her face up to his. "Is being my wife not work enough?"

The question hung between them like a cobweb, one she'd rather not touch, for it would be hard to shake off. Yet sometimes there was nothing for it but to charge head-on through a sticky web. "Are you saying that once we are wed, I am to live out the rest of my life in drudgery, chained to a hearth?"

"Oh, Kit. Such dramatics." Shaking his head, he offered an arm in invitation, yet she caught a faint muttering under his breath. "I doubt I could command you to do anything."

She grabbed his bicep and spun him around. "Jackson Forge! Are you having second thoughts about marrying me? Because I am beginning to have a few of my own."

"Of course not, my love." He smoothed his hands along her arms. "Were the date not already set at the church, I'd marry you tonight."

"Is that so?"

His lips came down hard. Fast. Consuming her in ways that drove any doubt she might have into oblivion. Or was that her own hunger that kissed with such passion? Either way, she melted against him, giving back as much as she took.

By the time he pulled away, she was breathless, and he was smug.

"There." He squared his shoulders. "Does that convince you of my desire?"

She snorted. No way would she feed that beast of an attitude. "It's a good start, I suppose."

"Oh?" The blue in his eyes gleamed electric in the streetlight. "I look forward to the day I can finish what I started."

"Jackson!"

He laughed. "You know, your nose crinkles in the most delightful way when you're incensed."

"It does not." She considered mashing his foot but, at the last moment, stomped the pavement instead.

Once again, he gathered her into his arms, the rogue twist to his lips almost too handsome to bear. "Do not fret, fair lady. Your virtue is safe with me, leastwise for another eleven days."

"And then?"

He pressed his forehead against hers, skin to skin. Heart to heart. "And then you'll be mine."

She snuggled against him. That was exactly what she wanted. Being this man's wife would fill her heart, make her whole. But what of those she loved on Blackfriars? She'd never considered that by marrying Jackson she might have to leave them behind.

Martha and Frankie. Joe and Natty Card. Her father.

Would she really have to?

Chapter Five

Something wasn't right. Something more than the chafe of the worn stocking that bunched in Jackson's shoe. For at least the tenth time since he'd left the boarding house, he wheeled about and scanned the pavement behind him.

Even though the grey of dawn had barely lightened to full day, the streets of London already crawled with people. Merchants opening shops. Stevedores scurrying towards the docks. A loaded omnibus hauling factory slogs to their monstrous machines of industry. Not one pair of eyeballs seemed to be focused on him, yet that did nothing to diminish the prickling at the nape of his neck.

Shoving aside the fruitless sensation, he continued on his way. Two blocks later, he neared the door of the Old Jewry police station, where a man-sized pile of rags shot out a dented tin cup as he passed. "Spare a farthing, guvnor?"

Jackson retrieved a penny and dropped it in with a clink, trying not to retch from the man's sharp stink of spoiled milk and onions.

Dark eyes, glassy as a bat's, peered out from a tatty black hood. "Bless ye, guvnor."

"And you." He nodded as he tucked away his money pouch. "But a word to the wise—you ought to shove off. The officers of this station don't take kindly to penny coves like you sniffing about. You're as like to find yourself locked up as to hear another coin in your cup."

Turning from the man, he was about to reach for the door when it swung open. Out strode a blue uniform bearing a golden sergeant's insignia on the upper arm. Immediately Jackson retreated a step and dipped his head in respect for his former boss and soon-to-be father-in-law. "Good morning, Sergeant Graybone."

"Forge." The sergeant nodded. "You're here early."

"I am." He inhaled a lungful of the brisk September air. Though he would be family, Graybone could still intimidate the quills off a hedgehog. "I've already been to Dedfield's Dust Yard and am now getting a final interrogation out of the way before accompanying your daughter and my brother to the zoo."

Graybone stroked his thick beard, the black bristles now threaded with grey. Though nearing retirement, he wore his years well. "No brigand chasing or murder solving on the docket?"

Jackson shook his head. "Not today. For once, Kit and I shall lead the life of a perfectly ordinary couple."

A snort puffed from Graybone's wide nose. "There is nothing ordinary about either of you. Still, I am glad to hear that for once my daughter will be out of harm's way."

Jackson tugged at his coat sleeve, straightening the hem. The sergeant sounded suspiciously like his own father. Had the two been talking? Not that he could blame them. He would as soon see Kit removed from danger, and with the earl's offer still weighing on his mind, the means to do so was yet within reach.

He met Graybone's always-intent gaze. "What if, sir, once Kit and I are married, I permanently remove your daughter from the hazards of the city? Would you abide such a move, even if it meant you didn't see her as often?"

"There's no doubt I'd miss the chit." Graybone sniffed, then rubbed the back of his hand across his bristly moustache. "But up until several months ago, I didn't know she even existed. So, while I cherish every moment I can get with her, yes, I believe for Kit's best interests, I could happily agree to not seeing her as often."

Jackson swallowed. Those words stung. It would be in Kit's best interest if he took that job with the earl, but could he as happily agree to not seeing her for an entire year?

"Why?" Another officer exited the station, and Graybone shuffled sideways before peering back at Jackson. "What have you in mind?"

"Oh, em. . ." Should he tell the sergeant about Gordon-Lennox's offer? It wasn't as if the earl had bound him to secrecy. Still, an earl's business ought not to be bandied about so freely, especially on the street where stray words could be gathered and used for ill intent. Who knew? Even the beggar might gain what information he could for some nefarious advantage.

With a noncommittal shrug of his shoulders, Jackson hedged. "No plans to move now, sir. Just dreaming."

"Dreaming has its place in front of a hearth, with a dog at your feet and a pipe in your mouth, not here at work—or you shall promptly find yourself out of a job. . .or worse. And that would do you nor my daughter any good. Stay focused, man."

"Sage advice, sir." Jackson squared his shoulders. "I shall take it to heart."

"I should hope so, for your sake and for Kit's. With that, I bid you good day."

"Thank you." Jackson stepped aside to allow him passage, remembering just in time to warn the sergeant about the beggar. "Oh, and sir? Go easy on the beggar. I already warned him. . ." As his gaze drifted over the sergeant's shoulder, his words faded.

The man was gone.

Graybone followed his gaze, then lifted a bushy brow back at him. "Dreaming of beggars as well, Forge?"

"No, sir. The man must've heeded my advice."

"Well, good luck with that questioning, then. I have a feeling you'll need it in your scattered state of mind." The sergeant strolled away.

Blowing out a sigh, Jackson yanked open the station door and strode in, tipping his hat at the front desk clerk as he passed. "Good morning, Smitty."

"Morning, Inspector."

The clerk's greeting blended with the usual hubbub. Constables shuffling criminals about. Citizens reporting crimes to be investigated. The squawk of the chief inspector's parrot winging down from an office upstairs.

Jackson left it all behind as he descended the back staircase to the holding cells, the air growing cooler, the stink of body odour more profound. The sounds were more raucous too, though no wonder, really. When a man had nothing to do all day but sit in a cage, it made sense that when he wasn't snoring, he'd take to spewing curses at all and sundry, sometimes even himself.

Halfway down, Jackson flattened against the wall as two constables hefted a stretcher between them, carrying a body up to either the hospital or the deadhouse. Judging by the full coverage of a brown woolen blanket, it would be the latter.

"Pardon, Inspector." The lead constable—Durry, if he wasn't mistaken—nodded at him.

"No trouble at all." Jackson lifted a prayer as the draped corpse passed. Whatever poor soul had expired, hopefully he was now at peace. . .though one could never be sure with the clientele this station served.

When the passageway cleared, he trotted down the rest of the steps and stopped at the tall desk on the bottom landing.

"Good morning, Mr. Barrycloth." He gave a sharp nod to the bear of a constable perched on his stool in front of the tall desk. It took a special man to fill this role, and mammoth-shouldered, one-eyed Barrycloth was just the fellow. Even a hardened street cully would think twice before giving him any trouble. Jackson held out his palm. "Keys for cell eight, please."

"No need, sir." The constable laid down his pen. "Cell's empty."

Jackson pulled back his hand, thoroughly confused. Sackett should not have been sent to the Old Bailey until after this morning's final interrogation. "Where is my prisoner?"

The constable's gaze drifted to the stairs. "I believe you just passed him, sir."

A charge jolted through him. The shape beneath that blanket had been the wily foreman of Dedfield's Dust Yard? But he'd been in perfect health when Jackson questioned him yesterday.

"What happened?" he asked.

Mr. Barrycloth shrugged, the stool beneath him groaning with the sudden movement. "Hung himself, sir. Found him strung up earlier."

"Surely someone saw or heard him in the act. How did that slip by you?"

"Sackett were in the end cell, no one next to him. Constable Toff forgot to turn in his Nightly—as the old badger is more than wont to do. If ye ask me, the ol' coot oughtta be put out to pasture."

Jackson drummed his fingers on Barrycloth's podium. "What has that to do with Sackett?"

"Oh, aye." Barrycloth scratched his jaw, eyes screwing up to the left as he recalled the past hours. "I ran that Nightly up to Smitty, and ye know how he is. Talk yer bleedin' leg off, he will. All to say, I were away from my post a fair bit o' time, more than enough for Sackett to tie himself up."

Jackson blew out a sigh. So much for all of the foreman's bold bluster. In the end, he hadn't been courageous enough to admit to his thievery. Disappointing, that. But with Sackett dead and the house-maid run off, it did put a finish to the case of Sir Culpepper's stolen goods. The chief would be happy, as would the superintendent. The only real loser here was Sackett.

"A rather harsh way to conclude an assignment," Jackson murmured. "He should have just confessed."

"Who knows, sir? The vicar was the last one to see him alive. Maybe he did come clean."

"We can only hope. Thank you, Mr. Barrycloth." Wheeling about, he made it up several stairs before the nipping at the back of his mind turned rabid. He retraced his steps. "This vicar. . .did Sackett ask for one?"

"No, sir." With his one good eye, Barrycloth stared at him as if he'd just waltzed out the door of Bedlam wearing nothing but a lampshade. "*You* asked for him, sir."

"I requested no such thing!"

The constable's thick lips pursed around a grunt. "Strange. The man gave your name. Even showed me a paper saying he was working with you as clergy to your convicts. Some sort of new liaison between the church and the police. Being that he'd missed you here, I heard he asked Cobb for a copy of your work roster for the week. You know, in case there were any more poor souls you were after that he should plan on visiting."

Quickly, Jackson reviewed his most recent meeting with the

chief. Had the man suggested he develop such a relationship with the church? Perhaps he'd been so preoccupied thinking of Kit that he'd not acted on the plan. . .and in his stead, the chief had? He scrubbed his jaw. No. He'd have remembered such a conversation. "What did this vicar look like?"

"Typical. Dressed in black. White collar. Smelled a bit funny, like he'd recently spent too much time near a furnace—kind of burnt like." The constable leaned aside, the stool tipping to a dangerous angle as he shouted towards the row of cells. "Hey! Quiet your yaps down there, or I'll come give you something to squall about."

Jackson waited a few beats for the last of the curses to fade away. "The vicar's face—a description, if you please."

Barrycloth shook his head. "Couldn't say with any certainty."

"Why not?"

"He wore a thick pox veil, sir, and was given to keeping his chin tucked. I imagine he's horribly disfigured, too far gone for viewing by the public."

"Interesting. His name?"

"It were Mort-something. Italian, I think. Maybe Portuguese." The constable flipped back a few pages in the big ledger on his desk. Tracing a podgy finger down the list, he finally stopped a third of the way down the page and turned the book for Jackson to see. "Here it is." He tapped the name for emphasis.

Jackson examined the fine penmanship. Elegant, really, and quite distinct with how each letter flowed effortlessly into the next.

L. Mortusagro.

He ran the name through a file in his head, and though he tried hard to connect it to any acquaintance, either recent or past, he came up woefully short. He straightened, despising the defeat of the moment. "Very good, Constable. Thank you. Oh, and if this vicar returns, hold him for me."

"Hold, sir?"

"Yes, Mr. Barrycloth. Detain him as long as possible and send for me." He turned on his heel. After all, it only made sense to meet with the man he was supposedly working alongside.

No belly should grumble this early, not powerfully enough to drive one from a warm bed to brave the chill of a September morn. Yet a whole line of empty stomachs dressed in tatty shawls and patched trousers stood outside the soup kitchen, which wouldn't even open for several more hours. Kit's step hitched, heart breaking as she passed by mothers with little ones hanging on their skirts and men whose shoulders bent beneath the ungodly weight of poverty. A few steps ahead of her stood several lads who ought to be on their way to school instead of waiting for a handout. One was taller, a bit more filled out, with an oversized flat cap pulled low. The boy closest to her was...no! Of all the ridiculous places to land this fish.

She tapped Frankie on the shoulder. "Just the fellow I was hoping to find."

The boy flinched, then cast a nervous glance at her over his shoulder. "Go away," he whispered.

Kit arched a brow. He should know better than to order her about. "What are you doing out here instead of helping your mother inside before school?"

"Shh."

It was more of a hiss than an actual plea for her to be quiet, but either way, it garnered the attention of the other boy, who turned. Kit studied the lad's slim nose and fine cheekbones. If she didn't know better, she'd swear that boy was a—

Her arm yanked sideways as Frankie bolted, dragging her along for a ride. Surprising how strong a freckle-faced nine-year-old could be, especially when catching one off guard. He dragged her clear into the mouth of the alley before she gained her footing and wrenched from his grip. Taking care to block the only exit back out to the street, she bent face-to-face with the little urchin. She'd give him no quarter whatsoever to make falsehoods an easy game.

"Listen here, my boy. I've had just about enough of this cloak and dagger business." She popped her fists onto her hips. "What's gotten into you? Tell me what you've been up to. All of it."

His pointy chin lifted a full inch. "Somethin' big, tha's what."

"Such as?"

For a long while, he said nothing, his nostrils flaring now and again. What was going on in that head of his?

"Too soon to tell," he said at length.

"Is that so? Well then, perhaps a night or two down at the police station will speed up time for you." She grabbed his arm.

He yanked away, a deep scowl adding years to his face. "Ye'd turn me in? What's got into *you*, Miss Kit?"

She sucked in a breath, utterly dumbstruck. The lad was right. What had she been thinking? Frankie was a former member of her crew—and a crew member *never* turned on another. A sigh leaked out of her. Perhaps she had been taking this whole law and order thing a bit too far.

Bypassing Frankie, she sank onto an overturned crate and fished out a stick of peppermint from the stash in her pocket, treats she intended to share with Jackson's brother. "You're right, my friend. I crossed a line. Forgive me?"

He snatched the offering. Closing his eyes, he drifted off to heaven with several long licks. Kit couldn't help but smile. This boy would sell his knickers for a piece of candy.

After a few more satisfied lip smacks, he gazed at her sideways. "Mum put ye up to this, din't she?"

"You make it sound as if that's a bad thing. The truth is, my boy, your mother loves you dearly. More than that, she needs you. As do I. The poor of Blackfriars depend upon this soup kitchen, and without your help, how are your mother and I to manage feeding them? You know what an empty belly feels like. It wasn't that long ago we were both scrabbling on the streets after a few crumbs."

His head hung, the candy forgotten for the moment. "Aye."

Reaching out, Kit straightened his cap then planted her hands on his shoulders. "I know you wouldn't wish that feeling on any of those people out there in line, would you?"

His head wagged side to side. "Never."

"Then can I count on you?"

"Ye can always count on me, Miss Kit." He pounded his thumb against his chest. "Ye should know that. Why, I wanna be like you and Mr. Jackson, tha's all."

The ferocity in his tone, the determination in his widened stance—all foretold of a boy who would grow to be a leader. . .but a leader of what? Of whom? Though he aspired to serve the law as she and Jackson did, how well she knew that the wrong sorts of influences could easily sway his heart.

Oh, God, keep this young one on the straight and narrow, for I cannot.

The heavy wheels of an omnibus ground past the alley opening, reminding her Frankie wasn't her only mission for the day. "Well then"—she tousled his hair—"I shall expect to hear no more reports from your mother of you skipping out on her, am I understood?"

Sucking hard on his candy, he scuffed his toe, following the movement with his gaze for a few kicks before his muddy-brown eyes flicked back to her. "All right. Mum shall have no cause to say any such thing. I'll go nowhere without her permission. Be that what ye'd like, Miss Kit?"

"Good man." She cuffed him on the arm. "Now off with you—and I mean off to help your mother."

"Aye, miss." He darted down the alley, hollering over his shoulder, "Thank ye for the sweet."

Kit dusted off the back of her gown, relieved at Frankie's change of heart. Thankfully, she and Martha had nipped this rebellious streak before he'd been ruined.

She sauntered out to the street, humming an old ditty from her past. She was ready for a day with nothing other to worry about than oohing and aahing over the bears and monkeys at the zoo, all while strolling at the side of a certain handsome inspector and his lovable brother.

Indeed. Today, she would be a proper young lady without a care in the world.

Chapter Six

This was time away from work? The monkey house was exactly like the London streets Jackson surveilled every blessed day. All the screeches and squawks blended into a clamor like a chorus of Blackfriars coster-mongers hawking their wares. Not to mention the press of the place with so many bodies milling about, stirring a host of rank odours into a stench. Why, he may as well have escorted Kit and James on a stroll through Bankside and saved the pennies he'd paid for this exhibition. Even so, Jackson grinned. Despite the bedlam, how could he begrudge spending time with those he loved most?

But his grin quickly faded as that recurring prickle spread over the back of his neck again. For at least the tenth time that afternoon, he snapped a glance over his shoulder and scanned the busy atrium behind them. Just like on the street that morning, no one paid him any heed, nor did anyone dodge from his line of sight. He blew out a long breath, releasing the tension in his shoulders. Was he losing his edge?

Kit's laughter pulled his gaze back around. Stretching over the railing, James waved a big square of red fabric in the air, frothing the monkeys behind the bars into a frenzy.

"James!" Lunging, Jackson snatched the old piece of blanket from his brother's hand before a zookeeper happened along and frog-marched them off the premises.

Two frowns turned his way, James's by far the most dour. His big hand reached for the material. "*My* silkie."

Jackson retreated a step, sweeping the tatty keepsake just beyond his brother's fingertips. "I told you your silkie must remain out of sight, did I not?"

Kit sidestepped between them, her big brown eyes pleading. "Your brother was only having a bit of sport, as were the baboons. Don't be so hard on him, hmm?" She blinked, a picture of innocence and purity.

Mimicking her, James tried to blink at him as well, but with a swath of hair covering half his face and the awkward angle of his head, the effect was more of a confused buck than a beseeching doe.

Bah! How was he to stand against this?

"Fine." Jackson huffed as he handed back the wad of fabric. "But make sure you tuck this away in a place where I shall not see it again for the rest of the day. Understood?"

James nodded solemnly as he spun around, shoulders hunched, to squirrel away his precious bit of blanket.

Kit beamed at Jackson. "Well done."

Jackson shook his head. "You dote on him far too much. He's a grown man, not a child."

"Come now." She stepped close, the alluring scent of tea rose soap yet lingering in her hair—a welcome contrast to the monkeys' earthy musk. "I've never had a brother, and I find I fancy it. He is so easy to love."

Jackson choked up. Most women in Haywards Heath looked the other way when James passed by. Whispering. Pitying. Judging. But not this sprite. Kit welcomed his broken-minded brother not only with open arms but with an open heart as well. It took all his self-restraint to keep from pulling her into his own arms.

"I am glad to hear you say so." The words came out husky, and he cleared his throat. "But loving James is one thing. Condoning his ill behaviour quite another."

"Don't be such a thundercloud. It's not as if he were breaking any laws."

"Oh?" He brushed his fingers over the brilliant scarlet flower tucked next to her ear. "And darting past a No Trespass sign to pick this blossom wasn't a breach of order?"

Kit shrugged, the silvery blue in her eyes flashing. "He merely wanted to give me a gift. I think it rather endearing."

"And when he ran off to see the elephant? We nearly lost him."

"Don't be silly." She tossed her head away from his hand, tenacious to a fault. "You cannot lose a grown man who towers over most of the patrons here today. And besides"—she speared him with an arch look—"even you laughed when we found him giving his own elephant rides to the children near the pachyderm pen."

"You are determined to defend him."

"And you are determined to be a curmudgeon."

James plowed through the thin space between them. "Turtles now."

Jackson watched his brother stroll ahead as if there were nothing more important in the world than finding some turtles—which likely, there wasn't. When James was on a mission, there was no stopping him.

Before his brother wandered too far away, Jackson offered his arm to Kit. "Looks like we're off to the Reptilium."

She pressed her fingers against his sleeve with a wicked smile. "Of course we are."

Cool air welcomed them the instant they strolled from the monkey house and set foot on one of the zoo's outdoor walkways. It was a pleasant day, what with the sun shining and the first yellow leaves of autumn drifting down one by one. The gravel path curved gently, lined with boxwood and perfumed by a row of shrub roses bearing a late bloom. James rambled ahead of them, humming a tune of his own creation. Kit's hand rested warm and steady on Jackson's sleeve, her steps in time with his. Save for the few incidents with James earlier and the racket of the monkey house, all in all, it truly was a perfect afternoon.

They passed a couple pushing a pram with a baby cooing inside, and for the first time, a rogue desire welled so strongly, Jackson couldn't help but press his hand against Kit's. That could be them someday. . . someday soon. God willing. He was about to whisper as much into her ear when the hairs at the nape of his neck once again stood on end. He glanced over his shoulder and—

Nothing. What the deuce? Was this what came of always having to be overly vigilant, that on a day off, the habit of looking for those bent on crime just wouldn't stop? That must be it. A hazard of the job. Relieved, he faced forward.

And was met by a narrow-eyed stare from Kit.

"Well?" she asked.

Dash it all. "Well what?"

"Is now the time to pull out my boot blade?"

So, she had noticed. But that didn't mean he must confess. He averted his gaze. "I cannot imagine what you're implying."

Kit snorted. "Can you not?"

He rubbed the back of his neck, working out a knotted muscle. The woman was far too canny, which—when working on a case—was an asset. But now? Blasted inconvenient. "It's nothing. Just spying for trouble where there is none."

His words circled back, this time smacking him right in the face. Was it not better to focus on the known problems in life instead of inventing more? Lord knows he had enough intrigue simply figuring out benign mysteries like where to take Kit and James for dinner or who in the world that vicar was with whom he was apparently working.

"By the by"—he glanced at Kit— "have you any acquaintance with a vicar who goes by the name Mortusagro?"

"Mortusagro." She tasted the name like an unripe pear, her lips twisting. "No. Why? Who is he?"

A capital question. . .one to which he should know the answer. He kicked an overlarge piece of gravel from the path. "It appears that this vicar is part of a new liaison between the police and the offenders who warm the station's cells. Being you have so many connections, I wondered if you knew him. That's all."

"I can ask around if you like."

"No need." He smiled. "I'm sure I'll meet him soon enough. Now then, here we are. James! What did I tell you about doors and ladies?"

Before James completely disappeared into the Reptilium, he swung his head back, confusion in the one eye not covered by hair. When his gaze drifted to Kit, a toothy grin lit his face. Retracing his steps, he held the door wide and stood aside. "For lady."

Kit dipped him a curtsy. "Thank you, kind sir."

Jackson clapped his brother on the shoulder. "Good work, Brother."

There was no atrium in this building. They merely stepped into a large room with glass panels lining the walls, each pane housing a variety of snakes and lizards. At center, five large cement circles penned other reptiles, a few with iron bars curved partway over the top so the most dangerous inhabitants could not escape. One of them held water. Large plants hung in baskets from the glass ceiling, and enormous potted greenery dotted the perimeter, making for a tropical feel. As in the monkey house, people milled about, but the noise level was far more tolerable—leastwise until James let out a whoop.

"Turtles!" His brother dashed ahead.

"James!" Jackson collared the man before he rammed into a portly woman using her parasol as a balancing stick. No wonder Father rarely took him out in public.

He tugged his brother aside with a quick "Forgive us" to the lady, then glowered at James. "I told you to stay with us. You cannot go tearing off like that."

Shoulders slumping, James hung his head.

Kit shot Jackson a dark look before gathering his brother's big hand in hers. "What your brother means to say is that he thinks it would be lovely if you showed us the turtles, but not at such a fast pace. Isn't that right, Jackson?"

Instant shame heated his gut. A fine man he was, treating his brother like a regular street cully. He softened his tone, grateful for Kit's gracious heart. "Yes, Brother, that's exactly what I meant. Being you know so much about animals, won't you show us?"

James scuffed his toe, refusing to look up.

Crooking her finger, Kit gently lifted his brother's face to hers. "Would you show me?"

A smile spread, ending with a nod.

"Good. It is settled then." Jackson swept his arm towards the cement pen at the farthest side of the room. "How about we—"

"My hat!" A child's cry rang to the rafters, followed by a few shouts and a woman screaming, "Auguste, no!"

Jackson turned towards the fracas, as did everyone else in the big room. Ten yards ahead, a boy had climbed over the waist-high wall, intent on retrieving his hat from a nest of sharp-toothed alligators. A problem easily remedied by snatching the child out—were the boy's mother, or governess, or whoever-she-was not swooning.

Jackson lunged forward—only to be yanked backwards in a

chokehold with a blade pressed to his side, hard enough to hurt but not to draw blood. Not yet, anyway.

The stink of spoiled milk and onions hit him as forcefully as the growl in his ear. "Ye'll be goin' with me, guvnor. Nice and quiet like."

Jackson stiffened. Only God knew what would happen should he comply with the brigand. A second crime scene was notoriously worse than a first. . .and there was no debating the knife to his ribs *was* a crime. No. He'd have to take down this villain here and now.

Parents these days. Could they not keep a more watchful eye on their offspring? Kit frowned. No wonder this sort made for easy marks on the street.

As she expected, Jackson darted ahead to rescue the hapless lad, then as suddenly, he was yanked back.

What?

She snapped her gaze sideways. A fellow dressed in rags had him in a headlock, shuffling him towards the entrance—just as a shrill scream erupted from the boy in the alligator pen. In the blink of an eye, she and Jackson held an entire conversation without a word, one that affirmed their love and his capability of dispatching his own attacker and indicated she should meet the need of the defenseless child.

She whirled back to James. "Don't move, Brother. Stay here!"

Without waiting for confirmation, she sprinted to the alligator pen. Several ladies had already swooned, filling the arms of nearby men. Posh! Those lizards weren't even full grown. Sure, their snappers could inflict some serious damage, breaking bones and the like, but to faint over such a thing? She'd seen worse threats at the Hogboggon Alley dog fight arena. Even so, she took great care as she hefted her skirts and climbed over the wall.

"I say! Whatever are you about?" A man with a cane grumbled while trying to hook the boy's arm with the curved end. . .which would take a miracle. The child was on the floor, having fallen and skinned his knee.

And one of the sharp-toothed reptiles was closing in fast with clacking jaws.

Shutting out the cries of the gathering crowd—and the crash of glass where she'd left James and Jackson—Kit snatched the boy up. In two steps, she tossed him over the ledge to one of the bystanders. Once again, she gathered her skirts—or tried to. A mighty tug at her hem jerked her backwards. Fabric ripped. She flailed for balance.

"Grab hold!" The man shoved his cane at her.

Did he seriously think he could pull her out before teeth sank into her ankles? No. She'd not be hobbling about for the next few weeks, especially not down the aisle in her new gown.

"Thanks!" Kit yanked the cane from the man's hand and wheeled about. With mighty whacks, she beat the ugly reptile across the head… which unfortunately attracted the other alligators in the pen. Four more sets of snapping white teeth inched her way, emboldening the one she'd been whacking to charge ahead.

She dropped the cane and bolted, barely clearing the wall ahead of scratching claws, popping jaws, and the distinct crunch of wood.

"My cane!" the man cried.

"My hat!" the boy wailed.

"My goodness." Kit blew a hank of hair out of her face, thoroughly winded. After a few bats to straighten her gown—now raggedy edged, with a big chunk of fabric having been bitten off—she straightened.

Only to face what appeared to be the end of the world.

All over the room, women screamed. Men ran helter-skelter, scooping up small children and dodging an influx of zookeepers shouldering large nets. To her left, Jackson crouch-circled his attacker. His sleeve was ripped. Blood dripped. From one of the broken reptile encasements or the slice of the knife now lying on the ground? Either way, that was the least of her concerns. More pressing was the snake coiled right where James should have been standing.

A host of emotions rushed through her as she picked her way over to a quiet corner near one of the overlarge pots that yet stood. She didn't know if she should be elated James had wandered off or piqued he hadn't obeyed. At least he was safe from the snake watching her with beady eyes and flickering tongue. An underlying worry for Jackson nagged, but not as prickly as the creepy-crawlies under her skin from the loose reptiles slithering about. But now was not the time to panic. Observation, that was the ticket. A cool head and methodical thinking must be maintained if she were to find James in this macabre circus.

Grabbing hold of the tree trunk, she pulled herself up to stand on the pot's edge. From such a bird's-eye view, she scanned past the chaos to the turtle pen, searching for a blue coat on a man who easily stood a head above the rest. But there was none. Not one blessed person stood by the turtles. Most patrons were fleeing out the doors, screaming. Kit's blood ran cold. Had Jackson's feeble-minded brother run off as well? It was dangerous enough in here, but out on the London streets, alone?

God, no. Please let him be here. Please, help me find him.

Her gaze drifted from pen to pen, and. . .there. Not far away, perhaps ten yards or so, she focused on a broad set of shoulders hunched over a dropped cone of sugared nuts. What a dear! He hadn't wandered far, after all.

Thank You, God.

She jumped down, nearly upsetting the pot. The second her feet hit the ground, something heavy whumped onto her shoulders. Kit stiffened as a long, scaly tail draped over her bodice. Hissing overrode the pandemonium. Swallowing hard, she slowly turned her head—and came face-to-face with a forked tongue.

Now was the time to panic.

Chapter Seven

He should've trusted his gut, the very instinct the sergeant—and Kit—had tried to get him to embrace time and again. Jackson scowled as he circled his assailant, the same supposed beggar he'd sent scurrying earlier this morn. "Who are you?"

The man spit out a mouthful of blood. "Just doin' a job, guvnor. Nothin' personal."

Claptrap. The way the slice on his arm ached, this was personal. Jackson swung.

The man dodged. A narrow miss.

Bouncing on his toes, Jackson regrouped. The blackguard was no boxer, but neither was he a pushover. "Who hired you?"

His lips spread in a wicked grin, exposing teeth the colour of a dormouse. "Wouldn't ye like to know, eh?"

Shrieks bounced from wall to wall in the huge room. An alligator snapped, too close for comfort. Some sort of lizard ran between them. How had things gotten so out of hand? Time to end this nonsense and get Kit and James to safety.

Jackson crouched lower and put his weight into his rear foot. He'd hinge off his front and throw everything—

The man lunged sideways, swiping up a dropped parasol. In that one swift movement, the sport changed from boxing to fencing.

And Jackson didn't have a sword.

A blink of an eye later, the parasol's pointy end stabbed into the gash on his arm. Pain exploded, radiating down to his fingertips. Biting back a howl, he retreated a step, then another when the next thrust came dangerously close to his left eye. Plunge after plunge drove him backwards, towards the glass door. This would never do.

On the next jab, instead of withdrawing, Jackson sprang, putting all his muscle into smacking the parasol from the fellow's grip. The makeshift weapon flew sideways and clattered to the floor, exactly as he'd planned.

But what he hadn't counted on was the flash of murder blazing in the man's gaze. The brute charged, a bull intent on flattening his prey.

At the last minute, Jackson pivoted and planted an undercut to the man's nether region, connecting hard with soft tissue. A primal groan ripped past the brute's thick lips.

Winding back once again, Jackson let loose a right cross. He hit just below the cheekbone, square on the jaw. The man staggered backwards, then sprawled to the ground like a felled tree.

Jackson's chest heaved, dragging air into his lungs as he stood over the lump of rags. Nothing whatsoever was familiar about him. Not the zigzag scar on his chin nor the distinctive way the skin pulled taut over his cheekbones, as if the fellow had been shorted an ounce or two of flesh. So, if not a personal vendetta, who had hired this assailant? And why? Jackson nudged the man's boot. No movement. Good. He wouldn't be coming around for some time, and when he did, he'd have a head banger the size of Bristol.

Whipping out his handkerchief to wrap his wounded arm, Jackson scanned for Kit and his brother. The eerie silence of the place hit him like another blow to the gut. The hysterical patrons had been replaced by zookeepers who prowled about quietly, bagging loose reptiles. Thirty or so paces from him he spied Kit, frozen statuesque, with impossibly wide eyes, a linen-white face—

And a viper draped over her shoulders.

All the air punched from his lungs. *God, no!*

He dashed ahead, unsure of how to help her yet determined to do everything—*anything!*—he could.

A zookeeper shot out his arm, blocking him. "Stop," he hissed. "No movement. No loud sounds."

Jackson froze, the hopelessness of the situation sucking the very marrow from his bones. Was he to simply stand idly by and watch the woman he loved die? No. He couldn't. He wouldn't!

"Tell me what to do," he whispered to the green-coated keeper.

"There is nothing to be done but wait until ol' Dory decides that plate o' mice be more temptin' than the little lady." The keeper tipped his head slightly.

Jackson slid a glance where he indicated. Sure enough, a platter of brown fur had been set out near the wall, a mere six feet from the hem of Kit's skirt. Close, but close enough? What kind of danger had it been to even move that lure there in the first place?

He shot his gaze back to Kit. The fear in her eyes nearly buckled his knees. Never had he seen such terror swimming in those blue pools. This brave, bold woman, who wouldn't think twice about hefting a knife against a pile of muscle twice her size, now stood like a frightened little girl.

And there wasn't a thing he could do about it.

Oh, God, more than ever, I need You. Kit needs You. Show Yourself mighty. Please, do not take her from me. Not yet. We've hardly begun.

His throat closed. No air going in. None out. He might never breathe again, especially if that viper buried its fangs in Kit's tender flesh. The side of his own neck stung, just imagining the razor-sharp punctures that might take her life any second now.

I love you, he mouthed.

From the corner of his eye, a dark shape arose. James. Sweet heavens! He'd forgotten all about his brother. Yet there he stood, tipping back his head and patting the last crumbs from a cone of nuts into his mouth.

"James," he whisper-growled. "Stay still."

His brother turned towards his voice. The snake reared its head towards James, and the movement attracted his brother's gaze.

Perspiration glistened on Kit's face. So did tears.

"Lady cry?" James's voice boomed in the silence. "Bad snake!"

A mighty scowl carved into his brother's face. James dropped the paper cone, then took off at a run, straight towards Kit.

She'd died a thousand times in the past few minutes, in small ways and big. But this was the real moment. Her final breath. Clenching every muscle, Kit braced herself for the bite. The closer James drew, the more agitated the scaly skin pressing against the back of her neck became. It wouldn't be long now.

She scrunched her eyes shut, refusing to take to the grave the pain in Jackson's gaze. Would that things had been different. Would that she'd been his wife, even just for a day, before leaving him behind.

"Bad snake!" James roared.

The heavy weight on her shoulders lifted. No more warm, dry skin slithered across her nape. Her eyes shot open.

And then she really did die.

James clutched the snake by the tail in one hand, but the wicked serpent's mouth was firmly locked onto his other arm.

"James!" Her cry blended on the air with Jackson's.

Had he saved her life only to lose his own?

"Bad, bad snake!" Dropping the tail, James grabbed the viper's head and pried open its jaws, then flung the thing to the ground.

Immediately a net crashed down upon the deadly vermin. The zookeeper snatched it away but too late. The deed had been done.

"Oh, James." Her voice broke, as shattered as the look on Jackson's face.

"What is to be done?" Jackson questioned the green-coated keeper as he wrapped an arm about his brother's shoulder.

The man shook his head. "There's nothing can be done but make him comfortable."

Hot tears filled her eyes. It wasn't fair. It wasn't right. This gentle giant had done nothing but come to her aid.

"Is there no doctor on the premises?" Jackson's voice crashed like thunder. "Can we not—"

"No doctor!" James pulled away from him.

"But, Brother." Kit laid what she hoped was a calming touch on his shoulder while Jackson ordered the keeper to fetch a surgeon. "Your arm needs tending. At the very least, let's go sit down." How all those words made it past the lump lodged in her throat was nothing short of a miracle.

Even more miraculous was the slow grin spreading on James's face. He shook his head as if she'd spouted the most fantastic jest. "Silly lady."

Her heart squeezed. What a dear soul he was, leaving them all with a smile, though in reality, the simple-minded man likely had no idea of what was to come, what agonies his final breaths might bring.

"Kit is right." Once again, Jackson reached for him. "Your arm must be tended. Let's get that coat off you and sit you down."

Jackson helped his brother ease his uninjured arm out of one sleeve. Then, so tenderly, Kit watched as he slid off the other sleeve. Or tried to. The thing wouldn't budge. Had his arm swollen so large already?

"Ow!" James hollered. "Me do!"

He jammed his fingers into the opening of the sleeve at the wrist. After a few contortions of his lips, twisting this way and that, he finally yanked out a long, fat wad of red fabric.

"Silkie." He rubbed the swath of old blanket against his cheek.

Kit sucked in a breath. Had that gob of material possibly prevented the snake's fangs from breaking his skin? Her gaze met Jackson's, the wonder in his eyes mirroring the question.

Without a word, Jackson yanked off the rest of James's coat and shoved up his brother's sleeve. Sure enough, though the flesh was creased from the pressure of the balled-up blanket fragment, no blood dotted the surface. Not one blessed drop.

Kit wobbled on her feet. *Thank God!*

James looked at them as if they both needed a quick ride to the asylum. "Turtles now?"

"You never quit, do you?" Jackson chuckled as he helped his brother back into his coat. "But I think it best if we return to the Reptilium another time. Father will be worried." Jackson whispered out of the side of his mouth for her alone, "Especially if he catches wind of the uproar here this afternoon."

James frowned, a protest sure to follow.

"Well, I am famished," Kit interrupted, hoping to ward off a possible tantrum. "How about we share a pasty on our way out?"

"Brilliant idea." Jackson retrieved his coin purse and handed her some pennies. "Would you see that James not only gets some refreshment but also take him back to the inn? I have an assailant to escort to his new quarters at the station." He hitched a thumb over his shoulder.

Kit's gaze followed the gesture, then snapped back to him. "Do you?"

He pivoted—to view the empty spot on the terrazzo where a body should have been.

Chapter Eight

The only thing better than a hot drink of tea on a cold morning was catching a glimpse of the one you loved most over the rim of the cup. Not that Jackson sat opposite her—nothing so conventional. . .yet convention had never been her strong suit.

Kit shook out the leafy dregs in her cup and set it on the street vendor's tray just as Jackson came into view. My, my. What a fine view indeed with his strong stride and chiseled good looks. Never had she dreamed such a gallant man could love the likes of her.

A smile spread on his face as he spied her, which boded well. She'd been hoping he'd be in a good mood this morning after all the hubbub of yesterday's zoo adventure, for she had a brilliant idea taking root. The trick would be getting enough information from him without hinting at what she was about, for above all, a wedding gift should be a surprise.

And what a gift it would be—*if* she could pull off the job in time.

As he neared, she linked arms with him, matching his pace. "This is a rather rough part of town, sir. Shall I accompany you to keep you from being accosted?"

A smirk twisted his lips, and before she could blink, he flipped her around and backed her against a wall, his palms planted on either side of her, effectively penning her in. This was no greenhorn rookie, not anymore.

He leaned in close, the scent of his bay rum shaving tonic spicy on the air. "How about I accost you instead?"

Goodness and light! In one sultry gaze, he stole the very breath from her lungs. Not that she'd let on, though. She angled her head to a superior tilt. "I suppose I cannot refuse such an offer."

After a stealthy glance around, he brushed his lips against hers. "So, am I to learn why you've lain in wait to waylay me this early in the day? My animal magnetism, perhaps?" He waggled his eyebrows.

"Something even better."

"Better than me?" He folded his arms with a huff, then winced and dropped them to his sides. Apparently he'd forgotten his injury.

Kit shook her head, unable to stop a smile. Was she marrying an inspector or an aspiring actor? "You are as gifted at sulking, my love, as your very accomplished brother. I will have you know James was cross the entire ride home from the zoo yesterday. Why, I doubt your father will have a moment's peace until he takes him back to the Reptilium. Speaking of which, did you ever find your missing assailant?"

"No." He sighed. "Not a sign of him. Shall we?" He offered his good arm.

Kit rested her hand atop his sleeve, admiring the thick cords of muscle beneath the fabric. "No leads?"

"Not a one."

And there she had it—an opening, packaged and delivered right to her door. "As I recall, you never told me if there were any leads on the people who attacked your brother all those years ago."

"Leads?" He snorted. "I was ten years old at the time, hardly of an age to pursue an investigation. As I recall, the police had no luck either. Why?"

Oh, no. She'd not meet that soul-exposing stare of his. Gathering this information was too vital to accomplishing all she hoped to attain. She made a production of lifting her hem to avoid tripping on an upraised cobble. "Simply wondering," she murmured.

Once again Jackson guided her aside, and then he tipped her face with a light touch to search her eyes. "You never idly wonder, my sweet. What is in that pretty little mind of yours?"

"I told you. I am curious about what happened to your brother, especially now that I've come to care for him." She shrugged. "He saved my life yesterday, despite his obvious mental challenges. . .which got me to thinking on what happened to him to put him in such a state to begin with. Hence my question. How many did you say were in on the crime the day James was attacked?"

"Does it matter?" Jackson eyed her more thoroughly than a cut-purse sizing up a crowd on market day.

Flit! She'd known extracting information from this man would be difficult, but not *this* difficult. She flashed him a smile, one that did nothing to untie the pinch of his brow. "In the grand scheme of things, I suppose it isn't of vital importance. Yet if I am to understand your brother, to learn to interact with him in ways that are meaningful to him, I should know exactly how he came to be the way he is. But if you don't think it as valuable as I do, then never mind."

Taking a risk, she tossed her head and made to sidestep him.

"Hold on." Jackson mirrored her movement, blocking her. "Since you put it that way, how can I refuse? Most women write James off, ignore or pity him, but never once has one sought to understand him. You know, you never stop surprising me, Kit Turner."

"I should hope not." She grinned, both from the admiration in his gaze and the fresh opening this created. "So, what were the details of that ill-fated day?"

Jackson sucked in an audible breath—and for the first time since she'd set this course, she wondered if she ought to turn back. Digging up the past would be painful for him, but in the end, the prize would outweigh the pain. Hopefully.

With a faraway glaze to his eyes, Jackson rubbed his knuckles along his jaw, a now-familiar habit.

"I cannot be sure," he said. "Two. Three? Seems that would be a typical setup." His blue gaze once again focused on her. "As you well know, for were there not three of you targeting me when we first met?"

"My, my. You do excel at sulking." She arched a brow. "Isn't it time you got over that little incident?"

"Isn't it time you told me what you're up to? Not that I doubt you care for James—and for that I *am* grateful—yet still, I cannot help but wonder. . .why the sudden urgency to know? Could this not have waited until dinner?"

"Justice is always a pressing matter." She smoothed a crease on his lapel, allowing him time to swallow that bait, then blinked up at him. "Do you not think those responsible for maiming your brother ought to be held accountable?"

"Mmm," he murmured. "I think of it every time I see him." He caught her hand and pressed a kiss to her wrist before releasing it. "But those men are long gone."

"Are they, though?"

"Kit, that was thirteen years ago." Plowing his fingers through his hair, he let out a long breath. "Even if they were still around—which is highly unlikely—there is no way to prove what they did. I never saw their faces. Those thugs knew what they were doing, coming up from behind, then keeping to the shadows in that passageway."

Clenching her jaw, she bit back a rather unsavory oath. She knew the type of scoundrels who would do just such a thing. Immoral, greedy jackanapes! They deserved to be locked up for stealing James's chance at a normal life. "You may not have seen the felons who attacked your brother," she ground out, "but no doubt there's a lookout somewhere who knows who did the deed. I know that setup well enough. Bullies bent on robbery always have an innocent as a spotter, ready to squawk should trouble show up."

"If that's so, then same as me, he was but a child at the time." His Adam's apple bobbed, and that, combined with the tic near his left eye, gave away a raging inner struggle.

Setting aside her anger, Kit studied him. What sort of demons tormented him? Guilt? Anger? Defeat? Shame? Likely all. Her heart squeezed. Would that she could remove such bitter memories or at least ease them—and by God's grace, she would.

At length, Jackson shook his head. "Thanks to you, I have made peace with the past. I see no point in revisiting it."

"Even if doing so brings criminals to justice?"

"As I've said, I have no doubt those men are long gone. There is no sense in wasting your time, and there is nothing more to be done for James. Love him as he is and leave the past in the past, where it belongs."

She stepped closer, resting her hands against his chest, hoping to drive home the importance of her query. "But Jackson, if you could just think back, even a snippet of memory concerning that lookout might be the key to—"

"Forge!"

Jackson wheeled about, and they both met the gaze of a brown-eyed blue-suit.

"You might want to save these dalliances for after the wedding, eh? The chief's bellowing for a certain inspector." Officer Baggett tipped his hat at her. "Mornin', Miss Turner."

"Good morning, Mr. Baggett." She dipped her head.

Jackson turned back to her with a light touch to her cheek. "I must run. See you tonight at the George?"

"Absolutely." She forced a smile, belying the disappointment sagging her shoulders from such a failed interview.

"Come along, Baggett." Jackson set off. "I may need you as a buffer."

Heaving a sigh, Kit watched them stride towards the Old Jewry Station, her gaze lingering on Jackson. Well. That hadn't gone as planned. Still, lack of information had never before proved too high a roadblock to hurdle. Despite Jackson's admonition to leave the past behind, she'd simply have to find a way to gain her historical evidence elsewhere.

Turning on her heel, she headed to the soup kitchen. Martha had asked her to keep Frankie busy, and now she had just the case for him. She already knew where James had been beaten. She knew when. All she had left to find out was who had committed the crime, and then she could bring the ruffians to justice.

After all, what better wedding gift could she give a man of the law, especially one who despite his objections still didn't seem to have quite as much peace with the past as he claimed? A compassionate man like Jackson not only needed that peace, he deserved it.

And she'd be the one to give it to him.

There was a certain odour that permeated Chief Inspector Theodore Ridley's office, so distinct it popped Jackson in the nose the moment he entered. Musky parrot droppings, sweet Turkish tobacco, and a sharp tang of comfrey liniment—quite the opposite to the dusty, stuffy little corner beneath the stairs that his own desk occupied.

Bypassing the enormous birdcage taking up half the office, Jackson straightened to full attention in front of the chief's desk. "Sorry I'm late, sir. I was conferring with Officer Baggett and—"

"Hang 'im up, boys! Hang 'im up!" An ear-screeching squawk followed the only line the bird knew.

Jackson schooled his face, denying the urge to scowl at the feathered menace. First Kit's shenanigans with dredging up the past, now the contempt of a bird. And judging by the glower on Ridley's face, the disapproval of his superior as well.

"Why you were delayed is neither here nor there, Forge. The fact remains you are late." It was arguable how old Ridley was, but the censure in the man's granite gaze left no quarter for debate. He was a full-faced man, clean-shaven, with rivers of quicksilver running through his once-dark hair. He wore it slicked back, not a strand out of place, every bit as controlled as the men he ruled over.

Jackson dipped his head. "I grant you that tardiness is unprofessional, sir, and I beg your pardon for my lapse."

Propping his elbows on the desk, the chief planted his chin atop his knuckles, beginning a round of uncomfortable silence. Moments like these, Jackson missed the stormy bluster of Sergeant Graybone. At least then he knew how many ways until Sunday he'd offended and what was to be suffered for the breach. Stiffening his shoulders, he prepared to weather Ridley's stare-down.

At length, the man inhaled so sharply, his nostrils contorted. "There is nothing to be done for it now, I suppose. I knew full well when I took you on of your unpunctual habits, thanks to Sergeant Graybone's thorough briefing. I suggest, however, you show up on time for your own wedding."

Jackson lifted his chin. "I shall do my utmost, sir."

"As well you should." Ridley drifted back in his chair, the obnoxious creak of the wood as unrelenting as the iron grey of his eyes. "Now then, since we're on the topic of your upcoming nuptials, I can spare you a few days off, as you requested, but as for a rise in wages, the answer is no. While the superintendent is pleased with your work on the Culpepper case, he was not of a mind to approve a higher salary."

"Hang 'im up, boys!" The parrot squawked again. "Hang 'im up!"

Indeed. Jackson shot the bird a sideways glance, fully agreeing with the sentiment. Surely the superintendent could have made a concession. It wasn't as if the man would have to pay the extra pennies from his own pocket. An inspector's wages were enough to support himself now, but with a wife and—Lord willing—a child? He'd have to be more creative with his finances. . .unless the earl was still interested in taking him on. Unbidden, Jackson's fingers clenched. He wasn't as resolved on the matter as he'd thought, and oh, how he hated to be double minded.

"Have you something to say, Inspector?"

Jackson snapped his gaze back to the chief. "Yes, sir. Thank you. I appreciate you inquiring with the superintendent."

"I should hope so." Ridley sniffed, his upper lip curling. "Ever since the man beat me at backgammon, he's been an insufferable boor."

"Hang 'im up, boys! Hang 'im up!" *Squawk.*

"Agreed, Dutchy." The chief rounded his desk and poked a small piece of dried fruit through the bars of the cage. "As for your workload over the next week, I doubt very much your mind will be on solving murders and the like. Still, you must earn your keep." He swiped a folder from the top of his desk. "This ought to keep you busy. It's a relatively mindless task, but one that needs doing. Sometimes one must be a gatherer instead of a hunter. Information is every bit as important before a crime is committed as after, and as you well know, there never has been nor ever will be a shortage of offenses on Holywell Street."

Jackson flipped the folder's cover to the first page. Columns lined the paper, one listing addresses, another, owners. The third column bore the heading of current occupant and was blank. His gut tightened. *This* was what his distinguished crime-fighting career had come to? Taking a census of all the flash houses and opium dens in the Holywell slum was as bad as guarding a fabric warehouse with a persnickety dog. The job with the earl was looking better every minute.

He tucked the folder under his arm and straightened his shoulders. Showing any sign of disappointment with the assignment would only earn him another round of the stare-the-subordinate-into-submission game.

"Thank you, sir," he said.

The chief sank into his chair. "That's all I have for you today, Forge. Dismissed."

Jackson shifted his weight, not quite prepared to lose such an opportunity to gain information—which was, as the chief said himself, important. "Excuse me, but one more thing, sir, being that I have your sole attention."

"Make it quick." Ridley tapped a thick ledger near his elbow. "With your days off, there is some schedule juggling to which I must attend."

"Yes, sir." He rubbed the back of his neck. Now, how to word the whole vicar conundrum without letting on he didn't have a clue as to the details of the clerical program? The sword-grey gaze of the chief would slice through any thin shield of purported knowledge he might try to take cover behind. Perhaps it would be better to question the vicar instead of the chief. Yes! Capital plan.

He met the chief's gaze. "I was wondering, sir, if you could provide the address of the vicar."

Ridley's brows pulled into a thick line. "There's practically a church on every corner, man. Can you not find one on your own?"

"Yes, sir, but I meant in reference to the newly formed liaison between the station and the clergy, specifically the vicar assigned to my detainees. I should like his contact information so I can meet with him. You know. Continue the lines of communication and all that."

"What the devil are you going on about, Forge?"

"The recently installed program for prisoners and—"

"Hang 'im up—"

Before the parrot could finish, Jackson flashed the bird a glare. He growled low in his throat, effectively silencing its unwelcome tirade, then turned back to the chief.

"Thunder and turf!" The chief pounded his fist on the desk.

Jackson squelched a flinch. Had he crossed some invisible line by calling his superior's pet to task?

"Did the superintendent put you up to this prank, Forge?" The chief's eyes blazed. "Because if he did, he's taken this backgammon business to a new low."

Jackson widened his stance, holding ground against the chief's glower. "No, sir. This is no jest, though it may be a case of misunderstanding. Perhaps I misconstrued what Constable Barrycloth told me. Might I ask if you are familiar with a vicar by the name of Mortusagro? He wears a pox veil and stopped by to see one of my convicts the other day."

"I have never heard the name. Now then, as I said"—Ridley reached for the ledger—"I have work to do."

"Very good, sir." Jackson gave a sharp nod. "Thank you."

He strode from the room, ignoring Dutchy's loud caws. More troubling than the gratuitous census in his hand was the chief's ignorance of a clerical liaison between church and gaol. If Chief Inspector Ridley hadn't authorized the vicar's visit—and he hadn't either—then who had?

And why?

Chapter Nine

Eight days should have been more than enough time to hunt down the pair of scummers who'd maimed James all those years ago. Eight full days! Kit stormed across Ironmonger Lane, ignoring an offensive jibe from the dray driver she cut off. Shouldn't the week before a wedding be light and happy? Hah! It had been anything but. After combing through countless ratholes and rookeries, scrapping for snippets of information, she was still empty-handed and cross. She'd so wanted to surprise Jackson tomorrow at their wedding breakfast by handing him the key to a cell housing those foul brigands, or at least give him a card with their names on it.

She hiked her skirts to long-step over a gutter of brackish muck, a sight as pleasant as the scowl on Mrs. Gilman's face this morn when she'd picked up her gown. The woman had made a last-gasp effort to cajole her into purchasing a white shawl, and when that hadn't worked, she'd offered to rent her one. Even now Kit smirked. She couldn't keep such a dainty clean if her life depended upon it.

By the time she reached the Old Jewry police station, her fractious mood was hardly improved, not with her shoes and hem covered in filth from a street sweeper. Before reaching for the door, she paused to brush off her shoulders and skirt. Meeting with her father in such a state would assuredly raise one of his bushy eyebrows.

"Allow me to get that for you, miss—though you'll not be a miss for much longer." Jackson's deep voice rumbled behind her, and as he opened the door, the gleam in his eyes made it hard to remember exactly why she'd been so churlish.

"Thank you, kind sir." She swept past him into the hubbub of the station, then followed the tip of his head to a quieter corridor off the side of the stairway.

After a sly glance side to side, Jackson pecked her on the cheek. While entirely chaste, it was a bold move. If one of the constables chanced to see, he'd no doubt bear a slew of crude jests later.

He retreated a pace, as if there were nothing more between them than a platonic how-do-you-do. "I didn't expect to see you here today." He tucked the folder he carried under his arm. "Shouldn't you be out doing whatever it is that brides do, buying fripperies or partaking of beauty treatments and the like?"

"Are you suggesting I need something to enhance this?" She circled her face with an open palm.

"No!" Red crept up his neck. "I didn't mean. . .I mean, I didn't. . . Scads! You *know* what I mean."

The first genuine smile of the day quirked her lips. "Well, aren't you the tongue-tied gent. I hope that's not a sign you won't be able to manage your 'I wills' at church."

"Never fear, my lady." He slapped his hand to his heart. "I vow I shall practice all evening."

"Good, then you shan't miss me when I don't show up for dinner tonight."

"Again?" He frowned while he waited for a few officers to pass by. "I am beginning to think you're avoiding my company—which doesn't bode well for a marriage partner."

"Pish." Spying another dusty smudge on her sleeve, she brushed it off. "You worry too much."

"With reason. You have missed the past four nights with me and my family. Even James has voiced his doubts on your flimsy excuses. So, let's have it. What have you been up to?" A muscle jumped in his jaw, a spasm meaning he'd not be trifled with for much longer.

"Very well. If you must know, I've been working on a wedding gift for my husband."

"Kit, you're the only gift I need." He stroked his thumb over the curve of her cheek. "Whatever it is you've been working on, leave it be. I'd rather have you at my side than some wrapped-up trifle in my hand."

The touch, the swell of love in his gaze, his scent of man and strength all left her a bit weak-kneed—but not feeble enough that she'd let go of her mission. She pressed her face into his touch. "Grant me this one last night of freedom, my love, won't you?"

He pulled back as boot heels pounded down the stairs. His chest expanded and deflated before he finally answered. "I suppose I can allow you one more night, but once you're my wife, I shall expect you safely at home with me, understood?"

It sounded wonderful, truly. Hours on end with the man she loved. Sitting at his side. Walking hand in hand. An absolute dream. Still. . .

Other than her tender years at the foundling home and that stint as a housemaid more than a decade ago, she'd not had to answer to anyone but herself. Coming and going on her own terms was her life-blood. A time of transition would be needed before she fully surrendered. Besides, she still had a soup kitchen to run and Frankie to keep out of mischief.

Jackson pulled out his pocket watch, and except for a brief glance at the time, his gaze bored into hers. "As much as I'd love to hear whatever objections you seem to be harbouring—which I am sure aren't anything we can't solve together—it will have to wait. I have an appointment with the chief and I'd best not be late. Was there something you wanted from me?"

She shook her head. "I have my own appointment, with my father."

"Give him my regards. And I shall see you tomorrow." The blue in his eyes glimmered with imminent possibility.

Mercy! Was it hot in here? Cheeks burning, she sucked in a breath, then tossed back her head as if they discussed nothing more than which variety of potato to purchase for dinner.

"You, sir, are incorrigible." She strode past him without a backwards glance, for to do so would steal the breath she had left.

Thankfully, by the time she reached her father's office, she'd cooled considerably. She frowned at the scarred door standing ajar. The bottom half of the S in Sergeant Henry Graybone still hadn't been repainted. Perhaps she ought to bring a brush and some bootblack to fix it herself. Now that she knew her father, she very much wished the best for him, even in something as slight as the letters on his door.

After a cursory rap on the frame and her father's bellowed "Enter," she slipped in. A desk sat at center, dwarfed by the man behind it.

"You asked to see me, Father?" *Father.* She could still hardly believe this gentle giant was her own flesh and blood.

"I did. Have a seat, please." He tapped a thick stack of papers into an orderly pile, then set them onto his desk while she sat.

And sat.

And sat.

All without one word from him. She cocked her head. "Did I catch you at an inopportune time?"

"No, no. Now's as good as any." One of his big fingers tapped on the tabletop, yet still the only thing that broke the silence was the shuffle of feet outside in the corridor and an occasional howl from the cells below.

Odd. Usually, the man was straight to the point. Unease crept up her spine. What wasn't he telling her? "Are you well, Father?"

"Fine, fine." *Tap-tap-tap.*

Despite his assurance, there was nothing fine about this meeting or the nervous beat of his finger. "Was there a particular reason you summoned me here, or am I merely to be an ornament for your office?"

The tapping stopped, replaced by a slap of his hand on the desk. "That tongue of yours! I wonder that Jackson is taking you on. I suspect your mother—God rest her—would have had plenty to say about such cheek, young lady."

She grinned. "This tongue of mine has kept me out of many a scrape. So, are we to have a discussion or not?"

"As you should know by now, I'm not much for talking. I just, em... well...I have something here." He retrieved a small black box from a top drawer and shoved it across the desk with a gruff "For you."

Her heart skipped a beat as she reached for it. In the four months since they'd been reunited, he'd not once given her a gift—unless she counted the return of his Coldstream Guard button that she'd carried since birth. She opened the lid, and her breath caught as she pulled out a blue velvet-ribbon necklace with a single pearl dangling from a cameo. The profile was the very image of herself. Or was it her mother? For she'd been told time and again she was a picture of the woman.

She clutched the keepsake to her chest and gazed at her father through a blur of tears. "It's beautiful."

He tugged at his collar. "It was your mother's. The ribbon, leastwise. She pulled it from her hair that day I shipped out. Pulled it right from her hair. . ." A faraway look glazed his eyes, and for a long moment she'd wager he stood on that briny wharf, the same as twenty-four years ago when he'd bid her mother goodbye.

Carefully, she folded the necklace back into the box, allowing him time to regroup.

At length, he cleared his throat. "I thought you should have it, so I had the ribbon made into something special for you to wear tomorrow. The cameo itself was a fortuitous find, for I'd say it looks exactly like you and your mother."

"I love it." Tucking the small box into her pocket, she rose and rounded the desk to plant a light kiss on his cheek.

He caught her hand before she pulled away. "Your mother would be proud of the woman you've become. I wish she were here to see you."

So did she. More than anything. Somehow, she managed a small "Me too."

Her father puffed out a breath and released her. "But the past is in the past."

She straightened, arching a brow down at him. "You sound like Jackson."

"Oh?" A storm brewed in his tone. "Has he some skeletons I should know about?"

"Straitlaced Jackson?" She laughed. "No, I was just looking into his brother's assailants."

"And he knows you're doing so?"

"Do you think I'd keep secrets from him?"

He slanted back in his chair, folding his arms. "You'd keep secrets from God Himself if you thought you could get away with it."

"You're beginning to know me far too well, I think. Or is it, perhaps, that though I look like my mother"—she bent close—"I have the cunning of my father?"

"Your deflection won't work. Leave the assailant hunting to Jackson and attend yourself to wedding matters. Now is not the time to nose about in past crimes. So, off with you." He flicked his hand in the air. "You have a ceremony to prepare for and I have paperwork to attend."

"Well, see that you get it all done. I would not have my father late to my wedding tomorrow morning."

With a reach of his arm, he tapped the pile of papers on his desk. "Neither reports nor brigands will keep me away."

Simple words, but even so, an unexpected surge of emotion once again brought the sting of tears to her eyes. What was this? Did being a bride mean she'd turned into a softhearted nimby-namby? Yet like it or not, there was nothing she could do to stop the rush of love she suddenly felt for this man.

"Father, I—" She choked up. Evidently, she wasn't much for talking either.

His bushy brows dipped low over his eyes. "Yes, Daughter?"

"Don't be late."

"It's your husband-to-be you ought to worry about. That man will be late to his own burial."

She paused on the threshold and tossed him a look over her shoulder. "If Jackson is late, it *will* be his burial. I'll see to that."

"I have no doubt. Now"—he reached for a pencil and drew the paper stack close—"off with you."

Kit smiled and closed the door quietly behind her. All the way to the front of the station she glanced about, hoping for a final glimpse of Jackson. Blue suits abounded on men of all statures, but none were as fine as the man she loved. Just as well. With less than twenty-four hours to complete her mission, she didn't have time for distraction.

She shoved open the station door and entered the fray of pedestrians, mulling over what stones were left to upturn to find the blackguards who'd maimed James.

"Been lookin' for ye, Miss Kit." A freckle-faced boy joined her side.

She glanced down at Frankie. The past week she'd kept him busy enough checking on rabbit trails to follow, and Martha had said the boy kept her informed of where he'd been and where he was going. Even so, every time she met Frankie's gaze, he made sure to shift his eyes to her forehead or nose. . .a trick she employed when wishing to keep something hidden.

She led him to the side of the pavement, stopping near a stack of apple crates by the greengrocer. "And now that you have found me, what have you to say?"

"More like what have I to give." He held up a slip of paper with a few words scrawled in what appeared to be charcoal.

Scampson Warehouse
5 pounds

She frowned. "What's this?"

"That lookout ye had me snufflin' 'round about, the one what saw who roughed up Mr. Jackson's brother?"

Her breath caught. Had the little street curmuffin uncovered a valuable tip? "Yes?"

Frankie nodded at the paper. "Someone knows who he is, miss. Someone who'll talk for a price."

A thrill zinged through her. Still, it paid to proceed with caution. Getting too excited only made one sloppy—and sloppiness was unforgivable on these streets. "How did you come by this information?"

"Em..." He twisted the toe of his shoe against the pavement, then lifted his face to hers, this time boldly meeting her gaze. "I can't rightly say, miss, other than I got it from a new acquaintance of mine—one who's as well connected and reliable as you. If ye trust me, ye'll leave it at that."

Deep inside those brown eyes of his, she caught another glimpse of the man this boy would become. A stalwart man, one who would allow no questioning of his integrity. And then the glimpse vanished, like the closing of a great pair of shutters over a window into a house that wasn't yet ready for company to view.

She tucked the paper into her pocket. As much as she wished to question the lad, to do so might wound the spirit inside those nine-year-old trappings who wanted—nay, needed—to be trusted.

"So," she said, "when am I to meet with this informant?"

"Tomorrow morning, miss. Just after daybreak."

"Tomorrow?" The word barely squeaked past her lips.

"Aye, miss."

She leaned against the grocer's wall, for the first time wondering if she ought to follow Jackson's instruction and *leave it be*. Should she really chance an appointment with an informant in a rat-infested, broken-down warehouse on her wedding day?

The Mayfair neighbourhood had a way of frowning down upon those who didn't belong, like a great aunt with a penchant for lip curling, making one feel the size of a grease ant for having shown up at the dinner table with a crooked collar. The same chagrin settled tidily in Jackson's gut as he entered the exclusive jeweler on Albemarle Street, particularly when the clerk eyed him from boot to bowler with thinly veiled disgust.

"May I be of service?" The man folded his hands primly atop the display case.

"Is Mr. Gerrard available?"

"He is not." The clerk sniffed, his sloping nose bobbing. "But if you go around to the back loading dock, our office manager, Mr. Candler, can help you sort out any transportation issues, provide you with the correct delivery addresses and the like."

Ahh. No wonder he'd been the recipient of such a mouldering look. Jackson smiled as he approached the counter. "I am not a delivery-man. I'm here to make a final payment and pick up a ring that's been set aside under the name of Forge."

"Is that so?"

The clerk might as well have called him a bald-faced liar, such was his tone. He ran his finger along a collection of boxes on the many shelves behind the counter. But even so occupied, the fellow cast frequent looks over his shoulder, silently warning Jackson not to so much as think of pilfering anything.

Purposely ignoring him, Jackson studied the sparkling baubles inside the glass case. Just one of those diamond bracelets or ruby necklaces was worth more than all the many hovels on Holywell Street. What a sorry state of affairs. It was neither right nor just that the men and women he'd documented over the past week must daily wonder where their next bite of gruel would come from when all this wealth sat idle. He'd been glad to put that assignment behind him, especially considering what he had to look forward to. For the next five days, he'd be a free man with nothing whatsoever to do but enjoy his new wife.

Wife!

His pulse took off at a gallop. This time tomorrow he'd be a married man.

The clerk opened the lid on a small black box. "Is this the piece?"

Chandelier light glistened off the many facets of a pink sapphire, which was quite a misnomer. The rare gem, set in a gold band and nestled atop white satin, glowed more purple than pink. Fitting that the name didn't begin to describe its true beauty. . .perfect for the woman who'd wear it.

"Yes, thank you." Jackson reached for the box.

The clerk beat him to it, sliding the thing back across the counter. "You owe ten more pounds before this may be removed from the store."

Jackson pulled out the banknotes he'd so carefully saved from the inside pocket of his suit coat. A hefty sum, one he could not have attained without the help of his father. But Kit was worth every penny in the world even if he had to borrow it. He laid the hard-earned money on the glass.

"There you have it. Paid in full." Once again, he reached for the box.

This time the clerk's bony fingers covered the container. "First I shall require your signature on a release form."

With his free hand, the man retrieved a half-sheet document from beneath the counter, then followed that up with a silver tray bearing a pen and ink.

Stifling a sigh, Jackson flourished his name on the line. He stabbed the paper with his forefinger and pushed it back. "I'll be taking that ring now, thank you."

The clerk's dark eyes drifted from his outstretched hand to his face, his long nose lifting into the air. "Not quite yet, I think. There are procedures to which one must adhere. Protocol to uphold, principally when a customer is unknown. . .and you are most certainly an unknown. I shall require some identification before I can release an item of such value."

"But I already paid you!" Who did this power-mongering little weasel think he was?

"You supplied me with the remainder of what was owed, sir, not the *full* amount, which had already been put on deposit. How am I to know you are who you say you are? That you're not some brigand who accosted the real Mr. Forge, lifted his money, and are now cashing in on a gem of considerable worth?"

Jackson clenched his jaw, restraining every muscle in his body to keep from snatching Kit's ring from the man's grip. He yanked out his badge and stiff-armed it in front of the man's eyes. "As you can see, sir, you may safely entrust that ring—*my* ring—into my care. That is, unless you have any more hoops you should like me to jump through?"

"Is there a problem here?" a deep voice boomed behind Jackson.

Jackson turned while the clerk spluttered, "Yes, Mr. Gerrard. This man is giving me quite the—"

"Young Mr. Forge? Alfred's boy?" The sharply dressed, grey-haired owner clapped Jackson on the shoulder. "Can it be?"

Jackson grinned. "One and the same, sir. And I am certain my father would wish to send you his warmest regards."

"Ha ha! No doubt about that, and over a mug of ale to boot. Give him my regards next time you see him, but for now I must be off. I am certain Mr. Harbald here will take good care of you."

"Yes, sir. I expect your clerk will treat me in the best possible fashion." He glanced at the fellow behind the counter, who suddenly blanched to a peculiar shade of grey. "Good day, Mr. Gerrard."

"To you as well." The older fellow clapped on his hat and disappeared out the door.

Jackson lifted a brow at the clerk as the man handed over the tiny ring box. "Thank you." Though much more could have been said, he chose the higher road with a sigh and left it at that.

The clerk practically broke his leg as he sped to the door, opening it with a bow grand enough for the Queen herself. "A very good day to you, Inspector."

Jackson tipped his hat at the man as he strolled out into the late afternoon. Hopefully in the future, the puffed-up clerk would think twice about treating a customer so poorly.

"Mr. Forge?"

He glanced over at a long-legged man exiting the tailor shop next door with the step of one who owned the world. . .for so he did, or at least a good portion of it. Of all the people to run into, it had to be the earl?

Jackson dipped his head. "Good afternoon, my lord."

"I did not realize Mayfair was part of your jurisdiction." The earl straightened his cuffs, a tilt to his head. "Unless you are simply out for a stroll."

"Neither, my lord."

"Then dare I hope you were on your way to call upon me?"

Jackson stepped closer, allowing an older couple to pass by on the pavement without having to break apart. "I am afraid I must disappoint you once again. I was picking up a ring I ordered for my bride." He swept his hand towards the jeweler's.

"Gerrard's, eh? Very nice. I did not realize the wages of an inspector allowed for purchases at the jeweler to the Crown."

Hah! He bit back a snort. His salary was more suited to a Clerkenwell pawnbroker. Were it not for the sizeable sum from his father and his family's long-standing friendship with the Gerrards, he'd never have been able to afford the silk-lined box warming his pocket.

"Yes," Jackson drawled, unsure how to unfurrow the earl's brows. "I, em—"

"No need to explain. I now understand more thoroughly why you turned down my offer. Not enough to entice you, eh?" Gordon-Lennox pursed his lips. "So, to what degree would you have me increase the amount?"

Jackson shook his head. "Your offer was more than generous. I have no hesitation whatsoever on that account. If you would reconsider permitting my bride to travel along with me, then I can say without pause that I am your man."

"Hmm." A gust of October wind curled around them both, and the earl reset his hat with a resounding tap to the top of it. "I am willing to negotiate remuneration, but I am afraid I must remain firm on my stance of no females. I shall give you seven more days to accept my offer. Otherwise, I must offer it to another man I have waiting in the wings."

"I understand, yet I am resolute in the fact that I cannot accept a position which would take me away from my new wife for so long. My best to you, however, and to the man you will hire." Stepping aside, he once again dipped his head. "Good day, my lord."

With a last enigmatic look, the earl strode past him. "Good day to you, Inspector."

Jackson stood near the tailor's great glass window, watching the fellow disappear into his shiny black barouche with green velvet curtains. A hard pit balled in his stomach. Was he making the right decision? And yet. . .instinctively, he shoved his hand into his pocket and fingered the ring box. The tightness in his belly loosened by increments. Once he put that gold band on Kit tomorrow morning, there was no way on God's green earth he would—or could—leave her.

The earl's carriage departed, giving him full view of the street, where his gaze snagged on a short man across the cobbles. A slight hump bulged his upper back, as if he'd spent years hefting a shovel. There was something familiar about that slightly hitched step, the white hair, the gnarled hands swinging back and forth as he walked. He'd seen him before. . .but where?

Instantly on alert, Jackson widened his stance, prepared for anything—anything except for the sudden realization of who the fellow was. The dust yard worker. The old duffer who'd snagged a silver napkin ring the week before he and Kit had taken down Sackett. What the deuce was he doing in the most affluent neighbourhood in all of London, dressed as if he were about to take in an opera?

Hmm. This bore looking into. Perhaps the Dedfield case wasn't as locked tight and tucked away as he'd imagined.

Chapter Ten

The thing about a life event was one could never sleep the night before it—a universal truth Kit had desperately tried to disprove as she'd tangled about in her sheets for hours. Yet she failed quite spectacularly. Every sheep counted turned into a chisel-jawed, blue-eyed, handsome Jackson Forge. The man would simply not be banished from her thoughts no matter how hard she tried to evict him.

Yawning, Kit bypassed her paper-wrapped wedding gown and pulled out her mud-brown skirt, hopelessly frayed at the hem from one too many treks down alleyways and gutter grates. Even a ragpicker would snub this sorry fabric. She stepped into the tatty garment and secured it at the waist, a smirk twisting her lips. This old street scamperer was the perfect attire for an early morning adventure.

And my, but it was early. She picked up her hairbrush and began untangling a few snarls. She'd considered trying to arrange another time to meet with the informant, but once she was married to Jackson, would another chance truly come? He'd already made clear his expectations. It would be far better to start their new life together with this behind them.

After a quick tussle with the brush and a few pins to snug back some stray locks, she turned from the mirror. Time later to fuss with her looks. For now, she had business to attend.

She tucked a five-jack into her corset, the paper of the banknote cool against her skin. It was an inordinate amount, one that could purchase buckets of pork bones and pounds of beans for the soup kitchen.

She really ought to haggle over the informant's fee, but there would be no wiggle room for negotiation, not if she wanted to make it back here in time to change for her wedding.

Wedding! My, how foreign the word sounded. She'd never allowed herself to imagine what life might be like as a married woman. She'd never thought anyone would choose the likes of her.

She paused with her hand on the doorknob, envisioning Jackson at the altar, his fingers entwined with hers, pledging the rest of his life to her alone before God and man. How was it she'd been so blessed?

"Thank You, God," she whispered, then pushed open the door. The sooner this rendezvous was over, the sooner she'd be on her way to Jackson's side—hopefully with the names of the ones responsible for his brother's attack.

She padded down the corridor, careful to avoid the creaky floorboard in front of Mistress Mayhew's bedroom. No sense waking the old bird. Suffering one of her long-winded orations on the deportment of a proper young lady would eat into an already tight schedule.

The passageway opened into the wider front hall. Though her eyes were adjusted to the predawn darkness, the coat tree in the corner loomed like a backstreet hackum bent on murder. Ack! What was she thinking? Wedding jitters were getting to her. She grabbed her shawl from the wooden stand and tied it tight at the neck, knowing that despite such precaution, the first blast of morning air would shiver through her as soon as she stepped outside.

"I was not aware daybreak weddings were in vogue, Miss Turner."

Kit spun, slapping a hand to her chest. How in the world had she not heard the approach of the hook-nosed matron of the house? Immediately, she ramrodded her posture into military perfection, lest she endure a tirade on the merits of a flawless bearing. "I beg your pardon, Mistress Mayhew. I hope my ramblings did not turn you from your bed."

A moot sentiment, that. This woman had been up long before one of Kit's muffled noises could have awakened her. She was already dressed head to toe in her usual pewter-grey bombazine. Not a hair strayed from the severe chignon at the back of her head, and even in the spare light beginning to leach through the transom window over the front door, the tips of her shoes shone without a scuff.

Mistress Mayhew tilted her head slightly. "I am not given to rising at the whims of others. Rather, I have a fully scheduled day ahead of me, including the preparation of your room to welcome the next boarder once your items are removed." Behind the woman's spectacles, her sharp little eyes narrowed on Kit's gown. "Please do not tell me *that* is what you are wearing to the ceremony."

"No, it is not." But all the same, a mischievous smile curved Kit's lips. What would Jackson say if she showed up in the very gown she'd worn when she'd swindled him out of some coins?

The silver-haired matron pursed her lips. "Have I, perhaps, gotten the date wrong?"

"Not at all."

"And yet I find you about to scurry off like a chimney sweep instead of preparing to look your best for your groom?" A fierce frown creased the woman's brow. "Have you learned nothing in your time here, Miss Turner?"

Kit folded her hands primly in front of her and straightened her shoulders in hopes of placating the old matron. For an added measure, she schooled her voice to a dulcet tone and parroted back words she'd heard a hundred times in her years living beneath Mistress Mayhew's roof. "A proper woman must dress properly for a proper occasion."

Surprisingly, her recitation had the opposite effect, for the woman's jaw completely unhinged as she flailed a hand towards Kit's gown. "And you think this is proper?"

Kit couldn't help but grin. "Without a doubt."

Before Mistress Mayhew could launch a full-fledged attack on her lack of decorum, Kit reached for the door and tossed a wink over her shoulder. "But you see, mistress, I am not going to the church."

She fled into the grey morn, leaving behind a woman who—despite her best efforts—would likely be spluttering unceremoniously about the house for the next hour. . .a wicked thought that lightened Kit's steps. It was cruel of her to tease the old matron so, but entirely satisfying after having lived the past seven years minding every aspect of her behaviour while in the old bird's presence.

Just past Lambeth bridge, Kit stopped in front of the old Scampson Warehouse, arriving at the same time as the rising sun. The orange wash of daylight did the ramshackle building no favours. High up, a row of broken windows gaped like empty eye sockets. A hefty smattering of roof tiles lay as corpses on the pavement, and the front door was secured with a rusty chain and saucer-sized padlock. Kit smirked. What a waste of effort and iron, for the entire south side had been burnt away, leaving huge gaps between the blistered timbers. Had the fire been put out sooner all those years ago, this structure would still be a hub of commerce.

Kit picked her way through one of those gaps. "Hello?" She stopped just inside the skeletal wall, scanning from shadow to shadow. "Anyone here?"

Nothing but the scurry of little feet answered. Rats. How she hated the beady-eyed menaces! Drawing her shawl tighter at the neck with one hand, she reached for her boot blade. Just let the little vermin try to attack, though like as not a kick to the head would work as swiftly as a jab of the knife and be far less messy. Still, it wouldn't hurt to be visibly armed for her meeting with an unknown informant.

"Hello," she called again, carefully stepping from one rotted board to another. "Hello?"

And so went the next half hour as she wandered through the bowels of the old warehouse. There weren't many places for a tipster to be lying in wait, the bulk of what had been inside Scampson's now picked clean by street scavengers. The top two levels had proven to be a thick congregation of spiderwebs and bird droppings, the chalky acridness making her sneeze repeatedly. Below stairs, she ventured only a few scant paces before deciding no informant in his right mind would risk a cave-in atop his head. So, where was the man?

Hefting a sigh, Kit worked her way back towards the light pouring in through the broken wall. Defeat was a caller she never welcomed with open arms—nor would she now. She'd wait, biding her time on the off chance the fellow had simply been detained, but she'd do so with a lungful of fresh air instead of the damp and mould of a warehouse that really ought to be torn down. And as she waited, she'd think of the officer who'd stolen her breath and heart—

A sharp crack split the air. The board beneath her feet gave way. Kit flailed her arms, knife flying as she leapt for solid ground. Her skirt snagged, stopping her short. Fabric ripped. Darkness sucked her down.

Down.

Down.

Her skull cracked against something hard.

And everything went black.

"Hold still!"

Jackson fisted his hands, quelling the urge to fidget while Baggett tied his cravat. An October chill sifted through cracks in the vestry window frame, yet it did nothing to stop the perspiration trickling down his brow. Father had warned him he might be nervous right before the ceremony. That it was only natural. He'd pooh-poohed such a reaction, for a man about to marry the love of his life would certainly not succumb to second thoughts. Nor did he. But he sweated all the same.

"There." His friend fluffed the knot just so then pulled out a handkerchief and offered it over. "You certain you're ready for this, old man?"

Jackson dabbed the cloth on his brow. "More certain than I've ever been about anything in my life."

Baggett brushed away any remnant of wrinkles on his shoulders and sleeves, then took a step back, appraising Jackson with a knowing look. "You'll have your hands full, you know. That bride of yours is anything but conventional."

"I would have it no other way." And he wouldn't. Yes, Kit could be exasperating, unpredictable, and even downright maddening. She kept a man on his toes, but that unexpectedness endeared her to him like nothing else. Life with Kit would never be dull.

"Well then, let's be about it, eh?" Baggett swept his hand towards the sanctuary door.

This was it. The moment his entire life would change.

With a deep breath and a sharp nod, he strode with sure steps into the chancel. The reverend stood at the front of the altar, prayer book in hand. Jackson's father and brother sat in the left front pew. Kit had hoped her friends the Cards would be able to join them, but across the aisle from his family, that pew remained empty. No surprise, though. Old Joe's rheumatism had been acting up something fierce since last spring's entanglement with criminals. The only other person missing was Kit's father, but no doubt the sergeant was even now having a final heart-to-heart with his daughter at the back of the sanctuary.

Jackson took his place in front of the altar, Baggett at his side, and after exchanging an affirming tip of the head with the Reverend Walker, he faced the aisle where his bride would appear any minute. Would she wear a white gown? Would her hair be pinned up tight or allow for her trademark tail trailing down her back? Not that any of it mattered. He'd take her in a burlap sack and a flat cap if he must, for it was the woman inside he cared about most.

"And so, we are ready to begin." The reverend's deep voice filled the big room.

Father and James rose, angling towards the back of the church. Jackson's heart took off at a gallop as he waited for the first hint of Kit's light steps.

And waited.

And waited.

Then waited some more.

"I said, we are ready to begin," Reverend Walker boomed.

Jackson stiffened, his muscles already feeling the strain from standing bowstring tight. But hang it all! He would look his best for his bride no matter the cost. Be a man she could be proud of. The only one to turn her head.

Once again, he waited.

And once again, no bride.

His father met his gaze with a concerned bend to his brow.

"Perhaps those aren't the exact words they are hoping to hear," the reverend murmured, then let loose a tone of biblical proportion, "Beloved, let us now gather in the sight of God and man."

The first bit of doubt crept in on spider feet, tickling the back of Jackson's mind. Was Kit having second thoughts about their union? Perhaps his father ought to have had the nervous conversation with her last evening, but she'd been absent, as she'd been on the previous four nights. . .had that been a sign of her doubts?

"Women are notorious for making a man wait, you know," Baggett whispered in his ear.

He latched on to the words with a death grip. That was it. It had to be. Kit was merely up to her usual shenanigans. There was nothing for it but to stay the course and stand tall until the whim took her to make a dramatic entrance.

Several minutes later, James whispered loudly, "Where is lady?"

"Shh," his father hissed.

But James couldn't be more right. Where *was* Kit? While drama was admittedly her style, this amount of theatrics crossed a line.

Jackson cracked his neck. "I'll go check to make sure all is well."

Baggett's grip on his shoulder halted him. "Allow me. It's bad luck for the groom to see his bride before the vows, especially if the groom is in a temper."

He smiled. Leave it to Baggett to provide a bit of levity. His friend loped down the aisle, and the tension in Jackson's shoulders eased. No doubt Baggett would return with a tale of a misplaced glove or a hair ribbon that wasn't sitting quite right, trifles only a woman could blow all out of proportion.

Baggett returned, however, with a grim-faced Graybone.

Jackson's heart slammed to a complete standstill. "What's happened?"

The sergeant looked everywhere but at Jackson. "She's not here."

Not here? What the deuce did that mean? He folded his arms to keep from throttling the man. "Where is she?"

"I don't know." This time the sergeant met his gaze head-on, and when he did, the concern in Graybone's eyes cut straight to the gut. He was worried. This big bear of a man who wrangled cutthroats and dealt with the most wicked-hearted cullions London had to offer without so much as batting an eyelash actually looked anxious, and all because of a slip of a woman. His daughter. Jackson's bride. God in heaven, if something had happened to her. . . Did the sergeant truly believe so?

The very floor seemed to drop beneath him, and it took all his strength and then some to remain standing. "When did you hear from her last?"

"Yesterday afternoon, at the station." Graybone ran a beefy hand over his face. "I knew I should have called on her at the boarding house this morning. I should have insisted. Dash it!"

The sergeant's oath violated the sanctuary, raising the reverend's brows and drawing Jackson's father and brother to the altar.

Father looked at them each in turn. "Is all a'right?"

No. It most certainly wasn't. Jackson scowled. He ought to be kissing his wife instead of conferring with a bunch of men in a brideless sanctuary.

"Kit is. . ." Jackson swallowed. What? Sick? Harmed? Looking down the muzzle of an eight-inch howitzer? It could be any or all, but he couldn't very well tell his father what he didn't know for certain. He'd have to try a different tack.

"Kit has—" He choked up. Where *was* she? If anything had happened to her. . . His heart seized, and he pressed a fist to his gut. "I'll go check at her boarding house."

Baggett nodded. "I'll cover Blackfriars."

Graybone clapped him on the back. "I'll pull a squad of men together at the station and send them out to inquire with her known contacts."

Father draped his arm around James's shoulder, pulling him close. "James and I shall wait at your residence in case she shows up there."

"And I shall pray," the reverend joined in. "May God's mercy rain down."

"Amen," said Jackson and then he stormed down the aisle.

If any ill had befallen Kit on her way to church, God help the one who'd caused it, for he'd show no mercy whatsoever.

Chapter Eleven

She'd had some head bangers in her day. Been walloped with a chair leg, an ox bone, and one time even with a cat, but never—*ever*—had Kit's skull ached so much she didn't want to open her eyes. Light would hurt. Bad.

Keeping her eyes squinched shut, she gingerly probed the back of her scalp. Sure enough, she fingered a welt the size of a chestnut. Bother! How was she to do up her hair for the wedding if—

The wedding! How long had she lain here? And where exactly was *here*?

Eyes popping open, she sat upright. Horrible idea. The whole world wobbled, and she flung out her hand for balance, grabbing hold of something cold and hard to ride out a wave of dizziness.

After a few steadying breaths, the woozy feeling passed, and she assessed her body for further damage. Her toes wriggled. Her legs moved. When she rolled her shoulder, her elbow stung as if it was scraped, but she appeared to be in one piece.

A stream of light oozed from a jagged hole in the ceiling, or what had been a floor—the floor she'd fallen through. Well, well. Next time she ventured about in a dilapidated warehouse she would definitely have to remember to use a prodding stick. For now, though, time to leave.

She shifted her weight to study the distance between herself and the opening, when a fresh pain cut into her backside. Whatever she'd landed on was hard and pokey. She glanced down—then shot to her feet and backed away until her shoulder blades hit a rock wall. Of all the things to cushion her fall!

Opposite her sat a reclining skeleton, head lolled to a dangerous angle. Goodness, had she nearly decapitated the poor soul?

Suddenly chilled, Kit turned her back on the bones and searched for a way out. The walls were slick with black mould. The door was even worse, but perhaps that was good. Weakened oak would be easier to bust through.

She took a few steps backwards, then charged ahead, ramming into the barricade with her shoulder. It didn't budge, but the room did. She flung out her hand against the wall as once again her vision swam.

It took a while for the throbbing in her head to simmer down and even longer for her to work up the oomph to give the door one more try. Not with her shoulder, though. It ached too much. She hefted her skirts and put all her weight into a full-heeled kick, a strong one.

But not strong enough to open the blasted door.

"Help! Get me out of here." She pounded her fists against the wood. Yet all her buffeting and battering accomplished was a few more bruises to match the ones she'd already acquired.

With a final roar, she dropped her hands—and was instantly ashamed. This was no way to behave in a crisis. She'd been in worse situations and never given in to such wild emotion, so why now?

And that's when it hit her. This predicament was of her own making. She was the one who'd gone against Jackson's wishes and her father's warnings to leave the past behind. Guilt scorched her chest. She should've listened. Should have heeded their counsel instead of going her own way, doing her own thing. She dipped her head, wincing from the movement.

Forgive me, God, for trying to bring about a justice that belongs to You alone. You have placed voices of caution in my life, restraint that I ignored. Grant me the wisdom to consider differing views, for if I had, I wouldn't be in this mess right now. . .a mess I very much need You to help me out of.

With a pleading gaze, she lifted her face to the heavens, or at least the rotted wood that composed her heavens. No guardian angel appeared to rescue her. Even so, a slow smile curved her lips. That hole in the ceiling meant escape.

She reached for her boot blade to use as a pick to climb her way up, but her fingers met an empty sheath. Dash and rot! She'd lost her grip on her knife when she'd fallen. A sigh ripped out of her. Of all the inconvenience.

There was nothing for it then but to dig her fingers into the cracks in the walls and pull her way up. Her boot slipped as she toed around for a hold, but after several tries, she finally made contact. Another reach, another toehold, and inch by inch, slowly she ascended.

By the halfway mark, her arms shook and her legs burned. Worse, the handholds petered out. Straining, she searched for the next available crevice—only to miss her mark and whump down several feet onto the hard-packed floor. *Oof!* Yet another bruise to add to the tally.

Catching her breath, she tried again—and again and again and again—until her body rebelled like a belligerent mule. She dropped on purpose the last time, lungs heaving, and glanced at the skeleton.

"I begin to see why you gave up," she murmured.

Oh, to what depths she'd fallen. Unarmed. Trapped in a hole and chilled to the marrow, with nothing but the remains of some unlucky scabber who'd gotten ensnared in the same situation as she. A shiver crept across her shoulders. Was she doomed to become a pile of bare bones like her companion here or. . .wait a minute. Was that *only* a pile of bones?

Kit edged a step closer. There was something more. Something that person had tried to hide during the last moments of life.

"Sorry," she whispered as she pried open the clutched fingers lying in the skeleton's lap. She'd never robbed a grave before. Then again, she'd never landed in one either.

They were fine bones. A woman's, no doubt. After lying in such an ignoble crypt for who knew how long, she certainly didn't deserve to have her one and only treasure taken from her. Still, the trinket might eventually identify the body, and the woman could finally be laid to rest in a more suitable place.

With as much care as possible, Kit disentangled a thin chain and held it up to the spare light. A tarnished locket dangled from the end. She tried to wedge it open with her fingernail, but the clasp would not give. Was the entire day doomed to failure?

She shoved the necklace into her pocket. "Just for safekeeping, my friend. I shall return it once I discover who you are and let your family know you've been—"

She froze. Something was at her back, staring with such intensity she could feel it in her soul. . .and that something was daring her to move.

Well, then. So be it.

Shoving down fear, she spun, wishing she clutched her knife, wishing even more that she'd never embarked on this ill-fated appointment.

But nothing was there, save for shadow and darkness. Her gaze drifted lower.

And that's when her heart stopped.

Eyes.

Small and round and glowing. Dozens of them.

A shriek pierced her ears—her own. She bolted, screaming as she jumped up the wall, scrambling for a hold. Any hold. Anything. Anyone.

"Help me! Somebody, get me out of here!"

"Kit? Kit!"

Jackson wasn't sure if his voice or his fist pounded harsher against the door of Mistress Mayhew's Boarding and School of Deportment. Either way, the racket earned him a sour "Men these days" from a passing matron with a peacock feather bobbing garishly on her hat.

He banged on the wood once again.

She'll be here. She will. Like a crazed incantation, he repeated the words over and over in his mind. It was a pointless exercise, and he knew it, but he still clung to the thought. She would be here. She had to be.

Yet no one answered.

As if he were on the mat with Baggett, he pummeled the oak. "Open this door immediately or I'll break it down!"

The door swung open to a thundercloud in a gunmetal-grey gown. Mistress Mayhew's usually pinched face nearly folded in on itself, so thick was her censure. "Mr. Forge." Her words clipped like the snip of garden shears. "I should think you would know a gentleman is never violent."

"That is a discussion for another time, mistress. I must know if Miss Turner is all right." He gawked past her shoulder, praying to catch a glimpse of his brown-haired imp. "Is Kit here? Is she ill?"

The woman's jaw tightened another notch. "I can hardly be expected to answer such a barrage of questions all at once, sir."

Dash it! He didn't have time for this. He shoved past her and strode down the corridor.

"Mr. Forge!" Mistress Mayhew blustered behind him. "May I remind you—"

"Yes, yes. A gentleman would not burst into a house uninvited." Neither would a gentleman know exactly where his love's bedroom would be. He'd felt guilty that night he'd insisted on escorting Kit home in the wee hours after chasing—and catching—the ringleader of a Cheapside cockfighting gang. He'd felt even more shameful watching her shimmy through her ground floor window and admiring her curves as she did so. But now all self-reproach fled as he rapped his fist against her door. "Kit?"

Silence—save for the thud of Mistress Mayhew's solid shoes against the floorboards.

"Kit!" He tried the knob.

It gave.

Jackson flung the door wide, the crash of it nicking into the plaster.

"This is highly irregular, sir." Mistress Mayhew's condemnation stabbed him in the back. "Had you a thimbleful of patience, I could have told you Miss Turner was not in residence. I insist you leave the premises at once."

Ignoring the woman, he scanned the room. The window was closed. No upturned furniture littered the floor. Other than a four-poster bed with a wad of tangled sheets near the foot and a pillow on the floor, there was no sign of a skirmish. He closed in on her dressing table. Kit's hairbrush lay half off the edge, as if she'd set it there with her mind on other things. As it should be. This was their wedding day!

The wardrobe hung open, so he fingered through the garments, disregarding Mistress Mayhew's continued huffing and puffing. One gown was wrapped in paper, suspended untouched—her wedding gown, no doubt—right next to an empty wooden hanger. His gaze drifted back to the bed, on to the dressing table, and returned to the wardrobe. By the looks of it, Kit had risen, done up her hair, then bypassed her wedding apparel and dressed for some other occasion before leaving the premises. But where had she gone? And why?

He turned to the glowering hook-nosed woman at the door. "A few questions, mistress, before I grant your request that I vacate the property. Did you see Miss Turner this morning?"

The woman's lips pursed, her gaze burning a hole right through him. "Yes, Miss Turner departed just before sunrise with about as much decorum as your entrance and this interrogation. I must say, you are quite the pair."

"Did she inform you where she was going?"

"She did not, nor did I pry, though judging by her appearance, she looked as if she were about to go mudlarking the Thames."

Jackson raked his fingers through his hair. Kit had been up to something. He spun in a slow circle, searching for further clues, but nothing hinted in the least of where she might have gone. A sense of helplessness draped over his shoulders, pulling him under, stealing his breath. Oh, how he hated such impotence. And hated even more the mocking scent of Kit's rose water, reminding him that even now he ought to be sweeping his bride off to a life of marital bliss. A sour taste twisted his mouth.

Kit, why are you not with me? Where could you be?

Chuffing a sigh, he jammed on his hat and wheeled about. "Please, think hard, mistress. Have you any idea of Miss Turner's whereabouts? Any indication whatsoever? No clue is too small, no inkling insignificant."

The woman sniffed, her curved nose bunching into a tighter crook. "All I know, Mr. Forge, is that she said she was not going to church."

A knife stuck him in the gut. "She did?"

"Most emphatically."

The knife twisted. Why would she say such a thing? A woman in love ought to fly to her beloved on such a happy day, not categorically flaunt the fact she would do no such thing. Unless. . . He sucked in air. Had she been forced into something against her will?

He locked gazes with the mistress of the house. "Did Miss Turner appear to be in any sort of distress when she left?"

"Not in the least." She folded her arms over her bosom, and it was hard to tell which looked more starched, the woman's skirts or her face. "The truth of the matter, Mr. Forge, is Miss Turner behaved rather flippantly, certainly not the blushing miss she should be on her wedding day. Not that she's ever been one for conformity, mind, but her performance this morning was beyond the pale."

He'd noticed the same. Kit had been acting strangely the past week. Almost as if she'd been avoiding him. Once again, his gaze drifted around the room, searching for answers he wasn't sure he wanted to discover, yet wanting—needing—to know.

"I am afraid I can offer you no further information on your missing bride, Mr. Forge. Should she happen to return, I shall send word. Good day, sir." Hand on the door, she inclined her head meaningfully.

He paused a moment more, letting the words bounce to the carpet like a handful of dropped marbles. It seemed like defeat, leaving here without Kit, yet there was nothing more to be done.

He gave Mistress Mayhew a curt nod and a "Thank you" then stalked from the house without looking back. Unsure where to go next, he let his mind turn over the possibilities while his feet led him to the soup kitchen on Blackfriars Lane.

A queue snaked out the door, which he shouldered past, and a chorus of hungry bellies griped at his boldness.

"I were here a'fore ye."

"Snipin' line cutter!"

"For shame. Can't ye see I've younglings who need a bite?"

Normally, guilt would have turned him right around to explain the situation or perhaps defend his rude manner, but there was nothing normal about today.

Inside the small front room, the reek of bodies that hadn't seen a bar of soap blended with cabbage soup, punching him square in the nose. He skimmed the area, from loaded benches of the poorest of the poor shoveling broth into their mouths to a willowy woman who bustled out from the kitchen with a pitcher in each hand. He caught her gaze with a tip of his head.

Setting the pitchers on the nearest table, Martha scurried over to where he stood near the door. "Mr. Forge. Is all a'right?"

"I was hoping you could tell me that. Have you seen Kit?"

She shook her head. "Not since yesterday. Did she not make it to the church?"

"No."

Martha's fingers fluttered to her chest. "Oh dear."

"Have you any idea where she might be?" He flung out his hands. "Any at all?"

"None, sir."

Regret furrowed her brow. A long breath deflated what was left of his confidence. "Martha, I must know. . .I mean, I know Kit confides in you somewhat."

"Hah! More like I share my secrets with her. Kit keeps her feelings close." Martha peered up at him, her blue eyes genuine. "Yer the only one she trusts."

He liked to think so. But that did not account for her unexplained disappearance. He met Martha's gaze. "Do you think she avoided the wedding on purpose?"

She stumbled back a step. "Saints above! Such a question. Kit loves you, as sure as the sun and moon. She probably got waylaid somehow, that's all. Something ye'll both share a laugh over when 'tis all sorted out." She smiled. "Don't fret, sir. Should Kit come 'round, I'll send word to the station straightaway. Ye have my word."

"Thank you." He tipped his hat. "I shall let you be about your business."

He worked his way out to the street and glanced up at the grey sky. Where was she? Shoring his shoulder against the soup kitchen's wall, he tried to recall snippets of conversations he'd recently shared with her. Anything that might give him a lead. True as a sparrow's call, he heard her voice in his mind, and the words tied his muscles into knots.

"Had I known a marriage ceremony would be such a bother, I'd have skipped the whole thing."

"Are you sure you asked the right woman to be your wife?"

"Are you having second thoughts about marrying me? Because I am beginning to have a few of my own."

And then he really did stiffen. She'd objected when he'd first mentioned moving from the city. At the George, she'd told his father quite adamantly she had no intention of giving up her lifestyle just because she was married. And afterwards, when he'd walked her home, she'd equated marriage with drudgery. Perhaps he had spoken too harshly with her on the matter, which might have led her to misunderstand his good intentions, but even so, she had no cause to doubt his love for her. Had she decided to maintain her freedom in lieu of the wedding?

He shoved away from the wall. He had no idea of the answer to that question, but he was certain of one thing. He would find her and hear the answer from her own sweet lips.

Chapter Twelve

It wasn't as if you could slam the door on fear's face when it came calling. You couldn't. Terror slid in whether you wanted it to or not, eking sideways through the slightest crack in your confidence. And that one small truth annoyed Kit as much as the ache in her fingers as she clung to the mouldy rock wall.

"Help!" Her voice echoed big in the small chamber. Was it big enough to climb out the hole in the floorboards, trot through the expanse of the warehouse, and snag a passerby out on the street?

Oh, God, please make it so.

Her calves shook with the strain of hanging on to such a precarious perch. How long had she been here, suspended between horror and safety? Too long. *Far* too long. One foot was about to slide out of the crevice where she'd wedged in the toe of her boot. The squeaks of the rats below crawled under her skin, shrill and ear-piercing, almost as if the little devils anticipated her fall. She'd spent time in sewers before, but she'd always had a way out, even a small means of escape. Never had she been cornered by such a pack of wicked furballs as this. Worse, the damp rot of the place tickled inside her nose. There was no way she could hold on through a sneeze. She barely held on as it was.

"Help!" she tried again.

"Hello?"

Her breath caught. Could it be? Either she was imagining things or that faint voice was a lifeline—one she'd grab on to with both bloodied hands. "I'm here. Jackson? I'm here!"

"Where is here?" The man's voice belted stronger this time. Not Jackson's, but a saviour nonetheless.

"Below the floor. I fell through." Putting all her muscle into her legs, she vaulted higher—and came up short when toeing about for another hold. She dangled by two hands, one foot, and a shredding hope that she'd remain thus until the man arrived.

"Hurry, please!" she cried.

A balding head peered over the opening, a very round head with tiny eyes rather like the rats below. He clutched a bowler in one hand and a walking stick in the other.

"The lady in red?" he murmured. "It can't be. Not after so many years."

Of all the luck. A colour-blind man with spindly arms was to be her rescuer? She'd laugh if she wouldn't lose her grip, but as it was, her fingers barely clung to the crumbly mortar. "Please hurry. I can't hold on much longer."

"Right-o. Let's see what can be done." The man's head disappeared, and after a bit of scuffling and what sounded like the drag of a board, he bellied over the edge with his arm extended. "Grasp on and I'll haul you up."

It was a risk, this letting go of a sure thing for the promise of something better. She'd never made it past this point without falling—and to fall now meant landing in a horde of teeth and claws. Below, a host of beady eyes latched on to her. The furry rats writhed in one big mass, their high-pitched screeches deafening. Despite the chilling scene and the cold dampness of her prison, sweat trickled down her spine. One fat rodent had lifted to its hind feet and was testing the wall with its forepaws. Then—horror of horrors—it started climbing.

Right towards her.

"Look up, child," the man commanded. "Look ever upwards, therein shall you be saved."

He was right. She knew it in her bones. Still, it was impossible to tear her gaze away from the rat closing in on the hem of her gown. If that thing scurried up her leg, she would be undone.

"You can do this, child. Come to me. Make haste!"

Rallying what little courage she had left, Kit lifted her face and put all she had into shooting upwards. Her arm extended. Her fingers stretched.

And the solid clasp of a hand gripped on to hers. With the man's help, she clambered the rest of the way out of the hole, scrambling past the solid board he'd braced over the rotted floor. For several breaths, she lay on her belly with closed eyes, gathering her wits. That'd been close—far too close.

Thank You, God, for deliverance even from a muddle of my own making.

Shaking off the last of her jitters, she opened her eyes and spied her errant knife just a few feet off. Oh, how she could've used that little gem! Then again, would she have called out to God so sincerely if she'd had it in hand? Her lips twisted into a smirk.

You always manage to turn me back to You, Lord. And for that I am ever grateful.

She snatched up her blade and tucked it safely away before turning to her rescuer. By now the man had replaced his hat and leaned on his walking stick. One leg was shorter than the other, not by much, but enough to list him sideways.

"Thank you, sir. I'd not have gotten out of there without your assistance, Mr.. . .?"

"Mr. Harpenny, at your service, madam." He dipped his head. "I am the recently hired vicar at Cripplegate."

"Oh, forgive me, Mr. Harpenny. I had no idea you were a clergyman." Made sense, though. She had asked God for help. Who better to send than one of His own?

"No offense taken, madam. And you are?"

"Kit Turner. Miss Kit Turner." As soon as the *miss* rolled off her tongue, her stomach flipped. Soon—very soon—she would be a missus.

"Pleased to make your acquaintance, Miss Turner." The reverend swept her face with a searching gaze. "Some medical attention is in order for you, I think. You've managed a few scrapes to your cheek and brow. And then how about I help you find a better shelter than this old warehouse? I'm new to the area, but I am sure I can manage a ticket to the casual ward for you until better lodging can be found."

What a kind soul. Mistaken, but kind. She smiled. "Oh, no. I don't live here. I was just poking about."

His brows drew together. "Not a very safe pastime for a young lady. Nor is it safe for us to remain. Who knows what brigands might chance their way in?" He tipped his head towards the charred wall where light poured in across the great expanse of the warehouse. "Shall we?"

She matched her pace to his thud-step-step gait and kept a look-out for weakened boards that might land them back in a rathole.

"What about you, sir?" she asked as they worked their way out. "Why would a clergyman be strolling in this area unless. . ." She bit her lip, chewing on a new thought. Could this man be the informant with whom she was supposed to rendezvous? She glanced sideways at him. "Were you here to meet someone?"

He chuckled, which came out more of a chirruping gurgle. For a man of the cloth, he was quite the odd duck.

"There are better places to counsel a parishioner, Miss Turner, than in this heap of worn boards. No, no. My church is but a few blocks away. I was merely passing by when I heard you."

She studied his profile a moment longer. If only he'd turn his head that she might probe the truth of those words in the depths of his eyes, for the statement didn't ring true. If—as he'd said—he'd been out on the street, there was no way he'd have heard her cry for help.

She opened her mouth, several questions about to launch from her tongue, when they stepped into what appeared to be the spare light of late afternoon.

"Oh dear," she breathed, then louder, "Do you have the time, Mr. Harpenny?"

He clicked open the lid of a silver pocket watch. "Time for a cup of tea, I'd say."

Four o'clock?

No!

She took off, calling over her shoulder, "Thank you, but I must dash."

"Farewell, Miss Turner," his voice followed, "and stay out of decrepit buildings from now on."

Heart in her throat and a stitch in her side, Kit tore down every side street and back alley she knew—and even some she didn't—to arrive at the church on Spafford as quickly as possible. She yanked open the front door and sped through the small foyer, lungs heaving.

"Jackson! I'm here," she called as she burst into the sanctuary. "Jackson?"

She stumbled to a stop, grabbing on to a pew to catch her breath. No groom stood at the altar, nor did any vicar garbed in vestments clutch a prayer book beside him. The place was empty as a robbed grave.

She lifted a shaky hand to her lips.

"What have I done?" she whispered. "Dear God, what have I done?"

Jackson rested his head against the jiggling wall of the hackney. Maybe all the rattling and battering would order his wild thoughts into some kind of sense. What a stretch. How was he to think straight when the love of his life was missing?

Oh Kit, where are you?

He closed his eyes, momentarily giving in to the fatigue of such worry. For the past four hours—or was it five?—he'd tramped from one end of London to the other. He'd braved the underground and queried Skaggs, stopped off at the Grouse and Gristle to question anyone coherent enough to put two words together, and inquired with every known crew member with whom Kit had ever worked. He even rendezvoused with Baggett, but his friend had uncovered nothing either. Not one man or woman admitted to knowing Kit's whereabouts. It was as if the earth had swallowed her, leaving only the devil himself to question.

So of course, that's exactly what he must do next.

Heaving a sigh, Jackson peered out the window, trying—and mostly failing—to ignore the stink of body odour that permeated the cracked leather seat. If this didn't work, he'd have nowhere else to turn.

The cab canted precariously around a corner, thanks to a broken spring, and he braced his hand against the wall. Shortly thereafter, the carriage slowed to a stop.

"'Ere we are, sir," called the jarvey.

Outside, Jackson flipped a farthing up to the driver and gave the man a sharp nod of dismissal. The cab rattled off, leaving him standing in front of a hulking building of iron and stone, made all the more threatening by the jagged-piked fence surrounding it.

Pulling out his badge, he strode to the front gate. Not just anyone could enter this place, nor would many wish to. The Quad, the Nick, or as some called it, the 'Ville was not a holiday destination. Indeed, most people stayed as far away as possible from Pentonville Prison.

Jackson hid his distaste as he cleared his entrance with the gate guard. Of all the ways he'd imagined celebrating his wedding day, tromping into the bowels of a gaol didn't come close to making the list.

Clouds punched down from the sky like grey fists, blocking out what little light remained of the day, as grim as the set of the officer's jaw at the main door.

"Inspector Forge." Jackson palmed his badge at the man. "Here to interrogate a prisoner."

"Little late for that, ain't it?" the man sneered. "Those what pass through these doors be already condemned. Not like ye'll be able to free one of the sods what's already locked up."

"I am well aware of that." Jackson advanced a step.

The guard jingled his keys on the ring yet made no move to open the door.

Brilliant. A self-important dragon who had nothing better to do but snort his rank breath on those who came calling. Jackson ground his teeth, stopping a few choice words he'd picked up on the street. He didn't have time for this!

"Are you going to let me in, or shall I return with a writ of assistance from Scotland Yard?"

The man's face darkened, but at least he finally inserted one of his infernal keys into the lock. "Most make haste to skip out this door, not wedge their royal highness inside it."

As soon as the guard pulled the door wide enough to slip through, Jackson stalked inside.

"Warden's office is the first door on the left," the man's voice called after him.

Jackson stopped in front of a goose-necked clerk sitting behind a desk littered with papers and—oddly enough—a collection of candle nubs that would be better melted down than lying in a great heap. Once again Jackson offered his badge. "Inspector Jackson Forge here to see the warden."

The clerk shook his head. "He's gone."

"Fore!" The shout rumbled from inside the warden's office, followed by a sharp thwack against the door. "Blast it."

Jackson cocked his head. "Obviously he is not."

The clerk tugged at his collar. "He is, sir."

"Fore!" Another shout. Another thwack.

Jackson cornered the clerk's desk and strode to the warden's office. "Someone's in there, and that someone is playing golf."

The clerk's voice rose a full octave. "I wouldn't do that if I were—"

Jackson opened the door then immediately ducked as a ball winged towards his skull.

The warden—a tufty little fellow dressed in navy, skittery as a blue jay—frowned past him and shouted out the now-open door. "Graves! I told you I was occupied."

Jackson held up his hand. "Your clerk bears no blame. I entered of my own accord. I am in a bit of a rush and should like to see a prisoner. Immediately."

"Of all the brass!" The warden huffed and lowered his club. "Who do you think you are, ordering about a principal officer? I ought to have you horsewhipped for such insubordination."

"I am Inspector Forge. And the sooner you help me, the more likely I am not to mention your golfing practice on company time to the superintendent."

The warden gripped his club with white knuckles, and for a minute Jackson wondered if he'd take a swing at his head. Thankfully, the fellow set it against the wall instead. "Very well, Mr. Forge. A prisoner, you say?"

"Yes."

The man strolled to a series of ledgers on a shelf behind his desk, then pulled one down and set it on the tabletop.

"Name?" he asked.

"Simon Poxley."

Jackson's blood instantly boiled at the mention of the scoundrel's name. The villain had sworn his revenge against him and Kit the day he'd been carted off to gaol, and by all appearances, he may have finally made good on his word. Quite an impressive feat for one who's backside warmed a Pentonville cell. Not surprising, though. Poxley had more reach than a stretch-armed freak in a sideshow. The zoo assailant, Kit's disappearance—both could be explained by the heinous puppet master who even now must be rubbing his hands in wicked glee. Jackson curled his fingers into tight fists. He'd choke the information from the man if he must, and if Poxley was responsible for harming one hair on Kit's precious head, he'd rip the throat right out of him.

"Your request is denied, Mr. Forge." The warden's words barely registered through his haze of anger.

He blinked and stepped closer to the desk. Had he heard correctly? "Pardon?"

"You may not speak with prisoner Poxley. Typhus took him not long after he arrived." The warden bent over the page, squinting. "June seventeenth to be exact."

Dead? Four months ago. The information went down as easily as a bite of rancid mutton. Poxley had been his last lead.

Now what?

Chapter Thirteen

Night fell as hard as the slap of Kit's shoes against the pavement. By the time she reached Old Jewry, her hair tumbled down her back and her skirts were soaked from the thick mist rolling off the cobbled streets. Mistress Mayhew would have plenty to say about her slovenly appearance, but it didn't matter. Nothing mattered save for finding Jackson.

Dodging a bluecoat, she scurried like a crazed squirrel inside the station, where she immediately bumped into a broad chest.

"Here now, miss," a low voice rumbled. "You're in quite the rush. Can I be of any—Miss Turner? Is it really you?"

Swiping away some hair plastered against her wet face, she peered up into a pair of eyes the rich brown of a whisky barrel. Not Jackson, but Officer Baggett was the next best thing. He'd know where to find her groom. He *had* to know.

God, please, let him know.

She pressed a hand to her chest, desperately trying to calm her pulse. "Where's Jackson? I've been looking for him everywhere."

He frowned. "Still scouring the streets, asking the same question about you, as I and half the force have been doing these past six hours. Where have you been, Miss Turner?"

"Half the force? Why?"

"Did you really think Jackson and your father wouldn't turn the city upside down to shake you out of whatever hidey-hole you burrowed in?" The vinegar in his gaze dissipated somewhat as he focused on her scraped cheek. "Are you all right?"

"I'm fine." Hah. What a lie. She wouldn't be fine until she sorted out this jumble, and what a sorry jumble it was! Her shoulders sagged under its weight.

Officer Baggett reached for her, as if to give her a reassuring pat on her arm, then pulled back. "You'd better go tell that to the sergeant, Miss Turner. He's been half out of his mind all day—"

"Kit!" Her name snapped as sharply as a sail in the wind.

Bracing herself, she turned to face her bushy-bearded father, who stood near the front desk. Such a visible wave of emotion washed across his face it broke her heart.

Her father closed his eyes, his lips moving in a clear "Thank God."

Kit's hand flew to her mouth. She was responsible for this display, for the anguish and grief that'd aged him years in mere hours. Never before had she seen this man reveal his true feelings in such a public fashion, yet here he was, stoop-shouldered and clench-jawed, shaken to the core.

"You might want to have this conversation inside the sergeant's office." Officer Baggett's whisper warmed her ear.

She slipped a glance around her. Goodness. How had so many constables gathered in such a short amount of time? Every last one of them watched with hawk eyes.

Leaving Jackson's friend behind, Kit snagged her father's sleeve. "I need to talk to you, Father. There is much to tell."

He fell into step silently beside her, but the second the door closed, he yanked her into a bear hug.

And that's when the gravity of what she'd done stole her breath as thoroughly as the crush of her father's embrace. She squeezed her eyes shut, fighting back a rare sting of tears.

At length, her father set her from him. "What happened?"

"I. . ." Every last syllable dried on her tongue. How was she to admit to foolhardiness? She lifted her chin—though she doubted very much she'd be holding her head high for much longer. "I fell through some floorboards and hit my head."

Her father scowled. With a firm yet gentle touch, he probed her scalp with his big fingers until he hit the tender spot at the back and she winced. He growled like an angry dog. "How did that happen?

Mistress Mayhew would not allow a bruised piece of fruit in her house, let alone a rotted floorboard. Where have you been?"

He guided her face to meet his gaze—a look that would make the devil himself drop to his knees and confess all.

She could do no less.

"The old Scampson Warehouse." Her voice was barely a mewl.

"Scampson!" He scowled. "What the blazes were you doing there? And on your wedding day no less?" His brows gathered into a black squall. "And do not think to hold anything back from me, young lady, for I will have the truth."

She retreated a few steps. It was a pigeon-livered response but altogether necessary. The turbulence in his eyes was enough to make an alley cat skitter behind a stack of crates.

"I was meeting an informant." Oh my. Was that small voice really hers?

"Jackson has a full five days off work. There's no reason you should be on a case. . .unless." His dark eyes hardened to two rocks. "You're still hunting those cullies who harmed his brother, aren't you?"

The next backwards step hit her shoulder blades against the wall, and she dipped her head, unable to face the censure in her father's gaze. "I wanted to surprise Jackson. That's all. I wanted to bring justice to those who harmed his family all those years ago. What better gift is there than that?"

"Oh, I don't know, how about a bride who shows up at her own wedding?" Her father puffed out a huge chuff of air as he sank onto his chair. "Sit down."

"Father, really, I know I—"

"Sit!"

A firing squad couldn't have knocked her down faster. She sat. Silently. Clutching her hands in her lap. She felt like a five-year-old and didn't like it, not one bit. . .but had she not brought this upon herself? And as such, she alone should bear the consequences—a lesson she'd learned all too well on the streets.

Her father pinned her in place with nothing more than the rod-like veins bulging on his neck. "Jackson is a bull on the loose, ready to kill anyone he suspects has had a hand in keeping you from the altar. How do you suppose he'll feel when he finds out you willingly missed the ceremony? That there is no one to blame but you for such a humiliation?"

She blinked, dumbfounded. Did her father seriously think she'd skipped out on marrying the man she loved?

"Of all the absurd lunacies, Father. It's not as if I deliberately stepped on a rotted board and knocked myself out cold. I'd have been at the church on time if it weren't for that."

Her father shook his head, his displeasure doing more to wound her than if he'd backhanded her across the cheek. Though she'd known him a scant four months, she'd come to respect this man in ways she hadn't anticipated.

For a long while he said nothing, then finally murmured, "That's not the point."

Truly? But she'd told him everything. She shoved back a piece of hair, annoyed. "Then what is the point?"

He ran his big hand over his face several times before once again staring her down. "It is you, Daughter, who put a case before the man you love. No matter how good your intentions were, the fact is that you did what you wanted while knowing Jackson would have said otherwise."

Hah! He *had* said otherwise. A snort passed her lips. She couldn't stop it. But as soon as the flippant noise hit the air, she wished more than anything she could take it back.

"You don't know that," she ended up murmuring.

"What I know is when Jackson discovers the true reason for your absence, it will cut him deep. He cares more for you and your future together than he does about past wrongs done to his family."

She frowned. "But what happened to James was not right."

"That's undeniable, but you cannot right all the wrongs in this world, my girl. The sooner you learn that truth, the better." He blew out another sigh, ruffling his moustache. "Look, Kit, you have been on your own for a long time. Far too long, much to my regret. I understand your independent streak, such as it is, but know this, Daughter... if you continue to cling to your pride and pursue what you deem to be right, without taking into consideration what Jackson wants, you'll lose him. More than anything, a husband must be able to trust his wife, for she holds his very heart in her hands. Respect that truth. Respect him. That is the most precious gift you can give."

Shame spread like a hot rash. She squirmed on the chair. "You're right, Father. I will apologize at once. . .as soon as I find him, that is. I've been to Jackson's lodgings once already, where his father informed me he hadn't been there since the wedding. Maybe by now, though, he is. And if not, I shall wait for him. I *will* make this right. You can count on that."

Rising, she smoothed her skirts with the flat of her hands, and her fingers brushed over a small lump in her pocket. "Oh, I nearly forgot!" She pulled out the necklace she'd found clutched in the skeleton's fingers. "This was in the hole where I landed. I suspect you might have a missing person case on your hands—though not one that shall be easily solved. The body below the floor is nothing but bones now." She set the necklace on the desk. "This may help you identify the owner."

Her father held up the locket, the colour in his face leaching out in increments. And that's what she loved most about this man. He took every case personally.

"*How* did this happen?" His words were barely a breath.

She bunched her nose. "As I said, Father, when I fell through the floor, I landed on a skeleton—a woman's, I believe. She must have been there for years—decades, maybe. It appeared she'd been locked in. The door was impossible to budge. Believe me, I tried." She absently rubbed her shoulder, the memory still an ache. "Can you open the clasp on the pendant? I wasn't able to, and it might have a miniature of the owner inside, maybe even of her lover or some other hint of identification."

Her father didn't even try to flip open the lid. He just sat there, staring, saying absolutely nothing.

"Father?" She angled her head. "Are you ill? You're as white as Saint John's robes."

His big fingers wrapped around the necklace, covering it completely with his meaty hand. "It's been a trying day, Daughter."

Another gust of shame hit her so strongly, she clutched the back of the chair. "Will you forgive me? I vow I shall never again be late to my wedding."

He shook his head, a small smile twitching his moustache. "It is not my pardon—which I full and freely give—that you should be fretting about."

"Even so, I value your acquittal just as much, and I thank you for—"

The door crashed open, followed by a rain of plaster hitting the floor from where the knob dug into the wall. "I heard Kit is—Kit?"

Jackson's ragged voice wrapped around her an instant before strong arms pulled her against his heaving chest.

"Thank God!" Jackson pressed a kiss to the crown of her head, his voice—even half-muffled—husky with emotion.

Relief rushed through her veins, and she nestled against him, relishing the strong beat of his heart beneath her ear. He wasn't angry. He wasn't even vexed. What a man of goodness! She nuzzled her cheek against his waistcoat. This was all just a horrible hitch that could—and would—be easily righted with a simple postponement of the ceremony until tomorrow. Yes, indeed.

Thank You, God.

He cupped her face with his hands, but when his fingers hit the tender flesh on her injured cheek, she winced.

His face instantly hardened as his gaze roamed from the scrape, to the bruise, to the small cut near her temple. Murder flashed dark in his eyes. "Who did this to you?"

She looked away. Judging by the vengeance turning the blue in Jackson's eyes to ice, he wasn't going to like her answer.

Chapter Fourteen

All at once, the hollow cavern in Jackson's chest filled with air and he could breathe again. Finally. Kit was here. She was here! In his arms, safe and whole. Well, mostly. Those scrapes and bruises concerned him. Nay, more than that. The sight of her injuries caused a righteous anger to kindle in his gut.

"Who caused you such harm?" He brushed his thumb across her cheek before pulling back. "Name the scoundrel, and I will see him brought to heel."

Her teeth worried her lower lip, but no words came out. Who was she protecting?

"Kit, tell me who did this." His voice thundered harsher than he intended, but Lord have mercy, how it cut to the quick to see the woman he loved battered and speechless. Whoever did this deserved to feel the cudgel of his fists.

"You'd better answer him," the sergeant's voice rumbled, "before the man tears out of here on a killing jag."

A visible lump traveled the length of Kit's neck before at last she spoke. "It was me. I mean. . .I did it."

He shook his head. Surely he hadn't heard right. "What did you say?"

She lifted her chin and met his gaze head-on. "I am to blame. I fell through some floorboards, that's all. It was but a terrible mishap, my love. Nothing more." Pressing her palms against his chest, she smoothed her hands along his collarbone, eyes pleading. "Jackson, please believe me when I say that I never meant for any of this to happen. I hate that I missed our wedding, but it's not too late. We shall marry tomorrow, and all will be right. I'll make it so, you'll see."

A strange tale, to be sure, but her words rang true. They could as easily wed the next day—though this time he'd escort her from the boarding house instead of meeting her at the church. He captured one of her hands, intending to press a kiss into her palm, but ended up frowning at the abrasions marring her fair skin. "You are certain that save for this and those few scuffs on your face you are well?"

"Besides those and a knot on the back of my head, I am just fine." A genuine smile lit her face—a beautiful face he'd never tire of seeing, one he longed to wake up to every morning. "And even better, I have learned to never again venture alone into a dilapidated building without a walking stick to test the flooring." Her smile twisted into a smirk.

He grinned back. "I am glad for that."

And he was. This little street urchin should have known better than to traipse about on shaky ground, but why had she been alone in some forsaken death trap to begin with? His grin faded. "So, you were not abducted as I feared?"

"Nothing of the sort." She brushed back the thick hank of hair that'd broken rank and sallied down his brow, her light touch blazing across his skin. "Is that not good news?"

It was, and yet her explanation felt a'kilter, like a picture frame off center just a hair. She was hiding something. He'd bet his great-grandfather's pocket watch on it. He pulled from her touch. "Mistress Mayhew said you left the boarding house early this morning. Where did you go?"

"The old Scampson Warehouse, but no matter now." She flashed a beguiling smile. "Like I said, tomorrow is a new day in which we shall begin our new life. Just think of it! Mr. and Mrs. Forge."

His surge of relief at finding her safe suddenly caught wind and sailed off. By now he knew her tricks, the rapid-fire change of subject, the mesmerizing way she tipped her head just so, the sudden blanching of the tiny crescent scar near her left eyebrow. The little jade was of a mind to swindle him, but for what purpose?

"Why were you at Scampson's?" he asked point-blank.

"Oh, you know. Nothing to concern you."

He looked past her shoulder to Graybone. "Why was she at Scampson's instead of at church?"

The sergeant's bushy beard made his face completely unreadable, but down to the very marrow of his bones, Jackson suspected her father owned all the details of where she'd been—and that stung as sharply as being abandoned at the altar.

The sergeant's chest rose and fell like a wave on a stormy sea. "The story is for Kit to tell, I think."

He *did* know!

Jackson tipped Kit's face up to his, trying desperately to return to the joy he'd felt mere moments ago. "Well?"

She averted her gaze. "If you must know, I was working a case."

"On our wedding day?" He dropped his hand, his heart falling right along with it. What woman went in search of cutthroats and criminals on the day she was to marry? "What compelled you to do such a thing?"

She lifted one shoulder in a maddeningly dismissive shrug. "It was an early meeting, one that would've easily been accomplished had I not fallen through the floor."

"Who were you meeting?"

"I. . .I don't actually know."

He folded his arms to keep from grabbing her and shaking out words that actually made sense. It was either that or give in to the mad desire to kiss her and pretend all was well.

Which it most certainly wasn't.

He drew in a few deep breaths, an effort—albeit vain—to quell the rising fire in his chest. "Are you saying you willingly gave up exchanging vows with me for some unknown man?"

She popped her fists on her hips. "It might have been a woman."

"It doesn't matter who it was. The fact is you chose someone else over me." The truth of it doubled back and walloped him right in the gut. Had he been wrong about this woman all along? Did Kit really love him as thoroughly as she'd professed?

"Don't be absurd." Her pert little nose wrinkled. "I would never do such a thing."

"But you did!"

The sergeant's baritone voice barged into what was promising to be quite the knock-down-drag-out. "This might be a good time to tell him you're sorry, Daughter."

The vexed lines on Kit's face instantly softened. "I am sorry." She came to him then, drawing so close he breathed in the faint scent of tea rose soap still lingering in her hair. At least she'd prepared somewhat for their wedding day.

But he still could not shake the image of her wedding gown hanging forlorn in its packaging, abandoned in her wardrobe.

"Jackson, please forgive me." She pressed her palm to his cheek. "I shouldn't have been working a case on the day of our wedding. I know that now."

"I think you should have known that sooner than this very minute." He sighed, all the angst and worry he'd suffered still a fresh wound, then finally gave in to the regret in Kit's eyes and the warmth of her touch. "Very well. I forgive you."

Rising to her toes, she planted a chaste kiss on his lips before backing away with a grin.

Little scamp! He may have forgiven her, but that didn't mean he'd let her off the hook.

"What case were you working on?" he asked.

"The case is of no consequence. What is important is that I am here now, and all will be made right tomorrow morning. And with that"—she turned to the sergeant—"I bid you good night, Father. I'll be turning in early. Can't risk oversleeping, you know."

She winked at Jackson and whirled away.

"Not so fast." Jackson tugged her back to himself. Did she really think he'd be put off so easily? "What case is it, Kit? I have a right to know what was more important to you than our wedding."

She frowned. "Nothing is more important."

"Obviously there was, for you weren't there." He upped her frown with a scowl of his own. Though he'd forgiven her, he hadn't forgotten the torment of the day. "I stood at that altar waiting, hoping, plagued beyond reason when you didn't come down the aisle. I flipped this town on its ear, looking in every crevice, scrounging through back lanes and rookeries." He released her and pushed one hand through his hair. "Blast it, Kit. I even trudged up to Pentonville to put the screws to Poxley. You owe me an explanation. I will have it, and I will have it now!"

The words came out harsher than he'd intended. Even so, the tone didn't negate the genuine need burning inside him to know what she'd been up to.

She jerked away from him, a fierce spark in her eyes. "Is this the sort of husband you'll make? You should know I will not submit to being dominated like a common scullery maid."

"And I will not be some pup kept on a lead that you yank about on a whim."

Her face flushed a murderous red. "Is that what you think of me? That I'm a scold? A regular fishwife?"

"There is nothing *regular* about you!"

"Careful, now. You are both on dangerous ground." Graybone's chair creaked as he planted his hands on the desk. "Take heed. Words once spoken cannot be unheard."

"Don't worry, Father." Kit flipped back her long tail of hair. "I have nothing more to say."

And just like that she stormed out, a tempest in a raggedy brown gown, leaving a riot of ugly emotions in her wake. Not only did Jackson not like it, he had no idea what to do with all the rage and shame and longing that balled into a prickly wad in the middle of his chest. He felt like a monster for upsetting her. But by all that was holy, he was the one wronged here!

Clenching his fist, he let loose and punched the wall. The plaster gave. So did his knuckles. He pulled away, skin broken, blood oozing, and all without quashing the white-hot agitation eating him alive.

"Well," Graybone grumbled. "That could've gone better."

Jackson wheeled about, aiming a finger at the man. "Do not think to blame me."

The sergeant merely shook his head as he sank back to his chair. "It takes two to quarrel. The sooner you learn that lesson, the better."

"You heard her." Incredulous, Jackson flapped his hand towards the door. "Kit not only stood me up at the altar, she refuses to tell me why she did so. But you know, don't you?"

A tic crinkled Graybone's left eyelid. Good. At least he recognized in some measure how unjust it was for him to be Kit's confidant instead of her own husband-to-be.

The sergeant averted his gaze, taking a sudden interest in the inkstand on his desk. "Again, it is Kit's place to say. This is a scrape you need to work out with her, not me."

"I am not so certain I want to anymore." Jackson plopped into the other chair, suddenly tired of love and promise. Truth be told, he was weary of everything. "Kit Turner just might be more trouble than she is worth."

The sergeant wagged his big head. "You don't mean that."

"Yes, I do."

Graybone sighed. "Give it time, man. Each morning brings fresh mercies, but for now, it's best you put your mind on other things instead of festering over today."

Jackson yanked off his cravat and wound it around his bloodied knuckles. "Today will not be so easily forgotten."

"It will when I charge you with a new murder case to work on."

He snorted. "You are not my superior anymore."

A strange light flared in Graybone's eyes. "This isn't an official case."

Jackson winced as he tucked in the ends of the cloth on his sore hand. "What are you talking about?"

The sergeant shoved a dainty bit of gold across the desk. "Kit found this on a dead body."

Jackson stared at the necklace. If he touched it, it was like committing to a job he didn't wish to take, and yet... Bah! Would the urge to bring about justice never stop burning in his soul?

He swiped the thing up and studied the thin chain, the tarnished locket, the broken clasp that would not allow him to pry the lid open. The tip of a knife—used carefully—would be needed. Who had this belonged to? What sort of death had the woman succumbed to at the hands of who-knew-whom? He'd have to question Kit where exactly she'd found—

No.

Absolutely not.

He pushed the necklace back to Graybone. "Nice try, but Kit will have to work on this case alone."

"On the contrary, Kit is to know nothing of it." The sergeant collected the necklace as if it were a precious gem instead of a forgotten relic. "You still have your five days off, so you can investigate without anyone knowing."

An alarm bell clanged inside Jackson's head. This was odd. Graybone followed rules. He abided authority at all costs. So why the sudden request for a covert operation? "What are you not telling me?"

The sergeant shifted on his chair as if the wooden seat had suddenly sprouted nails. "This is for your ears alone, understood?"

He pinched the bridge of his nose. Did he really want to hear this? It wasn't too late to stride out the door, for the truth in the sergeant's earlier admonition still rang clear and true.

Words once spoken cannot be unheard.

Dropping his hand, he nodded. He owed this man who—while brusque beyond measure—had taken him under his wing.

Graybone stared at the bauble, overly small in his big hand. "I know who this necklace belongs to. Or did." His fingers wrapped tight around the dainty chain. "Isabella Dalton."

Jackson blinked. Though he turned the name around, studying it from every possible angle, it meant nothing to him whatsoever.

But if the sheen in the sergeant's eyes was any indication, it most assuredly did to Graybone.

"Who is she?" Jackson asked.

After a sharp inhale, the man's gaze shot to his. "She is. . .was. . . Kit's mother."

"But I understood she jumped from a bridge, taking her own life."

"As did I." The sergeant's face turned to stone. "Apparently we were wrong."

Chapter Fifteen

Sometimes no matter how hard you scrubbed a burnt pot, the etched-in singe just would not be removed. The stain was too deep. The vessel too ruined. With a growl, Kit kicked the pot, embracing the pain in her big toe. . .anything to put her mind on something other than the ugly words that'd flown between her and Jackson.

Heaving a sigh, she planted her hands against the counter's solid framework, weary beyond measure. Though she'd tried, she'd not slept half a wink since their big fight, so here she was at the break of dawn, bleary-eyed in the Blackfriars soup kitchen, wishing to rewind the hands of time.

The back doorknob rattled, followed by a screech of hinges, the patter of several pairs of feet, and a gasp.

"Miss Kit?" Wonder threaded Martha's voice. "Oh, I was that worried about you!"

Kit barely had time to turn before her friend rushed over with a baby on her hip and pulled her into a side hug.

The second Martha released her hold, she stepped back and gave Kit a worried once-over. "But what are you doing here?"

Exactly. Why was she in the cramped rear room of a run-down heap of board and nails when she should be lying abed in her husband's arms, sated by a night of happily-ever-aftering? She grabbed a dishcloth off the counter, unwilling to meet Martha's gaze. "Thought I'd help you get an early start for once. You work too hard."

Without missing a beat, Martha unspooled a string of commands.

"Alice, see to little Hazel. Jane, a tea tray for Miss Kit and I. Anna, pick up that pot off the floor, and the rest of you be about your usual tasks. What do you say, girls?"

"Yes, mum," the children chorused in unison.

"There's my good girls." Martha tugged Kit towards the dining room, hardly waiting for Kit to sit before arching a brow at her from across the table. "Let's have it, then, aye?"

"There's nothing to have." The words were as hollow as her voice. The same sick feeling she'd had since sparring with Jackson churned in her belly once again. She fisted her hand against it and all the horrid emotions she'd bottled inside. "Turns out Jackson wasn't the man I thought he was."

"I don't believe that for one second, and neither do you. Tell me what happened."

Kit massaged little circles at her temple, as mystified now as she had been when Jackson had blown up at her. Sure, she'd arrived late at church—*very* late—but it wasn't as if she'd murdered anyone with a hatchet. "All I did was show up a bit tardy to the ceremony."

"Posh! Ye missed it altogether is what I heard." Martha smacked the table. "Why, yer man was fit to upend the city from Blackfriars to Greenwich to find ye."

The guilt she'd been trying to stave off all night slipped through a crack in her heart, and her shoulders drooped. "You're right. I did miss the wedding." She lifted her chin. "But I apologized as soon as Jackson found me."

"Then ye've been forgiven, Mr. Jackson loves ye that much." Martha clasped Kit's hands, giving a little squeeze, the pity in her eyes almost unbearable. "So why are ye not with him?"

Kit pulled away, the bitter truth of all that'd happened heaping coals upon her head. "I may have Jackson's pardon, but I most certainly do not have his good opinion."

"Nonsense. Mr. Jackson thinks the world of ye. Why, he could have no higher opinion of any woman on this patch o' earth and there's no denying it."

Perhaps at one time that had been true, but not now, and maybe not ever again. She fiddled with the cuffs of her sleeves as his words barreled back. "He said I wasn't *regular*." She scowled—a petulant response but wholly unstoppable. "I heard it from his own mouth."

Martha laughed, though the humour of it was lost on Kit. There was nothing amusing about this in the least.

"Oh, my sweet, headstrong friend." Once again she collected Kit's hands, and this time she held on tight. "Mr. Jackson couldn't be more spot-on, for there's not one blessed regular thing about ye. But don't ye see? That's what makes ye so special, love. Ye *are* unlike any other, and I daresay that's what yer man admires most, fer Mr. Jackson is no common suit either. Ye were meant for each other, and way deep down, I think ye know that."

Kit sucked in a breath as the reality of Martha's words tipped her world on end. Had she been wrong to take such affront when all Jackson had wanted was for her to share what she'd been up to? Perhaps *she* was the one who'd been too reactionary in the heat of the moment. Scab-nippity! She knew better. Why must that man always muddle her cool reserve? No other man ever had. . .

And then she knew.

Because she loved him, so much it was an ache in her bones, a need in her very soul. He was the one God had crafted just for her. Her alone. She buried her face in her hands.

Oh, God, forgive me.

A swish of skirts rounded the table. "There now, love." Martha patted her back. "It'll all work out, just you wait and see."

Would it, though? She knew how to handle a back-alley sharper bent on a slicer of a knife fight, but this?

A rattle of teacups entered the room. Kit lifted her face as young Jane set a tray on the table and poured her and Martha a steaming cup.

Kit arched a brow at Martha over the rim. "I don't suppose I can swindle my way out of this predicament, can I?"

Her friend's mouth twisted into a wry smile. "How about ye try humility instead? If there's one thing I've learned in marriage it's this. . . pride preserves yerself, humility preserves yer relationship. 'Tis a simple enough truth, but I daresay not an easy one."

"Nothing is easy, it seems." Sighing, Kit set down her cup. "And since I have no other ideas of how to make amends, I shall take your advice to heart and give it a try. . .if Jackson will have me, that is."

"Of that I have no doubt." Martha grinned, then instantly sobered. "But one more thing before you go, something unrelated, though I do hate to trifle ye with such, what with yer own messes to mop." Martha fumbled in her pocket and pulled out three pewter thimblerig cups.

With a frown, Kit reached for them, familiar with the weight and feel of the small gambling shells. "What are you doing with these?"

"Found 'em tucked a'neath Frankie's mattress."

The little scalawag. He'd vowed not to give his mother cause to report his skipping out, and now this? Kit tapped her lip with her forefinger, thinking hard. Then again, skipping out wasn't exactly what Martha was reporting now, was it? A slow smile spread beneath her finger. He was a nimble-tongued operator, that boy, exactly as she'd trained him. Why, Frankie's artful ways might even surpass her own in a few years.

Her grin faded, the sweet taste of pride turning to ashes in her mouth. Now that such a skill was turned against his own mother, she didn't like it. Not at all.

She met her friend's worried gaze. "Have you noticed any other unusual activity from him?"

"None. The lad's been a shiny-faced angel since ye talked with him. Why, he's even taken to helping old lady Crocker down on the docks every day. Between that, school, and lending me a hand, there's hardly a moment for him to scare up trouble. I can't cipher it, unless he's holding on to those cups for that new friend he's taken up with, Joe Something-or-other, if I remember right. That boy's been comin' 'round the soup kitchen more often of late, always when Frankie's about."

Hmm. Likely she referred to the lad next to Frankie in the soup kitchen queue nigh a fortnight ago. Were the pair up to shenanigans or merely friends?

She held up the cups. "Mind if I keep these?"

"Not at all. What will ye do?"

Kit shoved the thimblerigs into her pocket as she rose. "First I'll have a talk with Jackson, then I'll pay Frankie a visit at Fanny Crocker's."

A good plan. Solid, even.

But only God knew how either meeting would turn out.

Jackson pounded down the street, cross with Kit, irritated with himself, livid at whoever had murdered Kit's mother, and especially peeved about the way the morning sun hit him square in the eyes. To make matters worse, his feet hurt. He'd walked miles last night, unable to sleep, unwilling to go home. His trek to Mistress Mayhew's had been fruitless—Kit wasn't there—and he'd been forced to take a circuitous route to the old Scampson Warehouse to shake whoever it was that trailed him. Had he lost the blackguard bent on tracking his every move?

He stepped through the hole in the broken-down building, then just to play it safe, he immediately whipped around. Shading his eyes with one hand, he squinted. No one lurked at the edge of his line of sight. In truth the only thing on edge was him. He exhaled a lungful of disgust and readjusted the coil of rope he'd brought along, which had shifted on his shoulder. His sleuthing abilities were slipping away, and why not? The past fortnight he'd been so preoccupied with Kit, it was no wonder his senses were off-kilter. A low groan strangled in his throat, and he closed his eyes.

Oh, God, I know I really ought to be at church this morning, but even so, grant that I may be able to bring to justice the one responsible for Isabella Dalton's death. . .and since I'm asking for a miracle, please make things right between Kit and me.

In more ways than one, it was a desperate prayer, which did not sit well. Desperation was for those of little faith and weak of mind. Was that truly what he'd become?

Sighing, he turned—then immediately pulled back his fist to strike.

Stepping out of the shadows several paces away, a black-coated man clutched a stick in one hand that might easily crack his skull.

But the fellow made no move to take a swing and, in fact, shored himself up on what Jackson could now see was a cane.

"Have a care, sir!" The fellow held up a palm. "I mean no harm to you, and I pray you bring none to me."

Jackson lowered his arm, for now that daylight landed plainly on the man's form, the truth of his claim was apparent. Though tall, the fellow listed to the side, one leg shorter than the other. He was small boned, smaller eyed, and smelled as musty as a book that'd sat long forgotten on a shelf.

Even so, Jackson kept his feet firmly planted in a fighting stance in case the man was a decoy of some sort. "Who are you, and why are you poking about this warehouse?"

"How curious." The fellow cocked his head, eyeing Jackson as diligently as Jackson studied him. "You speak with the mien of a constable, yet you do not dress the part."

"Who I am and what I wear does not signify. I will have your identity and I will have it now."

"As you wish." The man shrugged. "I have nothing to conceal. Mr. Jacob Harpenny, vicar of Cripplegate, at your service, sir." He dipped a scant bow. "And with whom do I have the pleasure of speaking?"

Jackson swallowed a sour taste. He was the worst sort of monster, having bullied Kit last night and now a clergyman. He flexed the stress out of his fingers, wishing he could as easily remove the shame lodged in his chest. "I beg your pardon, sir. You must understand that one cannot be too careful when entering an abandoned building. And you weren't far off on your estimate of me, for I am an officer of the law, Inspector Jackson Forge. But I am afraid I must ask once again, what are you doing here?"

"There was a young lady caught in a hole here yesterday." He aimed the tip of his cane backwards, towards the shadowy corridor from which he'd emerged. "Highly irrational of me, I know, but I thought I should take a peek today to make sure there were no other damsels in distress."

Interesting. Kit hadn't mentioned anything about a saviour. Then again, there was likely much she'd omitted from her story. "Am I to understand you helped the young lady out of her predicament?"

"By God's grace, yes, and a good thing I happened along when I did, for the poor thing was fairly frantic."

Jackson snorted. Kit frantic? Perhaps she had realized the error of her ways in choosing to come here instead of the church. He offered Mr. Harpenny his hand. "I thank you for your service."

"No thanks needed, for I shall reap my rewards in heaven, but all the same"—he shook Jackson's hand with a surprisingly strong grip—"many thanks to you for keeping the streets of my parish safe."

Jackson pulled back, quickly rummaging through a storehouse of all the acquaintances he'd made in the past half year, and. . .yes. He had met the vicar of Cripplegate during the St. Giles grave-robbing case, but that man had been shorter, wider, and employed no cane—though he had really ought to. The fellow had been as old as Saint Peter himself. "*You* are the vicar of Cripplegate?"

"I am now, what with Mr. Spooner recently retired. I took up his duties just a week ago. And speaking of duties. . ." The vicar clapped his hat tighter atop his head. "If you have no further inquiries, I really should return for morning prayers."

"By all means." Jackson stepped aside.

Mr. Harpenny strode past him with an off-center gait, but before he got too far, Jackson called him back. "One last question, Vicar."

Harpenny turned with a raised brow. "Yes?"

"Did you notice anything other than the panicked young lady in the hole yesterday or spy anything amiss as you investigated today?"

The reverend shook his head. "It is quite dark down there, even in daylight. Had the woman not been so vocal, I am sure I would not have ventured so far inside. And so, have a care, sir."

"I have every intention of doing so, Mr. Harpenny. Good day."

With a tip of his head, Jackson picked his way down the bleak passageway. The man was right. This place was a death trap. Scant daylight filtered in through gaps in the roof, painting a striped walkway fraught with all manner of possible ankle twisters. He would be wise to measure each step.

After a few dead ends and a broken stairway leading to a loft full of bat droppings, he finally found the hole where Kit had taken her tumble. Two boards had cracked, leaving an opening with dagger-sharp edges. A makeshift platform lay across the top. Jackson eased himself onto the strong hunk of lumber and peered over the edge into a black pit. Of all the places to fall through! It was a wonder Kit hadn't broken her neck.

"Woman, what am I to do with you?" he growled under his breath.

Then he got to business, for there wouldn't be much time before the recovery team arrived from the station. That lot could upend a crime scene more thoroughly than a herd of Hampshire hogs.

He secured one end of the rope to a thick stud and laid his coat over the sharp edges of the floorboards, and then, grabbing hold of the rope, he worked his way down until his feet hit solid ground. It took a fair amount of blinking to acclimate to the darkness, and when he did, he squatted near the dull white of a pile of bones.

"Well, lady," he whispered. "Are you really Kit's mother, or did you steal that locket from her?" For according to Graybone, there was no disputing the locket had belonged to Kit's mother. As he'd said they would, once they'd pried open the broken catch, inside they'd found a snippet of the sergeant's hair, a keepsake he'd given Miss Dalton the day they'd parted forever on a blustery London dock.

Jackson examined the skeleton from head to toe, noting the missing canine tooth, a few threads caught on the ribs from fabric not scavenged by rats, and a clear break in the tibia—none of which would help identify the woman's abductor. He duck-walked back a few steps, widening his search. One odd-shaped bone lay at a perpendicular angle from the body—a bone that didn't belong to the skeleton.

It didn't belong to a human at all.

He swiped up the bleached bone, an inch wide, a foot long, and flat. Very flat. A woman's busk, and an ornate one at that. He held the piece up to the thin light dribbling in from the hole in the ceiling. The etching of a ship sailed across what appeared to be calm waters. A scrimshaw pattern, of sorts. Aha! Now this was something he could use.

Tucking the corset piece into his waistband, he searched the rest of the pit. The door would not be budged no matter how hard he rammed it—likely barred from the outside by whoever had imprisoned Kit's mother. A small hollow in the wall let loose a few rats, which he kicked right back inside. Part of a nest fell out, bits of twigs, blackened twine, and a small square of dirty red. He scuffed the fabric farther from the nest with the toe of his boot then collected it. Probably wasn't anything, but on the off chance, he tucked it into his pocket and went back to searching.

In the darkest corner of the tiny chamber, a few divots marred the wall. On instinct alone, Jackson brushed away the black mould from the stone, and after scraping one knuckle and snagging his thumbnail, he finally cleared what appeared to be tally marks. Seventeen crudely carved lines. Anger hardened his gut. Was that how long this poor woman huddled in this cell?

He yanked out his handkerchief and scrubbed the area with the fabric instead of his skin, searching for any other etchings. Minutes later, he uncovered coarse letters.

EFMANN

A clue. A valuable clue.

But what the devil did it mean?

Exhaling sharply through his nostrils, he returned to Isabella's body. "Very clever of you to leave me such a curious lead. Your daughter would have done the same. There is a crew on their way to lift you to a better resting place. In the meantime, I will find this Efmann and bring him to justice for you and the sergeant. And for Kit. But I suppose first I should make things right with her."

Rising, he snagged the rope, unsure which of his upcoming tasks would prove to be the biggest challenge: a final questioning of Dedfield about the possibility of more stolen goods showing up at his dust yard, solving a twenty-four-year-old murder case with nothing to go on but a whalebone busk and six carved letters. . .

Or tracking down Kit to apologize.

Chapter Sixteen

Riding an omnibus was a peculiar sort of torture for those too poor to own a private carriage. Normally, Kit didn't mind a good jostler of a ride, but today's bus was particularly crowded, and she was already emotionally on edge. The sharp-elbowed lady next to her had sown quite a garden of bruises on her arm, and nothing could quell the oily stench of the man seated across from her. Nor did she like the way he eyed her. Thankfully, the next stop was hers.

The second the lumbering coach heaved to a stop, elbow lady bolted to her feet and scurried past, knocking Kit's peace offering of *The Pickwick Papers* to the floor. Jackson loved Dickens. Hopefully, he still loved her as well. She swiped up the book and dusted off the cover, feeling the gaze of the large man across from her lingering far too long on her bodice. Too bad she didn't have time to teach the blackguard a few manners, yet the urge to find Jackson and apologize burned too hot in her heart to ignore any longer.

She tucked the book into her pocket as she rose, but by now the door was blocked with a broad set of shoulders and blue eyes that stared into her soul.

"Jackson?"

"Kit?"

Amidst street hawkers barking outside and a hearty cough inside, their names played a surprising harmony in the enclosed space.

Kit blinked as a hundred other words rose to the surface. She wanted to tell him how sorry she was, name all the reasons why she shouldn't have walked out of the station last night. Explain that she loved him more than the stars in the sky or the breath in her lungs. But now that Jackson was here, his chiseled jaw and dimpled chin right at eye level, her traitorous tongue lay fallow.

Surprisingly, his did too. He didn't scold. He didn't nag. He didn't... anything.

The omnibus lurched into motion, catching her quite off guard and off balance. She stumbled into Jackson's chest. For a heavenly moment, she breathed in his scent of cedarwood soap while his warm hands righted her. An unstoppable zing charged through her from head to toes.

She stepped back and grabbed the thick wooden pole next to the door.

Their gazes met, and once again they spoke in unison. "I—"

A small smile played on Jackson's lips. "Ladies first."

At least he was thinking of her as a lady and not a scoundrel. She returned his grin. "I was on my way to find you."

"Then we are on the same mission. I was seeking you out at Mistress Mayhew's."

"You would have been sorely disappointed." She clutched the pole tighter as the omnibus turned a corner. "I've not been to the boarding house since before dawn."

"So I discovered when I called earlier."

"You did?" What a good man. She'd been the one to let anger get the best of her, and yet he'd been out looking to make amends? "I thought you might still be cross with me."

One of his brows lifted.

A rude tug of her skirt, with fingers pressing far too intimately against her thigh, was immediately followed by a raspy voice. "If he be done wit' ye, luv, what say ye give it a go wit' me?"

Her skin prickled. Bother! She should have taught that blackguard a lesson when he'd ogled her. Well, he'd picked the wrong woman this time. She cocked her head down at the greasy-haired fellow, donning her street identity. "Like what ye see, do ye, ducky?"

"Kit," Jackson breathed a low warning. "Not here."

Both she and the big oaf ignored him.

"Ye look like a fine tasty to me, and I wouldn't mind seein' a bit more neither." The man waggled his eyebrows. "If ye take my meanin'.'"

"Oh?" She bared her teeth in a trap of a smile. "Like to see a bit o' skin, would ye, darlin'?"

"Don't do it," Jackson growled.

The man leered up at her, a disgusting amount of lust shining in his eyes. "You offering?"

"More than you know."

In a flash, she yanked out her boot knife and held it to his neck, the jostle of the omnibus causing the blade to nick into the fat folds on his skin. A collective gasp filled the small space. One lady squealed. The rest of the passengers scooted as far from the scene as possible.

Jackson hauled her out the door to the little platform at the back of the transport. "Come on. This is our stop."

The curses of the man inside collided with the shout of the conductor as Jackson leapt from the moving coach, tugging her through the air and down to the cobbles into the safety of his arms.

The conductor shook his fist over the railing. "I'll have you both hauled into the station if you ever ride my bus again."

Kit chuckled to herself. Wouldn't her father love that. Pulling away from Jackson, she tucked her knife into her boot sheath.

Jackson shook his head, lips flattened in annoyance. "We need to talk."

"That man needed to be taught a lesson and you know it."

"Agreed, but that's not what we need to talk about, and *you* know it." A ragged sigh whooshed out of him as he guided her to the pavement.

She sobered at the sound and at the shadowy crescents beneath his eyes, shadows no doubt put there by her. "You're right." She dipped her head. "I suppose I must once again beg for your pardon."

"I already told you I forgave you."

Kit scrunched her brow up at him. "But I didn't apologize for rushing out of my father's office in such a flurry last night. It was very wicked of me, especially after I missed our wedding."

"True." Grabbing her hand, he steered her into an alcove between buildings, out of the public eye. "But neither did I apologize for being the cause of that flurry. I should have been more kind to you, Kit."

She pressed her palm to his cheek. Stubble met her touch. "You were pretty harsh."

"And you were pretty. . .pretty." He nuzzled against her hand.

This—*this!*—was bliss. Reconciliation had been easier than she'd imagined—and far sweeter. She leaned closer. "So, all is well between us?"

He pressed a kiss to her hand, his thumb rubbing a delicious circle on her wrist the whole while. "As long as you mend your ways," he whispered against her skin. "Yes, all is well."

The amorous cadence of her pulse slowed to a dull thud. "What ways?"

"Your devil-may-care recklessness, for one." Dropping her hand, he tipped her face up to gaze directly into her eyes. "I saw the hole you fell into at Scampson's, Kit. You're lucky you didn't break your neck. You take too many risks, my love, and that must stop."

He'd actually checked up on her story? A brick to the head couldn't have stunned her more. "Did you not believe me?"

"Of course I believed you, the parts you told me at any rate." He glanced towards the pavement, where a particularly loud gaggle of schoolboys passed by, and when he looked back, he narrowed his eyes as if she were a criminal to be interrogated. "It is the things you leave out that give me doubt. How am I to trust you when I never know if you're telling me the full truth or not?"

She frowned. He didn't trust her? She'd taken him into her confidence. Shared her past, her dreams. Bared her soul as she'd done for none other. Anger boiled up from her belly. "Never once have I—"

"Pride preserves yerself, humility preserves yer relationship."

Martha's admonition surfaced, shutting her mouth. Was it true? Would a soft word ward off what promised to be another spectacular row? She took a deep breath. Then another. And though it galled her beyond reason, she finally tucked her chin in submission. "I shall try to do better in the future."

"Good." Jackson flashed a grin. "I am glad of it. If I am to keep you safe, I must know all."

"Must you?" She flipped back her tail of hair. "I am taking you as my husband, Jackson, not my warden."

"In your case, I suspect that will be one and the same." He laughed. Laughed!

And the sound rubbed her raw. "That's not funny."

"Oh, Kit." His laughter faded. "Don't you realize by now I merely want you out of harm's way? These streets are deadly."

A touching sentiment—truly—but did he really think she wasn't aware of how lethal this town was? She folded her arms. "I know the danger."

"And I know better." He tipped his chin. "Look what happened to my brother."

Hah! *He* knew better? She'd scrapped about in every nook and crook of this city since she'd been abandoned at a foundling hospital as a newborn babe, and he'd been here what? A scant six months? Something twisted in her chest, as if all the humility she'd harnessed was being slowly wrung out, drip by drip. "I am not some fluff-headed country boy wandering about as a sheep among wolves. I've lived these past twenty-four years quite nicely without your protection. Furthermore, if I recall properly, there was a certain raw recruit of a constable who required my assistance last spring. Why, you'd not have lasted a week here without me, and that's God's truth. So pardon me if I do not agree that you know better than I when it comes to keeping out of harm's way."

Jackson poked a finger in her chest. "I will not have my wife stabbed in the gut or shot in the head. Do you hear me?"

She glowered. The whole blessed parish of Cheapside could hear him.

"Nor will I be told what to do in my own home, and this *is* my home." She flailed her arms, indicating the ramshackle buildings, the manure-laden cobbles, the hubbub of what was and always had been her childhood playground.

Jackson's jaw hardened. "Your home is with me, Kit, wherever I decide that may be. That's what it means when you vow to honour and obey your husband."

Pah! Was he seriously playing the obedience card? With *her*?

"What a load of balderdash. Wives are not slaves to be strong-armed by a husband's will. Not to mention that you've conveniently omitted the part about a husband's vows to love his wife. It seems to me that any man making major life decisions without first consulting his wife is neither loving nor kind."

Jackson stilled, deadly calm. Good. Her words had hit home.

He lowered his voice. "After all we've been through, after all I've done for you, do you really think me such a harsh taskmaster?"

She stared deeply into his blue eyes, softening somewhat as memory after memory surfaced. Jackson following her into the underground train tunnel, sheltering her at the risk of his own life. Acquiescing to her hunch of working the dust yard and nearly getting himself brained because of it. And he did give her leave to run the soup kitchen as she saw fit without any interference whatsoever. But—and there was always a *but* when it came to men—he frequently made sure to remind her of the freedoms he allowed and the risks he took on her account.

"No, Jackson, you are not harsh," she admitted aloud. "You're worse. You're stubborn."

He snorted. "There is none more obstinate than you, my dear."

"I am not obstinate. I am determined, which is a virtue, not a vice."

"Determined to kill me, more often than not," he said under his breath.

"I heard that."

"Look, Kit." A great sigh rushed past his lips. "We both know were it not for your rash behaviour, neither of our lives would ever be in danger to begin with. You are the cause of most mishaps we encounter."

Of all the hog-brained accusations. So much for humility, for this was not to be borne. She popped her fists on her hips. "I am not to blame for *your* lack of street smarts."

An angry shade of scarlet crept up his neck. "Oh? So now you're saying I'm inept?"

"If the boot fits. . ."

She swallowed, stunned by the stricken look on his face. She should apologize again, but the words would not come. They heaped in her chest, right behind her heart, grey as ash. The clamor of the streets receded until all she could hear was the rush of her own blood in her ears.

"If that is truly how you feel"—his voice was ice, the blue in his eyes even colder—"then perhaps I am not the man for you."

Her heart froze, but all the same, a freakish resolve flowed strong in her veins. "Perhaps you are not."

For a long moment, he said nothing. Neither did she. It was a terrible silence, like the unnerving hush after the slamming of a great door.

"Well, there you have it then." He wheeled about. "Goodbye, Kit."

Panic pulsed through her veins. "Jackson, wait."

But he didn't. He stalked out of the alcove, out of her sight. Out of her life. What sort of man walked away like that? Poof. Gone.

And that's when the ugly truth hit her hard, stealing her breath. Jackson didn't love her. Not wholly. Not truly.

Just like her mother. The woman who'd walked away and left her at a foundling hospital to fend for herself. The woman who'd selfishly taken her own life.

Kit's eyes burned, the pressure of tears building until her jaw ached and her head throbbed. If one drop let loose, there'd be no stopping the torrent. So she swallowed the hot mass, forcing it down, burying it deep. Let it rot. Let it all rot.

Whirling, Kit pounded her fists against the wall until the fleshy sides of her hands were a bruised and battered mess.

So much for humility.

And so much for a marriage with Jackson Forge.

He'd been down before. Face to the sand. Belly to the dirt. But never—ever—had Jackson been so thoroughly gutted. A boning blade couldn't have done a better job of slicing the life out of his chest, leaving nothing behind but cold air and regret. And all because of a snip of a woman whose tongue was sharper than a Highlander's dirk, whose pride was larger than the heavens.

But not larger than his anger.

Or his hurt.

Jackson took the stairs two at a time up to the front door of the fancy Mayfair town house, blind to anything but the pain in his soul.

Kit didn't respect him. The woman he loved more than life didn't believe him to be competent. Well then, he'd prove her wrong and be glad for it!

Lifting a lion-headed knocker, Jackson banged the brass against the wood hard enough to rattle the glass in the mullioned windows on both sides of the entrance.

Moments later, a pinch-mouthed footman scoured him with a poisonous gaze. "The servant's entrance is at the back." With a white-gloved hand, he began to swing the door shut.

Oh, no. Not in the mood he was in.

Jackson shot the toe of his shoe in the ever-narrowing opening and snapped out the calling card the earl had given him at eye level.

Upper lip slightly curled, the footman glanced at the elegant script—and the curl instantly smoothed into an even line. He opened the door wide and gave a curt bow. "I beg your pardon, sir. Good day to you."

"Good day." Jackson strode past him, then followed him into a small sitting room just off the foyer, where he was offered a drink. He declined with a shake of his head. Mixing spirits with the foulness in his soul right now would be a deadly combination.

The footman paused on the threshold. "I shall inform my lord he has a caller. Whom do I have the pleasure of announcing?"

"Jackson Forge." There was a harshness to his tone, one that ought not to be there. One he doubted would ever go away.

"Very good, sir." The man walked off on silent feet, almost too silent. Part of a servant's job, though, appearing and disappearing like a ghost. Naturally, the earl would hire only those best suited to the task.

Jackson stalked to the window and parted the sheers with one finger, but he didn't see a thing. How could he? A cancerous red haze filtered everything. He'd never view life the same. Not without Kit. His fingers twisted in the filmy fabric. A perverse pastime, this strangling of curtains, but at least it gave him something to do other than pummel the next person that entered the room.

Good timing, too, for the earl's bass voice arrived hardly two breaths later.

"Mr. Forge? Quite a pleasant surprise."

Jackson spun, leaving the wrinkled sheers swinging behind him. "I shall be brief, my lord, for I daresay we both have business to attend."

Even at leisure in his own home, not a silver-tipped hair was amiss atop Gordon-Lennox's head. He lifted one hand in the air. "Then I can assume...?"

For one crazed second, the urge to run out the door itched in his feet. Just tear out of here and scoop up Kit to kiss away all the horrid barbs they'd flung at one another. But she'd said herself he wasn't the man for her. And why would he be? There could be no man for such a headstrong, spiky-tongued street princess. What a fool he'd been to ever think he could fill such a role.

Throwing back his shoulders, he met the earl's gaze head-on. "Yes. I will take the job and thank you for it."

"Very good." The man nodded once, sharply. "We sail in two weeks. I'll send word to you for times and dates of a few meetings beforehand. You ought to know the itinerary and details of where we'll be staying, and I shall expect you to submit a full report on how you intend to keep me safe for the next year of traveling."

"It shall be as you wish. Thank you." And that was it. In the space of a minute, his life changed onto a course that would take him to the other side of the world—which was fine by him. The voyage couldn't come soon enough. "Good day."

The sentiment barely made it past his lips. Good? Hardly. Nothing was good in this world. He strode to the door.

"Oh, Forge."

"Yes, my lord?" He paused without turning.

"May I be so bold as to ask what changed your mind?"

The question hit him like lightning to an old oak, one that'd long since rotted, with nothing left inside but splinters and dust. He grabbed on to the doorframe, grinding his nails into the wood.

"No, my lord," he murmured. "You may not."

Chapter Seventeen

Some days, especially the rainy ones, a man was better off just hanging up his hat and calling it quits. Steady drips rolled between Jackson's collar and hairline, leaking cold down his spine. And why not? The rest of his world was swirling down the gutter like the wash of grey water running along the kerb. Scowling, he jammed his hat on tighter and long-legged it over a puddle, wishing for the hundredth time he'd thought to grab an umbrella before he'd left the boarding house this morning.

After a night of wretched sleep—would he ever truly be at rest again?—he'd seen his father and brother off at the station, which was a particularly bitter moment. What should have been a happy send-off with his new bride turned into a solemn parting. The pity in his father's gaze would molest him for all eternity. But even worse had been the confusion plaguing James. His brother's wounded brain could not comprehend where the pretty lady had gone or why she wasn't at the platform to say goodbye. James had searched the face of every passing woman, and if that weren't bad enough, he'd eyed their bodices as well, hoping to catch sight of the watch brooch he'd given to Kit. What a stir that had caused. Jackson could only imagine the trouble Father would have on the train ride home.

Two soggy blocks later, Jackson stopped in front of a sooty-windowed rag-and-bottle shop pinched between two larger buildings. It was a seedy affair, with gaps in the brickwork where the mortar had crumbled away and a scabby front door blistered by weather. Fitting that this dump belonged to the owner of the derelict Scampson

Warehouse—which was Jackson's only lead thus far in the mystery of Isabella Dalton's murder. Hopefully, Baggett and Graybone would turn up something more. He'd asked Baggett to check into the identity of the mysterious Efmann while the sergeant investigated the busk manufacturer and looked into the coroner's report. Not much to go on, particularly when Jackson would leave the country in a little over two weeks, but it was something.

He lifted his hand to rap on the door, then thought the better of it. Banging on the rickety wood might collapse the whole blessed structure. The knob gave, so he shoved the door open. "Mr. Scampson?"

Two steps inside, Jackson immediately pressed the cuff of his sleeve to his nose. He'd been around decomposing corpses and open sewers, but dash and rot! This putrid stench beat all. His gaze drifted about for a dead body, maybe more than one tucked away in this chaos. Boxes of oily rags were stacked to the ceiling. Bins of half-filled bottles heaped one atop the other, creating a narrow and dangerous path to a crooked staircase against the back wall.

He edged towards the stairs. "Mr. Scampson?"

"One more step and I'll blast that pretty head off your shoulders, mate."

Rocks in a tin can couldn't have grated more than the gravelly voice at Jackson's back. He froze, annoyed with himself for not first checking behind the door. Kit would have plenty to say about—no. No, she wouldn't. His fingers clenched so tight his nails cut into the heels of his hands.

"I'm merely here to talk, Mr. Scampson." He measured out each word in a calm meter as he skimmed the crowded space for the thickest pile of cover. . .*if* he could even shimmy into one of the crevices.

"I got nothing to say but this," the man rumbled. "Tell Boniak he'll have his money by midnight tonight. Now, hands where I can see them while you get your scrawny backside out of my shop. You have ten seconds."

Jackson eased his hands into the air as he turned. The moment he faced the pile of pitted, peeling flesh aiming a pinfire revolver at his head, his gut lurched from a fresh wave of stink. Cod's heads! The man was a walking disease. His cheeks and nose were marred with great caverns and his bald head was scaly with some sort of flesh-eating malady.

"I do not work for Boniak, sir. I don't even know the man."

"Nine. Eight. Seven." Scampson stared him down, his sickly eyes filmed over as if they'd been dipped in milk. But sickly or not, the gun in his hand aimed true.

"Fine," Jackson conceded. "To the point, then. I am an inspector, Mr. Scampson. Jackson Forge, working out of the Old Jewry Station. There was a skeleton found on your property two days ago, and I intend to find out how it got there."

"A bobby? What do you know." The man shifted his weight, the bulk of his belly pressing into a tower of crates and shifting it towards Jackson's head. One wrong move and a load of bottles could take him out as quick as a shot from that gun. "Six."

If nothing else, the man knew how to hold a course. Jackson dared a step closer. "I need information, sir. To whom did you lease your warehouse twenty-four years ago? Or are you, perhaps, the one responsible for the woman's death?"

Jagged laughter filled the air, void of humour, from a mouth just as void of teeth. "Five. Four."

"Mr. Scampson, either you answer my questions here in your shop, or I shall have you hauled in for a proper interrogation at my leisure, which could take awhile. A very long while, if you catch my meaning."

Scampson spit out a curse. "You think your threat frightens me, bobby boy? Three."

"No, but I suspect Boniak worries you, or you'd not have been armed and ready for the arrival of one of his louts. And if this Boniak hears you ratted on him—and trust me, he will—well, well. . . I expect that is something you would fear."

The muzzle of his gun wavered, not much, but noticeable. "I ain't ratted on him."

"Do you think he'll believe that when a squad of bluecoats shows up at his door naming you as the snitch?"

The bluff flew out his mouth without a second thought, and he lifted his chin for emphasis. He had no way of knowing if this Boniak had cause for arrest, but if he'd learned anything from Kit, confidence was the key to success.

Scampson's pasty skin bleached a shade greyer. For a long while, he said nothing, the silence broken only by the pelt of rain against glass. It was a brittle sort of quiet, a thin sheet of ice just ready to crack. Jackson stared the man down.

Scampson lowered the gun. "What do you want, bobby?"

Jackson dropped his hands—but not his guard. "I require information, sir. Who worked for you twenty-four years ago? Who owned the cargo in your warehouse at the time? And more to the point, how did you not know there was a body rotting in your cellar?"

Scampson's lips parted in a slow smile, baring mottled gums. "I hardly know what I did last week let alone a score o' years ago, but I do know this." His head swiveled, revealing an earthworm of a scar crawling in a large C shape around the back of his skull.

Gads! The man had actually survived such an injury?

Scampson's hazy gaze returned to Jackson's. "Twenty-four years ago, a crane hook fell on me. Ended my business and nearly my life. But the bottle was my salvation." He indicated the precarious stack next to him. "In more ways than one, you could say."

Jackson sighed. What a sorry mess. It appeared Isabella Dalton wasn't the only victim of a twisted fate. "Granted you may have no recollection, Mr. Scampson, but what of records? Or ledgers? You must have kept track of invoices, payroll, and the like."

"You saw that burnt hull of a warehouse. Lost it all, along with my memory." He tapped his temple, the movement causing a few flakes of skin to fall to his shoulders. "Who knows?"

"*You* have to know. You're the owner of the property."

"Not anymore."

Jackson stilled. "What do you mean?"

"Sold it a few days ago."

"To whom?"

"Don't know. Don't care. A man offered me a tidy sum, and I snatched it up, no questions asked."

Jackson gritted his teeth, frustrated beyond measure. He'd come here for answers, not more avenues to investigate. "What did this man look like?"

Scampson's lower lip pooched out. "Bald fellow. Middling of years.

His eyes were pea-sized, and he walked with a stick, a big stick, making up for a short leg."

Interesting. If he didn't know better, he'd swear that vicar he'd met—Harpenny, was it?—was the purchaser of Scampson's Warehouse. But what the devil would a reverend want with such a worthless structure? It would cost more to raze it and rebuild than a clergyman could possibly have in his pocket.

Jackson headed towards the door. "Thank you, Mr. Scampson." He tipped his head at the man as he passed. "I leave you for now but will no doubt return with a few more questions. Do not try to skip out of town or I will hunt you down."

"You wouldn't be the only one." Scampson's gruff laughter followed him out the door.

Outside, rain still fell with a miserable steadiness, each black umbrella Jackson passed taunting him for his absentmindedness. Perhaps he ought to swing by home on his way to the station, but was it truly worth the effort? His wet trousers already clung to his legs like a second skin. If Kit saw him now, she'd laugh and—no! He ground his teeth. He had to quit thinking about that faithless sprite.

Ahead, a mammoth of a man stood near a lamppost, but oddly enough, the moment Jackson noticed him, the fellow closed his umbrella with a smirk—one that highlighted a zigzag scar on his chin.

And then he knew.

The man from the zoo.

Jackson dodged as the attacker lunged. Too late. The tip of the man's brolly seared hot pain across his shoulder. He crashed into a robust woman, sending them both stumbling. She screamed. He groaned. Blood oozed down his chest. That was no regular umbrella. The tip had been modified.

With a knife.

He whirled. Better to face the attacker than take a stab to the back and bleed out not knowing who or why.

The man sprang again.

This time Jackson took it in his upper arm. Dash it!

He wheeled back to the woman. "May I?" He snatched her umbrella as another scream ripped out. He'd take that as a yes.

Grasping each end, he held the thing out like a cudgel stick and repelled the next blow.

"Who are you?" Jackson roared.

"Your executioner." He slashed.

Jackson leaned into it, the woman's umbrella bearing the brunt. Fabric hung in shreds. If he didn't take down the man soon, he'd have nothing left with which to fight.

Jab after jab. Deflection after deflection. Quite the deadly game until the big man's shoe hit a puddle. Jackson put all he had into the next thrust.

The man flailed backwards, landing with a whump on the wet cobbles.

"Watch out!" a dray driver hollered.

The horses bolted. The driver's big wagon lurched ahead. Jackson grabbed for the attacker's leg—too late.

With a sickening roll-thud, the front wheel caught the man's neck.

Behind Jackson, another scream rent the air. "Ye killed him!"

The woman was right. The man who'd assaulted him was dead. . . but who was he? And why was he after him in the first place? He frowned down at the body. He'd be getting no answers from this fellow.

Indeed. Some days a man was better off just hanging up his hat and calling it quits.

Kit peered over the salt barrel's rim, scanning the docks for a chipped-tooth boy with a smattering of freckles. Her bonnet wilted over her brow, dripping rain down her nose. Good. She welcomed the annoyance. Anything to keep her from thinking of Jackson Forge, the tyrant who'd professed love but didn't really mean it. And here she was again, caught in the same angry eddy she'd been swirling in since yesterday.

Ooh, that Jackson! Would that she'd never met the blue-eyed enchanter.

With no glimpse of Frankie, she eased back into the narrow space between the barrel and the boathouse overhang. The book she'd bought for Jackson cut into her thigh as she settled. The sooner she returned that thorn in the flesh, the better. Though maybe she'd keep it. A morbid reminder, of sorts, to never again fall for a man. Men were a pack of liars, or so she'd keep telling herself. Better to hold on to her fury than for one second give way to the deep hurt festering in her heart.

Bah! What was wrong with her? Such conflict dulled the senses and ruined concentration, a deadly combination on the Wapping riverfront.

A door slapped closed, pulling her from her jumbled thoughts. She crept up once again to peer past the barrel, and this time she spied young Frankie Jones striding hunch-shouldered away from old lady Crocker's shack.

Kit waited until he passed by, then strolled up behind him. "Cutting out early, are you?"

Frankie spun, eyes wide. "Miss Kit!" His brow scrunched. "What ye doin' here?"

"Your mam told me you were helping old lady Crocker till dark." She tossed an exaggerated look at the bleak afternoon sky. "Grey as it may be, there's plenty of daylight left."

"I am helping Mrs. Crocker. I mean. . ." Frankie jammed his hands into his pockets, his toe scuffing a piece of gravel back and forth. "I—I did help her. Aye, that's right."

Fiddlesticks! If the lad wasn't careful, he might sprain his tongue with such verbal gymnastics. Did he really think he'd convince her so easily?

He lifted his face with a confident twist of his mouth. "I finished helping her early today, that's what."

"Good. Your mam could use another pair of hands in the dining room. A few of the benches need shoring up. You know how to use a hammer. Come, I shall accompany you." She draped her arm across his shoulders and set off down the worn board walkway.

Frankie pulled away. "Can't now. I'll meet ye back at Blackfriars, Miss Kit."

He dashed ahead.

So did she, linking arms with him when she caught up. "Not to worry, my friend. I have all the time in the world. Where are we going?"

He wrenched his arm from hers. "No!"

She arched a stern brow at him. "You know what happens to those who cross me, do you not?"

He immediately shrank. "I mean, no need, Miss Kit. Wouldn't want to trouble ye, tha's all."

She hid a wicked smile. Intimidating a nine-year-old was truly vile, but it wasn't hard. "It is no trouble, my young friend. I have no pressing engagements."

Rain dripped off Frankie's nose. He scrubbed away the moisture, gazing at the muck of low tide instead of meeting her eyes, enticing her to follow his lead and try to decipher what he found so interesting. A diversion tactic, one she'd taught him herself. If she gave in to so much as a glance away from him, he'd bolt.

Once again she bit back a smile. "Come now, do you really think that little trick will work on me? Let us be off instead of standing here in this miserable rain."

"Kipes!" His freckles gathered into a storm across the bridge of his nose, so scrunched was his face. "Ye can't come with me, and tha's the truth o' it."

"Oh?" She folded her arms. "And why is that? I wonder."

He waited until a muscle-bound stevedore stalked past them, then stepped close, his words for her ears alone. "'Tain't safe, miss."

She laughed, surprised she even remembered how after all the angst this week had delivered. "I've seen more danger in one day than you have in your whole life, my boy."

Were it not for your rash behaviour, neither of our lives would ever be in danger to begin with.

The sting of Jackson's words pricked just as sharp and stringent as the moment they'd passed his lips yesterday. She scowled, stiff-arming the accusation, holding it at bay lest it continue needling over and over again.

"Please, Miss Kit. Ye must let me go. Ye taught me well." Frankie's big brown eyes pleaded up at her. "Trust me."

She choked. This man-child, who was up to no good, expected her to trust him? Hah! What a ludicrous jest.

Shoving her hand into her pocket, she pulled out the pewter thimblerig cups. "Tell me, young Frankie, how exactly am I to trust you when you have obviously gone behind your mother's back and continued bibbing about with your wayward friends? For shame. And after you promised to give your mother no more cause to worry."

"Those are mine!" He swiped for the cups.

She held them just out of reach. "Not anymore."

"Give 'em back!" He jumped, again and again, all in vain. Comical, were it not for the feeling in Kit's heart that this boy was pursuing illegal gambling.

When his defeat finally sank in, he thrust out his lower lip. "Gimme those cups, Miss Kit, or I'll not tell ye what I know."

"About what?"

He pressed his lips so tight, little puckers gathered at the seam.

Kit flicked her fingers in the air, feigning indifference. "Maybe I do not want to know."

"Ye did last week."

Drat. That could only mean one thing. . .the boy had scrounged up information on the scoundrel who'd crippled Jackson's brother, a trail that had been dead cold since the missed meeting at Scampson's. But did she really want to pursue James's attackers anymore? She sighed, not wanting to admit the answer—yet it surfaced anyway.

Just because she was done with Jackson didn't mean she ought to abandon the pursuit of justice. For James's sake and others like him. And it wouldn't hurt to prove to Jackson that she had gone to the warehouse for a good reason after all.

Even if what Frankie had to share was a small morsel of information, it was still something, which was more than she had now.

Reluctantly, she lowered her arm.

Frankie seized the cups with a grin. "That bird ye were s'posed to meet still wants to sing, long as yer offering the same reward. You want I should find out when and where?"

Hmm. Second chances didn't often come knocking at the same door. She'd be a fool not to open it. "Yes, but this time, please arrange for a place less likely to break my neck."

"Aye, Miss Kit. Will do. See ye back at Blackfriars, then." He tore down the slick boardwalk, feet now and then slipping sideways.

Kit took a step towards him, then hesitated. She could follow at a distance, find out where he was going and what sort of mischief he was about. Come to his rescue should he get tangled up in a life-threatening snarl. But he'd said the danger was for her, not for him. And he had asked her to trust him. . .just as she had asked Jackson to trust her?

She never should have given Frankie back those thimblerigs.

She never should have taught him the cunning guiles of a swindler.

Closing her eyes, she lifted her face and let the rain wash the wayward tears slipping from the corners of her eyes. Maybe there was a smidgen of truth to Jackson's words after all.

Maybe she was a bit rash sometimes.

Chapter Eighteen

In the space of two days, Jackson's arm quit bleeding every time he made a quick movement. The skin had knit together, scabbed over quite nicely actually, and was well on the way to healing. Too bad he couldn't say the same for his heart. But in just under two weeks, he'd leave that pain behind.

Ducking his head against a brisk October wind, Jackson strode along a row of immaculate white-brick town houses, each door fronted by Roman columns. While not as fashionable as Mayfair, Kensington held its own. Baggett had pinpointed the residence of the mysterious Efmann—Edward Francis Mann—to this neighbourhood. How the man could be connected to Isabella Dalton was anybody's guess, but that's what he aimed to find out. *If* the man was indeed Efmann. But Baggett had assured him the fellow was the only solid match to be made. Hopefully, his friend would have as much luck in tracking down the name of the umbrella attacker, though that might prove to be an impossible task. The villain hadn't had a snippet of identification on his body, and no missing men bearing the corpse's description had been reported.

Jackson scanned each house number he passed. Spying three-twelve, he jogged up the few stairs and rapped the knocker.

Moments later, a housekeeper with a lace kerchief perched atop her grey head answered the door. She was a timeless sort of servant, somewhere between fifty and seventy, one who gave the distinct impression she would face death with as much calm certainty as she did life.

"Good day, sir." She dipped her head in greeting, the kerchief not daring to slide so much as a squidge.

"Good day, madam." Jackson removed the hat from his head and held out his calling card. "I am here to see Mr. Mann."

The woman's sharp gaze skimmed the print. "I hate to disappoint you, Inspector, but I am afraid Mr. Mann is out of town. He will not return until Friday."

Botheration. That would set back his investigation. He replaced his hat with a curt nod. "Very well. I suppose I shall have to question him then. Please pass along my card when he returns."

"As you wish, Inspector."

She made to shut the door, but he wasn't quite ready to admit full defeat. He shot out his palm, stopping the wood from closing completely. "Pardon me, madam, but how long have you been in Mr. Mann's employ?"

Her brows pulled into a line of censure, yet her voice gave no hint of irritation. "I have served this household nigh on thirty years now, sir."

Aha! Perhaps the woman could prove to be a fount of intelligence. He donned his most enticing smile. "May I step in and ask you a few questions?"

"Me? Goodness." She clucked her tongue. "I am sure I would not know a thing about Mr. Mann's business."

"Do not be so quick to discredit yourself." He curved his lips into a smile with all the charm Kit had taught him to wield. "A housekeeper such as yourself is the true backbone of a home. I'd wager you know more than you think you do." He added a wink.

Amusement twinkled in the housekeeper's eyes as she squeaked a tiny giggle, quite the breach of protocol for an upper servant. At least his charm hadn't been too damaged by Kit's rejection.

"I suppose I have a few minutes to spare." The woman opened the door wide. "Follow me."

She led him through an expansive hall, a chatelaine of keys swinging gently back and forth at her waist with each step. "The downstairs is currently undergoing renovations, so the master has given me leave to receive guests here." She swept out her hand, and he entered a spacious sitting room done up in powder blue from carpet to curtains.

She indicated a settee of the same hue. "Please have a seat, Inspector."

He shook his head. "After you, Mrs. . . . ?"

"Margaret Grady." She settled on a wing chair and waited for him to sit before asking, "What is it you wish to know?"

Jackson pulled out a small notepad and pencil to jot down her name. "I am seeking information on a certain woman who may have been connected with Mr. Mann. Have you any knowledge of an Isabella Dalton?"

"Dalton. Dalton." She repeated the name as if speaking Kit's mother back into existence. "No, nothing comes to mind."

"This would have been twenty-four years ago. The spring of 1861, April, to be exact."

"Sixty-one? La!" Her hand fluttered to her bosom, then as if caught in the act of pilfering a sack of coins, she immediately folded her hands in her lap, once again the consummate housekeeper in charge. An interesting reaction.

"The date means something to you."

"Not me so much as the family. The missus. . ." Memories ran like ripples across her face. "Well, suffice it to say that was a sorry time around here."

Jackson edged forward on the sofa cushion. "How so?"

"It all started with the master's fall from grace and—" Eyes wide, she shot to her feet. "I won't be a moment, Inspector."

She swirled out the door, skirts swishing, keys jing-jangling. Evidently, he'd hit some sort of nerve.

He rose and strolled the perimeter of the room. One could tell a lot about a man by the trinkets in his house. An ornate wood and brass humidor sat on a small table in the corner. Jackson lifted the lid and sniffed the tangy aroma of hand-cut tobacco. Windsor cigars, if he didn't miss his mark. Mr. Mann had expensive taste. Another glass-topped cart held an array of crystal decanters. No cheap gin here, but a collection of rich amber scotches. Fine drink and fine smokes? Had he a penchant for fine women as well?

Several gilt-framed portraits lined the mantel, some artistic renderings, others actual photographic images. Jackson studied one after the other. He'd been correct. The same stunner of a woman graced each one.

"I see you've found the mistress, God rest her."

Jackson turned at Mrs. Grady's voice. "Mrs. Mann is deceased?"

"Yes. God rest them both, I should say."

"Mr. Mann has had two wives?"

"Yes, but"—she waved a book—"you were asking about Isabella Dalton. My memory may not be so good, but my accounting is impeccable. Come see, Inspector."

Before he followed the woman, he wrote down the tidbit of information that Mr. Mann had been married twice.

Mrs. Grady strolled over to the sofa table and opened her book, her finger skimming down a page. "There."

Jackson studied the neat handwriting.

April 25. Isabella Dalton hired as scullery maid.

Strange. Hadn't Graybone said Miss Dalton came from a family of means? A woman like that would not willingly take on such a backbreaking duty. "Miss Dalton served here?"

"She was supposed to."

"What do you mean?"

"Normally, I wouldn't remember such trivialities as the details of a scullery maid, but this one…" With a sigh, Mrs. Grady closed the book and held it like a shield over her chest. "I hired the girl to help with an important dinner. She was a sickly little thing, pale as a half moon, and her reference was from a house I'd never heard of, but I was desperate. Mr. Mann made it very clear the dinner included some powerful men who could make or break him. We were sorely understaffed, and he was of a sharp temper, which was to be fully understood, considering."

Jackson cocked his head. "Considering what?"

"Oh. . .no matter." Mrs. Grady clutched the book tight enough to flatten her bosom. "It does not signify. You were asking of Miss Dalton. Cook trained the woman, but everything she touched went awry. She brought the wrong cut of meat from the butcher's. Burnt the pudding. Soured the milk when she spilled vinegar into the vat. But worst of all, she disappeared the afternoon of the big event. She went to the baker for Cook's special order and never returned. Ruined the whole dinner, she did."

It was no wonder she'd not come back, not after all those mishaps. But could a spoiled meal be a cause for murder? "Excuse me, Mrs. Grady, but how does that relate to Mr. Mann's 'fall from grace,' as you put it?"

She lowered her book, her brow sinking as well. "The investors he wished to impress that evening were not pleased, so they withdrew all financial backing from the master's enterprises."

"A meal gone wrong is hardly grounds for such vindictiveness."

The housekeeper shrugged. "I suppose it could have been more than the dismal food on the table, but that is what Mr. Mann laid the blame to. He remained in a foul disposition for weeks and. . .well, there were family matters going on at the time."

"What sort of matters?" He studied her face carefully. The contraction of a neck muscle, the pursing of the lips, any little movement might add meaning to her words.

"Personal matters, Inspector." She whirled the moment she answered, hiding her face as she stalked to the door. "And now, I really must be getting back to work. I shall see you out."

Once again, another nerve, and both tying back to whatever happened twenty-four years ago, something he suspected went well beyond Kit's mother. But what?

He followed Mrs. Grady then paused on the stoop before she shut the door. "One last question, Mrs. Grady. You mentioned Miss Dalton was sickly at the time. Was she, by any chance, with child?"

Her nostrils flared. From the delicate question or something else?

"I may have been in need of help at the time, Inspector, but not that desperate."

"I meant no offense." He tipped his hat. "Thank you, Mrs. Grady."

"Good day, Inspector."

He trotted down the stairs then gave the town house a last glance, from shiny brass house numbers to the clay-shingled roof without a divot or chip. It was a fine home. Well maintained. Smacking of wealth, which begged the question. . .

If Mr. Mann lost so much money all those years ago, how did he still manage to live in this part of town?

Usually, Borough Market put a spring in Kit's step. The bustle of shoppers never failed to invigorate, lending the place an electric feel. And if that weren't reason enough to be glad one was alive, the tantalizing aromas of roasted meats and sugared dough balls and the sharp tang of pickles in great glass jars made a person thankful for a mouth to taste and belly to fill. But not today. Kit scowled as she anchored herself against a pillar, keeping her distance from the flurry. Even London's simple pleasures had lost their appeal.

And all because of a blue-eyed law man who'd carved out her heart and trampled it under his feet.

"You be Turner?"

She turned at the sound of a scratchy voice. Either the fellow in front of her had yelled an excessive amount in his two decades—for he could hardly be much older—or he'd been born with the froggy tone. A scar rippled the left side of his mouth, giving him a perpetual leer. He had a cagey air about him, his gaze darting everywhere and nowhere all at once, and he leaned into the balls of his feet, ready to tear off in a blink. He had to be a streeter. But just to be sure, Kit whipped out her knife and held it blade down between them.

He matched her move, his crusty knuckles pressed against hers.

She raised a brow. "On three?"

He gave a sharp nod.

"One," she began. "Two—"

He sprang into action, as did she—with the first real grin of the day. He *was* a streeter, for no self-respecting gutter runner would have waited until the finish of the count. Even so, she easily pinned the fellow against the stone wall with a sharp edge to his neck. Point made, she pulled back.

Admiration flashed in his dark eyes as he tucked away his knife. "Yer better 'n what Frankie said."

Pleasure flushed her cheeks. At least this young man appreciated her skill with a blade instead of coddling her as if she were some precious porcelain teacup. She sheathed her knife. "You'd have found that out had you shown up at our previous meeting."

His lips twitched. "Couldn't be helped. Got waylaid."

She studied him, deciding by the hump on his nose, which had been freshly broken, that he spoke truth. "Your name?"

"Tazz."

She tried hard not to wince when he spoke. His rough voice was like nails on slate, grating strongly despite the background noise of hawkers and shoppers. "All right then, Tazz, what do you have for me?"

"Let's start with what you have for me."

She pulled out a small coin purse and handed it over. "Half now. The rest after I hear what you have to say."

He fingered through the sovereigns then met her gaze, a steely set to his jaw. "I could just as easily leave with this, you know."

"And I could just as easily bury my blade in your back."

He grinned then, the puckered side of his mouth not quite matching the other side. "You got a man?"

"Do you think I need one?"

His gaze dropped to her bodice as he tucked away the cloth pouch. "You might think otherwise after a tumble with me."

She sighed, tired of defending her virtue at every turn. "To business, please. Frankie said you know what happened on Skullcap Lane thirteen years ago. Or you know of someone who does. Tell me all and I'll give you the rest of the coin."

Tazz ran his tongue over his teeth a few times before answering. "I were working third wheel to a pair o' devils. They fed me and kept me in rags, so least I din't starve. I weren't naught but six at the time. That whole wing o' Whitechapel were Gwince and Skarm's playground, and I did their bidding."

"Mmm." She nodded. That would explain the wildness engrained in the young man. "So, this Gwince and Skarm liked to play rough, and while they did the deed, you kept lookout for trouble, eh?"

"That's the size o' it." Once again Tazz sucked on his teeth. Perhaps a bit of gristle or bone was stuck. Or maybe the aromas of the marketplace were getting to him. "Gwince were a jollocks of a man, Skarm the real brains. Both were mafficking ruffians, if ye know what I mean."

Kit inhaled sharply. She knew the type. Predatory beasts who collared little boys and forced them into slavery. Men who owned all the morals of a jackal, just waiting to sink their teeth into the next vulnerable lad who crossed their path. . .a lad such as James Forge. Devils, indeed. "Do you remember a time, Tazz, when those masters of yours mig-mauled a youngish lad, 'round thirteen or fourteen years old? Toward dusk. Had another boy with him. Two greenies ripe for the plucking."

Tazz shook his head, his raggedy hair scraping his collar. "Too many to remember."

"This one wouldn't have walked away. Not dead, mind, but thrashed enough that he'd never be the same."

"Mebbe. . .lemme think." Tazz scratched the scruff on his chin, gaze drifting to the semi-roof of the market. "Could be the one what put up a fight, I suppose. They did a regular boot jabbin' to the head on him. Blood were everywhere. If that fellow lived, he likely has a scar right about here." He swept his index finger from brow to chin, slashing across the right eye, exactly the same shape as the disfigurement on James's face.

Anger licked like fire through her bones, and it took several deep breaths before she could speak. "Where can I find these men now?"

Tazz's sharp shoulders lifted. "Pit o' hell, leastwise for Skarm. Drank away his bloody innards, he did."

"And Gwince?"

"Lost track o' him when he went black. His brother would know, though, for he were the one who finally snagged him and sent him away."

Interesting. Gwince's brother must be an equal force to be reckoned with. Kit nibbled her lower lip, trying hard to recall anyone who might fit that description, someone who could cow a brigand but that'd been well before her rise to power in Blackfriars.

She stepped aside, allowing the passage of a woman loaded down with packages, then once again faced Tazz. "This brother, is he still here in the city?"

"Aye. Phineas Gwince runs some gentleman's club, last I heard."

This just kept getting more curious. Gwince's brother was an upstanding citizen? "Where does he live?"

"Dunno." Tazz ran a dirty sleeve across his nose. "He don't surface much, and when he does, he keeps to the shadows. But one thing I do know is he ne'er misses a club meeting. It's a. . .special club. Real exclusive, like."

Well, that could be a problem. "What is the name of this club?"

Tazz's head swiveled, his gaze scanning left and right, then he whispered, "Tenebrous, but ye din't hear it from me."

Kit scrunched her nose, both from his rank breath and the name of the club. She'd heard of Whites, Boodles, the Carlton and Brookes, but not Tenebrous. Oh well. Maybe that would make it easier to get into.

She retrieved the other pouch of money. "Thank you, Tazz. You have been more than generous with your information."

"I could be generous with a lot more, if ye like." Again the lustful gleam in his eyes.

"Go home, Tazz. I am not the woman for you."

She shoved her way into the fray of the market, saddened by the truth in her own words. She wasn't the woman for anyone, not anymore.

Chapter Nineteen

Grit in his eyes and cotton in his mouth, Jackson dragged his empty shell into the station. One of these nights he'd sleep. He'd have to. His body couldn't take much more of this. But every time he closed his eyes, all he could see was a loose-haired wildcat in a brown skirt. Gads! He had been right all along.

Kit would be the death of him.

Keeping to the far wall, he evaded eye contact while avoiding the stairway leading up to the chief's office. Come Monday morning, he'd have to inform his superior of his intention to leave the force. But not today. He'd need all his wits about him for that little tête-à-tête.

"Oy, Forge!" The clerk at the front counter waved him over.

So much for beelining it to the sergeant's office unaccosted. "Yes, Smitty?"

"From Baggett." He shoved a folded slip of paper across the scarred countertop.

"Thank you." Jackson scooped it up then continued down the corridor, opening the note as he went.

Still at it.

Frowning, Jackson shoved the paper into his pocket. Though no more attempts on his life had occurred in the past three days, neither had Baggett been able to discover the blackguard at the root of it all. Dash it. Perhaps if he created a timeline of when the attacks had begun, the location of each, the frequency and such, he might have a better idea of who wished him dead.

But for now, he rapped his knuckles against Sergeant Graybone's closed door and waited for a corresponding "Enter." Once inside, he pulled off his hat while purposely taking the chair farthest from the door. Kit always sat in the other, with a proud toss of her head and a bounce to her toes as she settled onto the leather seat.

"You look like a dog's dinner," Graybone rumbled. "Haven't slept in days, have you?"

Oh, no. He'd not dive down that rabbit hole with the man who would've been his father-in-law. "My sleeping habits have no bearing on the investigation of Miss Dalton. Now, shall we compare notes, or would you also like to question my dental hygiene practices?"

A merlot-coloured flush ran up the sergeant's neck, stark against the deep blue collar of his uniform. "I've thrashed men for lesser cheek than that."

Jackson scraped his nails along his scalp. The sergeant was right. He ought to receive a whack with a truncheon for such insolence. Dropping his hand, he dipped his head as well. "I beg your pardon, sir."

Graybone grunted. "What did you discover at the Mann residence yesterday?"

"That he is absent until Friday. I queried the housekeeper, though. She provided written records of hiring Isabella Dalton on April twenty-fifth as a scullery maid."

"Scullery!" Graybone slammed his meaty fist against the desk, rattling the inkwell. For a few moments, his nostrils flared large above his bushy moustache. "I never should have left her, but there's naught to be done for it now."

Pain ran husky in the man's tone. After two decades, he still grieved the loss of his love. Jackson fisted his hands, fighting off the thought that twenty years from now, his own heart might very well still bleed for Kit.

"Anything else?"

Jackson jerked his attention back to Graybone. "Yes, Mann's housekeeper also said Miss Dalton was not with child when she hired her, but she did look sickly. I imagine that would've been shortly after Kit's birth. She went missing on the twenty-seventh, never returned from an errand."

"The date of her abduction, no doubt."

"Could be. And this may or may not be related, but the house-keeper also mentioned there was some sort of turmoil going on in the home at the time, something having to do with Mr. Mann's finances."

"Hmph." Graybone grunted. "And his wife."

Jackson tipped his head. "How so?"

"The whalebone busk you found was sold to a Mrs. Henrietta Mann."

"An interesting twist." Jackson tapped his finger atop his hat. "But why would Miss Dalton have had it? Was it given to her, a castoff from the mistress, perhaps? It seems an odd thing to steal."

Graybone slapped his palms against the table, half-rising from his chair, a volcano about to blow. "Bella would never—*ever*—take that which didn't belong to her. I will not sit here and listen to such slander."

Jackson shot up his palm, warding the man off. "No disrespect intended, Sergeant. Just trying to piece together what happened. You have had longer to dwell on the situation. How do you account for Mrs. Mann's busk?"

Graybone sank back into his seat. "I don't. Unless for some unknown reason Mrs. Mann accompanied Bella on her errand and they were both taken."

"Yet there was only one body in that hole, and the housekeeper said nothing about a missing Mrs. Mann."

"That's troubling." The sergeant rubbed the back of his neck several times before continuing. "Also troubling is the coroner's report from that year, or lack thereof, I should say. The whole box of records suffered water damage in a flood. The box was salvaged, but the contents are completely unreadable. As such, I have no idea why the body dragged from the Thames that Bella's father acknowledged as hers could have been found twenty-four years later at an old riverside warehouse."

Indeed. "So, we've got Miss Dalton's locket, Mrs. Mann's busk, and one body. Oh, and a small scrap of faded red fabric from the rat's nest." He blew out a long breath. "Guess I'll be visiting Mr. Mann when he returns. And though it's a grisly request, I shall need you to re-examine that corpse more closely, see if there's any other positive identification besides the locket."

Graybone scowled. "Not a task I relish."

"Nor will this be...I think you should tell Kit. It will go harder on her if she gets wind of this from anyone other than you."

The sergeant shook his head. "Other than the locket, we have no definitive proof. I will not subject her to a broil of unnecessary emotion, not yet."

Good point. Jamming on his hat, Jackson stood. "As you wish. And with that, I think we are finished for now. Good day, Sergeant."

"Hold up there, Forge."

"Is there something I missed, sir?"

"Yes." Graybone drummed his fingers atop the desk, each tap overly loud in the small office. "It's been five days and you've yet to make things right with my daughter."

Jackson flattened his lips to keep from gaping. The man seriously expected him to make things right? He was the one who'd been jilted! "Sometimes there is just no righting a wrong, sir."

"Good thing God doesn't hold that view." Graybone speared him with a sharp look.

Jackson parried with a piercing gaze of his own. "I am not God."

"No, you are not. But that doesn't excuse you from offering an olive branch."

He ground his teeth. It was Kit who should be seeking peace with him. She was the one who'd labeled him inept. Who'd blatantly said he was not the man for her. The sergeant was wrong. It wasn't the injured who'd sent an olive branch in the beak of a dove, but the one who'd destroyed the whole blasted earth with a flood. Kit was the one who'd destroyed his heart. Let her make the first move. "I cannot have a relationship with a woman who does not respect me."

"Don't be daft. Kit holds you in the highest regard."

"I have it from her own mouth I am not the man for her. That doesn't sound like respect to me."

Graybone flicked his podgy fingers. "Angry words from a hot-headed young woman, nothing more. Go after her, Forge. Love is always worth fighting for."

"A noble platitude, one I might consider if Kit actually loved me."

"But do you love her?"

Thunderation! This—*this!*—was exactly what kept him flipping like a beached mackerel half the night. Deep down, in a crevice he'd rather not crawl into, he knew there was a part of him that would always love the woman, blindly, madly. Eternally. Which was probably why he'd not returned the ring yet. Oh, he'd told himself he'd been too busy, but perhaps that wasn't the real reason.

He headed for the door. "It does not matter. I set sail in a week and a half."

"Coward."

The accusation hit right between the shoulder blades. Jackson gripped the knob so hard, the veins on his hand popped two sizes larger.

The sergeant didn't have the slightest clue of how wrong he was. There was nothing faint-hearted about traveling halfway across the world, nothing gutless about putting one's life on the line to protect a man for an entire year. He yanked open the door and stalked out without a word. There was nothing cowardly in the least about such an endeavor.

But Jackson suspected he would be trying to prove the sergeant wrong for the rest of his life.

It took bravado to smile when what you really wanted to do was pin someone's hand to the tabletop with your knife. And yet Kit kept her grin firmly in place as she removed the old lecher's fingers from her knee. Stars and glory! Who'd have thought that sharing a cup of Earl Grey at a teahouse with an upstanding gentleman—or so she'd been told—might threaten her virtue?

"Now, now, Mr. Nettles." She forced a coy laugh. "We cannot provide Mrs. Nettles cause for becoming jealous, can we?"

"Pish-posh! The old cow doesn't know a thing about my dalliances. Too busy with her infernal feline menagerie at home." He plucked a particularly large cat hair from his sleeve and flicked the offense to the floor.

Glancing at the ornate case clock near the window, Kit stifled a sigh. Nearly half an hour had gone by since she'd arrived, and all she had to show for her efforts was a half-drunk cup of cold tea and the beginnings of a magnificent headache. Enough with the small talk.

"So, Mr. Nettles, to business, shall we?"

"By all means, my dear." He ran his tongue over lips as thin and purple as two angleworms. Perhaps the gesture had been flirtatious fifty years ago when the old fellow had been in the throes of youth. Now it was anything but enticing, not from a malmsey-nosed sexagenarian wearing a horsehair wig that'd gone out of style when the prince regent had still been alive.

Kit took a sip of her cold tea, wishing for the hundredth time they'd been seated at a table near the front window instead of in the back corner of the shop. "I have it on good authority, sir, that you are a member of a particular gentlemen's club, one which my younger brother dearly wishes to join."

"Your brother, you say?" He scratched behind his ear, knocking the ridiculous wig askew. "So why am I not having a conversation with him? Not that I frown upon taking tea with such a delicious pastry as yourself, mind."

It took every bit of self-control Kit owned not to roll her eyes. "Yes, well, you must understand that my brother has been abroad these past few years. He is only now on his way home to London, arriving the day after tomorrow. His most recent correspondence urged me to, oh, what did he say?" She tapped her chin for the right effect, as if she were remembering a letter. Guilt nipped as she did so, but this fabrication was ultimately for justice, which made it a worthy pursuit.

Did it not?

Strangling the scream of her conscience, she snapped her fingers. "Aha! I remember. My brother said I should inquire for him to schedule an initiatory visit as soon as possible after he arrives. You know, to get the wheels in motion, so to speak, save him lead time in application and the like. Some clubs have such ridiculously long waiting lists. I do hope yours is not one of *those*." She drawled the word as if it were a rag dragged through the dirt, adding just the right amount of nasal intonation to her voice without overdoing it.

Mr. Nettles chuckled. "I should say not." Beckoning her close with a crook of his finger, he whispered, "Tenebrous is unlike any other."

A shiver spidered across her shoulders, and not just from the rank whiff of cats on his clothing. Tazz had whispered the club's name as well, as if speaking it aloud might swing open the door to a cage of demons.

Fidgeting with a loose lock of hair to shake the uneasy feeling, she sank back in her seat. "I am happy to hear your club is so unique. Makes it all the more exclusive. I wonder, sir, if there is any way I might beseech you for a nomination of my dear brother. He would be most appreciative for your sponsorship, willing to make room in his busy schedule at your earliest convenience for an initial visit. And a more qualified candidate you will not find. Here are his credentials." She offered a few sheets of paper from a leather portfolio.

As the old fellow scanned the information, another pang of conscience pricked her heart. Jackson would never have approved such means to an end. . .and she had a dark suspicion neither did God.

"Yes, yes. Very good, very good," the old fellow mumbled as he read. "Don't say?" A surprise snort of air rushed out his nose.

Kit bit her lip. Had she embellished a tad too much, perhaps?

At length, the old fellow set the papers on the tea table and folded his hands over his belly. "Your brother appears to be quite the illustrious fellow. I should have no qualms whatsoever in sponsoring him, but I must ask. . .are you certain this is the club for him? Did you read the name correctly, my dear?"

Rather had she *heard* the name correctly. Either way, it was an odd question, but in all due diligence, she mentally revisited the meeting with Tazz, then immediately nodded her head. "Without a doubt, sir. My brother said this would be—and I quote—'a gilded ticket into the society with which I not only desire to rub shoulders, but a fellowship I feel fate has directed me towards.' "

Mr. Nettles's bristly eyebrows shot clear up to his scruffy wig.

She pressed her lips tight. Had she overdone it?

"Well, well." He plucked one more cat hair from his sleeve. "Far be it from me to tempt Lady Fate."

"So, you shall nominate him, then?"

"Better than that, my dear. With this profile"—he tapped the papers—"and such inherent enthusiasm on your brother's part, there is no need to waste time on trivialities." Though there was still plenty of tea in the pot, he waved down a server. "A pen, if you please."

The white-aproned woman looked as confused as Kit felt, nevertheless she bobbed her head. "Right away, sir."

"Do you mind?" He pointed at the faux summary on the table.

"Not at all." Naturally, he'd take the bait back to the other members, a nominating committee perhaps.

But Mr. Nettles ripped the top page into quarters.

Kit grabbed her cup simply to give her hands something to do other than startle from the odd action.

The server returned posthaste with a silver tray bearing an ink bottle and feather pen. "Here you are, sir."

"Thank you." He licked the nib, his tongue darting out again and again while he batted his eyelids at Kit.

Really. This was getting to be a bit much. She looked away.

After a few scribbles and much folding and creasing, then some more folding, he reached for her hand and wrapped her fingers around the small square of paper. His touch was not only cold as a river mist, it was just as pervasive, encompassing her entire fist.

"This is very important, my dear." He gave a little squeeze. "You must see that your brother—your brother alone—digests this information for the time and place of the next meeting. We cannot have the men in blue wise to our whereabouts."

An exceedingly strange request, but a victory nonetheless. She tucked the tiny missive into her reticule. "My brother shall be most appreciative, sir. I thank you."

Mr. Nettles nodded, his wig falling forward on his brow. "Remind him to dress appropriately."

Mercy, there was a dress code? She hadn't thought to ask. Did most clubs have uniforms? She hadn't expected men would care a fig for such trifles.

"Forgive me, Mr. Nettles, being I'm a woman and all, I am curious if there is anything in particular—a colour or pattern, say—that an initiate should wear? Granted, I am certain my brother already knows of your standards and such." She fluttered her fingers to her chest. "I merely ask out of my own interest."

His gaze roved from her bodice to her face, an odd glint in his eyes.

"Your brother should wear something that can be easily removed."

She tipped her chin. "Removed?"

"Ho ho!" He slapped his knee, bumping the table in the process and rattling their teacups—which swiveled the heads of several ladies nearby.

Mr. Nettles gave them a little wave before once again tilting closer to Kit. Too close.

"You see, my dear, the fellows are always eager for an old-fashioned paddling. It will be all the worse for your brother's backside if he keeps them waiting any lengthy period, hence the need for loose-fitting garments that don't require a lot of fuss."

She blinked. She'd heard a lot of quirky talk in her day, coded words and veiled innuendo, but this? He couldn't have meant what she thought. "Pardon?"

The old fellow guffawed. "Oh, the look on your face is quite priceless, Miss Turner. I realize this subject is rather coarse for one as delicate as yourself. But then"—he ran his finger along her sleeve—"one cannot speak of a hellfire club without a bit of indecency, can one?"

She yanked her arm from his touch. By all that was right and good! What had she gotten herself into this time? She'd heard rumours of such secret brotherhoods, but the stories were too fantastic to believe. Rituals bordering on the occult. Indulgences that would make a doxie's cheeks redden. If such hearsay was true, no wonder Mr. Nettles didn't want the police tipped off to their whereabouts.

Then again, it was also said such secret societies had died out in the last century. Surely this was something else. She shot to her feet, snatching up her portfolio as she went. "Thank you, Mr. Nettles. I shall see that my brother is informed. Good day."

The old fellow stood as well. Reaching for her hand, he planted his cold lips on her skin. "It has been entirely my pleasure."

She clenched her fingers lest she whip out her boot blade. Was every man in the city nothing but a debaucher? With a tight smile, she fled to the street. She didn't stop until she reached a quiet corner near a soap seller's window.

What was she to do? Her plan of going incognito as her own brother would not work, not if she had to shed her clothes for some perverse initiation rite. Quickly, she rifled through the names of her former crew members, but what a farce that would be. Not one of those men would be able to converse without slinging some street slang. That would be a tip-off. Nor could she ask her father. Even with a liberal amount of bootblack, he was much too silver threaded in the hair and beard to pose as her younger sibling. Not to mention the tongue-thrashing she'd receive for coming up with such a slip-brained plan in the first place. No, the only one she could ask who stood a chance of pulling this off was. . .

She deflated against the shop. Jackson truly was the only viable candidate, yet there was no way on this side of the Thames or the other that he would agree to do it for her. But would he agree to do it for his brother?

Chapter Twenty

Finally, Jackson slept. Passed out, more like it. The moment he'd stumbled home last night, he'd collapsed like an uneven pile of stones, half-on and half-off the bed. But it hadn't helped his fatigue. Not a whit. When he'd arrived at the Mann home this morning, he barely kept from yawning in Mrs. Grady's face. And now, the instant the housekeeper exited the sitting room to retrieve Mr. Mann, he gave into that yawn, a real jaw popper, which annoyed him. Deuced inconvenient time not to be at his sharpest.

Shaking off the mental fog—but would he truly ever?—he strolled the length of the mantel, studying each picture. In one, Mrs. Mann brandished a parasol over her shoulder. In another, she perched on a velvet cushion with a sour-faced pug on her lap. The next showed her kneeling next to a. . .no, it couldn't be. Was that a peacock?

He reached for the silver frame, but in doing so, he knocked the neighbouring photo to the marble tile in front of the hearth. Dash and rot! It couldn't have landed on the nearby Turkish rug? By some great miracle, the glass didn't break, but a big dent marred one corner, the backing fell off, and the photograph slipped sideways out of its place.

He flipped over the image only to discover there wasn't one picture but two—and the other wasn't the same woman nor a photograph. A watercoloured beauty stared languidly from beneath a large red hat in a matching red gown. The first Mrs. Mann, perhaps?

Footsteps clipped out in the corridor. Mr. Mann would stride in here before those images could be reseated and the frame replaced. What to do?

Gaze darting wild, Jackson narrowed in on an overly large potted fern to the side of the hearth. He shoved the picture frame mess behind the big planter and rose, just as an imposing man of magnificent height entered the room.

"Inspector." Mr. Mann dipped his head, the gesture lending him a more manageable stature until he straightened. "My housekeeper says you wish to speak with me?"

"I do, sir. Just a few questions. Shouldn't take long."

"Very well. Shall we?" He swept one long arm towards the sofa and chair collection. Jackson swallowed hard. If the fellow took the high-back on the right, he'd see the broken frame.

"By all means." Jackson scooted to the chair and sank into it before Mr. Mann could commandeer the spot.

The fellow sniffed at Jackson's manners as he sat on the edge of the sofa. "What is this about? Am I in some sort of legal danger?"

"I should think not. Currently, I am working on a murder case that is somehow tied to your former wife."

As the words sank in, a faint ripple of confusion worked its way across Mr. Mann's brow. As soon as he noticed Jackson watching him, he instantly schooled his face into a placid mask with a hint of a smile. "I regret to inform you that you must have received some false information. I fail to see how Alexandra could have had anything to do with a crime."

"I was speaking of Henrietta."

The man's left eye twitched. Not much, but enough to give away the fact he'd been surprised, and judging by the downturn of his mouth, Jackson got the distinct impression he abhorred surprises.

"I see," Mr. Mann drawled, the tone indicating he neither saw nor truly wished to see whatever crawled beneath the rock Jackson had lifted.

Intriguing. Jackson jotted it down on his notepad, along with the name of the second Mrs. Mann, before looking up. "Can you tell me a bit about your first wife, sir?"

An iceberg couldn't have looked any colder or harder than the lines on Mr. Mann's face. "There is not much to say except Henrietta was a quiet soul who has been gone these past twenty-four years." He stood. "Now if you will excuse me, I have business to attend."

Jackson rose, lobbing a last question before the man could escape out the door. "Can you tell me why I found Henrietta's whalebone busk next to a skeleton in a warehouse down by the south bank?"

The fabric across Mr. Mann's shoulders pulled tight as a sail in a squall. "As I said, Inspector, I have business."

"And I have a murder case to solve. Either I question you here in the sanctity of your own home or I escort you to the station."

The tension in the room increased tenfold, as if all the air had been sucked out. If Mr. Mann's shoulders strained any more, the seams of his fine suit would rip wide open.

Without warning, he deflated. "Follow me."

He strode off, not waiting for a response. Jackson didn't hesitate to follow. The second they entered a walnut-paneled study, Mr. Mann sailed straight to the drink table and held up a decanter as an offering.

Jackson shook his head. "Thank you, but I am on the clock."

With a shrug, Mr. Mann poured a stout glass of amber liquid before he indicated they should sit. This time Jackson allowed the man to choose his own seat first, a posh leather armchair next to a small table with an ashtray that smelled of raw cut tobacco.

Mr. Mann took a swallow of his drink then pursed his lips. "You must understand I am a very private man, Inspector. I should not like my personal matters aired on the street."

"I assure you, sir, any information you provide shall remain confidential, unless what you share is a direct offense to the Crown."

"I am the one who suffered offense, Mr. Forge." There was a sudden edge to his voice, a sharpened dagger ready to strike.

An interesting response. "What happened in April of 1861?"

"Right for the jugular, eh?" The man swigged down the remainder of his drink in one great gulp. He returned to the decanter, speaking while his back was turned. "Sixty-one was a dark period in my life. One I would rather forget. But the past is not so easily left in the past, is it?" A huge sigh whooshed out of him, his shoulders sagging as he returned to his seat. "My first wife, Henrietta, was kidnapped that spring."

Jackson scribbled down the information, speaking in time with the scratch of his pencil. "I am sorry to hear it, sir."

"As I said, it was a dark time."

"How and when did she go missing?"

He swirled the liquid, gaze fixed on the golden tornado. "On a Thursday, I believe. Yes, that's it, because I'd returned home from a board meeting, which convenes only on the third Thursday of the month. Instead of being greeted by my wife, as was her wont, a smudge-faced street boy dropped off a note, informing me of her abduction."

Jackson diligently wrote down each crumb of information. "And how did the authorities handle the case?"

"There were no authorities." Mr. Mann's gaze shot to his, a flinty gleam in his eyes. "I never informed the police. The note was quite clear that any involvement of law enforcement would mean Henrietta's swift demise. I may have had my differences with the woman, but never once did I wish her dead."

"So, you paid the ransom."

"I did." He slugged back the drink and set it on the table with a bang. "Not that it did any good."

Aha. After noting the payment, Jackson edged forward on the cushion. "What happened, Mr. Mann?"

"I sent the money along with my valet to the stated drop-off point at the specified time. Once the money was transferred, the brigands not only killed my faithful servant but my wife as well."

Jackson's gut twisted. Vile men. It was foul crimes such as this that'd compelled him to take on a badge. "My sincere condolences, sir. Were the villains apprehended?"

"As I said, Inspector, the authorities were never involved."

"But after you discovered the bodies. . .there were two murders for which to account!"

"I had the matter taken care of quietly." He rubbed his hand along the leather arm of the chair, and only then did Jackson notice the darkened stain where he'd made habit of just such an action. "My wife and valet were properly buried, I assure you. To this day I see that Henrietta's grave is maintained at Kensal Green."

That didn't make sense. He scratched down the name of the grave-yard, trying to understand why the man hadn't gone to the authorities after the deed had been done. There was nothing to lose at that point.

Something didn't add up. He rolled the pencil between finger and thumb, thinking aloud. "The money was never recovered?"

"No, and it was a tidy sum indeed."

So, not only had Mr. Mann been out the ransom money, but Mrs. Grady had said he'd lost his investor funding as well. Were those two events somehow related? "What date did your wife go missing?"

"April twenty-third."

Jackson flipped back a few pages, where he'd written down Mrs. Grady's information. That would've been four days before the dinner. He lifted his gaze to Mr. Mann. "Did your wife's absence, perhaps, influence the investors you'd hoped would fund your business?"

A tempest couldn't have looked blacker. "What would you know about that?"

"I am an inspector, sir. It is my job to know."

"And it is my job to—" He pressed his lips into a thin line, trapping whatever retort had tried to escape. "No, Mr. Forge. My business associates knew nothing of my wife's disappearance. At the time, no one did, save for my valet and me."

Jackson jotted that down. "And yet you financially recovered from the blow."

"Thanks to an insurance policy on my wife, yes, I did." Mr. Mann's dark eyes narrowed. "Though I suppose you already know that as well. Records of such payouts would have to be released to the Yard, I assume."

And there he had it. Maybe. Jackson tapped his pencil on the paper, debating the best way to snare the man before landing on the most direct approach. "What is to keep me from thinking you simply had your wife killed for that payment?"

"Because I have proof." Mr. Mann circled his desk. After unlocking a bottom drawer and retrieving two small papers, he returned to Jackson. "I saved these for just such a moment."

Jackson glanced at the first, a handwritten withdrawal slip from the Bank of England. The other paper was torn on one end, grease smeared, and with some words crossed off and rewritten. The best he could make of the scrawl was

1000 kwid to Crawley Allee
Dark o nite on the 27th
No bobbeez

So, the date Isabella Dalton went missing was the same as not only the ruined dinner but the money exchange and the murders. They *had* to be related. . .but how?

Jackson tapped the ransom note. "Do you mind if I keep this for further study, Mr. Mann?"

"I suppose it has served its purpose." He slanted back against his desk and folded his arms. "Have you any further questions, Inspector? I really do need to attend some business."

"A few. What exactly is your business, sir?"

"Not that it signifies, but I am an accountant of sorts."

"What sort?"

"The kind that deals with the investments of powerful men—*very* powerful. Tut-tut, Inspector." He wagged a finger. "Do not think to question me any further on the topic. My clients' anonymity is of the utmost importance. They keep a low profile and expect the same of me. Hence my need for personal privacy."

Jackson tucked away the ransom note along with his notepad. Better to allow the man to think he was nearly finished while casting a sharpened hook. "Does the name Isabella Dalton mean anything to you?"

"No. Should it?" His lips didn't pinch. His gaze held steady. There was no nervous scratch behind the ear or a shifting of weight. Mr. Mann spoke the truth.

But that didn't mean he didn't know her.

"Miss Dalton served a short while as your scullery maid, namely the day before and morning of your investment dinner."

Ever so slightly, the man's nostrils flared. He stalked to the big seat behind his desk, putting the large piece of mahogany between them. "You would have to take that up with Mrs. Grady. I keep my distance from the lower staff. Now if you will excuse me, Mr. Forge." He gave a curt nod towards the door.

Well, if that whole maneuver didn't scream the man knew her, Jackson would be hog-tied to know what did. Making a mental note of it, he strode to the door and paused on the threshold. "One last thing, sir. On the day Mrs. Mann went missing, do you recall what she was wearing?"

The man's jaw hardened. "I shall never forget it. Her red gown, one that drew attention. One I never should have allowed her to purchase. Good day, Inspector." He dropped to his chair and picked up a newspaper, stretching it open as a shield between them.

"Thank you, Mr. Mann." Jackson smiled. "You have been most helpful."

More than the man could possibly know, actually. Jackson mulled over the information as he padded his way back to the sitting room. Mr. Mann had indirectly admitted he'd been in financial trouble, and though he'd paid the ransom to keep the kidnapping matter hush-hush, somehow the investors must've gotten wind of his lackluster bank account.

Jackson feigned interest in a large portrait as a servant trotted by with an armload of linens. Once she passed, he continued down the corridor, closing in on the sitting room and the rest of what he'd discovered. The insurance windfall had been a surprise. Interesting timing, that. Might Mr. Mann have been so financially desperate he'd had his own wife abducted and murdered? But that made no sense, not since he'd paid the ransom and subsequently had the sum stolen. Perplexing at best. And at worst. . .

Jackson sighed as he neared the hearth in the sitting room. He hadn't a clue as to how all this tied in with the bones of Kit's mother, for if Henrietta Mann were in Kensal Green, then that skeleton must be Isabella Dalton. How that fact fit with the body the authorities had dredged from the river all those years ago, he couldn't yet say.

He *had* to solve this tangle, but first he needed a second look at that picture and a quick fix to that frame.

Dropping to one knee, he dug out the dented frame and the pictures from behind the fern. He pressed his thumb against the divot and pushed, which worked a bit to restore it, but not fully. Mrs. Grady would be sure to notice—

A soft jingle of keys entered the room.

"What are you doing, Inspector?"

Chapter Twenty-One

Jackson froze right there on the sitting room floor, as crouched and culpable as a schoolboy who'd slid down a banister—but that didn't mean he had to 'fess up to his wrongdoing. Not yet, and had he any say in the matter, he never would...a lesson he'd learned well from Kit.

He jammed the frame and the pictures into his pocket, guilt a sour taste on his tongue. If he walked out the door with some of Mann's belongings, he'd be no better than a common thief. But no, there was no theft involved. He was a borrower, plain and simple, keeping the frame for only as long as it took to pound out the dent and replace the back clasp, at which point he'd return it to its rightful place on the mantel—maybe even better than it was to begin with. Why, he was practically doing the man a favour.

Heaven and earth! What was he thinking? He'd hung around Kit so long he was starting to think like the little scamp.

"Well, Inspector, have you a reason for inhabiting Mr. Mann's sitting room?" Mrs. Grady's footsteps clipped closer.

Jackson pivoted to an angle where Mrs. Grady would not see the bulge in his pocket. "I beg your pardon, Mrs. Grady. I thought I might have dropped my notepad, but now I realize I've had it all along." He patted his other pocket, drawing her attention away from the contraband. With a sweep of his hand towards the mantel, he redirected her gaze off him. "I also thought I recognized the late Mrs. Mann. Turns out I was mistaken."

The housekeeper's puckered lips evened out. "Aye, the missus had that effect on many a man, especially those who frequented Blackfriars."

"Oh? I did not realize the elite had much to do with that neighbourhood."

"Some do, leastwise the gentlemen, though only by cover of night."

He studied her carefully. "What has that to do with Mrs. Mann? A lady of her stature must have preferred the west end."

"Naturally, she did, after Mr. Mann. . ." The matron's gaze skittered between him and the mantel. "As far as I know, she maintained a different lifestyle once they were married."

"Once they were married?" Jackson stepped closer, listening with his whole body. "And before?"

"Before? She—" Mrs. Grady's lips clamped shut. She fluttered a hand in the air, employing the same redirection technique he'd used on her. "Now, Inspector, don't go minding me. I'll just be seeing you to the door, then."

She whirled, her chatelaine bouncing against her hip.

He followed, glad the woman couldn't see the frame in his pocket or smirk on his face. She'd handed him enough intelligence to conclude a few things. The second Mrs. Mann must have come from a lowly background, one she'd endeavored to distance herself from after her advantageous marriage. And if she'd been highly recognizable to other men, she hadn't been a simple shopkeeper's daughter. At best she'd been a tavern server. At worst, a strumpet. Perhaps even Mr. Mann's personal mistress until Henrietta Mann was murdered. A stretch, but not an impossibility. He'd have to take care investigating such a delicate angle. The easiest route would be to ask Kit, for she knew everyone in Blackfriars, past and present.

Too bad he wasn't speaking to her anymore.

"Good day, Inspector." The housekeeper held the door wide.

"To you as well." He stepped outside, leaving with more questions than he'd had when he'd arrived. The only thing he knew for certain right now was that he had a picture frame to fix. The small kit of watchmaking tools his father had insisted he pack along for his new life as a London constable had seemed ludicrous at the time, but not now. Jackson glanced at the overcast sky.

Thank You, God, for a father with the foresight of a prophet.

He snagged a hack and returned to the boarding house, mind whirring with all he'd learned at the Mann household. For now, Mr. Mann seemed to have far more connection to the death of Isabella Dalton than the former warehouse owner, Willard Scampson. It was still curious timing on the sale of that building, though, as fishy as the whiff of bad salmon leaching out the door of room number three. Jackson upped his pace, leaving behind the stink. Hopefully, Baggett had finished the legwork on culling out the name of the new warehouse owner, someone who perhaps might shed some light on the matter.

Jackson put his key into the lock, then froze. An odd twinge— nearly imperceptible—pinched his gut. Immediately, he wheeled about, pulling his knife in one swift movement.

But no rogue crouched ready to strike. No man-sized shadow crept up the stairs. The window at the end of the passage wasn't open, so no soul could've crawled in to attack him. Truth be told, there was nothing more dangerous here than the curled corner of the passage runner.

He sheathed his blade and turned the key, still a bit on edge, yet was that not to be wholly expected? Tomorrow would be but seven days since the great wedding debacle. It was no wonder he wasn't fully mentally acute. It would take longer than a week to recover from such a blow.

Shoving open the door, he slipped into the sanctity of the familiar room, sweeping the corners with a glance to be sure no one lurked inside. No body bulged the faded blue draperies. The lumpy bed in the corner remained flat, save for the counterpane that refused to lie evenly. Everything appeared exactly as he'd left it, even the leftover soapy water in the washbasin he'd meant to empty.

The tension in his shoulders eased. He crossed to the window, pulled the frame and pictures from his pocket, and laid them on a small table, when he heard it.

A breath, ever so slight.

He whipped out his knife and spun. A cold sweat beaded on his brow. Of all the bad pennies to show up in his private quarters.

Why? Why!

The knife shook in his hand. This was not to be borne.

Sitting in the chair near the hearth was a blue-eyed, pert-nosed pixie.

Crouched like a panther ready to spring, Jackson was a sleek animal to be admired, which only added to the melancholy that had already punched Kit in the gut when she'd breathed in his familiar scent of cedarwood and smoke. Oh, that she might simply open a vein and purge Jackson Forge from her blood.

"What the devil are you doing here?" he rumbled.

"Hello to you too." She arched a brow at his knife. "I knew you were cross with me, but really?"

His lips flattened to a thin line while he sheathed the blade. How many demons was he fighting at the moment? As many as her? Seeing him standing there, so close that in the blink of an eye she could be in his arms, only reminded her he *was* her lifeblood.

"How did you get in?" His voice was as tight as the line of his lips.

With her fingertip, she ran a languid pattern on the arm of the chair. No sense letting him know the pull of him was nearly too much to bear. "Your landlady is ever so kind, especially to your sister."

"I have no—"

Jackson's face darkened so fiercely she nearly regretted having come in the first place.

His heels thudded hard against the boards, and he flung the door open wide. "It is not seemly for you to be here. Go."

"Seemly or not, here I am. I realize my presence galls you, likely just as much as it does me. But you know me well enough to understand that if I did not have good reason to speak with you in private, I would not have come."

For a long while he said nothing. Just stood there. Gaze of ice. Rock-hard jaw. Staring at her as if she were some sort of monster to be slayed.

She met that cold gaze with a frigid one of her own, otherwise she might melt into a puddle of ridiculous tears right here.

At length, he shut the door. Snagging the wooden chair from the desk, he dragged it to sit opposite her, spine stiff as a carpenter's beam. "So, I ask again, what are you doing here, Miss Turner?"

She welcomed the sting of his rebuff, for it would be far easier to dwell on business than the soft feelings she believed he'd once harboured for her.

Keep your distance, girl. Remember, he was the one who walked away from you.

"I am in need, Mr. Forge"—she put just as much vinegar into his name as he'd poured into hers—"of a man who is capable of playing the part of a gentleman yet who is also skilled in the art of interrogation."

He snorted. "What's to stop you from putting on a pair of trousers?"

"It's not the putting on but the taking off that concerns me."

"Kit," he growled—more of a snarl, really—cementing her preference that they stick to surnames. "What have you gotten yourself into this time? No. Do not answer that. The less I know of your hijinks, the better." He rocketed to his feet. "Leave, please. Now."

Stubborn man! So much for keeping this professional.

She closed the distance between them and laid her hand atop his sleeve. "Hear me out, not for my sake, but for your brother's."

For a long time, he stared at her fingers on his arm, his chest heaving. His silence was as thick as a bowl of day-old pea soup and every bit as appealing. She braced herself against his reaction.

"Do you really think me weak enough to succumb so blindly to your wiles?" His whisper was wretched.

"No, I believe you smart enough to recognize the truth when it's spoken." The words slipped out before she realized she'd even thought them.

Jackson slammed the door. He stalked to the table and planted his hands on it, back towards her. Two small papers rose and fell from the movement, catching her attention. No, not papers. Pictures, likely having something to do with the dented silver frame he'd deposited upon entrance.

"Before you begin spinning a story in which you no doubt hope to entrap me, a forewarning." His voice dropped an octave. "I will have every scrap of information from you, every morsel, every crumb, and if I suspect you are withholding anything, I will heave you over my shoulder and toss you out in the street. Is that completely understood?"

He meant it. Every last word. Of that she had no doubt. "Yes, Jackson."

He whirled, eyes sparking. "Do not lie to me!"

The words ricocheted from wall to wall, landing in her heart like a lead shot. Goodness, was *that* what Jackson felt she had done to him? No wonder he had been so upset when she refused to disclose why she had been at the warehouse. She swallowed the big lump that swelled in her throat, but it refused to stay there, squeezing her next words. "I have tied the truth into many a pretty bow to serve my purposes, and upon occasion withheld information when I felt it necessary, but never once—not ever—have I lied to you." She squared her shoulders. "And this time I vow I shall give you every detail."

He narrowed his eyes. "No matter the consequence?"

"No matter the consequence."

"Everything?"

"Everything."

He studied her a moment longer, then returned to the wooden chair near the hearth, wherein the ashes heaped with only a memory of warmth. "I know I'm going to regret this, but tell me all."

"Remember when I told you I was checking into who'd been responsible for James's assault? I am this close," she held up her thumb and forefinger a paper's width apart, "to finding the villain who beat your brother senseless."

"You never quit, do you? I told you to leave it alone."

"Yes, well. . ." Why was this so difficult?

Rising, she paced the length of the small hearth, glad now that it didn't kick out any heat. Sweat dampened her gown, her corset suddenly far too tightly cinched. There'd be no skip-stepping around any details this time, not if she hoped to gain his help in the matter. Dare she be so vulnerable with this man once again? Open herself up for another possible emotional blow? "As we both agree that justice is a lady worth serving, indeed a value higher than any other to—"

"Get to the point, Kit. I am beyond the power of your pretty words."

She frowned down at him. "I wanted to give you a wedding gift of finding who maimed James."

"I would prefer not to speak of anything even remotely related to what should have been our wedding." The temperature in the room dropped ten degrees, so frosty was his tone.

"You wanted the full truth. And the full truth is that although you say it doesn't matter, it still haunts you. I saw it in your eyes. Was I so terrible for wanting to free you from that once and for all so we could begin our life together unfettered? It might be too late for us, but justice still should be served—for James, for others like him." She almost added *and for you*, but the words caught on her teeth.

For a long while he said nothing; he just sat there, clenching and unclenching his hands as if wanting to hold on to what she'd said but at the same time wishing to let it all go.

"Go on," he said at length.

She sank back to her seat. "I was given the name of an informant who knew the identity of the assailants. A meeting was set at Scampson's the morning of. . ." Oh dear. Now that she laid things out, speaking aloud exactly what she'd done, it did sound rather bad.

A muscle on Jackson's jaw jumped. "The morning of our wedding, is that what you were going to say?"

She tipped her chin, refusing to be cowed. "Yes."

"And you went."

She focused on the neat crease of his trousers, tempted to touch his knee for emphasis. But she didn't. He'd likely see the action as another use of her feminine *wiles*. "Jackson, I swear had I known I'd fall through a rotted board, I never would have gone."

"A rotted board is why you shouldn't have gone? Oh, that's a ripe one, that is." He stormed across the room, and when he wheeled around, fury radiated off him in waves. "You shouldn't have gone because it was a foolish and dangerous thing to do! You're lucky you didn't suffer more than a crack to the head, meeting alone with God knows who. But you wouldn't listen because you know infinitely more than I do. The truth of the entire matter is that you did not respect my wishes. You did not respect *me*."

His words hit dead center, piercing her heart. He was right, God love him. He was more than right. She had cast aside his instruction. But she wasn't about to admit that here. Especially now that it no longer mattered. She met his stare. "Please, let us move forward in the account."

Plowing his fingers through his hair, he dropped to his seat. "I'm listening."

"I admit the Scampson rendezvous was a failure, but I caught up with the cully later at Borough Market. Turns out the man was a crow."

"A what?"

"A crow."

Jackson blinked. So, he'd heard her but didn't understand. He'd come a long way in his knowledge of street cant, but not as far as she'd credited.

"A crow is a lookout while a crime is being committed," she explained. "He caws when the first sniff of trouble comes along. This man, Tazz, was a chavy at the time—a child—and at the mercy of two bludgers who ran a skull-cracking robbery ring. Tazz recalls the men dishing out a particularly brutal beating to a young man, detailing a scar that—" She shut her mouth. No sense revisiting the horrid event. "Suffice it to say that from what Tazz related, the resulting disfigurement matched perfectly the slice on your brother's face."

A deep flush rose up Jackson's neck. "And you got the names of these men?"

"I did. One of them is dead. The other was sent away by his brother to an undisclosed location."

Jackson planted his forearms on his thighs, hands hanging between his legs—a favourite thinking position of his, one she hadn't realized she missed seeing until now.

"So," he said, "the location of the brigand must be extracted from this brother you're talking about, and that's where you need my help."

She nodded. "Phineas Gwince is the manager of a gentlemen's club here in London. He's a recluse, one who chooses not to be found, but he never misses a club meeting."

"When is the next meeting and who is the sponsor?"

"You're to meet a Mr. Stanley Nettles tomorrow night, half past ten, on Pickering Place in St. James."

He straightened, rubbing the back of his neck while working out a kink. "I don't recall a club tucked into that back alley."

"I am not surprised you haven't heard of it. Evidently the Tenebrous Club is very exclusive."

"Tenebrous?" He dropped his hand, his blue gaze seeking hers. "You're right. I haven't heard of it."

"There you have it, then. Play the part of William Turner, aspiring initiate, and as you're doing whatever it is that gentlemen do in their masculine lair, find a way to get Gwince alone and extract the information about his brother."

"How do my trousers fit in?"

Heat flared in her belly. Of all the things she most certainly did not want to think about, Jackson's trousers topped the list. "Pardon?"

He aimed his finger at her. "You said, and I quote, 'It's not the putting on but the taking off that concerns me.'"

"Oh, that." She forced a small laugh, thinking wildly. If she told him about the purported paddling he was to receive, he'd recant at once. Yet had she not moments ago vowed she'd give him every detail? What a pickle!

She went to the window and stared out blindly at a passing dray. Speaking what she must would be hard enough without having to face Jackson. "I have it on good authority that there may be a paddling involved."

"What did you say?" His voice was deadly.

Oh, that she could jump through the glass and land on that wagon, drive off and not have to finish this conversation. Still, that wouldn't help her—or him—in finding James's attacker. Gritting her teeth, she wheeled about. "Horseplay is part of any gentlemen's club, is it not?"

"Drinking games and whatnot, but this is too. . ." He cocked his head, his rogue curl flopping onto his brow. "Are you trying to get a rise out of me?"

She shrugged. "I am merely telling you all I know—which is what you requested."

"I find it hard to believe such an activity would be part of an upstanding men's club."

"Believe what you like, but don't say I didn't warn you." She took a sudden interest in the cuffs of her sleeves, tugging one down after the other, once again preferring anything but the sharp gleam in Jackson's eyes. "Now then, the password is *Have you any frilly pantaloons, my good fellow?* And—"

"Stop right there. You are poking about for a reaction. You'll not have one. Not from me."

Hah! The folding of his arms and smug lift of his chin *was* a reaction.

She smiled. "Good. Then it won't bother you in the least to know Tenebrous is a hellfire club."

A bittersweet chuckle rumbled out of him. "I thought you never lied to me."

Her smile vanished. Here she was serving up a platter of truth and he dared to slap it away as nothing but a meal of falsities? She'd stomp her foot, but like him, she'd not give the satisfaction of such a visible response. "Will you go to that meeting, or shall I play the part of an initiate?"

He stared at her long and hard, until finally he let out a low breath. "I'll do it. But to be clear, I do so only for my brother."

Of course he did. It would be folly to think otherwise.

She strolled to the door but couldn't resist pausing at the table and examining the two images, one a painting, the other a photograph. Both beautiful. One somewhat familiar. She squinted at the woman in a red gown. Hadn't the vicar said something about a woman in a red gown when he'd first spied her in that warehouse hole? Could be connected—or maybe not—but truly, it didn't concern her in the least.

Turning, she was surprised to find Jackson hardly a step away from her. When had he learned to move so quietly? "Well, well." She arched a brow. "I see you've taken no time at all in reassigning your affections."

"Now there's a headliner for you. Kit Turner, jealous." He underlined an imaginary news breaker with a sweep of his hand through the air.

"Don't flatter yourself, sir. Just curious. This one. . ." She swiped up the photograph. "Do you know her?"

"Maybe."

She smiled. What a change from the rookie constable of last spring. "Evasive." Her grin flattened. "Good training."

Her training.

"Actually"—Jackson plucked the image from her hand and frowned down at it—"I was hoping you could tell me more about this woman, a Mrs. Mann."

"A missus?"

"Yes, I'm working a case."

Now there was the real headliner. She hadn't been informed of any new cases. The Home Office had cut her out. Maybe even at Jackson's request.

She flexed her hands to keep from balling her fists. "What case?"

"One that doesn't concern you other than this." He waved the photo in front of her face. "What is this woman's connection to Blackfriars?"

Kit focused on the image. Though past her prime, the woman was a looker, employing a practiced tilt of the head, sultry pout of her lips, and. . . Kit leaned closer, squinting. That wasn't just a speck on the picture but a beauty mark near the woman's left eyebrow. A unique spot. A memorable one. Could this be the famed Xanadu? And if so, why would Jackson want to know? What mysterious case was he working on?

"Well?" he prodded.

She shrugged. "I cannot be sure without a little digging."

"Would you?" He offered the image on an open palm.

She looked from the photo to him, pulling it from his hand as she did so. "I suppose then we'll be even, will we not?"

He gazed down his nose at her. "If that's how you look at it, then yes."

"How do you see it?"

He inhaled so deeply, his waistcoat stretched taut over his chest. "Look, Kit, I am not an enemy to be met fist for fist. If we are to cohabit this city, at least for the next few weeks, then let us be civil."

"I thought that's what I was doing." She cocked her head. "Wait a minute. . . What happens after a *few weeks*?"

His face went blank. "It is time you leave."

And he complained about her withholding information? She lifted the photo to within an inch of his eyes. "Does it have something to do with this case?"

He batted away her arm, scowling. "I've given you all the information I intend to. Go." He jerked his chin towards the door.

So, there was a clear connection. Satisfied, she flounced out as if she didn't have a care in the world, but once in the corridor, she slowed her pace. She did have a care. Several, actually.

Where might he be going?

And most importantly, why did it matter so much to her?

Chapter Twenty-Two

There was a fine line between wealth and poverty, one that never failed to surprise Jackson, especially in the St. James district. A mere half block after he passed by the Atheneum's golden statue of Athena, her gilded robes proudly glinting by streetlight, he turned into a dark passageway—and immediately scowled. The stench of urine in this narrow neck was no different than in the rabbit warrens of Seven Dials. Indeed, save for the pristine storefronts lining Pall Mall, the alleys and poorly lit mews riddling this playground of the rich were no different than a slum.

Two blocks later, Jackson swung into the bleak tunnel of Pickering Place, trying hard not to consider what the heel of his left shoe had just squished. As the note Kit had shown him instructed, he counted ten paces, faced left, then crouched and fingered the paneling for a loose board. A hand-sized square of wood near his knee gave, so he shoved the piece in with all his might. Something clicked. Gears whirled. Pulleys squeaked, and behind him hinges groaned. He wheeled about. A false part of the opposite wall opened, revealing a hidden door.

Impressive.

Yet the pitted wood he pounded his fist against was anything but remarkable. He might as well be knocking at a sailor's watering hole near Limehouse instead of seeking entrance to an exclusive gentlemen's club.

An instant later, a slot opened at eye level. Two rather bloodshot peepers stared out, somewhat ghoulish in the tenuous light from an inside lantern. "Password?"

Jackson sucked in a breath. He'd heard of ridiculous watchwords before, but nothing quite like the embarrassment he was expected to say. Oh, how it vexed that Kit had once again convinced him to do her bidding. He lowered his voice. "Have you any frilly pantaloons, my good fellow?"

"Eh?" The eyes squinted. "What's that you say?"

Jackson scanned the passage to make sure no one lurked at his back. Satisfied, he stepped closer to the door and spoke a little louder. "Have you any frilly pantaloons, my good fellow?"

The man merely blinked. "Speak up, if you please."

No, he most certainly did not please! Jackson ground his teeth. Next time he saw Kit, he'd throttle the little nymph for this indignation. "Have you any frilly pantaloons, my good fellow!" he blasted.

The words reverberated in the small space. The slot slammed shut, a bolt shot open, and the door swung inward to the boisterous laughter of a man with chipmunk teeth.

"You are William Turner?" the man asked between chuckles.

"I am." Despite the good this visit might yield, it was still a lie, one that tasted like a fatty bit of gristle. The sooner this charade was over, the better. And if this cherry-cheeked fellow was Gwince, hopefully it might be over before it began.

"You are. . . ?" Jackson asked.

The man offered his hand for a hearty shake. "Poppet."

Jackson lifted a brow as he pumped the fellow's moist fingers.

Poppet winked. "You shall receive your own club name soon enough."

Dash it! How was he to find Gwince if everyone went by a nom de guerre?

"Follow me, Turner." Poppet grabbed a lantern off a hook and descended a flight of stairs smelling of damp rot. After a small landing, an adjoining set of steps hairpinned the other direction, down, down, down. Then the process repeated yet again. Of all the convoluted entrances! If this turned out to be another excursion into the sewers of London, he really would throttle Kit.

"Fresh fish!" Poppet bellowed at the bottom of the stairs, then stepped aside.

Several men set down their drinks and swiveled their heads in what appeared to be a huge vault, at least eighty paces wide. Sconces cast golden light against walls honeycombed with wine bottles. A few lit passages spindled out like the spokes of a great wheel. At center, plush chairs were grouped in threes and fours around small tables, a huge chandelier dazzling over all. The gaze of eighteen or so men glinted with interest. One fellow with rather purplish lips stood, clutching his drink as if it were a life preserver—and it was, judging by the carbuncled nose on the man. What an ocean of spirits the fellow must down each day. No wonder his wig sat askew.

"You must be William Turner." The man eyed him from head to toe, then draped an arm around his shoulder. "I say, you are as fine a looking fellow as your sister is beautiful."

Jackson's gut roiled. When Kit said it was a hellfire club he would be visiting, he assumed she was just trying to goad him. Prove he was as inept as she once claimed. Now he wasn't so sure. He pulled away. "Mr. Nettles, I assume?"

"Up there"—Nettles aimed his thumb towards the ceiling— "but down here I am Ruffles."

Jackson stifled a snort. The absurd monikers might be some sort of ruse to evoke a reaction from him, but he was in no mood to deliver. All he wanted was to find Gwince and leave this strange underworld.

Nettles clapped his hands, the sound oddly muffled by the thick layer of rugs spread across every inch of the vault. "Ready to begin, lads?"

As the men rose, so did Jackson's alarm. They all leered at him as if he were a rare moth to be dissected. He angled close to Nettles, speaking for him alone. "I should meet with the manager before we start. You know, check in and the like. Where is he?"

"Very conscientious of you, my friend, but not to worry. I already passed on your credentials. Besides, Gwince runs things behind the scenes, preferring to move seamlessly in and out during meetings instead of getting bogged down with business. You know how it is."

No, actually he didn't, but at least he now knew that Gwince didn't have a silly made-up name. Jackson scanned the shadowy alcoves of the great space, hoping to spy a man "behind the scenes."

Before he could finish, Nettles pulled him into the center of the room. "And so the games begin." Nettles released him as the men circled about. "Remove your right shoe, if you please."

Jackson hesitated, wondering if all were to go shoeless, but when no man bent to the task, he did. It was a strange request to be sure, but it wasn't as if he'd been asked to strip his knickers for a paddling like Kit had insinuated. Proving she had been playing games with him.

He held out his shoe.

At the far end of the room, a man in a green frock coat carrying a bowl emerged from a passageway. As he slipped through the circle, Jackson studied him. Same height, same build as himself. He even wore a similar moustache—but in quite a different colour. The man's hair was a lightly creamed tea to Jackson's coffee brown. The elusive Gwince, perhaps?

The question perched on Jackson's tongue, then quickly flew away as the fellow poured the contents of the bowl into his shoe and a chant began.

"Drink. Drink. Drink. Drink."

Jackson stared at the mess in his best oxford. Ten goldfish swam in a bubbly fizz—champagne? They couldn't expect him to drink this. He glanced up at Nettles, anticipating the older fellow might instead hand him a stout glass of whisky.

Nettles merely cuffed him on the shoulder. "Down the hatch, old man!"

Jackson ground his teeth. *Blast that Kit!*

"Drink. Drink. Drink. Drink!"

There'd be no getting out of this. Licking his lips, he mentally prepared for the abomination, then lifted his shoe.

Oh, how wrong he'd been. Dreadfully wrong. There was no way he could ever be prepared for the little lumps cascading over his tongue and diving down his throat. He nearly gagged as he tipped back his head to finish the foul concoction.

A cheer rang out, sickeningly gleeful.

Jackson bent, hiding a scowl, and shook out his shoe, making sure no fish remained before he shoved it back on his foot.

"Bully for you!" Nettles beamed at him.

As did Poppet, his chipmunk teeth surprisingly white in the golden light.

"Is the iron ready, Gwince?"

The green-coated man gave a sharp nod as he disappeared down a passageway.

So, that *was* Gwince! Jackson took a step towards him.

Nettles snagged his arm. "This way, Turner. Time for some real merriment."

He stiffened, and though it cost him all his self-restraint and then some, he allowed himself to be led in the opposite direction of Gwince. Timing mattered, a fact Kit had bludgeoned him with on many an occasion.

The entire group of men followed them into a large alcove where a chair sat at center next to a bucket of what appeared to be white-hot coals. A thick metal rod protruded from the center. The fish in Jackson's gut swam laps. Surely this wasn't what it appeared.

The men ringed the room, shoulder to shoulder, three of them stepping forward with arms crooked, each with an expectant tilt to his head. Nettles elbowed him. "Bunny shall take your coat, Dotty your waistcoat, and Pigsqueak your shirt. Chop, chop. We haven't got all night."

If he made a break for it now, he'd leave unscathed—but also without the information he needed. Warily, Jackson peeled off article after article, hanging each item over one of the men's arms.

"Very good." Nettles pointed at the chair. "Have a seat, Turner."

He lowered to the velvet cushion, trying to ignore the heat radiating against his calf from the nearby bucket.

The circle of men closed in. The only way out now would be at knifepoint.

The bulbous-nosed Nettles lifted his arms to the low ceiling. "Bite of dragon, singe of flesh, mark you now for Tenebrous." Drawing his hands into prayer, Nettles eyed Jackson. "Do you agree to join the brotherhood?"

Sweat trickled between his shoulder blades. He really would throttle Kit for this. Drawing in a deep breath, he forced out, "Yes."

But only for the night. And may God forgive me.

Hands grabbed his shoulders, pressing him down, cementing

him into the chair. Nettles removed the rod from the bucket, one end glowing with an ornate letter *T*. A branding iron, the tip as red as the flames of hell.

The fish in Jackson's gut went belly-up.

Oh, God. A way out if You please?

A cloth sack dropped over his head, black as burnt flesh and smelling as fetid. Another low chant began.

"Burn. Burn. Burn. Burn."

Jackson clamped his jaw so tightly it crackled in his ears. Every muscle in his body clenched, preparing for a sickening sizzle and searing agony.

Metal hit his chest.

Iron hard.

Freezing cold.

Freezing—*what?*

The sack was yanked off. The red-hot brand hung low in Nettles's hand, and in his other waved a dripping wet duplicate, a bucket of ice water having somehow magically appeared near the entry.

Great guffaws filled the small space. Some fellows even clouted him on the back. Jackson was hard-pressed to decide if he should land a few uppercuts to work out his stress or collapse against the cushion of the high-back.

"Cracking good form, man!" Nettles dropped both branding irons into the icy bucket, a hiss of steam arising. "Not a cry nor a whimper. Why, you have not even soiled your trousers, unlike when Lacey, here, was initiated." He hitched his thumb at the man next to him. "Up you go, now. One last rite until you're a tried-and-true member, my boy, and then the real games begin."

"I can hardly wait," Jackson grumbled under his breath, then strained a smile as he stood. "I am your servant, gentlemen." He flourished a deep bow.

More laughs pealed.

"Hah! He's been practicing."

"Wish I'd brought my cricket bat."

"Now there's a solid target."

Amidst more crude remarks, they returned to the main vault.

Nettles ushered him across the thick rugs to the same passageway where Gwince had earlier disappeared and shoved his discarded clothes at him.

"You'll find the changing room just down this passage, first door on the right, where there are pegs for all of your garments. Off with you now. We eagerly await your return." The man winked, his pitted nose scrunching with the gesture. Then he pulled out a small paddle and whacked Jackson on the backside.

The sting instantly curled Jackson's fingers into tight fists. Oh, how he'd love to bash the big red target in the middle of Nettles's face. Dash that Kit! She *had* been telling him the truth, but with such fits and starts, it was no wonder he'd not believed her.

He stormed down the corridor, blind to everything but the scarlet rage rushing through his veins. Not even the chilly air against his bare chest cooled his fury. How he'd get out of this predicament was a quandary, but he was sure of one thing. He was done. Finished with this whole insane evening. He'd find Gwince elsewhere, even if he had to scare up a writ of assistance to do so.

But first he had to get out of this twisted looney bin.

He glanced into the changing room, which held a pair of white knickers hanging on a peg. A bright red target was painted on the middle of the backside. What sort of twisted men were these? Scowling, he glanced around for a door through which to escape. Nothing. Just whitewashed walls.

Quickly, he shrugged into his shirt and threw on his waistcoat and dress coat, then backed out of the room and dashed to the next door. Locked. Farther down on the other side, a door stood open, light spilling a triangle onto the carpet. Jackson approached on cat feet and peered around the side jamb.

Inside, a man stood with his back to the entrance, pouring red liquid into little vials. Jackson stifled a snort. After his experiences thus far, it was probably monkey blood. But that didn't interest him nearly so much as the green of the man's coat.

Gwince.

Jackson stepped into the room. "Excuse me."

Setting down the carafe, Gwince turned. A slight frown creased his brow. "I am afraid you have taken a wrong turn, sir. Allow me to redirect you."

"No, I'm in the right place. Just a few questions, Mr. Gwince. Shouldn't take long."

"I think not." His face hardened. "Rather it is time you join the others." He advanced.

No matter how hard Jackson had been trying to block his memories of Kit, her voice flowed unhindered in his head.

"Hold. Hold. Timing is everything."

Bad memory. Good advice.

Just before Gwince grabbed for his arm, Jackson sprang. In a swift movement, he whipped out his knife with one hand, and with the other, he wrenched Gwince's arm behind his back. Before the man could regain his balance, he shoved in the tip of his blade, ripping fabric, penetrating skin, just deep enough to prevent Gwince from breaking away. "If you'd like to keep your liver intact, I suggest you answer me."

Cords popped out on Gwince's neck, bulging against his neckcloth. "Who are you? What do you want?"

"Information." Jackson twisted the knife. "Where is your brother?"

A wince curled the man's upper lip. "You are a year too late to catch that train."

He jammed the blade deeper, just a bit. Any farther and he really would cause some damage. Hopefully, Gwince would take the bluff. "I'm not playing."

"Neither am I," Gwince snarled. "My mongrel of a brother died of the pox last summer, and the world is a better place for it."

Dead? Dash it! But indeed, the world was a better place without that garrotter. "Agreed," Jackson grumbled.

"Being we are in agreement, then would you kindly remove your knife?"

He could. He should.

But not quite yet.

"I am afraid there are some gentlemen in need of entertainment, and as manager, I suspect you would not wish them to be disappointed. Come along." Jackson wrenched the man's arm harder while simultaneously loosening the pressure of his blade—not completely, yet enough to shuffle the man to the door without actually spearing his liver. Men milled at the end of the passageway, but by God's good grace, none looked their way.

"Make one sound and I'll serve your innards as a late-night appetizer. Now move." Jackson steered the man into the changing room, then gave him a shove and crouched in front of the door, ready to spring if need be. "Off with your coat, please."

Pressing his palm against the blood oozing onto his waistcoat, Gwince glowered. "You'll never make it out of here."

"That remains to be seen." He flipped the blade around in his hand, illustrating who yet held the power in the room.

Gwince shrugged out of his coat.

"Drop it," Jackson ordered.

The green fabric pooled on the floor.

"Your neckcloth, as well."

The second the long strip of white silk touched ground, Jackson smiled. "Very good. Now kick it to me."

Gwince did, with more force than necessary. The fellow had every right to be upset, especially for the headache he was soon to own.

"Turn around, hands behind your back, wrists together."

No sooner did the man comply than Jackson snatched up the silk and secured his hands. "Hate to do this, but. . ." With the hilt of the knife, he thwacked Gwince atop the head. Hard. Then guided his limp body to the floor.

With no time to waste, Jackson exchanged his best dress coat with Gwince's, the fabric still warm from the man's body. If he stuck to the shadows, hopefully no one would notice him.

He tore out of the room and retrieved the tray of blood-coloured drinks. Already catcalls bounced from wall to wall, Nettles especially loud.

"Turner! We're waiting." The old fellow smacked his paddle against his palm, the sound rising above the other men's voices.

Jackson turned his back to them all, and just in time, for Nettles's voice once again rang out.

"Gwince! Is the new fish nearly ready?"

Jackson ducked his head, hoping they'd not notice his brown hair. He gave a noncommittal wave with one hand, praying that would suffice.

Then he held his breath.

"I say we go help the kipper!" A shout from the other side of the room was met with a cheer. Feet shushed over the carpet. Voices faded.

Jackson dropped the tray and bolted for the stairs. It wouldn't take long before they discovered his duplicity. By the time he slid open the bolt on the door at the top of the stairs, shoes pounded from below.

Jackson fled into the night. Far and fast. Not stopping until he crossed London Bridge and scampered beneath it. Lungs heaving, he sank onto the damp gravel, not caring a fig for how the green slime would muck up his trousers.

What a waste. This whole evening had been for nothing, save for a possible future bust on a club that ought not to be in operation. Even though God was sovereign and justice was His alone, it still rankled that those brigands who'd maimed his brother would not be brought to heel on this side of heaven.

He stared out at the dark waters, the river deceptively still yet with a powerful undercurrent for the unsuspecting. And in the darkness of his mind, an equally powerful current rose to the surface. Perhaps the night hadn't been for naught. It did bring an end to the wondering he'd tried to ignore these past years, just not in a way he'd expected—or hoped. At the very least, he now knew who was responsible for maiming his brother and had the assurance they'd not commit the same crime on someone else's brother. Perhaps Kit had gone about things the wrong way, but she might have been right in pursuing this after all.

Disappointment tasted sour in his mouth. Kit would be equally upset about the matter.

He tugged his collar tight against the chill of the October night, knowing he ought not to consider what Kit thought or felt, especially after the humiliation he'd suffered in that club. But the truth was. . .

He did.

Chapter Twenty-Three

Going to church was a bad idea. Kit squirmed on the pew, thankful she'd chosen the back row, out of Jackson's line of sight and where no one would see her fidgeting. The vicar, draped in his black cassock and white surplice, lifted his hands in supplication at the altar—the very place she should have stood with Jackson last week. Holy words filled the sanctuary, words that stung.

"Truth may sometimes bleed the soul, yet it is also a balm, healing that same wound when spoken in love. It is falsity which betrays, bringing comfort to the ear while driving a knife in the heart. Therefore, Beloved, as Paul so aptly states in Ephesians, we ought to put away lying and speak truth with our neighbours, for we are members of one another, set apart as the family of God." The vicar swept a gaze over the congregation, landing on Kit as if God Himself were singling her out. "Let us not grieve our great and gracious Creator by deceiving one another, but rather let us go forth boldly into the world, speaking truth, and that abundantly."

Kit bit her lip, barely hearing the benediction. How could she? Too much conviction pulsed through her veins. She hadn't boldly spoken truth to Jackson. La! She'd not have spoken it at all had she felt there was any other choice. The real truth was ever since she'd met the man, she'd been skip-stepping around facts and details, telling him only what she thought he needed to know at any given moment. In essence, she made herself a god by deciding what he should hear and when he should hear it. What sort of arrogant monster had she become? Her chin dropped to her chest.

Oh, God, grant Your pardon for my prideful ways. You gave me a man of integrity to love and be loved by, and I threw Your gift right back in Your face. But if there's a chance, Lord, any chance at all, would You make things right between Jackson and me? Because the truth is, God, that I love him . . . and I always shall.

Feet shuffled by, and she immediately doubled over, feigning a sudden interest in the laces of her half boot. Better to accost Jackson outside than here in the sight of God and the vicar. As soon as the last footsteps stamped past, she dashed outside. Rising to her toes, she shaded her eyes from the late morning sun and glanced down the street. No set of broad shoulders stood out from the crowd. She pivoted and—there. Down the block, near a lamppost, Jackson hailed a hackney, looking far too handsome even in an ill-fitting coat that flapped in the wind. How had he gotten so far so fast?

She dashed ahead, catching up to him just as he was about to shut the cab door. His brow arched as she hoisted herself inside. Surprisingly, he said nothing as he secured the latch and sank to the seat.

Catching her breath, Kit smoothed her skirts. "You are in quite a hurry this morning. Was the sermon so very vexing?"

He folded his arms, a magnificent scowl darkening his face. "I could ask the same of you."

She met his challenge, mirroring the tip of his head. "What's stopping you then?"

"Because I doubt I'd get a straight answer."

She bit the inside of her cheek to keep from cringing as she pulled the photograph from her pocket. "Here's your picture."

He stared at the image a moment before flicking his gaze to her. "Did you learn anything about Alexandra Mann?"

She shoved a wayward piece of hair beneath her hat, annoyed. "As I suspected, you are looking at the famed Xanadu. Leastwise, years ago she was notorious."

"Oh? How so?"

The cab veered around a corner, and Kit flung out her hand, grabbing hold of the windowsill for balance. Must every London cabbie drive like a wild banshee? "There used to be an introducing house over on The Green Walk. As a girl, I sometimes loitered in the area, hoping to catch a glimpse of the pretty ladies who worked for the madam. There were many, but none so legendary as Xanadu." She pointed at the photograph in Jackson's grip. "Her fame lived on long after she'd been bought up, such was her beauty. Her portrait hung prominently in the front room for years beyond her employ. As a girl, I used to press my face against the glass, dreaming I might grow up to be such a looker."

Jackson rubbed his brow with one finger. "Bought up? I am not familiar with the term."

"I should hope not. It means some wealthy gent wished to have Xanadu for his personal pleasure. The women who work for introduction houses are free agents, paying only for rental of their room, so she must have agreed to the man's terms. And why not? Women like that are often put up in luxury. Some of them even manage to marry the man who keeps them."

"Do they? Interesting." His gaze drifted out the window, but judging by his deadpan stare, he wasn't admiring the tinker shop or the bakery that the hack rattled past. She'd bet her best handkerchief he was stitching together the threads of information she'd just given him, embroidering some sort of picture that would solve his case—a case he had yet to share with her.

"What are you thinking?" She kept her tone dulcet. If she played her hand right—calmly and carefully—she might find out what he was working on.

Absently, Jackson rubbed his knuckles along his jawline. "Either he did not know of his wife's past, or he was the one who purchased her services for himself."

Who is he? The question burned on her tongue, but better to swallow it than remind Jackson she wasn't working this mystery with him.

Leather creaked as he shifted on the seat. "What year did Alexandra quit working for the introducing house?"

"1860."

"Which would be the year before Mr. Mann's first wife was murdered."

Aha. Now she had a name. How much more could she fish out of him? "Do you think he arranged for that murder?"

"It's not out of the realm of possibility, I suppose, not if Mr. Mann wished to marry this mistress." The blue of Jackson's eyes grew in intensity the more he thought aloud. "If that's the case, then he'd have been forced to get rid of his wife. Still, it doesn't fully add up. Assuming he was behind the whole scheme, why would he pay the ransom money her kidnappers demanded, allowing his valet to be murdered in the process?"

"The valet died and she was kidnapped?"

The wheels dipped into a rut, jostling the carriage. Bad timing. The unexpected lurch pulled Jackson into the present, for he tucked the photo into his pocket and glowered at her. "You just don't quit, do you?"

"Information—no matter how it is gained—is power. I have given you the information you wanted." She lifted her chin. "So, your turn. What did you learn at the Tenebrous Club last night?"

"That there are a lot of sick and twisted people in this world." His face darkened.

She snorted. "I could have told you that."

"And yet you knew all along what I'd be walking into when I set foot in that place!" His tone dropped dangerously low. "You tricked me, Kit, just as you've been tricking me since the day we met."

"That's not fair, nor is it true." She cut her hand through the air, frustrated beyond measure. "I told you everything down to the last detail, but a lot of good it did me. You're as cross with me now as if I hadn't shared anything with you. It seems no matter how honest I am, there is no way for me to earn the trust of someone who *refuses* to trust."

His chest swelled, so deeply did he inhale. Hopefully from conviction and not more anger. Hard to tell though, for he said nothing.

"Jackson, please try to understand." She reached for his knee, hoping to soothe instead of fan the flames of the hot contention between them. "I know it wasn't a pleasant experience, but I had every confidence you would have exacted an escape before the paddling."

"I did. Even so, I am out my best dress coat thanks to you, hence this monstrosity." He flicked his fingers at the pea soup–coloured coat which—now that she looked closer—was threadbare at the cuffs and collar.

And all because of her.

"I am sorry. Truly. I shall see it is replaced." She opened the drawstring on her purse, but before she could withdraw any coins, his big hand closed over hers.

"I can manage new garments on my own," he grumbled.

She stared at his hand, the bitten nails, the tiny scar at the base of his thumb almost too beautiful to bear. Oh, how she missed his touch. Shoving down a rising melancholia, she pinned on a smile as if he had no effect on her whatsoever. It was either that or weep. "More importantly, then, what did you learn of your brother's attacker?"

Jackson pulled back. "He's dead."

Dead? The word hooked her deeply. Sharply. She squeezed her reticule, giving her hands something to do other than strangle the life out of her small purse. "It was all for nothing? They are both beyond the reach of the law?" Her voice sounded flat even to her own ears.

"They are beyond man's law, yes. But we may safely leave their punishment in God's hands. . .though I admit I am as disappointed as you." Lifting his hat, Jackson raked his fingers through his hair. "Look, Kit, while I cannot pretend I wasn't cross with you for pursuing this case, as it turns out, I am glad you did and that I can finally put this behind me. Thank you."

She gaped at the raw emotion deepening the blue in his eyes. Such a vulnerability was surprising, considering she'd gone against his wishes in the first place.

"I am glad for you. Truly." Once again she reached for his knee.

But then like the closing of a great pair of shutters, he looked away and pounded his fist against the roof.

"I believe this is your stop." He flung open the door before the wheels even quit moving, then sank back to his seat, refusing to look at her. "Good day, Miss Turner."

"Good day to you." The words slid out in a choked whisper as she climbed down to the cobbles. No sooner did her feet land than the door slammed shut, and the driver clicked his tongue at the horses.

Kit watched the black cab lumber off, a hollow feeling growing in her chest. Tears burned at the back of her eyes, building like too much steam in a boiler, so hot that if one slipped loose, it would blister her cheek. They'd been so close to reconciling. She felt it. She *knew* it! So why had he turned her out of the cab?

Pressing the back of her hand to her mouth, she swallowed down the ugly burn, each tear landing as a cold, hard stone in her belly.

Jackson mashed the heels of his hands against his eyes, preventing him from snapping his gaze to the window for a last glimpse of Kit. What a cad he'd been, giving her such a churlish dismissal. The hurt in her voice—though she'd tried to hide it—couldn't be denied.

He loosened his collar, finding it suddenly hard to breathe. The sooner he sailed from England with the earl, the better—and it couldn't be soon enough, not with Kit continuing to bob in and out of his life, churning up feelings he'd rather not name.

Several bone-rattling blocks later, he alighted from the weak-springed hackney, his old coat flapping in the breeze for want of some missing buttons. Other than his constable blues, the worn suit coat was the best he now owned, but he'd be hog-tied before taking money from Kit to purchase a new one.

After flipping the jarvey a coin, he trotted up the few steps to Number Seven, Tweed Lane, and pounded on a door as weathered as he felt after last night's scant sleep. Those goldfish in his gut had kept him up till the wee hours.

The door opened to the bristly bearded sergeant. Jackson blinked. Dressed in a grey waistcoat and shirtsleeves instead of buttoned tight in his police uniform, this version of Graybone was a stranger.

But the censure in his dark gaze was a familiar friend. "You look like you've been keelhauled."

He felt like it too. What a day this was turning out to be. "Kit has that effect on people."

"Oh?" Graybone's bushy eyebrows lifted. "Dare I hope you've finally made things right with her?"

The shrill laughter of a pedestrian behind him grated as much as Graybone's expectation that he be the one to pursue reconciliation with Kit instead of the other way around. Admittedly, though, she had told him the whole truth about the hellfire club, even though she had every reason not to. In the past she wouldn't have done such a thing. Perhaps she was right. Maybe he was refusing to trust her.

But that was a rock to look under at another time.

He shook his head at the sergeant. "You are as tenacious as your daughter, and that is all I have to say on the matter."

"But it's not all *I* have to say. Yes, you were wronged, but that doesn't mean you must spend the rest of your life playing the victim. You weren't the only one injured. Kit feels it too. We both know she's sorry. It's time you gave her a second chance. At the very least, think on the possibility."

Jackson swallowed the admonition, the old feeling of being the new recruit facing the indomitable sergeant rising from the past. The man was probably right, though. He should seriously consider reconciling with Kit.

But not now.

"Point taken, sir." He lifted his chin. "Now then, are we also to share information about the Dalton case out here on the stoop?"

"You know, somehow I prefer the fresh-faced rookie to the carping fishwife you've become." Graybone held the door wider.

Jackson bypassed the man, removing his hat as he entered a surprisingly neat front room. A polished stove sat in one corner, practically gleaming in the late morning light. Nearby was an overlarge, blue-striped chair, a lacey antimacassar draped over the top. In front of the window was a settee with a tea table sporting a doily. The opposite wall held a glass-doored bookshelf, but it wasn't the titles that astonished as much as the porcelain figurines atop it. Huh. If Jackson didn't know any better, he'd guess a spinster lived here instead of a fifty-something bachelor.

Graybone entered, swinging his hand towards the sofa. Jackson sat. The sergeant followed suit. "It's not her."

Jackson set his hat atop the tea table. "Pardon?"

"The body you found." He snatched up the hat and strode to a coat tree Jackson hadn't noticed behind the door, mumbling as he hung the bowler on a hook. "It's not my Bella."

"You are certain?"

"I am!" Graybone wheeled about, a glower drawing his brows into a thick line. "As far as I know, Bella hadn't lost any teeth, and she had a certain defect. As a young child, an andiron fell on her foot. She lost her pinky toe in that incident. There were no bones missing on the right foot of that skeleton."

Jackson scrubbed a hand over his face, stubble roughening his palm. "Whom did Kit find, then?"

"And how did the woman get ahold of Bella's locket?"

Jackson pondered the question, his hand running along the sofa, bunching and unbunching an embroidered arm protector as he worked through the puzzle.

"The body could be Mrs. Mann's," he said at last. "It was her busk we found, and Miss Dalton did work for the household. Not to mention the scrap of red fabric that might very well be from the same gown as in the picture I have of her. But no. It still makes no sense."

"Your babbling doesn't make sense either, Forge." Graybone rescued the arm protector, frowning at him as he smoothed the thing flat where it belonged.

My, my. The man was certainly fastidious about his furnishings. Lest he earn the barbed side of Graybone's tongue, Jackson folded his hands in his lap. "That's right. I suppose I haven't spoken with you since I met with Mr. Mann. I learned a lot from what he said. . .and from what he didn't say. Turns out his first wife, Henrietta—"

"The owner of the whalebone busk?" The sergeant resumed his seat.

"The very same. She went missing two days before Miss Dalton, a victim of kidnapping. Mr. Mann sent his valet with the ransom money to the prescribed exchange, but either he or the brigands got greedy. Mr. Mann's servant and his wife were both shot and killed on the scene. Their bodies were recovered, but not the money. Leastwise that's what he said."

"Have you not already checked into the records to verify?"

"He never reported the crime."

Graybone's head reared back. "Why the devil not?"

"Business reasons. According to Baggett, Mr. Mann is a bookkeeper and moneylender to aristocrats who wish to keep their gambling habits off their ledgers yet still must keep track of their funds. Such powerful men expect their accountant to keep a low profile. A kidnapping would've drawn far too much attention, let alone a murder."

Rising, Jackson paced the length of the small room, catching a whiff of linseed oil as he turned about. "Mr. Mann's story is overly tidy. What sort of man would not wish retribution on those who'd murdered his wife?"

"You believe he told you only what he wanted you to hear?"

"Perhaps."

Graybone grunted, his lips pursing. "What is your theory, then?"

"It is not fully formed. After checking marriage records, I learned Mr. Mann remarried shortly after the death of Henrietta. . .wedding a known harlot, though by then she'd been out of public service for some time. It is very possible he made a lady of the strumpet, so much so that they fooled everyone." He handed Alexandra's photograph over to Graybone.

Holding the image at arm's length, the sergeant squinted as he studied the picture, then offered it back. "Are you saying Mr. Mann had his wife murdered under the guise of kidnapping in order to marry his mistress?"

Jackson tucked away the photo, taking care with the creased corner. "It wouldn't be the first time for such an event. Perhaps his valet got in the way somehow, and Mr. Mann had him killed as well."

"Yet we only found one body."

"There is that." He sighed. "There is also the fact that Mr. Mann claims his wife was buried at. . ." Retrieving his small notepad, he paged through it to the last bit of scribbling. "Kensal Green. She is buried at Kensal Green."

"Or is she?"

Of course! He should've thought of that himself. Jackson strode to the coat tree and snatched his hat off the hook so forcefully the whole thing wobbled. "There is only one way to find out."

"Hold it right there, Forge." Graybone rose like a thundercloud. "Before you go digging up the past of a powerful man, you'd first better clear it with the chief, though I would prefer it if you do so without Ridley discovering what you're working on. I don't wish to lose my jurisdiction on this one, which I will if the chief finds out this is a murder case."

Jackson jammed on his hat. As usual, Graybone was right. What a firework show it would be in Ridley's office tomorrow. Not only would he have to inform his superior of his resignation but get permission to exhume the body of Henrietta Mann as well.

Chapter Twenty-Four

Monday mornings were notoriously hard, but this one was worthy of a trophy. Jackson grumbled to himself all the way down Brackley Street. He'd overslept then spilled his tea and stained his white shirt. And if that weren't bad enough, he'd slipped in a pile of rotting fish guts and ripped the hem of his trousers when he'd dashed to the omnibus stand—only to find the bus had already departed.

And now this.

Pennies to pounds, someone tagged his heels. He was sure of it, especially after trying to shake the fellow by weaving in and out of the early shoppers at Borough Market. He'd added in a few more complexities to his route, using every evasion tactic Kit had ever shown him, and still he hadn't lost his tracker. . .which could only mean one thing.

It was Kit. The little vixen had been far too curious yesterday about his case. He'd have to mind his step until he figured out the whole Dalton/Mann mess. If Kit caught the slightest breath that it had anything to do with her mother's death, there'd be no keeping her nose out of it—and he could only imagine the pain which might result. She'd already come to grips with her mother's supposed suicide, but to discover it was instead murder would rip that wound wide open again. As much as she'd hurt him, he'd not willingly see her suffer any further pain on the matter of her mother. . .or anything else, for that matter.

He slowed his pace. Feigning interest in a nearby haberdasher's window, he paused long enough for Kit to draw closer without providing her time to take cover. . .which ought to be just about now.

He wheeled about, a harsh chastisement perched on the tip of his tongue—then shut his mouth. Lord, have mercy. He'd nearly rebuked a passing clergyman whose nose was stuck in a psalter. So hidden was the fellow's face—by the book and the dark hood on his head—how could he even see to walk? Curious, Jackson watched as he passed, the hem of his black cassock swinging with his long-legged steps. Curious, also, that the reverend was out in public in his Sunday vestments, for it was neither Sunday nor a holy day—but that mystery had nothing to do with who'd been following him.

Jackson snapped his gaze back down the street until he was satisfied no brown skirt lurked among the shoppers, then upped his pace. If Kit was tracking him, she'd be sorely disappointed with his destination.

On Old Jewry, he tipped his hat at a few huddled officers near the station's front door, then trotted inside and up the steps to the chief inspector's office. Hesitating on the landing, he drew in a deep breath then blew out a prayer for God's favour.

After a rap on the door and the resultant "Enter," Jackson strode into Ridley's domain, giving the birdcage a wide berth. "Inspector Forge reporting for duty, sir."

Oddly enough, no "Hang 'im up, boys" squawked at his back. Hopefully, the parrot's usual dire prediction would not come true today.

Ridley peered at him over the top edge of the daily news and frowned at the ill-fitting coat. Maybe he should've visited the tailor before coming here instead of vice versa. Scads! "Maybe he should have" seemed to be the chant of his life these days. Like maybe he should have stayed in Haywards Heath. Maybe he should have refused Kit as a partner. Maybe he should have returned the ring still buried in the drawer back at his home. Yet how could he relinquish the one thing yet wrapped in hope, crushed as that hope now may be?

Ever so slowly, the chief made a production of folding the paper before finally setting it down. "I should have thought you'd report last Monday, Forge, what with your wedding upset. My condolences, by the way."

Jackson flexed his fingers, working out the tension. "Thank you, sir."

"No time for wound licking, though. We here at the Old Jewry are made of sterner stuff. I insist you purchase yourself a new coat and move on with life." Ridley pivoted in his chair, wood creaking a complaint, and retrieved a fat file from a stack on the table behind him. "And in that vein, I have just the case to keep your mind occupied. A real heel pounder that ought to put your thoughts on other things." He held out the folder.

Jackson glanced at the file. Oh, what he wouldn't give to already be breathing in salty air aboard the ship bound for Africa. Anchoring his elbows to his sides, he met the chief's curious gaze. "Pardon, sir, but I must decline."

Immediately he widened his stance, fully expecting the parrot's "Hang 'im up, boys" to stab him between the shoulder blades.

But not so much as the ruffle of feathers disturbed the silence. All that filled the empty air was the thud of boots outside in the corridor and the sharp inhale of the chief inspector. "What did you say?"

It was a boom of thunder, not a question.

Jackson clenched his jaw. Despite the coming storm, he would face this as a man, not some sniveling milksop. He stepped closer and lifted his chin. "I am officially putting in my notice, sir. I have taken a new position and shall sail next week with the Earl of March as his bodyguard. I expect to be gone for a year."

"And do you also expect to resume your job here once you return?" The chief slapped down the file, the resounding *thwack* of it sharp as gunfire. "Because that will not be an option. One does not merely waltz in and out of an inspector position like some giddy debutante!"

Ridley's rant reverberated in Jackson's chest.

And still the parrot didn't squawk.

"I understand, sir." He clenched his hands to keep from swiping away the perspiration on his brow.

Ridley shook his head, not one of his slicked-back hairs daring to break rank. "You have put me in a bad position, Forge. How am I to replace you on such short notice?"

He shoved down a smile. Providing a suitable replacement might not only pacify but redirect Ridley's attention. And he had just the right man in mind. "If I could be so bold as to recommend Charles

Baggett, sir? He's a crack officer, already at level one. More than capable and highly dependable."

"That is what the superintendent said about you. Yet here you are, hardly five months into the job and already jumping ship. Do not presume to tell me this is all because of that skirt you were supposed to marry."

Fire ignited in his gut. Was that what men would think? That Kit had driven him to run away? As if that had anything to do with it! He'd considered the proposal *before* the wedding, not afterwards. Either way, he'd have been a fool to turn down such a lucrative offer.

"My departure is strictly for personal gain, sir. The earl was very persuasive monetarily. I assure you this has nothing to do with Miss Turner, my position, or my coworkers. Nor with you. You have been a fair-handed superior with whom it's been a pleasure to work."

"I should say so!"

Again, not one parroty peep screeched behind him. Jackson glanced over his shoulder. Shiny round eyes stared at him from the wood swing inside the cage, but the bird's beak didn't open. "Is something wrong with your parrot, sir?"

Instantly, the deep lines carved into Ridley's brow softened. The chief crossed to the cage, pulling a piece of dried apple from his pocket as he went. "Hear that, Dutchy?" He poked the treat through the bars. "Someone besides me misses your chatter."

He pivoted back to Jackson, gesturing towards the parrot. "Dutchy suffers from a minor lung infection. The veterinarian assures me my compatriot will be back to his talkative self in no time. I appreciate your concern, Forge. Very thoughtful of you."

Jackson gave a sharp nod. Why the deuce had he not thought of utilizing the chief's soft spot earlier?

Ridley strolled past him and once again held out the file. "Being you still have some time here, see how much headway you and Baggett can make on this."

Jackson accepted the packet while scrambling to hitch it to his next request. "I shall be happy to oversee the management of this case, sir, but there are a few loose ends on a pending matter I needs must tie up first."

"Oh? What matter?"

He clenched his jaw. Graybone would have his head on a platter if he breathed a word to Ridley. Though he hated to resort to such lowly tactics, some street-smart sleights of hand might be his only way out. Jackson tipped his head towards the parrot, redirecting the chief's gaze. "I shouldn't like to trouble you with the details, sir, with your parrot being ill and all."

Producing the already drawn-up request to exhume Mrs. Mann's body, Jackson flourished the paper in the air, once again diverting the chief's attention. "I merely need you to sign this disinterment form, as standard and trivial as it is."

Jackson fluttered the paper all the way to its resting place on the desk.

Then froze.

Egads!

Ridley's spectacles sat right next to the inkwell. If the man read the details on the form, he'd never approve the request to remove a body from such an illustrious graveyard. Jackson made to turn, then carefully knocked the glasses and a nearby book to the floor. "I beg your pardon, sir."

"What an oaf!" Ridley rumbled.

Blocking the man's view with his back, Jackson crouched and flicked the spectacles under the desk, retrieving only the worn copy of *Avian Lore*. He stepped away with what he hoped was a sheepish smile. "Indeed, sir. I am a bit off today. So, if you'll just sign, I will be gone and trouble you no more."

Scowling, Ridley scanned the desk, then patted his pockets before swinging back to Jackson. "I cannot seem to find my glasses. You shall have to wait for your warrant."

"I'm afraid haste is of the essence in this matter." He stabbed his finger on the signature line. "Just your name here, if you please, sir."

Ridley glanced at the document before glowering back up at him. "This is highly irregular, Forge."

"Simply trying to do my job to the best of my ability, sir, and I shall continue to do so until the day I sail."

A great snort puffed out the chief's nose. "I should hope so." Despite his obvious disdain, Ridley dipped the tip in ink and scratched his name.

The pen barely left the paper before Jackson snatched it away and instead held up the folder. "Thank you, sir. Now if you don't mind, I shall inform Officer Baggett he is to work on this case."

He was two steps to the door when Ridley's voice stopped him. "Hold it right there, Forge."

Gritting his teeth, Jackson swung back around. "Yes, sir?"

The chief strode over and plucked the file from his grip. "Send Baggett to my office. *I* shall inform him he is to work on this case."

He breathed lighter. That'd been close. "As you wish, sir."

Just before he shut the door, he'd swear to a magistrate that the parrot whisper-squawked, "Hang 'im up, boys. Hang 'im up." Jackson tugged his collar looser as he trotted down the stairs. Ridley really would have him hung if Mr. Mann found out he was on his way to dig up his dead first wife.

Somewhere between her bite of boiled cod and sip of cider, Kit knew. All the pieces of information she'd gathered from her father during supper, added with the snippets she'd already gleaned from Jackson, left her with no doubt. They were working on a case together—one that excluded her. The thought landed as hard and uncomfortable as the rough wooden pub chair on which she sat.

She laid down her fork, shutting out the background chatter in the taproom. "You met with Jackson on a Sunday in your own home. Why?"

Eyeing her, he took his time gnawing the meat off a mutton bone. "What are you going on about?"

"When the server first brought out your plate, you mumbled that the potatoes looked as green as Jackson's old coat."

He scooped up a forkful from the pile of mash sitting abandoned on one side of his dish and held it up. "Whoever stored these potatoes didn't take care to keep his vegetables in the dark. Only a fool or a beggar would risk such a bellyful of hurt."

"That is entirely beside the point. The fact is you couldn't have known Jackson was wearing his old coat any sooner than yesterday because that's when he started doing so. Furthermore"—she leaned closer, taking care not to upset her cider mug—"you also said you spent your entire Sunday with a pipe and a book. Hence, Jackson must have stopped off for some sort of meeting of the minds at your home."

"Bah." Her father's fork clattered to his plate, and he picked up his own mug, tossing back a hearty swallow before thudding it onto the table. "I believe we were speaking of your soup kitchen. I certainly hope your cook takes better care with the potatoes. It'd be a crime to add pain upon pain to those already suffering."

Did he really think to put her off so easily? "You and Jackson are working the same case. Which one? What are the details?"

He stabbed his finger towards her plate. "The only detail you need concern yourself with is finishing your supper."

"I am finished." She nudged the dish away. "I am also tired of being under Martha's feet at the soup kitchen. I was never meant to stir a pot of stew or bake loaves upon loaves of bread." She softened her gaze and pushed her lips into a smile. "Let me help you with whatever it is you're working on, Father. Chief Inspector Ridley tolerates me helping Jackson, but he'd never give me an assignment of my own. And what with Jackson, well. . .you know."

"Take heart, Daughter." Her father patted her arm. "Perhaps I can scrape together something for you to investigate or—here's a wild thought—maybe even help you start your own detective service. Why, I might even think of retiring from the force to join you in such a venture. In the meanwhile, it just may be that some time and space is for the best. I have no doubt Jackson will see the folly of his ways and return next year a changed man. . .though I admit I had hoped he'd make things right with you before setting sail."

She jerked up her chin, the information hitting her like a hammer to the head. She'd suspected Jackson was going somewhere, but for a whole year? "When does he leave?"

"Has he not told you?"

"Of all the ridiculous double standards! No, he most certainly has not." She balled up the napkin and slammed it onto the table, drawing a malignant eye from a nearby diner. Well, let him look. She had other scoundrels to worry about—namely Jackson Forge.

She shoved back her chair and stood. "It appears the man who expected me to share every blessed detail of my life could not be bothered to be held to the same standard. Pardon me, Father, but I believe I need some air."

Clutching her skirt, she whizzed past the other diners and fled outside, angry beyond reason—which irritated her even more. Truly, it should not have caught her so off guard that Jackson was skip-footing it to who-knew-where. But there had been that moment in the hack when he'd softened and thanked her for helping put the ghost of his past to rest. Those few words had given her hope that maybe God had heard her plea for reconciliation after all. Had it been a false hope? She choked back a sob as she stalked down the street, preferring the darkness between streetlights. Black suited her mood.

"Hold on, Kit."

Her father's voice boomed at her back, but she didn't slow, not a whit. She couldn't. Too much emotion bubbled inside now that she knew for certain Jackson was lost to her.

Strong fingers clutched her arm, forcing her to stop. She broke free of her father's hold and faced him. "I should like to go home, Father."

He sighed. "As you wish, but first, humour me. There is something I would like to show you."

"Father, I really don't think—"

He shot out his arm, crooked and at the ready for her to take it. "I wasn't asking."

There was iron in that voice, brooking no refusal. She grabbed his sleeve, annoyed yet unable to stop the slight curve of her lips. He was a determined bull, this man, set on having his own way. She was far too much like him.

Five blocks later, he released her with a low "Follow me." After a sideways glance down each side of the street, he ducked into an inky passageway.

What was her cagey father up to? She edged into the narrow space, her heels immediately sinking into some sort of muck. Drat. She should have worn her half boots instead of her shoes. Dampness leaked into her stockings, chilling her toes. Lifting each foot in turn, she gave them a good shake, not fully removing the scum, but it would have to do. She'd lost sight of Father. Squinting into the darkness, she vainly tried to make out the silhouette of his broad shoulders.

"Up here, girl."

The flash of a hand reached down towards her. Well, well. Not only was her father as determined as she but obviously as light on his feet as well.

His strong grip hoisted her up until her toes caught on the rungs of a wooden ladder. "I trust you are able to climb?"

She stifled a snort. The very hair on his head would rise if he knew half of the gutter pipes she'd scaled in her time. "I shouldn't think it will be a problem."

After a short ascent, he grunted over the top of a ledge, then once again aided her to do the same.

When she landed on solid ground—or roof, more like—she smoothed her skirts while her father pressed his back against a chimney and sank to sit. He patted the space beside him. "Come and see."

A smattering of curiosity shot holes into her earlier ire. Hiking her skirts, she dropped next to him.

"What are we looking at exactly? The missing shingles on the neighbouring roof or the heap of crumbled lime here by the flashing?" She brushed away fallen mortar chunks lest her gown take any more of a beating.

"Neither." His calloused fingers, rough and warm against the chill of the October evening, tipped her head to the heavens. "There. What do you see?"

She sighed, tiring of this child's game. Not that she didn't understand well enough he'd been trying to make up for lost time ever since he discovered she was his daughter. But this? Honestly, sometimes he treated her as if she were six years old.

She stared into the darkness. "I see a black sky."

"Then you are not as insightful as I credited," he grumbled.

That stung. She snapped her gaze to him, but the retort she'd intended melted away. Her father sat with his head tilted back and his eyes wide, a supreme look of peace softening the usual harsh lines near his temples.

"What do you see?" she wondered aloud.

"Hope," he said simply, then lifted his arm and pointed. "See that star right there?"

She followed the length of his arm, staring hard past the tip of his finger. Sure enough, a bright bead of light hung there in the blackness. "Yes, I see it."

"That's the one I railed against the night your grandfather told me your mother had died."

She scrunched her nose at him. "Why did you not rail against God?"

A small chuckle rumbled in his throat. "Never raise a fist against one who is more powerful than you. I should have thought you'd learned that lesson on the streets."

Indeed, she had, when as a chit of no more than seven she'd dared to cross words with a nine-year-old street sweeper who wielded an iron-hard broomstick—and she had the jagged scar on the back of her hand to prove it.

She scooted closer to her father, drawing from his warmth. "If, as you said, you ranted against that star, then how is it that now you see hope?"

For a long while he said nothing. The clopping of horse hooves pulling a carriage rolled by below them. A baby's wail leached out a window of the next-door building. Somewhere down on the streets, several men were in their cups, belting out a boisterous ditty. But all those noises sounded eerily small and far away from this rooftop island where she sat next to the father she hadn't realized she'd needed.

"I have learned," he said at length, "to look past the darkness of my anger and see the light of creation. To choose to think on the good my Creator has brought into my life rather than the hardships. Anger and bitterness are a choice. Either you may dwell on your losses or you may be grateful for what you have. I eventually learned to be grateful, and now I have you. You never know what gift God will birth out of the darkness, Daughter."

Warmth flared in her chest as he brushed his thumb across her cheek. Leaning her head against his shoulder, she peered up at her father's star, hoping to gain the same hope he owned. But the longer she stared, the heavier a scowl weighed on her brow. Her ruined marriage, Jackson's leaving, a career that seemed to be over almost before it began—none of that was a gift. She squeezed her eyes tight, shutting out the pinhole in the night sky.

Help me to see hope in the dark like my father does, Lord, because right now all I see is black.

Chapter Twenty-Five

A fine mist fell, cold as death and thick enough to merit an umbrella. Miserable, yet entirely apropos for a dreary afternoon in a cemetery. Jackson upped his pace down the aisle of ornate crypts clustered so closely together they looked like little beach houses of the departed. Embellished wrought-iron fences adorned several of them, which never did make any sense to him. It wasn't as if the bones next door were going to make a land grab, so what was the point?

"Hold up there, Forge." Baggett dashed towards him along the row of elaborate tombs, his black umbrella bobbing with each stride. "You're a slippery eel to catch lately."

"Just trying to finish this case." As soon as Baggett fell into step beside him, he slid his friend a sideways glance. "I'm assuming you didn't come all the way out here to admire the crypts."

"I have a few things for you. One fruitful, the other not so much."

"You might have left me a note at the station."

Baggett shrugged, cascades of little droplets falling from his coat to the gravel path. "You've not been at your desk for over a week."

"There is that, I suppose. All right, let's have the bad news first."

"I can find nothing on that umbrella attacker of yours. Not a name. Not any next of kin. Nothing."

Curious. Absently, Jackson gazed at the many names engraved on the tombstones they passed. How many of these poor souls had departed the earth with no one to mourn them? "So, the man is a ghost?"

"I suspect the man is a hired killer."

He shot Baggett a look. "How so?"

"His clothing was finely made, which means he had money, so he wasn't some desperate jake on a random killing spree. Besides that, most assassins take care to remain anonymous for the very purpose of leaving no trail for the law to follow should they get caught or killed."

"Who would hire someone to kill me?"

Baggett grinned, the tip of his nose turning red from the chill mist. "Kit."

"You must be jesting."

"Don't look so horrified, old man. I'm merely having a bit of sport." Baggett's grin faded. "But I do think you should make amends with her before you leave."

"You know I'm leaving?"

Baggett nodded, sending a shower of moisture from the brim of his hat onto his coat collar. "Ridley informed me of your upcoming departure when he briefed me on a new case. Which reminds me, thanks for the recommendation."

Jackson clapped his friend on the back. "You'll make a fine inspector."

"And you'll make for a miserable bodyguard if you do not reconcile with the woman you love."

Jackson gritted his teeth. Had his friend seriously come all the way to Kensal Green to lecture him about Kit? "You're as dogged as Graybone."

"I just hate to see you make the biggest mistake of your life." Baggett sniffled, his nose growing redder. "Remember that time we were going to rescue her from those thugs and she took one out with her knife before we could even pull our guns?"

He stifled a chuckle. "I do."

"And when she had the idea of hiding in a dragon costume in the Limehouse parade to gain intelligence on the opium den murders? Sheer brilliance."

This time he scowled. "You wouldn't think so if you'd had to be the backside of that dragon."

Baggett elbowed him. "But it solved the case, did it not?"

"What is your point, Baggett?"

The gravel crunching beneath their shoes was the only answer for quite a while, until at length his friend broke the silence. "Forgive me if this is too forward, but better I be forthright than regretful. It seems to me the very things you used to admire about Kit—her daring, quick thinking, bravery—are the same attributes you now eschew. Wildcats are not easily tamed, and honestly, would you truly want a domesticated Kit? I think you'd be unhappy, and she'd be resentful. You were never meant for a dull life, and neither is she. At least think on it."

"You even sound the same as Graybone." A disgusted sigh slipped out of him. "But yes, you—and he—have given me much to think on. For now, though, I have a grave to visit." Veering off the crushed stone walkway, Jackson tromped through the wet grass to where two men, thigh deep in a hole, hefted shovels.

A craggy-faced fellow peered up at their approach, the mist sluicing off his waxed-canvas coat like tears falling into the grave. How many decades had those gnarled fingers of his hefted a shovel?

"You the inspector?" His voice was as ancient as his wiry white eyebrows.

Jackson stopped a few paces from the upturned earth. "I am Inspector Forge, and this is Constable Baggett."

The digger leaned on his shovel. "We ought to be paid double for the bruisin' this one is. Ne'er seen a hole so fortified. Neither has Billy here. Right, Billy?" He hitched his thumb at the other filthy man shoveling in the mud.

Billy didn't so much as pause, just gave a sharp nod and kept right on eating up dirt a spadeful at a time.

Jackson scanned the gash in the earth. The rich scent of wet soil was thick on the air, as it should be. Nothing seemed out of the ordinary. "How is this grave any different than the others?"

The craggy digger pointed at a pile of metal rods heaped near the headstone. "This ground 'ere were fortified. Near to broke my shovel head when I hit the first bit o' iron, and that's the truth."

Jackson exchanged a look with Baggett, who appeared to be as clueless as himself. "Why would such reinforcements be installed?"

"Keeps out the likes o' the body snatchers, though judging by the date on the headstone, t'weren't necessary. This one 'ere"—he pounded the tip of his shovel into the ground a few times—"were put under during the big cholera scare of '61. No one willingly carts off the blue death. Regardless, some Joe dealt out a pretty penny to keep anyone from diggin' up this beauty. Right, Billy?"

Billy dipped another dutiful nod.

Interesting. Why would Mr. Mann—who'd admittedly bemoaned his financial woes during that time—have paid extra for such an extravagance?

"Thank you for the information. I shall pass it along." He turned back to Baggett. "Now then, what else do you have for me?"

"I thought to let you know that I found out who purchased the old Scampson Warehouse. Turns out it's a vicar—a Mr. Jacob Harpenny. No sooner did the man take up his position over at Cripplegate than he bought the property, a curious choice for a clergyman." Sniffling again, Baggett pulled a white handkerchief from his pocket and dabbed his nose.

Mr. Jacob Harpenny, vicar of Cripplegate, at your service, sir.

The introduction barreled back as did a mental visual of a balding man with a Cheshire grin. *He* bought the warehouse? "Why do you suppose a vicar would want to purchase a dilapidated old building?"

Baggett shook his head. "It is an oddity, I grant you, but who knows? Maybe the fellow has a grand scheme to house the poor or start a hospital."

"Would a vicar truly have such deep pockets?"

"I suppose that depends upon his family's wealth. It would be worth checking into. I'd do so for you, but that brings up the other reason I sought you out today."

Aha. Baggett hadn't gotten soaked to the teeth for him alone. Jackson arched a brow. "Which is?"

"That case Ridley handed me is as full of holes as a slab of fontina. I hardly know where to begin and yet the old man expects me to have a perpetrator in a pair of darbies by Friday. Friday!" He ground his heel into the damp ground. "You've worked with Ridley for some time now. Have you any advice for putting off the chief while carrying out an investigation?"

"Avoidance." A lot of Kit's savvy had rubbed off on him, and though it was hard to admit, he did truly owe her for all she had taught him. "Ridley can't dress you down if you're not at the station."

"Devious." Baggett cocked his head, an appreciative gleam in his eyes. "But clever."

A loud grunt and even louder "Put yer muscle into it, Billy!" drew both of their gazes to the diggers. Each man strained as they wrestled a coffin over the lip of the freshly dug pit. The muddy box finally came to rest atop the earth instead of below.

The older digger grabbed a pry bar from off the ground and worked his way around the top of the lid. With each ram of the bar and accompanying upward jolt, nails screeched like a summoned demon.

"Heave now, Billy!"

Despite the men's red faces and bulging muscles, the lid refused to budge.

Jackson glanced at Baggett. "Shall we?"

"Why not? I'm wet through anyway." He folded up his umbrella and set it down.

Jackson followed suit, and between the four of them, they worked off the cover and whumped it to the ground.

Billy let out a low whistle.

The older digger shook his head. "Well, that were a waste of iron bars."

Baggett's gaze shot from the casket to Jackson, questions in his keen brown eyes. And no wonder.

The coffin was empty.

Stretching over the railing of Blackfriars Bridge, Kit stared down into the murky water, letting drops of mist fall freely from her hair, her nose, her chin. Drip. Drip. Drip. After wandering the streets all day, she must look more bedraggled than a sewer rat, but she didn't care.

A shiver tickled along her shoulders, but she did not snug her coat tighter at the neck. In truth, she barely even registered it. Somewhere in a far corner of her mind, she knew she should go home and change into dry garments. Maybe then go to the soup kitchen and put her hands to work. She should do something—anything—other than stand here in such wretched weather and dwell on her father's words from last night.

. . .be grateful for what you have. . .be grateful. . .be grateful. . .be—

She wasn't. Not one little bit.

Gripping the railing, she lifted her face and roared at the leaden sky, no doubt drawing furrowed brows from those in the carriage rumbling behind her. So be it. What did she have to be grateful about? Not for the loss of a mother who'd hefted her skirts and flown off a bridge just like this one. Or was she to be thankful she'd ruined the one chance at marriage she'd likely ever have? And how exactly was she to appreciate that the only man she'd ever loved would soon flee the country—flee *her*?

A hostile laugh threatened to bubble up. She swallowed it. Anger and bitterness may be a choice as her father had said, but sorrow wasn't. No one ever chose woe, and she could no more shake the sadness settling deep in her soul than she could push back the clouds and stop the infernal mist from coating the world with a damp melancholy.

She gazed down at the water. Restless. Aimless. Hopeless. Was this how her mother had felt just before she'd jumped? Kit roughly shoved back a wet hank of hair from her brow. First her mother left her life. Now Jackson. Must she drive everyone to the water?

"Kit! Oh, Miss Kit!"

She glanced aside. A grey gown, draped over with a long black shawl, emerged from the brume. Martha dashed towards her, one hand pressed to her side as if a stitch needled her, and at the rate her feet scurried, no doubt it did.

"I been. . .whew!" Martha clutched the rail with one hand, bending double and catching her breath. "I been lookin' for ye."

Alarm instantly straightened Kit's backbone. Martha would never leave the kitchen unattended just before the supper rush. "What is it? What has happened?"

Red-rimmed eyes stared into hers. "It's my boy."

"Frankie? What's he done now?"

"I don't know where he is, and I'm that heartsore about it!" Martha cast a wild look about, as if the very act might make her boy miraculously appear. "I ne'er shoulda said the things I did. It's my fault. It's all my fault!" She pressed the back of her hand to her mouth, muting a ragged cry.

Kit glowered, doubting very much that Frank ran off because of his mother, for Martha was ever fair handed in the management of her children. Rather, she never should have given those thimblerig cups back to the boy. No, worse. She never should have trained him in the ways of the street.

She wrapped her arm around Martha's shoulders, shoring up the poor woman. "All right, my friend. Calm down. I am certain you are not to blame. Tell me what happened. Tell me everything."

"My Frankie and I had a row yesterday morn." Martha strangled fistfuls of her gown as she spoke. "Turns out the sly nipper weren't the helping hand for Mrs. Crocker that I believed him to be. I called him out on the matter quite harshly. Too harsh, I'm afraid. To his credit, he didn't deny his lacking service, but neither did he confess where he'd been spending his time. . .so I forbade him from leaving the house until I could sort things out." She wagged her head, a forlorn sight that tugged at Kit's heart.

"Oh, how I wish my husband were here," she wailed. "I need him! Frankie needs him. The lad ne'er woulda run off had he a father to face instead of me."

"Now, now, I'll have none of that." Kit gave her friend a little squeeze. "You've a nursling to manage, and your older girls require your time as well. You work dawn till dark and that after having barely recovered from the wasting sickness. I'd say you're doing a bang-up job with your brood."

"Maybe so, but that doesn't change the fact my boy didn't come home last night. And out on these streets, well. . ." Martha sucked in a choppy breath. "God help him."

Kit hid a shudder. God help him, indeed. She knew better than most the evils lurking about in London's back alleys, especially after dark. But she couldn't very well tell Martha that. Instead, she pinned on a smile. "God will help him, and so shall I. There are a few hidey-holes where he might have tucked off to. I'm sure I'll find him in no time."

A small spark of hope flickered in Martha's brown eyes. "I knew you'd be of help. Bless you, miss."

"Think nothing of it." She tugged her friend's shawl tighter about her shoulders, then brushed away the excess moisture. "Now off with you before you catch your death. I'll bring Frankie 'round to the kitchen, so have a bowl of soup or two ready, aye?"

Martha nodded. "Yer a gem, you are."

Kit strode the opposite way, fleeing her friend's kind words. She didn't feel like a gem—but no more time for floundering in self-pity. She had a chip-toothed rapscallion to locate. But first, some dry clothes were in order or her prophecy of illness for Martha would hairpin right back at her.

By the time she reached Mistress Mayhew's, the mist had thickened into a ghostly fog, lifting gooseflesh from one end of her body to the other. A lamp glowed in the boarding house's front window—the one where Mistress Mayhew took her tea. Drat. There'd be no hiding from the woman. If she waltzed through the front door dripping all over the runner, she'd waste a good fifteen minutes stiff-lipping it through one of the woman's lectures.

Leaving the gravel walkway, Kit dodged around the boxwood and picked her way along the side of the house, brushing her fingertips against the siding as she went. It was nearly impossible to see. When she hit the lilac bush, she felt around behind it for the stepping rock she kept hidden. She lugged the thing over to her bedroom window, then hoisted herself—and the sash—up.

Ahh. How good it felt to be out of that incessant bone-chilling dampness. The scent of supper lingered in the air, beefy, yeasty. . .stew and bread if she didn't miss her mark. She pressed a hand to her belly, beating back a ferocious growl. That chunk of cheese she'd snagged for lunch had been hours ago.

But no time for eating now, not when she'd promised to find Martha's little rapscallion. Kit lit the lamp on the stand next to the window, then turned.

And gasped.

A bloody-lipped boy perched on the end of her bed, one eye blackened nearly shut, the other gazing at her.

Chapter Twenty-Six

Evening slipped in like a drunkard having lost one shoe, teetering sideways and with a sour reek. Not surprising after such a damp day, but still annoying—which added to Jackson's foul mood. Paperwork at the station had delayed him all afternoon, but now—finally—he closed in on Mr. Mann's town house, where a hulk of a carriage crouched out front, the shape of the coach and the four black horses blurred by fog.

He made it to the carriage door just before Mr. Mann could reach for the handle. "Pardon me, but I would have a word with you, sir."

Though the glow from a nearby gas lamp was dismal at best, a distinct curl lifted the man's upper lip. "Step aside, Inspector. I have a meeting to attend."

"And I have a murder to solve—your wife's."

Little droplets collected on Mr. Mann's hat and shoulders, not one of them breaking rank. "You have apprehended the brigand who abducted Henrietta?"

"I believe I am looking at him right now."

The air turned noticeably colder, which could be blamed on the deepening murk, but down in Jackson's gut, he knew better. His words had hit home.

"Absurd!" Mr. Mann pounded the tip of his unopened umbrella against the pavement.

"Is it?" Jackson stepped closer, catching a whiff of the man's bay rum aftershave. "You have already admitted you kept a mistress while your first wife lived. What better motive to do away with Henrietta?

The question is, sir, how was Isabella Dalton involved?"

"I don't know what you are talking about." The queen's lions couldn't have growled any more ferociously.

Jackson reached for the man's arm. "Then allow me to enlighten you on our way to the station."

"I will do no such thing!" Mr. Mann wrenched away, rubbing at his sleeve as if it were tainted. "Five minutes, Forge. I shall give you that and nothing more." He stormed to his town house, the black tails of his coat swishing ominously.

Jackson caught up to the man just inside the foyer, where Mrs. Grady puckered her lips in confusion. "Back so soon, Mr. Mann? Shall I—"

"Nothing is required of you, Mrs. Grady," Mr. Mann barked as he stomped past her.

Jackson pulled off his hat, dipping his head at the wide-eyed housekeeper as he passed.

Mr. Mann barely took two strides into the sitting room before he wheeled about and jabbed his umbrella in the air like a bayonet. "You have crossed a line, Inspector."

Refusing to be drawn into a fight by the man's display of aggression, Jackson measured his gaze and his words. "As have you, sir. Your wife's grave is empty."

"How the devil would you know such a thing?"

"I had the casket exhumed earlier today."

Mr. Mann's umbrella dropped to the floor. His lips pressed into a line so thin and tight they'd have to be pried open. After a few nostril-flaring inhales and exhales, he stalked to the mantel, grabbing hold of the thing as if it were the horns of an altar. His head dropped, as did the timbre of his voice. "I wondered when that would come back to haunt me. Not that it matters anymore."

Jackson studied the fellow, from the taut fabric of his coat stretched across his shoulders to the slight quiver in the legs of his trousers. "Did you have your wife killed, Mr. Mann?"

The question hit like a branding iron. Mr. Mann spun, eyes wild, jaw clenched. "No, I most emphatically did not. Etta and I had our differences, but I swear I never paid anyone to harm her in any way."

Jackson spread his hands, inviting the fellow's full confidence. "Then how about the truth this time? Tell me what happened, sir. *Everything* that happened."

Mr. Mann aged visibly as he folded into a nearby chair. "It is much as I said." His words were so quiet Jackson stepped closer to hear.

"Etta was abducted," he continued. "A boy delivered the ransom note you yet have in your possession. I sent the payoff with my valet, who was murdered in an alley and the money taken. After that. . ." He shook his head. "My valet's body was recovered, but Henrietta's was not. I tried to find her. God knows I did."

His gaze suddenly burned into Jackson's. "There was nothing more I could do. The only way to make the whole affair go away without scandal was to allow the world to think Henrietta had died, as I had every reason to believe she had. Hence the grave. Yes, the ugly occurrence allowed me to marry my mistress, but I did not have Etta killed in order to do so."

Jackson edged his fingers along the brim of his hat, turning the wet felt round and round while he thought on all Mr. Mann had given him. The story was plausible—but was it true? He clenched his bowler, stopping the movement. "Why should I believe you? Better yet, why should the court believe you?"

"Because had I orchestrated such a crime, my own life would have been forfeit." Mr. Mann shot to his feet and, curling his fingers around his coat lapels, transformed back into the man of confidence.

Jackson narrowed his eyes. "How so?"

"I wasn't jesting when I told you the men whose funds I manage are powerful—more so than you can imagine." A mirthless chuckle escaped him. "They will stop at nothing to keep their questionable holdings private, including taking the life of the one who moves and hides their money without notice of the Crown. I know too much about the affairs of these men, and not one of them would suffer me to serve a stint in prison where many of their enemies now reside. Nor would they stand idly by if there were even so much as a chance of my books going public. So you see, Inspector, I may as well have signed my own death warrant as have had Henrietta murdered."

Mr. Mann fell silent, and in the quiet, Jackson studied him more carefully than ever. It was the thin space immediately following an alibi that counted most. The time when a flutter of an eyelid or a ripple of a lip gave away the falsity of a story. But through it all, Mr. Mann held steady, his dark eyes fixed on Jackson, his chest neither shrinking nor swelling with mock bravado. Perhaps he was speaking truth—which only served to sicken Jackson as much as if the man *had* done away with his wife. "How could you live with yourself all these years, not knowing what became of your wife?"

"Because the life I had with Henrietta was no life at all!" His voice ricocheted around the room. He drew in a great gulp of air, then another, until finally he calmed. "You may think me heartless, Mr. Forge, and perhaps I am, but while I am horrified at what sort of end Etta may have suffered, I did not miss her. There. I have been more than plain with you." He swiped his umbrella from off the floor. "Have you any further questions?"

Yes. Many. All of them slipping in through the closing gap of the door that was slowly shutting on Mr. Mann's having had anything to do with his wife's or Isabella Dalton's death.

Jackson clapped on his hat. "Not at the moment. I shall detain you no longer, Mr. Mann. Good evening."

Pivoting, Jackson strode to the door. He'd felt so certain Mann was to blame for that corpse he'd found, but now? He stepped out into the night, his preconceived notions curling away into the fog. All he had left was to question the new vicar in town, the one who'd happened to buy the wrong warehouse at the wrong time.

A lead so laughable, he might as well call it quits on the whole case right now.

A mouse. A frog. One time Kit had even been surprised to find a bandy-legged chicken clucking about in her bedroom. But never had she entered the confines of her private sanctuary to find a blood-smeared boy with a blackened eye whose rain-soaked clothes had dampened a circle into her counterpane. Worse, he smelled like a wet dog. Kit scrunched her nose.

"Oh, Frankie." It was more a sigh than words. Bending, she dabbed a moist cloth against the gash on the boy's lip. "What happened? And don't you dare keep anything back, understood?"

He nodded, then winced when his fat lip scraped against the cloth. She eased off a bit so he could speak.

"Jo and I were running a shell game." A slight lisp couched his words. To be expected, though, with the banger he'd taken to his mouth. "We made lots o' coin, taking from those what looked like they could afford to play."

A noble effort—yet it didn't ring true.

"The rich never play thimblerig." She went back to daubing off the dried blood, harder this time, working off the crusty bits.

"Ow!" Frankie pulled away and pressed his knuckles to his sore lip. "Din't say it were rich folk," he mumbled. "Said it were those what could afford it."

Stepping back from the boy, Kit scanned her handiwork—what she could see around his fist, at any rate—and chewed on the information he'd fed her. Save for the wealthy, the only other people walking around London with spare change jingling in their pockets were the chancers and cheats. And if that was indeed the clientele Frankie had been engaging, then the boy was lucky to have made it here with only these slight cuts and bruises.

She returned the cloth to the basin and wrung it out, turning the water pink. "You should know better than to swindle a swindler."

"Weren't no swindle about it. Me and Jo run a fair game."

She skewered him with a sharp look over her shoulder. "So why the split lip?"

"Made too much coin, I guess." He jumped off the bed, desperation shimmering in the one eye not swollen shut. "They took it all, Miss Kit. And they took Jo too."

Her brows bunched. "What do you mean they took Jo?"

"It's why I'm here. I saw where they tied up my friend. Ye gotta help Jo." He grabbed her arm and squeezed, driving home his point. "Ye just gotta!"

A tear leaked out his good eye. Kit brushed the drop away with the pad of her thumb, smearing dirt on his cheek. Such loyalty to a friend was rare—and heartwarming. "Don't fret, my boy. Think on what I taught you. What's the number one rule in a crisis?"

His lower lip quivered, drawing a fresh bead of blood from the gash now broken open. "Think and breathe," he said bravely.

"Good. Do so." Retrieving the cloth, she pressed the damp rag against his lip until the wildness in his gaze calmed down. She tossed the cloth back into the basin. "So, let's sort this out. Who are we dealing with, where can we find them, and why would your Jo have been taken?"

The toe of his shoe scuffed against the edge of the braided rug, curling it up from the floor. "Yer not gonna like it."

She flipped back the edge with her heel, then crooked her finger beneath Frankie's chin, forcing him to look up. "Like it or not, I would hear all."

Bosh! She sounded just like Jackson. And yet perhaps that wasn't such a bad thing.

Frankie's nostrils flared as if courage might be gathered in from thin air. "It were the Elephant and Castle gang."

"The Elephant Boys!" Kit whirled lest the lad see the grimace that would not be stopped. Of all the gangs to tangle with, it had to be that one? The Boys were the very reason she'd set up shop in Blackfriars, keeping her distance from the bloodthirsty mob. "Oh, Frankie. You should have known better."

"Knew ye weren't gonna like it, miss." Frankie's voice was impossibly small. "But they got my Jo, and you always say, 'Never leave a crew member behind.'"

She stared down at the bloodied water, a shiver creeping along her spine. It could've been worse—*much* worse—now that she knew with whom he'd crossed paths. "That's just it, Frankie. You shouldn't have a crew. You're nine years old."

"I'll be ten next week!" His foot stomped the floorboards.

Kit hid a smile. The little marauder had picked up many of her ways. "Well, what's done is done. And knowing the Boys, there's no time to waste. It's a good twenty-minute walk from here. You can fill me in on the way." She shoved open the window. Instantly, chill evening air swirled in on a waft of fog. "Out you go. Just give me a moment to put on some dry garments. I'll meet you in front."

He wasted no time fleeing into the gloom. Neither did she tarry in donning a fresh set of street clothes. They rendezvoused beneath the pole lamp just outside the boarding house, though in the drifts of grey mist, the light hovered hardly more than a foot from the globe.

She set off at a good clip, Frankie's legs pumping hard to keep up with her. "When did they take Jo?"

"Last night. We was about to close up when three o' the Boys come by and kicked over our crate. They were big."

Lowlifes. Calling out brute enforcers for a pair of kids collecting pennies on a street corner. She booted aside a broken bottle, crashing it against a wall. "What did the men look like?"

"Weren't men. Old enough fer chin hair, though, leastwise near as I could tell in the dark. The one I got away from had a pocked face." Sniffling, he dabbed his sleeve against his nose. "I shouldn'ta run though. I shoulda protected Jo. Tha's why I doubled back and followed 'em."

Kit glanced at the lad while they dodged around a rain barrel. Dampness already soaked into her coat. "What were the Boys after?"

"Money." Night shadows painted Frankie's bruised eye all the darker. "They took what we had but wanted the rest o' our stash. Thing is, we ain't got one. Jo and I gives our coins to the waifs o'er at the Buckle Street orphanage."

"You—what?" She stopped right there in the middle of Blackfriars Bridge and crouched eye level with the boy. Martha had been agonizing about the scandalous behaviour of her son when all along he'd been walking in the woman's own compassionate footsteps. Unless he was simply trying to tongue-wag his way out of her displeasure—a distinct possibility. "Do you mean to tell me you've been swindling the swindlers and giving the profits to the poor? And I will have the truth, young man, nothing more or less."

She swallowed. She really *did* sound like Jackson. Was this truly how hard it was to get information out of her? Guilt swirled through her gut. No wonder he had become so angry with her for withholding information, after having to extract the truth from her like this time after time. The man had more patience than she had credited.

"Aye, Miss Kit." Frankie bobbed his head. "Jo and I were just tryin' to be like you and Mr. Forge."

Her heart warmed—then instantly chilled. The boy had no idea of what a fine line it was to walk between the worlds of justice and injustice, crime and law keeping. . .truth and deception.

"I see." She straightened, brushing the excess fog droplets from her sleeves. "So, from what I've gathered, the Elephant Boys are trying to break your Jo for the location of your earnings, but there is no location, for you've given it all away. Is that the sum of it?"

His big brown eyes blinked, innocent as a newborn calf. "Aye, miss."

At the passing of a hackney, she pulled Frankie aside, avoiding the back splash of wet muck from the wheels. "Where is your friend being held?"

Hat askew from the sudden movement, Frankie jammed his flat-cap lower on his brow. "Jo's in the back room of the Lowry Street pawnshop. When I left nigh on an hour ago, only one of the Boys was there—the one I wriggled away from. Heard the others was goin' to get more muscle."

"Likely one of their elders, which means we have no time to waste." She grabbed his hand. "Come on."

As they dashed down one bleak lane after another, Kit formulated a plan then discarded it, time and again, until she finally decided on the one most likely to work. And the most dangerous. Especially for Frankie. No doubt Jackson would scoff at such a wild scheme—yet how many times had he gone along with her harebrained ideas anyway?

Arriving on Lowry Street, they split up to inspect the pawnshop, peering in windows, listening at the back door, until Kit was satisfied there was only one Elephant Boy guarding Jo. Kit stopped at the corner of the building, halting Frankie with a touch to his shoulder. "Are you sure you wish to go through with this?"

"'Course I do." A lopsided smile slanted his wounded mouth. Brave boy!

"Very well. May God go with us."

"And be with Jo," he added.

She smiled in full. "Amen."

Grabbing a fistful of his collar, she hauled him to the front door. With one hand, she pounded on the wooden frame, rattling the glass panes. With her other hand, she yanked Frankie upwards, the tips of his toes barely grazing the wet pavement. Her arm shook with the effort. My, but he'd grown. Hopefully, this wouldn't take long.

Moments later, lamplight appeared inside the shop, bouncing macabre shadows on the shelving as a young man strode from the back room. The second he opened the door, Kit donned her street persona.

"I got something 'ere ye might want, luv." She tipped her head down at the boy, then shoved him behind her and shot out her palm. "But the kipper will cost ye a coin or two."

The young thug's gaze scuffed along her outstretched hand. He was a gangly limbed boy-man, his cheeks pocked with scars and pimples. He might have fifteen or sixteen years on him, if that. He was well-dressed, though. The Boys always were a dapper lot. Lantern light sliced along the edge of his chin, sharp as the blade Kit slowly reached for behind her back.

"Yer a bold doxie." He barked a harsh laugh. "What's to stop me from just taking that prize?"

"This." She whipped out her knife, the cool hilt of it molding against her fingers.

The thug spit at her feet, the splatter of it tainting her hem. "You think I'm a'feared of a wench with a pocketknife?"

"You should be."

Before he could so much as blink, Kit sliced the fellow on the arm, then crouched, ready to spring and really do some damage if need be.

A roar ripped out of him. He thwunked his lantern on a nearby shelf and pressed his hand against the gash. Murder flashed in his dark eyes. "Why, I ought to—"

"My offer is time sensitive, luv. Do you want this nipper or not?" She gave the thug another peek at Frankie.

The young man's upper lip curled, lifting the shadow of a sprouting moustache. "How much?"

Kit cocked her head. "How much is he worth to ye?"

"Half a crown," he snarled. "Nothing more."

She held still one moment to make him think she was considering the offer, two to make him sweat a bit, and three just because. "Deal. But it's wet as a dog's jowls out here. I'll do me business inside, luv."

"Demanding little harpy, aren't ye?" He spit again, this time a direct hit on her skirt. Nevertheless, he stood aside. "But put that knife away or there'll be a price on yer head."

"As ye wish." She made a dramatic sweep of her hand to her waistband, but instead slid the blade up her sleeve. Grabbing hold of Frankie's collar once again, she yanked him inside so harshly, he stumbled. Regrettable but necessary.

The second the door closed, she winked at Frankie. His turn now.

He shrieked like a stuck pig. Flailing his arms. Kicking his legs. A little froth at the mouth and one would lock him up at Bedlam.

The thug wheeled about from the door. "Get that boy under control!"

Kit gave a few dramatic flails of her own. "I can't hold 'im."

And with that, she let the lad loose.

Frankie tore off, sweeping his arms along the shelves, clattering merchandise to the floor. Shattering clockfaces. Denting pewter mugs. Books and brushes and candles went flying. Kit secreted a smile. The boy was quite a tempest.

A string of profanity untwined from the young man as he charged after Frankie. As soon as he passed by Kit, she snatched out her knife and walloped him on the head. He pivoted, teetering for a few breaths before his eyes rolled back. His body crashed to the floor with a hearty *whump*.

She nudged him with her toe just to make sure he was well and truly out. "Sorry, lad. I daresay you'll have quite the headache when you wake."

Frankie flung open the door to the back room and raced over to his friend, who sat tied to a chair in the middle of the room. Nose bloody. Coat torn. Defiant green eyes blazing despite the bruised brow and cut chin.

And long, golden hair hanging loose about her shoulders.

Kit swallowed. Sweet heavens. Frankie had not been embellishing when he'd said he and his friend wished to be like her and Jackson.

For Jo—Johanna, more like—was a girl.

Chapter Twenty-Seven

"You will have no milk?"

The woman's question hung like a noose in the quiet of Reverend Harpenny's front sitting room. Jackson tugged at his collar, annoyed he felt the need to do so. She was a slip of a lady, fine-boned and white-haired. She lived in a cloud of lavender perfume and a neatly buttoned green gown, but even so, the stern set of her jaw said she'd have no trouble whatsoever giving a scar-faced knuckle-buster a good go-around should she wish.

Jackson covered his cup with his hand, feeling like a giant holding such a delicate piece of porcelain, which was quite the expense for a clergyman. "No, thank you, madam. I take my tea black."

Mrs. Harpenny's face remained placid, but he got the distinct impression she judged him as soundly as a magistrate. Just one more of the shortcomings he suspected she'd already gathered into quite a collection, keeping them on a hidden shelf next to the jars where she stored other people's deficiencies.

Lips pinched, she set down the creamer and picked up the teapot, pouring another serving for the vicar. "My Jacob says it is milk which whitens the sins of such a black brew." She handed the cup to her son. "Do you not, Jacob?"

"Yes, Mother." He waited while she added a splash of milk before shifting on the sofa—a Chippendale if Jackson didn't miss his mark. "Now then, Inspector, to what do we owe this visit? Are you in need of spiritual counseling?"

"No, no. Nothing of the sort." Jackson set down his cup, done with the preliminaries. "Just a few questions. I was surprised to discover you are the new owner of the Scampson Warehouse. I am curious as to why—"

"Did you know, Inspector, that my son's congregation has already grown by eight new parishioners?" Mrs. Harpenny sank onto the sofa next to her son, beaming at him. "And those numbers in merely the past fortnight."

A deep flush spread up the reverend's neck. "Mother, I hardly think the inspector is interested in a tally of the attendance at Cripplegate."

Hah! No wonder the thirty-something fellow was not yet married. He had no need with the way his mother doted on him.

Jackson straightened the left cuff on his new suit coat. "Your mother is proud of your accomplishments, Vicar, which brings me to my point. What do you intend to accomplish with the old Scampson warehouse?"

"For now, a simple tear down. I shouldn't like to see anyone hurt in such a derelict building." After one more sip of his tea, the reverend set his cup on the knee-high table at center. "After that, I hope to find financial backing to establish housing for the poor."

Mrs. Harpenny patted her son's knee, her leathery skin speaking of a hardscrabble life, which was quite the contrast to the exquisitely decorated sitting room. "There is no finer clergyman in all of London than you see here, Inspector."

This time the flush spread past the vicar's neck to his face. He tugged his own collar. "Mother, please. Praise our Lord, not me."

Jackson rubbed his jaw. All was as it should be. The devoted mother. The God-fearing son. Far too perfect. Which one of them was playacting? Both?

He dropped his hand, conviction settling in his gut. How cynical he'd become. "Yours is an ambitious plan, Mr. Harpenny, for one so new to the area. There are plenty of other buildings that would not have first required demolition."

"Yes, but not in that area. The place holds a certain charm. You see, Inspector, my mother and I are originally from there and—"

"Oh! The sandwiches. What an error." Mrs. Harpenny shot up in a waft of lavender and hustled over to a bell pull. Hardly a breath later, a white-aproned serving woman entered and dipped a slight curtsy.

"Our guest has not yet been served," the vicar's mother instructed.

Immediately, the woman retrieved a silver platter of sandwiches from a marble-topped sideboard and offered it to Jackson.

His gut turned. Little round cucumber slices sat atop bread slathered with butter. Just the thought of biting into one of those green demons made him reach for his cup. "Thank you, but tea is quite enough."

"I insist, Inspector." Mrs. Harpenny rapped her finger on the tea table. "They are Cook's specialty."

Interesting. Thus far he'd been greeted by a butler, served by a housemaid, and now to find out they also employed a cook? One would think the Harpennys were Grosvenor Square neighbours to the earl. If, as the vicar had said, they were from this area, how could they afford such niceties?

The reverend's eyebrows rose. "Is something wrong, Inspector?"

"Not at all." Forcing a smile, Jackson took the smallest sandwich possible—then quickly set it down and rose. It wasn't scrupulous, this sleight of hand with a finger sandwich, but better a swindle than a cucumber in the mouth.

"This may be of no consequence, but I wonder if either of you might be able to identify this woman." He pulled out the watercolour of Henrietta Mann. A smaller slip of paper came out along with it and fluttered to the floor. Blast! He never should have put the ransom note in the same pocket as the picture. He reached for it.

The vicar beat him to it. "I believe you dropped. . ."

The man's words faded as he stared at the note. He held it out, the paper quivering between his fingers. "Well, here you are."

"Jacob? You look positively grey." Mrs. Harpenny rushed to his side, attempting to press her palm against his brow.

He ducked away. "I am fine, Mother."

Jackson shoved the note into his coat and held out the image of Henrietta Mann. "Do either of you recognize this lady?"

The reverend's eyes widened slightly, and though Jackson couldn't be certain, it sounded as if the man whispered, "The lady in red."

Real or not, Jackson jumped on the lead. "So, you do know her?"

Harpenny bent over the image. "I cannot be sure, but—"

"Oh, do have a sandwich, Jacob." His mother nudged him away as she plucked the picture from Jackson's grasp. "Let me have a look."

She held the image an inch from her nose, her gaze sweeping over Henrietta Mann with a noncommittal *humph*. At length, she offered the picture back to Jackson. "I am sorry, Inspector, but this woman is not familiar in the least. Furthermore—oh, dear."

The older lady pressed the back of her hand to her forehead and sank into a nearby chair.

"Mrs. Harpenny?"

"Mother?"

They rushed to her side, the vicar snatching up her free hand and patting it, Jackson fanning her with a napkin.

Mrs. Harpenny appeared to be in good colour, but even so, Jackson asked, "Shall I ring for a physician?"

"No need." Her gaze flicked to his. "Just feeling a bit faint is all."

Her son shook his head. "I told you you've been overdoing it, Mother. I insist you take a rest. Despite your protest, I think we ought to send for a doctor."

His mother snagged his sleeve and tugged him back. "Don't trouble yourself, dear." She shifted to face Jackson. "If you wouldn't mind, Inspector, I should like my son to see me to my room now."

"Yes, madam. Fully understandable. I wish you the best of health. Vicar. Mrs. Harpenny." He dipped his head at each in turn. "Good day to you both."

He strode from the room, leaving behind the ailing woman, the horrid cucumber sandwich, and the vicar who knew Mrs. Henrietta Mann. And more than likely, so did Mrs. Harpenny.

First a bloody-lipped boy in her room. Now this. Pausing on the threshold, Kit frowned at the sleeping girl on her bed, her nose swollen, her cheek bruised, and a slicer of a gash on her jaw that Kit had hastily sewn last evening. She may as well hang a hospital shingle over her door.

Carefully balancing a pot of tea and platter of fresh scones, Kit pushed the door shut with her toe, then padded over to the dressing table and set down the tray. The battered Johanna had already slept through breakfast and lunch—which was just as well. Kit had needed the time to think up a plan. The girl had no home. No parents. No family whatsoever. Leastwise that's the story Johanna had fed Martha last night when Kit had brought her and Frankie to the Jones's household. True or not, the girl couldn't stay here. Mistress Mayhew would toss them both out, for the woman most emphatically and repeatedly told all her boarders, "No men. No strays. And above all, no children."

Kit glanced at the ceiling, ignoring the eerie crack in the plaster that always reminded her of a giant spider.

Well Lord, this is an interesting turn. What am I to do with a street waif?

Though she listened, no answer came. But what was she expecting? A lightning bolt with a note skewered onto the end? Puffing her cheeks, she blew out a sigh—and heard an accompanying creak of the bedsprings behind her.

She whirled to see eyes green as a cat's staring at her from the pillow. She relaxed her shoulders. "Well, well. . . I was beginning to wonder if you'd ever wake."

Johanna's gaze drifted from her to take in the small bedroom. "Where am I?"

"Don't remember, eh? Not surprising, what with those blows to your head. You're a scrapper, I'll give you that." Kit poured a cup of tea and set it on the nightstand. "You are currently residing at Mistress Mayhew's Boarding and School of Deportment—though old Mayhew doesn't know you're here and I doubt you care a fig about your deportment."

Kit winked as she set about fluffing the pillows behind Johanna's head so the girl could sit up.

Johanna winced as she dragged her rake-thin body upright. "Yer really Kit Turner?"

"Yes, we established that last night." Kit pressed her fingers to the girl's brow. "No fever, which is good, but your lack of memory worries me."

"I'll be fine."

Kit grinned. The girl had grit, just as she'd had at her age. Retrieving the cup, she offered it to Johanna. "No doubt in time you shall be fine. For now, let's get some tea into you."

The girl chugged down the whole blessed cup then held it out for more.

Grit indeed.

"What do you remember?" Kit returned to the dressing table for a refill.

Johanna thrust out her bottom lip. "A few ugly blighters thinkin' they could best me. But I din't sing for 'em. Not a word. I'm no tipster."

"Brave girl. I see now why Frankie took up with you." Kit set a scone on a plate, then thought better of it and brought the entire tray over to the nightstand.

She'd barely set it down when Johanna grabbed a pastry in each hand. The girl grunted while she ate, that slice on her jaw more than likely stinging something fierce. Not that it stopped her, though. The girl had learned to compartmentalize—a trait that either made or broke a street urchin.

Kit brushed crumbs from the counterpane. "What about afterwards? I brought you to Frankie's home before coming here. Do you remember that?"

"Aye." Johanna swallowed a huge mouthful. "Frankie's mum still rankled?"

"She has every right to be. You and Frankie ought not have been operating on the sly like you did."

Anger flashed in the girl's green eyes. "It were for the orphans."

Kit shifted on the mattress, admiration for the girl building. She knew that fire. The same craving to help the downtrodden burned in her own veins. But Johanna could hardly be more than eleven or twelve years of age. She had no idea of the dangers on the streets for a girl on the cusp of womanhood—or maybe she did and ignored them. Either way, Kit wouldn't allow this girl to hold hands with such hazard.

She took the empty plate from the girl's lap and set it aside. "I understand your desire to help those in need. I truly do. But I may have a less dangerous proposition for you that will accomplish the same purpose."

"I ain't no soup kitchen drudge." The girl's pointy little jaw jutted. "And neither are you."

Kit laughed. "On that we are agreed."

Wariness lived in that green gaze. Unblinking. Unvarnished. Not astounding, really, considering this girl had likely been propositioned before—and those offers would have been dripping with lust or greed.

"What's yer game, miss?"

The question prodded Kit to rise. She didn't actually have a plan yet, not fully.

She rummaged through her wardrobe, searching for one of her old romping skirts while studiously avoiding the paper-wrapped wedding gown. "I am working out the finer details of a proposal I am sure you will not turn down. You may trust that I have your best interests in mind, and it does not involve dishing up cabbage stew."

Aha. There it was. Kit pulled out her trusty brown-striped gown. "Now then, let's get you into some proper garments and dash off before Mistress Mayhew sticks her nose in the door."

The girl was surprisingly modest, asking Kit to turn about as she slipped out of bed and donned the skirt. Moments later, she sucked in a breath.

Kit whirled. "Are you all right?"

Johanna stared in the mirror, twisting this way and that. "This feels... well. . .I can hardly believe it." She shook her head, her blonde hair wagging. "I look like a girl, but this gown feels as if I could shimmy up a drainpipe or skip-scab through a gutter grate."

Gratification sent a flush of warmth to Kit's cheeks. Not just any girl would appreciate a gown modified by unorthodox nips and tucks. "You're not far off." She straightened the girl's collar. "I reconfigure all my garments for ease of movement. A girl never knows when she must fleet-foot it from a bad situation, eh?"

She may as well have been a reigning warrior returning from a victory, so much hero worship radiated from Johanna's eyes. "Will ye teach me?"

"In time." She turned the girl about. "Now then, how about we put those skirts to work and dodge out the window?"

Johanna's brow scrunched. "Where are we going?"

"To some old friends of mine. I sent word to Mr. and Mrs. Card, and they are happy to take you in until I arrange for a better situation."

Johanna averted her gaze. "I dunno. . ."

"It's a warm bed and a full belly each night."

The girl snapped her face back to Kit. "Why?"

"Why what?"

Sudden tears shimmered in Johanna's eyes. "Why ye bein' so good to me?"

Kit's heart melted at the show of emotion, yet at the same time an itchy sort of discomfort crept up her backbone. The girl was getting too attached to her. She could feel it. And that would never do for two loners who faced the world on their own terms. "Only God is good, love. Thank Him, not me. You ready?"

Johanna nodded.

In a trice, they slipped out the window and joined the early evening throng of shift workers on their way home. In this neighbourhood, most wore patched coats in varying shades of dirty dishwater, but as they passed a fellow in smart sky-blue trousers and a green-checkered overcoat, Kit's steps slowed. There was nothing wrong with the man. Not overtly. But something was off. Kit glanced over her shoulder. Indeed. That off-beat gait and slightly crooked spine were familiar.

"Wait here," she instructed Johanna as she doubled back. "Excuse me!"

When the fellow turned, she knew. "You're one of the sifters over at the dust yard."

"Mebbe. Mebbe not." The old fellow squinted at her a moment before his eyes widened. "Why, I knows you. Yer the dust girl what got the hi-ho from Dedfield."

Kit nodded. "You still work there?"

"Do I!" He elbowed her. "The pickin's is better than ever, a small trinket here, a dented dainty there. Adds up. One more piece and I'll be outta there for good, long as no one calls me out a'fore that."

That explained the man's new garments, but how? And who? If Sackett hadn't been the linchpin for the thieving ring, then who was?

"Could you help me get back in on it?" she asked.

"Sorry, ducky." The man shook his head. "Ain't worth the risk."

"But if I did manage to get inside, you wouldn't squeal, would you?"

"I'm no piglet." He chuckled.

"Good man. I'll be seeing you, then." She tipped her head and strode back to Johanna, thoughts rattling like a runaway carriage.

Such a return visit would have to be in disguise—*and* be sanctioned by the chief himself lest she find herself on the wrong side of the law. She glanced over at Johanna, who gazed up at her. Bother. What a time to have a pseudo protégé looking to her as a role model.

"This way." She turned onto the narrow lane where the Cards' flat slanted lopsided. With Johanna taken care of for now, she could easily meet with the chief tomorrow. . .though there would be nothing easy about it. Chief Inspector Ridley would not be pleased to reopen a case he'd already officially closed.

And he especially wouldn't like that she'd dare to enter his manly realm without Jackson as a buffer.

Chapter Twenty-Eight

Of all the banes of existence, paperwork had to be foremost. Jackson sat at his desk, wallowing in misery as he flipped through marriage records, glad for once he'd been shoved into a back corner. Behind him, the pulse of the station thrummed with constables—men he'd rather not encounter. The great wedding debacle was still too fresh.

Focusing on the job at hand, he ran his finger down a column of surnames, scanning for Harpenny.

Haggeth.

Halbert.

Hatterly.

He slammed the ledger shut. That did it. He'd gone through two decades of the St. Giles parish registry without a Harpenny to be found. . .which either meant Mrs. Agnes Harpenny had married in a different parish or hadn't legally married at all—which wouldn't be a stretch. Most residents in that area didn't bother with such legalities, choosing instead to spend the registration fee on a pint of gin.

Jackson returned the ledger to the big box on the floor and whumped a different fat book onto the desk, jiggling loose a lip-curling odour of sweat and despair. The embossed title was scuffed flat in places, making the *Newgate Prison Register 1860–1880* nearly impossible to read. Hopefully, the inside pages would be more legible.

A rumbling laugh drew near. Another joined in. If he darted off now, he'd most certainly garner the attention he'd been hoping to avoid. Nothing for it, then. He face-planted his head atop folded arms, feigning sleep.

"Would you look at that?" The footsteps paused at his back. "Forge. Haven't seen him in a while."

"To be expected." A different voice this time. Tinnier and slightly scraping to the ear. Dennison, if Jackson wasn't mistaken.

Dennison continued, "You heard, din't ye?"

"Aye, the whole station did. Poor sot. Quite the gutting, being stood up like that. It's either drink it off or sleep it off, I suppose. Cheaper this way, at least."

The footsteps thudded into action once more, passing near Jackson's elbow.

"It's a rare sorrow when a woman bests you. The ol' bloke took quite the blow. Kit Turner marked him, and that's a fact." Dennison's voice faded.

The sting of his words didn't.

Glowering, Jackson flipped open the record book with more force than necessary. Better to bury himself in the monotony of name scanning than to revisit the festering wound in his heart. Yes, Kit had hurt him—marked him, as Dennison said. But a layer below that hurt all the words of admonition from Baggett and Graybone had taken root. He ought to make things right between him and Kit before sailing off for a year...but how to go about doing so when the very thought of it chafed?

Chuffing a low breath, he paged through the ledger and started scanning name after name under the year 1875. By the time he made it to 1870, he couldn't stop yawning. At 1865, his eyes drooped, heavy with sleep. Perhaps a little shut-eye on the desktop was a good idea. He toyed with the idea as his gaze slid from name to name, then promptly forgot all about it when he hit 1862. Eagerly, he ran his finger along a line of interest. This could be it, but he re-read the faded ink just to be sure.

> *Reuben Harpenny. Theft. Died April*
> *1862, Gaol Fever.*
> *Effects: broken pocket watch,*
> *bone-handled pocketknife, two pence.*
> *Released to Agnes Sallow.*

Lacing his fingers behind his head, Jackson closed his eyes. Might the good Reverend Jacob Harpenny have been born out of wedlock to a convict and a liar? Quite the contradiction to his current lot in life, what with all his fine furniture, impeccable clothing, and a house employing three servants. The average St. Giles resident would never be able to afford such luxuries. Then there was the whole matter of Cambridge or Oxford tuition—which was not cheap. Unless there was a rich uncle somewhere in the picture, the numbers didn't add up. Had the reverend—then a boy—and his mother been involved with the Mann abduction and somehow ended up with the ransom money?

Jackson yanked the ransom note from his pocket and smoothed it out on the desktop. Between the misspellings and poor penmanship, this note might very well have been written by a child or an uneducated adult.

"There you are, Forge. Didn't think you'd actually be here." Constable Cullimore—a snub-nosed monkey of a man—stood at his elbow.

Dash it. He should've been paying better attention. Jackson dipped his head. "Cullimore."

"Heard you were a bit upended about the whole, well. . .you know." Cullimore cuffed him on the arm. "But don't let that guttersnipe get you down. Such a skirt weren't worth your time, anyway. We all thought you could do better than a Blackfriars' street rat."

Jackson's hands instantly curled into fists, the urge to flatten Cullimore's pug nose rushing through his veins. Kit was many things—fearless, headstrong, defiant—but beneath it all, she was still a lady. "Did you want something, Constable?"

"Oh, yes." Cullimore held out a slip of paper. "Just dropping off this message for you. Smitty's out of commission. His ankle's swelled up, purple as a plum. Took a tumble down a staircase. One too many mugs at the pub if you ask me." The constable waggled his eyebrows. "The flow of paperwork will be sluggish at best for the next several days, I imagine."

"Thank you." Jackson snatched the note. "Now if you'll excuse me, I am in the middle of something. Good day."

"More like good night now. The evening shift is about to come on." Another cuff on the shoulder. "But good to see you back in the thick of things, Forge. Cheers."

Jackson waited until Cullimore's blue coat rounded the corner, then unfolded the note. Capital letters scrawled across the middle of the page, all in unfamiliar handwriting.

TODAY
POLK ALLEY FLATS #2
6:00 PM
THE MAN YOU'VE BEEN LOOKING FOR

He flipped it over. Blank. No name. No signature. Clever place to meet, though. The entire four block area of Polk Street was slated to be demolished tomorrow. No one would chance being there tonight... save for someone wishing for a clandestine meeting. But who would give him a tip-off of the umbrella man's identity? If indeed that's what this was about.

Only one way to find out.

Pulling his pocket watch from his waistcoat, he opened the lid. 5:35. Thunderation! How long had Cullimore been sitting on this note?

Jackson jammed his hat on his head, then snatched his coat from the back of his chair. Lastly, he seized his umbrella and dashed out of the station into the chill of early evening.

And bowled right into Kit.

She teetered one way. He the other. Both grabbing the other's arms for balance.

Kit frowned up into his face. "You should look where you're going, Inspector."

"And you shouldn't be loitering in front of the station door." He released her, the scent of her rose water perfume sending a rush of heat through his body. "What are you doing here, anyway?"

"Not that it signifies, but I was pondering the best way to approach the chief." She swung her hand towards the station. "He's not left for the night, has he?"

Jackson snorted. Ridley was notoriously cantankerous by the end of the day. He'd eat her like a kipper snack. "As far as I know he is still in his office. He doesn't usually leave until the new shift arrives. But why the deuce would you want to—" He pressed his mouth shut. This was none of his concern. *She* was none of his concern—even though he still yearned to make her so. The thought nearly knocked him over. Despite all the hurt she had caused him, all the betrayal he still felt, he yet wished to actually make her his concern. But now was not the time to figure out what to do with that. All that mattered was making it to Polk Alley. He dipped his head stiffly towards her. "Good luck."

He strode away, flexing his fingers, trying to shake the memory of how good Kit had felt to his touch.

Light footsteps scurried at his back, coming fast, catching up. "Actually"—Kit blinked at him—"now that I think on it, a little insider information would be helpful. What is the best way to handle Ridley?"

Jackson crossed the street, long-legging it, unwilling to waste any more time and miss meeting with the informant—if it was an informant.

Kit trotted along beside him, lips twisted into a smirk. "Surely you won't pass up the opportunity to tell me what to do, Inspector."

His lips started to twist into a smile. How he had missed her sharp wit! No one else could parry words like Kit, for good—or for ill. His smile flattened. "My best advice is to avoid the chief at all costs. It was the superintendent who wanted you working with me, not Ridley."

Her voice lowered. "Only the superintendent?"

Was that a hint of hurt behind her words? Jackson shook his head. "I never objected to working with you. I objected to you taking unnecessary risks."

"Unnecessary risks?" Kit's eyes rolled, the whites stark against the dark of the early evening. "Like what? Walking across the street?"

Jackson bristled. "Like putting yourself in dangerous situations with no backup."

"Really? Are you going to start that again?"

He veered left, swinging onto a narrower lane, half-hoping Kit would turn around and leave him be, the other half of him enjoying the familiarity of her stride matching his. "What are you talking about? Start what again?"

"You know. That thing you do." She circled her fingers in the air. "The *oh-the-dainty-little-trivet-might-get-broken* routine." Kit stepped over a pile of fallen shingles, kicking one so hard it skittered into the gutter. "I never asked for your protection, Jackson."

And she never would. The sharp-clawed kitten was far too proud for her own good. He shook his head, muttering, "Asked for or not, that's what you do for someone you love."

Kit's steps stopped, and he strode ahead without her, immediately missing her presence at his side. But that was for the best. He again turned, this time leaving behind the streetlamps of the main thoroughfare.

Kit came pattering up then, and again that annoying flare of admiration for her determination resurfaced.

"Back to the point, Jackson. I should like some inside information on how to persuade Ridley. You've dealt with the man. What is his Achilles heel? Flattery? Boldness? A pocket full of treats for his parrot?"

He hunched against the barrage of questions. "Even were I inclined to tell you, I really don't have the time for this. I'm sure you'll think of something."

"No doubt I will, but it would be faster if you simply told me what works best for you so I can employ the same tactic."

"I don't have a tactic. You're on your own, which is usually how you like it, is it not?" The moment the acerbic words slipped his tongue, he winced. True or not, she didn't deserve that. It wasn't her fault she'd had only herself to depend on for so many years. Still, Jackson had hoped that she had started to change, had begun to see him as a partner she could depend on. But leopards cannot change their spots, so why had he expected otherwise of Kit? He swallowed the fresh wave of grief and tipped his hat at her. "And here is where we part ways, Miss Turner. I've a meeting to attend. Good evening."

He stalked into the shadows until he hit a wall of roughly sawn wood. Each board carried a warning. DANGER. KEEP OUT. NO TRESPASSING. All in red paint with some of the letters dripping like blood. Either the painter had been overzealous or in a hurry. Using his umbrella as a pry bar, Jackson began systematically removing board after board.

"This is quite a dubious place to meet." Kit's voice bounced off his back in the narrow channel. "Even dangerous, especially without backup."

He yanked off one last board, clearing a space just large enough to wedge his body through. "Go home, Kit."

Without so much as a glance at her, he dove in, his shoulders scraping against splinters as he shimmied through the hole. On the other side lay an empty road, or more of a pathway, really. The whole place was a graveyard of buildings, lit only by the pale light of a waxing moon. Each tenement leaned into another, bowing over what used to be a residential street. It was pungent here. Hundreds of years of humanity pressed into such a tiny space had a way of imprinting the breath and death of thousands of people. The only thing living here now, though, were feral cats and rats—until tomorrow, when it all would go up in smoke and rubble.

His boots crunched against broken glass. Footsteps behind him did the same.

Sighing, Jackson stopped in front of a half-hung sign dangling in the night. The faded letters of POLK STREET ALLEY were barely legible in the rising moonlight. It had to be close on 6:00. Kit had to go, dogged woman, but she'd only do so with some sort of bone.

So, facing her, he tossed her one. "Ask Ridley about his parrot. He dotes on the thing. Your concern will earn you an unbiased moment of his time, but that is all you'll have, so speak your piece and get out. The man has little patience for me. He will have none for you."

Kit jutted her jaw. "Perhaps he would if you had seen fit to include me on the briefings when we were working together."

"Sour grapes ill become you."

"What's the difference?" She popped her fists onto her hips. "You've made it very clear you do not find me attractive anymore, anyway."

Oh, but she couldn't be more wrong. Even here in the shadowy ruins of a dead neighbourhood, she was a beauty with her blue eyes blazing in the moonlight. The curves of her body filled out her gown in ways he shouldn't notice. . .but he did. An undeniable bond yet tethered him to her, heating his belly, rushing in his ears.

"You got what you wanted, so go." He stalked into the darkness, not stopping until the thin drain of a passageway opened into a miniscule courtyard. Squinting, he scanned from door to door, trying to locate flat number two while holding his breath against the stink of coal gas wafting out of an open door. Gas? That could be dangerous if—

Skirts swished behind him.

Jackson gritted his teeth. Would the woman never give up?

"Kit!" He wheeled about, a growl vibrating in his throat. "I said go—"

His admonition died the second a spare flash of moonlight glinted on the blade in her hand. Instantly he scanned the area, the hair on the nape of his neck bristling.

Yet nothing but shadows threatened.

"What are you doing?" he whispered harshly.

Kit's gaze bounced from corner to corner. "Protecting you."

"From what?"

"Shh!" She shot up her hand, wide-eyed. "Do you hear that?"

He frowned. What sort of game was she playing now? "What are you talking about?"

She angled her head. "A shooshing noise. Listen."

He stilled. Inside the tenements, water dripped. A faint gurgle rumbled in his stomach, having missed lunch and breakfast. Claws scratched. Bat wings flapped. Other than that. . .

Nothing.

This was silly. He had a meeting to attend! He opened his mouth—then as quickly shut it when a high-pitched *hissss* caught his attention. A leaking boiler, perhaps. But here? In this abandoned collection of broken-down buildings?

"I also heard footsteps," Kit whispered. "And I don't like the sound or smell of a broken gas line. Shouldn't the gas be shut off? Whom did you say you're meeting?"

"I was hoping to find that out when—"

Gravel crunched at the opposite end of the passage. Could be his informant. Jackson stepped in front of Kit, blocking her. "Who's there? Who summoned me?"

Kit's arm shot out at his side, pointing down the dark passage. "Looks like God did."

Jackson narrowed his eyes, straining to see past the blackness to the dim grey at the end. Sure enough, a clergyman in an ankle-length cassock and a pox veil rose from a crouching position. A tiny pinpoint of light flashed at his feet, burning in a straight line towards them. The man disappeared. The burning line sizzled closer. If he didn't know any better, he'd say that was a—Lord, have mercy!

He grabbed Kit's arm. "Run!"

They tore off. Fled past the fuse. Legs pumping hard. Fast. Not fast enough.

The world exploded.

Chapter Twenty-Nine

Black. Everything was black. And oh, Kit was so tired of darkness. Of gloom and murk and shadows. Would she never escape such a pitch-painted world? She should try, she supposed, but her arms wouldn't move. Neither would her legs.

She swallowed.

Why did she not feel her legs?

A scream burned in her throat. Lodged sideways. Prickled. Poked. She'd give anything to drink some air. Soothe the pain. Release the awful weight pressing on her chest like a pile of stones. But though she tried, her lungs refused to work.

Somewhere an annoying alarm buzzed. The piercing sound wriggled in her ear like a worm and crawled about, driving her mad. Was that it, then? *Had* she gone mad? It would explain the rocking motion. The back and forth, back and forth.

Or perhaps she was in the arms of God.

A beautiful thought.

She gave in to the invisible strength cradling her. Limp and broken, she was more than ready for eternal rest. Yes, what a blessing to finally be at peace.

"Kit."

She startled. Of all the ways she'd imagined God's voice, never once had she supposed it to be so scratchy and ragged.

"Kit, please. Come back to me. I can bear anything but this. *Never* this!"

Anguish ran hot through the words. The voice was not God's but a man's—a frantic man. One who sounded as if lightning had struck and burned the heart right out of his chest, leaving his soul an ash heap.

She strained to lift her head. She should say something. Try to bring some sort of comfort. No one deserved to suffer such torment all alone.

"Oh, my love. Don't go."

Warm breath feathered against her cheek. She nestled into it, drawing life, gaining fortitude.

"Kit?"

Slowly, her eyelids fluttered open. The world emerged from black to grey to the brilliant blue of a worried gaze fixed on her. She pressed her palm against the battered cheek of a man who looked as if he'd been lost and wandering on a battlefield.

"Jackson," she whispered.

"I thought you were—" A shudder ran through his arms. Jackson's eyes glassed over with tears, and he swallowed, again and again. "Are you all right?"

She pushed her lips into a small smile, the vigor of life returning stronger and more fully with every breath. "I'm fine."

"Thunder and turf, Kit." A dark scowl creased his brow. "You are not *fine*. You've been out cold so long I thought you were dead."

Her grin grew. "So, you do care about me."

"Of course I care." He settled her at his side instead of holding her in his lap—quite the feat in the pile of rubble where they sat. "My loyalty was never in question. You're the one who stood me up, remember?"

She shoved back her, then winced as her fingers grazed against an abrasion. "How could I forget with you always reminding me?"

A sigh huffed out of him. "Now is not the time." He rose, broken bricks and pulverized mortar crunching beneath his boots. Dust particles hung thick in the air, coating Jackson's torn coat, falling from his sleeve as his big hand shot down towards her. "If you truly are as fine as you say, then let's get out of here."

She stared at his blackened knuckles, pride tempting her to refuse the offer, a sore body and an aching head arguing otherwise. She put her hand in his.

Glass ground with each step as they attempted to scale a huge pile of wreckage. She tripped, bloodying her hand on a board with nails sticking out.

Before she could even wince, Jackson led her back to the bottom, grumbling all the way. "We cannot safely climb such a treacherous heap. Besides, even cresting it won't get us anywhere but higher up in this mess. We've got to find another way."

He ducked under a rat's nest of jagged timber and entered a dark tunnel of building debris—a route that ended in a wall.

Frustrated, Kit banged her good fist against it, matching the beat of the horrid throbbing in her skull. "Someone? Anyone? Help us!"

"Hollering won't do any good." Jackson pulled her back. "If we cannot hear the sounds of life outside of this neighbourhood, then no one will hear us."

An ugly truth, but he was right. She shook out her hand. "Have you a better idea?"

"Let's try another direction. Perhaps if we work our way back towards where the blast originated, a different route might appear."

Carefully, they retraced their steps through the wooden tunnel. Someone had certainly gone to great lengths to put an end to the lawman in the ripped coat and torn trousers ahead of her. "What did you do to enrage a vicar so heartily that he's keen on blowing you to kingdom come?"

"I got too close to the truth." Jackson stooped under a beam.

"The truth of what?"

He flung a broken board out of their way with more force than necessary. "It's none of your concern."

"It is now." She frowned up at him, scowling as darkly as the soot smudged on his nose.

"I didn't ask you to tag along, Kit."

She stopped dead in her tracks. Of all the ungrateful things to say! "You're the one that said it was reckless to go to dangerous places without backup." Hiking her skirt, she sidestepped a tangle of rusted metal and caught up to him. "And it's a good thing I followed you or you never would have heard the break in the gas line. You'd have run headlong into that building and been blown to bits."

"I'm sure I would have heard it."

"Are you?"

"This is absurd. No matter which one of us is right, it's a moot point now anyway." Grunting, he heaved a splintered timber from their path—only to face another mountain of powdery plaster, jagged glass, metal rods, and more planks with treacherous nails poking out like the thorns in the Saviour's crown. "I'll shove aside what I can and hand you the larger pieces to pitch."

Without waiting for her to answer, he bent to the task.

Kit thought aloud as he intermittently passed her chunks that weren't so easily batted away. "Let me guess...the vicar sent you a note to meet in this out-of-the-way place, and you walked right into his trap."

He handed her a broken cylinder of clay pipe. "Your commentary is not helping the matter."

She chucked the pipe like a javelin, squeezing her eyes shut as the movement increased her headache. "Then you do the talking. I suspect this all has something to do with your poking about for information on Xanadu."

"Originally, I didn't think so. But now..."

"Why did you have me identify her? What is she tied into?"

For a while he said nothing, just kept sweeping aside rubbish, until finally his voice blended with the scrape of his sleeve against debris. "There was a woman—Henrietta Mann—who was abducted and murdered twenty-four years ago. I thought perhaps her husband had done away with her for the sake of the woman you call Xanadu, but I was wrong."

"Are you saying a vicar is responsible for such a heinous crime?"

"He wasn't a vicar back then." Jackson glanced over his shoulder, pausing his labour. "Tell me, have you ever known a boy of eleven or twelve to commit a murder?"

She nudged away pottery shards with her toe. "I can do you one better. I knew a nine-year-old who slipped rat poison in his father's ale. No mercy was shown the lad for his tender age when he stood trial, either. The judge said it is the amount of wickedness in a heart that makes a murderer, not how many years you've walked the earth."

"Interesting." Jackson dug back into the pile with more vigor.

Interesting, indeed. Absently, Kit rubbed an ache in her shoulder. "I assume, then, that it is Henrietta Mann I discovered in the Scampson Warehouse."

"It is, or rather it was."

"And that's the case you've been working on."

Again he said nothing, which confirmed her deduction—but made absolutely no sense as to why he'd been so clamp-lipped about the whole thing. "I was the one who found the body, so why all the secrecy?"

"It's complicated." Jackson hoisted a big rock from the pile with a grunt. He threw it hard, landing the thing with a resounding crash-thud—and stared at it for just a beat too long.

A diversion tactic? Had Jackson, perhaps, gleaned more from her than she'd realized?

She eyed him. "There is something you're not telling me."

He arched a brow, the smug twist of his lips as annoying as the throbbing in her temples. "So now you know how it feels, eh?"

"That's not fair."

"No? Why is it somehow all right for you to withhold information from me, yet when I do the very same it is unjust?"

Such a truth smarted. Still, she lifted her chin. "I am not withholding anything from you."

"Maybe not now, but you have in the past." Even by the spare light of the moon, hurt flashed visibly in his eyes. "Which is why I no longer trust you."

She swiped at her nose, feigning a cough from all the dust, anything to keep from sobbing at the loss of this man's good graces. Better to put her mind—and his—on the trouble at hand.

"If this vicar killed Henrietta Mann, then I fail to see how or why the case must be hidden from me unless. . ." She kicked a part of a windowsill out of the way as she added up all the pieces of information she'd collected. "This murder was twenty-four years ago, down by the river—the exact time frame and place where my mother's body was found." She sucked in a breath, suddenly short of air. "This has something to do with my mother, doesn't it?"

Jackson kept digging, moonlight stretching across the flex of his broad shoulders.

Kit propped her hand onto her hips. "Doesn't it!"

He stilled, his voice low. "I never said that."

"You don't have to. Is this vicar responsible for my mother's death as well? Is that what you and my father have been keeping from me?"

Rising, he reached for her, pulling her close enough to read the sincerity in his eyes. "I don't know about that, but I do know this. Your father and I only ever wanted to spare you from any further hurt on your mother's behalf."

There he went again, trying to order her world into how it should be instead of what it was. A noble gesture, to be sure, but after so many years on her own, it still chafed. "I am not a wounded bird to be swaddled and protected, Jackson. Life is pain. You cannot shield me from that."

"Would that I could." His shoulders sank. There was something spent about him, something older, something worn.

And she knew in her very marrow that she was the cause. Her pride was the cause. Oh, that she had heeded Martha's advice about humility sooner! There was nothing she could do about the past, but now? She stepped tentatively towards him, rested a hand on his shoulder, and forced out perhaps the two hardest words of her life. "Thank you."

His head jerked up. "For what?"

"For *wanting* to protect me. I just wish. . ." She bit her lip.

"Wish what?" His gaze burned into hers. "What do you wish for, Kit?"

Dare she be honest with him? But how could she ever hope to win his trust again if she wasn't? "I wish you would have chosen to walk with me through the pain rather than trying to shield me from it." Pulling away from him, she dug into the rubble. "And I wish to get out of here. I have a vicar to speak with. Ouch!"

She shoved her torn-open knuckle into her mouth, sucking away the blood while digging all the harder with her other hand.

A strong grip eased her backwards. "It's not doing any good. We can dig all night in this pile and still not make it through. We've got to find another way."

"Like what? We can't just fly out of here. These piles are too high and dangerous." She swept her hand to the sky, her gaze following the action—and snagging on a paper-wrapped cable attached to the side of a wall that yet stood. Something wasn't right about that line. She squinted. Indeed, it was too symmetrical for such a ramshackle neighbourhood. Newly placed, by the looks of it. But for what purpose?

"What's that?" She pointed.

Jackson's gaze followed her gesture. Too much debris blocked his path to climb up for a good look, but apparently he didn't need an up-close inspection. A flush darkened his face. "Dash it!"

He scrambled over another pile, gazing up. Then another. And another.

Kit followed, asking him time after time, "What is it?" or "What do you see?"

He said nothing. Absolutely nothing. And no wonder, for the tight line of his mouth wouldn't let a single syllable squeak through.

She grabbed his sleeve. "Jackson, you're scaring me."

"You should be." His nostrils flared as his chest heaved. He hitched his thumb over his shoulder. "Those are charging lines. This whole place is wired for demolition. Kit, if we don't get out of here by sunrise when this neighbourhood is slated for destruction, we'll go down with the rest of these buildings."

Chapter Thirty

Jackson stared at the moon, eagle-eyeing how much longer he and Kit would have to draw breath. Three hours—maybe. Could be less. He'd scoffed at Father's old-fashioned ways of reading the sky when he should have paid attention. Stupid youth. . .stupider man. Why had he run headlong into this disaster? He swiped the grit off his face, annoyed with the situation and even more so with himself.

Beside him, Kit grumbled an oath as she shook the dust from her skirts. "I knew this place was to be torn down, but with explosives? I've never heard of such a thing."

"Not many have. A few years ago, some engineer over in Hungary used dynamite blasts to fell a two-hundred-foot chimney." He scanned the nearest wall for a way out. "The developer of this wretched area intends to do the same but on a larger scale. It's a fool's game, if you ask me, trying such a novelty this close to the population."

"But if, as you say, these buildings are already prepared to explode, why didn't the blast set off the whole thing?"

He shook his head; the very same question had been nettling him for some time. "I don't know. Maybe it was a loose connection. Or perhaps one of their staggered detonations was misplaced. Who knows? The vicar may have even purposely rerouted the charge line to ensure his own escape before it blew. Whatever the reason, though, I believe God had a hand in it, leastwise the sparing of our lives."

"Agreed. And being He has spared us, surely He does not intend to abandon us here. We must trust—and look for another way out."

He stared at her, astonishment and admiration blending so thoroughly that he could savor the sweet taste. "You've changed, you know."

She scrunched her nose, all rabbity and adorable despite the scrape on her cheek and grime on her face. "What do you mean?"

"The swindler I once knew lived by her wits alone, charging ahead on her own instead of trusting for provision."

"Sometimes she still does, more often than she ought, to the pain of those who care about her." She looked at him, almost pleadingly, if the moonlight and shadows weren't playing tricks on him. "But anyone can change, Jackson. By God's grace, who we are today is not who we will become."

His breath caught, something stirring in his chest. Hope perhaps? Because a woman who had learned to trust God could not be wholly untrustworthy, could she? He edged near, brushing a hair away from her brow. "Who are you and what have you done with Kit Turner?"

"Pish." She dropped her gaze, hiding her luminous blue eyes from his sight. "I'm naught but a pile of dust if we don't get out of here. So, while we wait for the Almighty to intervene, we've got to try to find another way out."

He tore his gaze from the soft curve of her cheek to the elements of their prison. Where solid walls didn't hem them in, mountains of jagged debris did. No matter which way they turned, they were trapped. Peril on one side, ruin on the other. Hanging his head, he rubbed the back of his neck, thinking, praying, desperate for a way of escape. He focused on his shoes, the thick coating of dust, the littered earth beneath that, and. . .now hold on. That might work—leastwise it was something they'd not yet tried.

He shot his gaze to Kit. "I cannot believe what I'm about to say, but since we've already tried climbing up and digging through to no avail, that leaves us no choice but to go under."

She tipped her head to a rakish angle. "Well, well. It appears you have changed as well, sir. As I recall, you weren't an enthusiast for underground tunnels."

Better a crawl through a mucky sewer pipe than being blown to bits. He coughed, lungs rattling, cementing his decision. "In this instance, there's no place I'd rather be."

Her lips curved in a dirt-crusted grin. "Well then, let's find a sewer grate."

"You pinpoint the spot, I'll do the grunt work." He swept out his hand. "After you."

Kit grabbed a thin board and began poking about, step by step. "I am curious about one thing, and I would appreciate your true thoughts on the matter." She glanced at him, the whites of her eyes stark against the dirt on her face. "Do you think my mother was murdered?"

The question was as charged as the detonating lines above their heads. Yea or nay, he suspected neither answer would satisfy her. No matter. He hadn't drawn a definitive conclusion anyway. "Honestly, I don't know. We only have one body on our hands, Henrietta Mann."

"Then what made you suspect my mother was somehow connected?"

He grabbed his own stick and started poking, avoiding eye contact. "Remember the locket you found? It belonged to your mother."

"My—" Her prodding-pole clattered to the ground. "Are you saying that at first you thought those bones were my mother's? How could you have possibly kept that from me?"

And here it was, the reckoning he'd known deep down in his soul he'd have to one day face. He jammed his stick into a pile of broken wreckage and met Kit's fierce gaze head-on. "Your father thought it best—and I agreed—that until we had more information, you didn't need to know."

"That's a ripe one!" she spluttered. "And you complained about me withholding information? First you refuse to tell your father about who I am—really am—and then you hide this from me? Seriously, Jackson! It's enough to make me wonder why I should trust *you*."

Her accusation struck him in the chest, and instantly a dozen justifications launched to his lips. Yet even while preparing his defense, he realized in every situation he was about to cite she had also done something to prove why he should trust her, except for the wedding itself. And now knowing everything about why she missed that. . .well. Perhaps he had been too quick to jump to conclusions. And anger.

Besides, she had a point—a very good point.

A sigh ripped out of him. "You're right, Kit. We should have told you. But the skeleton wasn't your mother, so are you not the least little bit thankful you were spared the anguish of thinking it was?"

"I suppose so," she mumbled after a long moment, and then she eyed him. "But how did my mother's locket end up on Mrs. Mann's body?"

He shook his head. "That part remains a mystery."

"Until we question the vicar."

There she went again, assuming he'd so much as let her near that vicar. He opened his mouth to correct her—that he would be the one doing the questioning—then thought better of it. He retrieved his stick. It was her mother they were talking about, and it might not be bad to have Kit along; she could distract Mrs. Harpenny—alias Agnes Sallow—during the interview. If he could convince her to keep her knife sheathed, that is. Interrogation of a vicar at knifepoint. Wouldn't the chief love that? Which reminded him. . .

"Why are you wanting to meet with Ridley anyway? What sort of new scheme are you cooking up now?"

"Something old, actually." She ground the tip of her pole into the debris. "A return to Dedfield's Dust Yard is in order. Turns out that theft ring we thought we solved is still in operation."

"I've wondered about that ever since I went back to question Dedfield." He paused. "What makes you say so now?"

"I ran into that old shoveler, who confirmed it."

"But the foreman—Sackett—committed suicide. If that's not an admission of guilt, I don't know what is."

Bending nearly double, Kit ran her hand through the gravel, shoving it aside as she spoke. "Maybe he didn't take his own life."

"He was in jail, Kit. Alone in a cell. There's no way someone else strung him up, unless. . ." A vicar in a pox veil visited the cell just before Sackett hung—and now a vicar in a pox veil just tried to blow him to smithereens. Coincidence?

"Never rule out any possibility based on mere assumption." Kit spoke as if she'd read his mind. "Want to give me a hand here?"

Dropping his pole, he began digging alongside her. "Speaking of assumptions, I suppose you intend to single-handedly resolve the case?"

"Someone has to do it."

"True, but. . ." He stopped digging and faced her. "Why are you seeking out Ridley's blessing on the matter? That's not like you. Kit Turner charges ahead and asks for forgiveness later."

She lifted her pert little nose. "Maybe I've mended my ways."

True, she might have, but more than likely that wasn't all there was to it. What would compel her to—aha! He smirked at her. "You need Ridley to supply backup, don't you?"

She shoved a hank of hair behind her ear—a dead giveaway he truly was getting only half the truth. "I'm just used to working in a crew, is all."

"Mm-hmm. And if Ridley doesn't agree? Or worse, he orders you to stand down from the case? But that's not what you really fear, is it? You're afraid he'll boot you from the force once I'm—" He clamped his mouth tight. Thunderation! He'd nearly given away his own plans.

"Once you're what?" she prodded.

"Nothing." He started digging with a vengeance, cramming all manner of slivers and sand beneath his nails.

"When were you going to tell me, Jackson? Or didn't you plan to?"

He froze. "Tell you what?"

"That you're leaving. For a whole year." Her voice ran colder than ice water over his head. "You could at least have the decency to own up to it."

His heart seized. He should have known. If the scamp in a skirt wanted to find something out, a steam train couldn't stop her.

But how to tell her the truth without shattering his own heart into a million shards?

Kit sank back on her haunches, studying Jackson's face in what spare light remained from the moon. It would be daylight soon. The desire to escape pulsed strong through her veins, but the need to know the truth of where, why, and when Jackson was leaving was a craving that would not be denied.

He didn't so much as look at her as he started paddling away great handfuls of gravel like a dog in the dirt.

She poked him in the arm. "Well?"

A gusty sigh deflated his shoulders, and finally he gave her the courtesy of facing her. "Yes, if you must know. I am leaving."

Though she'd already known so, his admission carved a hole in her chest, right where her heart had once beat. "Where are you going?"

His blue eyes stared into her own, first the left, then the right, as if he weighed and sifted not only how much information to tell her but how she would react.

"Africa," he said at length.

She sucked in a breath, stunned. "Africa? Why not the North Pole?" She flapped her arms. "Why not fly straight to the blessed moon if you must put so much space between us?"

"Come on, Kit. You're being overly dramatic."

"I'm being dramatic? *I* am? I'm not the one who booked a ticket away from civilization all for the sake of wounded pride." She shot to her feet and paced in a tight circle. "When do you leave?"

He rose as well, his big frame blocking her path. "Three days."

She shook her head, completely unhinged. Unmoored.

Unloved.

Tears burned her eyes. "You truly can't get far enough away from me fast enough, can you?" Even to herself, her voice sounded impossibly small. "I know I made a muck of things, but for you to hate me that much. . .did you ever love me?"

His jaw clenched. "I'm not the one who—"

"Who stood you up. So you keep telling me. But at least I'm here now. You're the one fleeing to the farthest reaches of civilization to get away, not even bothering to try to make amends." So many emotions assaulted her at once, she grabbed on to the one that felt safest. . .fury. Her hands curled into fists. "Or is that the whole problem? I'm not good enough? Not good enough to present before Ridley. Not good enough to tell your father about. Not good enough. . .for you?"

She held her breath, fearing—yet needing—the answer.

Jackson reached for her, but inches from contact, his hand fell away. "It's not like that, not at all."

Another evasion tactic. . .or truth? She studied him, hard. "Then what is it like, Jackson? What am I to think?"

"You are to think that I was presented an opportunity I dared not turn down. The Earl of March approached me before the. . . Before we. . ." He shook his head. "Well, it doesn't matter when. He offered me a job as his personal guard during his year abroad. The wages are more than I'll ever see here in London, a small fortune, actually. So, I accepted. That's all there is to it." He reached for the board he'd used as a shovel and scraped it around in the rubble. "A business deal, nothing more."

She gaped. "You mean to say this business deal was proposed before our wedding and you didn't bother to tell me? You didn't even ask what I might think of the matter? Unbelievable." She whirled, lest he see her pain. This was too much—entirely too much.

"It wasn't worth mentioning because I didn't seriously consider it. There was no way I'd part from my wife—from you—having just been married. I wouldn't do that." The crash of his board hit the wreckage yards away.

She fumed a moment more until his words soaked in. He wouldn't have parted from her, not even for a great sum of wealth, the sentiment of which did much to water the hard ground in her heart. Many a man would have jumped at the chance. Slowly, she rubbed her arms. Perhaps she had thought the worst of him instead of the best.

She whirled about, facing him. "Fair enough, but you still should have told me. Part of loving someone is sharing events, no matter how big or small. I know that now. And I sincerely hope you do too."

He held up both hands. "You're right. It seems we both committed the same crime, for which—to your credit—you have already apologized. And. . . I suspect it is time I do the same." He lifted his chin, holding her gaze. "I'm sorry, Kit. I'm sorry for not telling you. I'm sorry for—" His voice broke, chipping off yet another piece of her heart. "Well, I'm sorry for the way things are. I never imagined it would turn out like this."

"Neither did I." She turned then, head hanging, not quite able to face him anymore. Too much sorrow and regret pressed in on her from all sides, as real and ragged as the ruined buildings around her. "I never meant to hurt you, Jackson."

"I know," he breathed.

He said no more, just grabbed another board and scuffed the

ground with the end of it, the gravelly noise sharp. She deserved this, his silence. She was the one who'd let him down. Flit! She'd let herself down with her own bullheadedness.

His board clattered to the ground behind her. "I cannot bear the thought of leaving you with this dark cloud between us. I was a cad; I admit it. I wallowed in my own hurt while totally ignoring your feelings. Will you—can you—forgive me?"

Her heart skipped a beat, hope flaring anew. Barely breathing, she wheeled about, pressing her hands to her chest while melting at the sight of repentance in his eyes. "Of course I forgive you." How could she not? She loved him to the very marrow of her bones. "Do you think we—do you think *I* could start over? That things could change between us? Please, can we try?"

His fingers flexed at his side, an entirely new sort of grief stiffening his body. "I don't know, Kit. Forgiveness is one thing, trust quite another. How can we try when there is no trust?"

She advanced, tripping on a bent iron rod and stumbling against him. His strong grip righted her as she peered up at him, thankful to God for the last bit of moonlight to plead her case. Surely Jackson must see the sincerity in her gaze.

Oh, God, please, make him see.

"I will earn back your trust, Jackson. Give me a test—any test— and I'll prove it."

The muscles in his arms quaked with strain as he set her from him. "Trust is not a carnival trinket to be given as a prize for winning a game." He raked his fingers through his hair, a shower of ash and dirt raining down on his shoulders. "You cannot force such a thing. It won't work."

"But I have changed, Jackson. You said so yourself." She flailed her arms. "I told you the whole truth about the club. I didn't hold anything back about why I want to meet with Ridley. I admit I have blundered in the past, but can you not see that I am trying to mend my ways? Can you not give me a second chance?"

He closed his eyes. No, more than that. He scrunched them shut. Tight. Stars and banners! Had she finally pushed him to his breaking point?

Then just like that, his eyelids flicked open, his eyes gleaming with a love so pure she sucked in a breath. "I shall try, Kit. For you, for us, I vow I will try to trust again."

"Thank you, Jackson, I. . ." She looked away, suddenly shy, unsure of just about everything save for the single truth pulsing through her veins. "I still love you."

Gently, he guided her face to his, the touch of his calloused fingers on her chin so warm and strong she could weep. Or was it the heat in his eyes that touched her so? The bend of his brow? The quiver of his lips.

"I shall always love you, Kit. Trust or not, there will never be another woman for me."

The air between them charged. Sizzled. Exploded when he pulled her to him and his mouth burned against hers.

And just like that, she was whole again. She would always be whole in this man's arms. Grabbing great handfuls of his coat, she clung to him, tasting his familiar flavor of cloves and spice, sweet and bitter. A tremor ran the length of her, settling low in her belly when Jackson trailed kisses down her neck. She could live here, in this moment, *needed* to live here.

Needed him.

A deep moan escaped her.

Releasing his hold, Jackson stepped back, chest heaving. The loss of his touch was more than she could bear. How could she possibly live without him for a full year?

"Don't go to Africa." Desperation thickened her voice. "Stay here and let's try again."

His smile faded, and even in the dark, she could see the pain etched into the grime on his brow. Whatever he had to say would cost him. "I wish I could. But I promised the earl. I have to go."

"Then maybe I can—"

"Go with? I already tried. He's adamant. No females." He swiped his brow with the back of his hand, leaving a smear of soot, then met her gaze, tentative, as if he were afraid she would now reject him. "But would you meet me at the dock on Monday? Be there to say goodbye?"

Rot! That's exactly what she *didn't* want to do. She'd much rather sneak aboard and prove to this earl how ridiculous his rule was. But her defiance of Jackson's wishes was exactly what had landed her in this kettle of fish in the first place. She lifted her chin. "Yes, I shall be there, and I shall also be there waiting when your ship returns. In this, you can count on me."

Timber creaked. Behind them a wall gave way, caving in with a crash. Kit jumped, as did Jackson.

She grinned. "But if you hope to board that ship, we best find a way out of here—fast."

A breath later, Jackson joined her side and they dug through the debris near the kerb until the moon went dark. If they didn't hit a void soon, they'd both be dead. Frustrated, she punched the rubble, heedless of the scrape against her knuckles.

And her fist went through, clear up to her elbow.

She stared at Jackson, who stared right back at her, but only for a second. They tore into that pile until a sewer grate appeared.

"Stand aside," Jackson ordered. With a great grunt and a heave, he worked the lid open and cast it off, then grinned up at her.

"You did it!" she cried.

"No, we did it."

We. Who would have thought such a simple word could have such power? Warmth blazed in her chest. "Yes"—she grinned—"we did."

"Just as we'll figure out the mystery at Dedfield's." He winked at her.

Kit inhaled sharply. "You mean—"

"Don't bother with trying to wheedle your way into Ridley's good graces. I'll give you the backup you need." He shot up his hand just as the first hint of grey lightened the gloom above them. "Ready?"

She grasped it, a smile stretching her mouth so large her jaw ached. "I thought you'd never ask."

With Jackson's help, she descended into the abyss.

Boots splashed into the muck next to her, followed by a pained grunt.

"Are you all right?" Her voice had the strange mix of being muffled and echoey at the same time.

"Something sliced my arm on the way down, but no time for that now. Which way?"

"I've never been in this tunnel. Let me get my bearings." She flung out her hand, steeling herself for the first touch of cold slime. But was one ever prepared for that slippery sludge? Inch by inch she probed the wall, not daring to move her feet and lose Jackson. Eventually, her fingertips hit metal, a brass rod—the linkage pipe used by flushers to guide themselves should their headlamp burn out.

"This way. Find my hand."

His strong fingers gripped hers, and they took off, just like old times. Other feet scurried in the darkness as well, but this time a cold sweat didn't bead on her brow. Was it that she couldn't see the rats or because the man she loved had given her a second chance? Her heart soared. Her feet flew. But not for long, not when she caught the barest hint of an odd whooshing noise coming out of the dark, blowing damp air against her face.

Oh. No.

She stopped, practically yanking Jackson's arm out of its socket.

"What the deuce?" His voice rang off the close walls.

"We've got to climb up. Get out. Now. Here." She guided him so that they were back-to-back. "Don't lose touch of me, but quickly feel along that wall for a ladder. I'll do this side. Go."

"How do you know we're far enough away from Polk Street to go topside?" he grumbled. "If you're wrong and we surface too early, we'll be caught in the blast. We're safe down here. We should take our time, go farther, make sure we've put enough space behind us."

"There is no time." She clawed at the wall, frantic. "Feel that breeze? Hear that whoosh? There's water coming, and by water I mean a great rushing flood. We won't stand a chance."

"Are you jest—?"

The whoosh changed to a roar. The first mist of water hit Kit's face. Just as her fingers clasped iron. "I've got it! Follow me."

She scrambled up the rungs and hit a metal ceiling. Bad idea. Why hadn't she let Jackson go first? How would she ever get that manhole off by herself?

God, please. A little help, here—and thank You.

She shoved with all her might.

It didn't budge.

"Kit, that water is nearly upon us!"

Her blood rushed as she sucked in a great, lung-burning breath, and then she tried again. The metal gave a little, but not enough.

"God!" she cried. "Help!"

Whether it was supernatural aid or the thrust of Jackson's body upwards against hers which supplied the most power, she'd never know. The manhole gave. She hefted herself out, Jackson at her heels.

Below them, a surge of water splashed out of the hole.

And at their backs, close enough for their ears to ring, the Polk Street neighbourhood collapsed in a series of fiery booms.

Chapter Thirty-One

Jackson could've used a shave, a bite of breakfast, and a stitch or two in the gash on his arm, which still leaked blood when he moved too fast. Not necessarily in that order, however, especially not with the way his gut rumbled as he strode down Pringle Street.

Kit glanced at him sideways. "I told you we should have bought some rolls off that cart." She tipped her head back towards the vendor they'd passed moments ago. "The vicar will hear you coming from blocks away."

"Only if he's in residence. Were the man smart, he'd be halfway to Dover by now, shipping out on the next ferry."

"True." Late morning sunlight lit a halo on her bare head. Neither of them had taken the time to clean up from their all-night trial, let alone thought to grab hats—and he loved her that way, with her brown hair flowing down her back in a loose finger braid.

She smirked up at him, a charming smudge of ash on the tip of her nose. "Even if he has run, that won't stop me. I've always had a craving to see the white cliffs for myself."

Though she tried to make light of things, weariness dogged her voice and her steps dragged. Jackson adjusted his gait despite the gnawing desire to get his hands on that criminal vicar.

He eyed Kit, frowning at the bruise darkening her cheek and scrape marring her brow. "Are you sure you're up for this? Peters is on a beat just a few blocks over."

"And miss the arrest of the man responsible for nearly killing us?

The one who may even be accountable for my mother's death?" She shook her head. "Not a chance."

"As you wish. I suspect were I to forbid you, you'd manage a way to turn up in Harpenny's house anyway."

A knowing grin curved her lips—one he matched with his own.

Two blocks later, he handed her a pair of darbies and swept his hand towards the vicar's white-stone town house. "Here we are. I shall question the vicar. You make sure Mrs. Harpenny does not escape; use those irons if you must. Things could turn ugly, and if they do, I want you gone. Understood?"

A nun couldn't have looked more innocent as she batted her eyelashes at him. "Completely. Lead on, sir."

Bah! The woman had no notion whatsoever to do as he said. But Baggett was right. That independent streak was one of the reasons he loved and admired her. How could he refuse her the satisfaction of seeing him clap irons on Harpenny?

Jackson pounded the knocker.

Several moments later, the door swung open to the butler. He was a goose of a man with his long neck and lips that stuck out like a bill—lips that rippled with censure as he laid eyes on their rumpled appearance.

Jackson cut the man off before he could direct them to the servant's entrance—or worse, the poorhouse. "I should like an audience with Mr. Harpenny and his mother."

"Church matters are dealt with at the church, not at..." The butler's eyes narrowed until recognition raised his brows. "Inspector Forge?"

"Is your employer at home or is he not?" The question barked out of him harsher than intended, but so be it. Niceties were for gentlefolk, and he was feeling anything but gentle.

The butler fiddled with his cravat. "Yes, however he is not taking any—"

Jackson shoved past him, Kit's footsteps tagging his heels. "Harpenny! I would have a word with you." He stuck his head into the sitting room. Empty.

"Stop right there!" the butler bellowed.

Jackson tromped down the corridor, smiling at Kit's snappy

suggestion that the fellow should go polish some silver instead of hounding them.

The door to the next room was shut. Jackson opened it to walls lined with books, the smell of leather and madeira, and small, dark eyes that blinked up at him from behind a massive desk.

The vicar set down his pen. "Inspector Forge and. . . ?" He squinted at Kit. "Miss Turner, is it not?"

A rustle of skirts flurried into the room behind him and Kit. Mrs. Harpenny stopped near the door in a sweetly scented puff of lavender and talcum, the butler huffing at her elbow. Her gaze drifted from person to person. "What is going on here?"

"No need for panic, Mother. It is merely the inspector." Harpenny waved his hand at the butler. "You are dismissed, Benson."

As soon as the butler grumbled away, Jackson shot a look at Kit, who immediately blocked the door, preventing either Harpenny from escaping. She patted the bulge in her pocket, reassuring him the darbies he'd given her were still in place.

So far, so good. Jackson pulled out his own pair of irons as he rounded the desk. "You are under arrest, Mr. Harpenny, for the attempted murder of Miss Turner and me and for the killing of Henrietta Mann twenty-four years ago."

"Absurd!" Mrs. Harpenny's shrill voice exploded. "My son is a man of God. I will have your job for this outrage."

"Mother, please. Let me handle this." The reverend folded his hands as if he were about to enlighten the entire room on a finer point of theology instead of plead for his life. "Your accusation is highly upsetting, Inspector Forge. Explain yourself at once."

Jackson whipped out the picture of Henrietta Mann, the darbies in his other hand clinking ominously with the movement. "You know this woman, do you not? And before you answer, I suggest you choose your words carefully, for as your mother so succinctly put it, you are a man of God."

Harpenny glanced at the picture, then met Jackson's stare without flinching. "I do not deny I know who she is."

Mrs. Harpenny huffed an unladylike snort. "That proves nothing."

"What about this, then?" Jackson fished out the ransom note, waving it in front of Harpenny's eyes. "When you first saw this slip of paper, you stammered and blanched. I believe you wrote it, didn't you?"

The reverend had the decency to pale. "I did, but—"

"See here, Inspector!" Mrs. Harpenny strode to the desk, jamming her finger against the wood with each word. "A slip of paper does not make my son a murderer."

"Nor does your defense prove his innocence," Kit called from the door. "Pipe down and let the inspector continue."

Kit's support went deep, filling more of the cracks caused by her betrayal at the altar. He retrieved the image of Mrs. Mann and once again held it up to Harpenny. "You knew this woman was being held in the cellar of the Scampson Warehouse, did you not?"

"I did," he said slowly, tugging at his collar. "But I swear I had no idea she'd been abducted. Father told me she was on the run from the law and that he was helping her to hide."

"Do not say another word, Jacob." Mrs. Harpenny's icy tone dropped the temperature in the room.

Jackson shoved the papers into his pocket. "He doesn't need to. I've heard enough." He hauled Harpenny to his feet, slapping on the darbies with a satisfying click. "I have more than I need to piece together a plausible case against you. Not only does the ransom note link you to the crime, but so does your admission to knowing of Mrs. Mann's captivity."

"He was a boy at the time. An innocent!" The reverend's mother flapped her arms. "He had no idea the note he wrote had anything to do with that woman. He couldn't have committed such an offense."

"Not alone." Jackson tipped his head at Kit, signaling her to be on guard lest Mrs. Harpenny run for help from the butler. Then he faced the reverend, who'd not moved a whit since being shackled. All he did was stare at the irons, jaw slack, his small eyes abnormally large behind his spectacles.

"I believe you worked along with your father, Mr. Harpenny, a convicted criminal who got greedy. After collecting the ransom, your father—perhaps even with a hand from you—murdered Mrs. Mann, then set fire to the warehouse to hide the odious deed. Shortly after, when your father was arrested on an unrelated charge, you fled the city with your mother, using the funds to start a new life. A better life. Who knows?" Jackson shrugged a shoulder. "Perhaps you returned to

St. Giles parish because of a spiritual awakening."

"Oh brother," Kit breathed out loud enough to be heard.

Jackson continued, undaunted. "But what a rude surprise it must have been to find Scampson's still standing. Hence, you immediately bought the property with the express intent of final demolition, erasing any ties to Mrs. Mann and yourself. And you might have succeeded too had not Miss Turner inadvertently fallen into your crime scene."

Harpenny shook his head, passion bleeding colour into his face and spreading over his entire bald scalp. "I swear upon my honour and God's Word that I did not kill Mrs. Mann or her maid!"

Jackson stilled at the confession. Finally—finally!—an admission of Kit's mother in connection to the crime. "You mean Miss Dalton?"

Kit sucked in an audible breath. "Mother?"

Harpenny glanced from her to Jackson. "I don't know. I never knew the other woman's name."

He may not have, but this was the crucial moment Jackson had been waiting for. If he played his hand right, he'd bag two blackguards for the price of one. With a glance at Kit for her to stand down, he roughly pulled Harpenny around the desk. "Let's go."

The reverend's mother shrieked, bustling her slight figure to block their way. "Jacob!" Tears garbled her voice and dampened her cheeks. "Not my boy. Not my only son!"

"It's all right, Mother." Harpenny lifted his chin. "God knows I am innocent."

"The magistrate will decide that." Jackson jerked the fellow tight to his side, growling into Harpenny's face. "But were it up to me, I'd lock you away in the deepest cell and forget where I put the key."

"Hah!" Kit spit out. "I would have him swing from a rope, and I'll do everything in my power to see it happens."

"No!" Mrs. Harpenny wailed. "I cannot let you take my son. It is as he says, he is innocent." Her chest heaved with a great sob. "I am the one you want."

And there it was. A double confession. Exactly as he'd hoped, for he'd had a gut feeling she'd taken part in the crime. It was ludicrous to think anything else.

Jackson nodded at Kit, who pulled out her set of darbies and made short work of clapping them on to Mrs. Harpenny's wrists.

The reverend wagged his head from side to side, spluttering. "Mother, what are you saying?"

"I will not see you meet the same end as your father." Her voice crackled with emotion. Red rimmed her eyes as her gaze burned into Jackson's. "Release my son at once, Inspector, or I shall take the truth of what happened to my grave. I vow it. My Jacob knows only what his father told him. I know the rest."

Now here was a turn. Might the scarecrow of a vicar actually be innocent? But if so, then why try to kill him and Kit?

He unlocked the darbies and swung them in the air, earning a black glower from Kit and a relieved whoosh of air from Mrs. Harpenny. "There you have it. Start talking."

"You already know the story in part." Mrs. Harpenny lifted her chin. "My Reuben was a hard man to live with and possessed an even harder backhand. One simply didn't say no to him, did one, Jacob?"

"Mother, you don't have to—"

"He beat us, Jacob. You know he did."

The reverend hung his head. "Only after too much drink."

"Of all the bloomin' porkies." Kit paced behind Mrs. Harpenny, the fire on her cheeks as crimson as the rug. "Do you really expect us to believe you were coerced into committing murder?"

Mrs. Harpenny scowled over her shoulder at her. "Believe what you like. I am telling you the truth." She faced Jackson again. "It was a hard life in St. Giles. Many a night my boy and I went to bed with nothing in our bellies." Her voice quieted some, and she clasped her hands at her midriff, chains rattling. "Starvation drives you to sins you vow you'll never commit. So, when Reuben came up with a plan to make money by abducting Mrs. Mann, I went along—but only if he promised no harm would come to the woman and that we'd keep Jacob in the dark. To his credit, he agreed on both points."

Harpenny stepped towards her, compassion folding his brow. "Mother? Is this true?"

Jackson narrowed his eyes, trying to decipher if indeed she spoke truth or if the woman was merely a good playactor. "Why Mrs. Mann in particular?"

"Do you mind?" Shoulders drooping, she tipped her head at a nearby high-back. At Jackson's nod, she sank heavily into the chair.

"Please continue," Kit prodded.

Mrs. Harpenny stared woefully at the shackles on her wrists. "It was nothing personal. My Reuben eyed up some wealthy homes, choosing the Manns' when he noted the moneyed clientele serviced there at odd hours. It wasn't known as a brothel, so he dug deeper and found out about Mr. Mann's notorious ties—ties that would keep him from going public with an abduction. He snatched the woman one night as she returned from one of her many ladies' meetings. Reuben made Jacob write the note, for neither of us could, you see. My son didn't have a choice in the matter. His father would have beat him senseless had he refused."

"Oh Mother." The reverend dropped to his knees at her side. "Had I known the trouble that note would cause, I never would have written it. I would have gladly taken the beating."

Fierce love blazed in her eyes. "The deed had already been done. You had no part in it but putting down words that, in and of themselves, could not incriminate you. I made sure of it."

Kit popped her fists on her hips. "Let's not forget that two women lost their lives. What happened to Miss Dalton, my mother?"

Jackson joined her side, which would do nothing to ease her loss but hopefully might lend some support. "Yes, Mrs. Harpenny. Tell us what happened to Mrs. Mann's maid."

The reverend's mother heaved a great sigh as she pulled her gaze away from her son. Something new lurked behind those eyes, something hard. Sinister. Like a shadow skulking in a cellar—one that clutched a knife.

"The night Reuben and I went to collect the ransom, Mr. Mann's valet decided to become a hero. He pulled a gun on my man and threatened to shoot Reuben unless he released Mrs. Mann into his care posthaste. Naturally, I couldn't let that happen, so I hit the valet in the head with a brick, dropping him flat to the ground. I didn't mean to kill him, but. . . Well, we all know that wouldn't have stopped a judge from condemning me." She shook her head. "Reuben would have done away with his body then and there, but it turns out Miss Dalton had followed the man in hopes of begging for a coin or two and saw the whole thing. We couldn't let her go. So, Reuben locked her up with Mrs. Mann. By the time he went back for the valet, his body had been removed."

Kit shoved her hair behind her ear. "But there was only one skeleton in that cellar. I should know. I explored every corner of it."

"I am sorry, Miss Turner, but your mother died before we could think of what to do with her and Mrs. Mann. She was sickly, you see. I suspect from a recent birth, if the blood staining her skirts was any clue. We held her in the same chamber as Mrs. Mann, debating if we ought to bring in a surgeon, but we simply couldn't take the risk. She died of natural causes, and Reuben tossed her body into the river. I vow her death was by God's hand, not ours. We may have been abductors, but we were never murderers. Not on purpose."

Beside him, Kit sagged. Jackson edged closer to her. "That explains one death but not the other. How did you kill Mrs. Mann?"

"I didn't." Mrs. Harpenny jutted her jaw, stiff as the starch in her collar. "Nor did Reuben. Oh, he talked about it many a time. I'll not deny that. But for all his violent ways, he never killed anyone. Defending my man with a brick was one thing, but outright murder, well. . ." A deep sorrow suddenly creased lines on her brow, and her voice dropped. "Reuben—in his usual fashion—raised a fist when I suggested letting the woman go and fleeing the city. I stumbled into a lantern, which overturned. We couldn't stop the resulting fire even if we wanted to. There was no time to get the woman out. We barely escaped with our own lives."

"It's true." The reverend glanced from his mother to Jackson. "My mother has a scar on her leg to prove it."

Kit snorted. "But you did escape with the money."

"Yes, for it wasn't kept at the warehouse." Mrs. Harpenny skewered Kit with a pointed look. "I did it for my son, and I daresay you would have done the same to protect a child of your own."

"Oh Mother." Jacob pulled her into his arms.

She nuzzled her face against his collar. "How you turned out to be such an angel never ceases to amaze me."

"He's not that innocent." Once again Jackson hauled the man to his feet and reassigned the darbies on his wrists. "You're still under arrest for my attempted murder and nearly killing Miss Turner as well."

"I did not—nor would not—try to kill anyone!"

Jackson exchanged a glance with Kit. If the twist of her lips was any indication, she believed him about as much as he did. "Where were you last night at six o'clock, Reverend?"

"Conducting a prayer service at church. My parishioners will vouch for me. I'm telling you, Inspector, you have the wrong man."

A surprising rash of doubt prickled along Jackson's arms. Could it be true? Was this man as innocent as he and his mother claimed?

He signaled for Kit to escort Mrs. Harpenny while he once again grasped the reverend's arm. "We'll see about that."

And he would—or perhaps die trying, for if this man had not set off that explosion. . .then someone else was out there still gunning for him.

Chapter Thirty-Two

What a mistake. Blackening her teeth had seemed like a good idea this morning. Not so much anymore. Kit spit out another chunk of wax darkened with charcoal. Her whole mouth tasted like a hearth. But worse, the pillows she'd shoved into Martha's old maternity gown itched like a nest of lice. Bother! The things she did for a chief who wouldn't even acknowledge her were beyond the pale. No doubt Jackson would get the credit when they nabbed the dust yard culprit.

If they nabbed him.

Kit shifted her position, easing the cramp in her leg from crouching so long. After an entire morning of sifting through a rubbish pile taller than her head, she and Jackson had uncovered nothing but bones, broken pottery, and some old shoes.

She glanced at him and a smile twitched her lips. A straw-coloured wig hung low over his brow. When she'd first pulled the tatty old thing out of a sack and handed it to him, he'd balked—but not nearly as much as when she'd asked him to shave off his moustache. Though she'd hated to see his familiar whiskers go down the drain nearly as much as he did, it had been necessary.

And it had also worked. Hillwoman hadn't blinked twice at them when they'd shuffled in with the rest of the workers at the crack of dawn.

Jackson's shovel ate up another bite of rubbish. She scratched her belly, taking care not to shift one of the hidden cushions. She really should be working as diligently as he was, but oh how hard it was to pull her gaze from the flex of his muscles as he laboured. She'd miss the long lines of this man's body, the blue of his eyes, the lips she longed to kiss. Most of all she'd miss the compassion in his voice and all the ways he showed his love, even the small things like when he insisted on walking near the traffic side of the pavement whenever they were out and about. Yes, his protective ways sometimes chafed, but in truth, she would mourn the loss of them. The loss of him. How would she even breathe when he was gone?

He jammed the tip of his shovel into the pile. "Stop looking at me like that."

Drat. Caught in the act. She smiled sweetly. "Like what?"

"Like I have one foot in the grave and the other in a patch of wheel grease. I'll only be gone a year, not forever."

She arched out a kink in her back. "Don't be ridiculous." Rising to her tiptoes, she straightened his wig. "I was merely noting your hairpiece is askew."

"Is it really?"

She looked away, avoiding the knowing lift of his brow. Near the rear gate with her back towards them, hillwoman hunkered on an overturned bucket, a pipe in her mouth and wreath of smoke hovering over her head.

Kit set down her sieve. "If I don't return before ol' dragon breath over there finds me gone"—she hitched her thumb at hillwoman—"cover for me, will you?"

Jackson frowned. "Where are you going?"

"To dig in a different pile."

"Without a shovel?"

She shrugged as she strode away. She couldn't very well explain to Jackson where she intended to look when she didn't really know herself.

Circling the yard, she took care to avoid hillwoman and the corner where several men as lusty as a shipload of sailors unloaded carts full of the Polk Street building debris. At the base of the stairs leading up to the main office, she sank down next to the ragpicker. From this vantage point, she could see the whole plot of refuse, which meant the ragpicker saw all as well.

"Need a hand, luv?" Kit discreetly nudged one of her pillows back into place—though she needn't have been so subtle. The woman took no interest in her whatsoever, just kept winding a sour-smelling strip of filthy cloth into a ball.

"Stick to yer sifting," she grumbled.

Well then. This might not be as easy as she'd hoped. Kit yanked a brown-stained length of fabric from the huge basket in front of the woman and began winding as well. "There's not a trinket to be found in that heap o' dust I been siftin', if ye know what I mean. And I'm sure ye do, aye?"

The ragpicker cut her a glance, sharp as the point of the woman's chin.

Botheration! Kit pulled a coin from her pocket and tossed it in the basket.

The ragpicker's greedy gaze followed the movement, hesitating hardly a breath before snatching it out and squirreling it away. She went back to winding without a word.

Kit waited.

And waited.

Finally the woman mumbled, "What ye want, then?"

Kit grabbed another strip of fabric, mimicking the woman's silence. More often than not, it paid to match the mark's rhythm when fishing about for information.

"What I really want, luv," she said at length, "is an in. You know, to be a major player. Is hillwoman the lead? She the one what I oughtta shimmy up to?"

The ragpicker shook her head, little puffs of dust wafting off her dirty kerchief. "Don't know what ye're talking about."

Sighing, Kit flipped another coin in the basket.

Which once again opened the woman's mouth. "That ol' sack o' beans don't have the brains to lead nothin'."

"Then who?"

Wind. Wind. The ragpicker's ball grew. Kit set down her own lopsided ball. At this rate, she'd not have enough money left for a pork pie at dinner.

The ragpicker pocketed the coin with the others, took a few

minutes to pick something out of her teeth, then finally answered, "I dunno who 'xactly, but I do know this. . .hillwoman was replaced just a'fore Sackett got snagged, and the goods didn't slow one drop. Don' seem to matter what bodies work the yard, so can't be any o' them."

Interesting. Kit spit out another broken hunk of wax. Perhaps she and Jackson had been looking in the dust when they should've lifted their gaze to a more heavenly view. "Who is at the top of the ladder, then?"

The woman's lips rippled into a tight clamshell.

Greedy goblin! Kit pulled out her last two coins then as quickly shoved them back. It had to be Dedfield. He had the means to establish a network of thieves in wealthy homes *and* the power of coercion or maybe a sovereign or two to keep those working for him quiet. Maybe permanently quiet. Was it fear that killed Dedfield's foreman in his jail cell, or had a constable done the deed for him?

"Thanks, luv," Kit murmured as she rose, all the while planning her next move. Dedfield had strolled through the front gates an hour ago and hadn't returned. Hillwoman yet puffed on her pipe. Jackson was in conversation with one of the rock pickers. Now was as good a time as any to hatch her next move.

Kit scurried up the wooden stairs and peeked in the front window. Empty. She tried the door. Locked. A slow smile lifted her lips a she pulled out her modified lock-picking set. Most light fingers carried a standard set of five tools, which was far too bulky in one's pocket. All she needed was her trusty L-wrench and a hook. Two quick jiggles, a slide with a sharp upward jerk, and the bolt gave.

"Mr. Dedfield?" she called as she entered. It always paid to feign innocence when busting into a secured area. "Beggin' yer pardon for a minute o' yer time, sir."

No bushy-chopped man answered. Save for an overloud mantel clock and the braying of a donkey outside, all was quiet.

She dashed to the desk and gave the littered papers a cursory glance on the off chance he was of the mind to hide things in plain sight. No good. Each consecutive drawer she pulled out yielded only the usual invoices, rubber stamps, ink pads, a half-full bottle of single malt whisky, and a nearly empty flask of what smelled like Old Tom.

Rising, she scanned the small room and fixed her gaze on a chest-high cabinet. She'd assumed it housed liquor, but the man kept his drink within reach. She tugged on the glass knobs. The doors didn't give—and the lock on this piece of furniture was a whole different animal compared to a regular bolt.

She dashed over to the window and peeked out. No snappily dressed business owner strolled in through the front gate. Hillwoman was nowhere to be seen—but at least she wasn't tromping up the stairs. Jackson appeared to be striding off, sandwiched between two of the rock pickers. Strange he'd leave his post, but perhaps a cart had overturned, and they'd snagged him for his muscle. Either way, she'd not be missed for a few more minutes.

It took more than that. By the time a small click broke the silence, sweat beaded on her brow. She flung open the cabinet doors to some very expensive silver pieces on the top shelf. A fat book sat on the second. She retrieved it and thumbed through. Column after column listed the names of fine houses, contacts, and an itemized list of stolen goods, leastwise what she assumed were stolen goods until. . .aha! She squinted, thankful Jackson had taught her to read. Written in slanted handwriting was *Culpepper* and the same items the baronet had reported missing. Dedfield would serve a very long stint in Newgate for this.

She shoved the whole ledger into her bodice, glad now for all the extra padding. No one would be the wiser. She shut one cabinet door, and then her gaze landed on a folded pile of black fabric on the bottom shelf. Curious, she lifted up the thick cloth, giving it a little shake as she did so. A dark veil fell to the ground, and she blinked at the cassock in her grip.

A shiver spidered up her spine. The alley. The explosion. The vicar who'd nearly blown them to the glorious kingdom.

"That man of yours just won't die, will he?" a man's voice rumbled behind her. "And neither will you."

She whirled, clutching the fabric to her chest. Dedfield loomed on the threshold, his small eyes smouldering with rage.

A fair amount of fury burned in her belly as well. "You're the one who's been trying to kill Jackson! Why? And why me?"

Dedfield pressed the door shut, methodically pulling down the shade on the glass panel and the front windows. "You were simply in the wrong place at the wrong time. As for the inspector, I couldn't very well take the risk that Sackett had told him everything, yet even after that leak was plugged he came sniffing about, asking questions, probing too deeply. I hired a cutthroat to silence Forge, but I should've realized after the zoo fiasco just what a bumbler he was. The truth is if you want someone killed, you must do the job yourself." He produced a length of rope from his pocket. "A job I shall finish today. Better you and the inspector should rot in the ground than me in gaol."

The hairs at the nape of her neck stood up like wires. Dedfield was a desperate man—and cornered desperation was never a badger to be poked. "There will be no rotting required, Mr. Dedfield." She used her most soothing tone. "Simply cut me in on the deal. A mere thirty percent would be worth your while to keep from rotting, as you put it."

He snorted as he secured the rope around both hands, leaving an ominous length to fit exactly around her neck. "Not a chance. I keep my payroll to a minimum, and I've got all the employees I need."

The icy gleam in his eyes was a dead giveaway he'd not be moved. She'd have to try another tack. She widened her stance, feet itchy to flee. "You're not guilty of murder yet, though. The judge will be lenient on you for simple thievery."

A crazed smile stretched his lips. "But that would end my production, and you see, Miss Turner, I am not ready to stop. There is so much more to be had from this world."

Kit dropped the cassock, edging closer to the door while keeping the desk between them. "This world will pass away, Mr. Dedfield, and then what? You cannot take any of your ill-gotten gain into eternity."

He sidestepped, his big frame cutting off any chance of an escape out the door. "I didn't figure you as the religious sort."

"You didn't figure me as the law-keeping sort either," she stalled, gaze wildly scanning for an escape. Oh, where was Jackson when she needed his muscle?

But no broad-shouldered saviour burst through the door. She was on her own.

There was nothing for it, then.

Drawing from all the bluster she'd learned on the streets, she stomped over to Dedfield, vainly trying not to note how he towered above her by a handspan. "Your thieving days are done. You are under arrest, Mr. Dedfield."

He laughed, fish and chips wafting on his breath. "You're a bold one, Miss Turner. I'll give you that. But do you really think a chit like you can best a full-grown man?"

He was right. She couldn't—but neither could David slay a giant unless he hit the right spot. Kit ripped the ledger from her bodice and swung hard, cracking Dedfield's skull.

The man oophed out a rush of air as his head snapped aside. He teetered.

Kit dodged. Grabbed the doorknob. Yanked it open. She breathed in a draught of cool air—then stopped breathing altogether as a rope at her neck jerked her backwards. She grabbed at the rough hemp.

In vain.

Hot breath defiled her ear. "It will be a real pleasure to add your bones to those of the inspector in one of my dust piles."

Steely fingers sank like teeth into Jackson's upper arms as two men hauled him towards a back shed. It didn't take a genius to know that once they shoved him inside, he'd never walk out. Using all his strength, he wrenched one way and twisted another.

The fingers dug deeper.

"Don't make this harder than it has to be, mate." The man on his left walloped him with a clout to the face.

Jackson's head jerked sideways, the hated wig Kit had coerced him into wearing slipping, blocking half his vision. Blood tasted briny on his lips, and he spit, aiming for the shoes of the bully.

The other man chuckled as they neared the shed door. He pulled out a lumpy stocking weighted with some sort of nuts and bolts assortment. "Jago's right. 'Twill be a right easy piece o' work if ye just let it happen. Then again, don't mind me a bit o' sport, neither." He jingled the makeshift weapon.

Jackson's gut cinched. This wouldn't be a fair fight. But he hadn't trained so hard in the ring with Baggett just to be taken down by two Neanderthals bent on murder.

A few paces from the door, Jago's grip slackened. "In you go."

Jackson waited for the brute's grasp to lessen. When it did, he lunged and spun, fists at the ready, taking care to plant himself in front of Jago. "Give it your best shot, my friends, because you'll only have one."

Jago smiled like a jack-o'-lantern with a few missing teeth, then nodded at the other man.

He swung back his weapon.

Time slowed. Sound magnified. Jackson measured every breath as the heavy stocking hurtled through the air. At the last instant, he ducked.

Jago's mouth dropped as he flinched away.

Too late.

The sock of metal took him in the side of the neck. He spun askew, hitting the gravel hard, while Jackson simultaneously struck the other blackguard. He grabbed the sock-swinging arm and hooked his foot behind the behemoth's knee, rotating him off balance.

The man landed face-first. Jackson dropped atop him and, with one well-placed punch, struck the tender spot behind the man's ear, rendering him motionless. Breathing hard, Jackson rose, swiping up the metal-filled pouch on his way.

"That were a fine piece o' knuckle-bustin'." A dust-covered onlooker nodded at him. "I'da helped but ye had that lot in hand."

"Thanks." Stepping over the hated wig—which he was more than happy to let die on the ground—Jackson strode off, searching for Kit.

If these two were on to him, she might be in danger as well.

Two seconds. Maybe three. That's all Kit had before passing out.

And she'd be hanged if she passed out.

Fighting the strong instinct to lurch as far as possible from the madman behind her, she leaned into Dedfield, twisting sideways. Sucking in a much-needed breath, she drove the heel of her hand full force into Dedfield's nose. Cartilage gave. His head snapped back. The rope went slack.

Victory!

She wriggled away, but no time to gloat. No time to flee, either. Hillwoman blocked the stairway, a knife in her hand.

And there Kit stood, caught between a dog-faced woman brandishing a blade and a roaring Dedfield, furious as a wounded bear.

Kit darted sideways, lungs burning as she scurried behind the desk. There'd be no blustering this time. There would be blood and lots of it.

She yanked out her own knife.

And crouched.

Jackson strode the length of the dust yard, searching for Kit. No brown skirt swirled about. No nimble-footed sprite flitted around any corner. Where was she?

Flexing his fingers, he worked out the ache as he doubled back to the ragpicker. He'd last seen Kit conversing with the woman. Maybe she'd have a clue. He planted his boots in front of her, and she glanced up from where she sat, every bit the heap of scrap and patch as the basket of fabric.

He tipped his head. "Have you seen the sifter who worked alongside me?"

She eyed him, lips pursed so tightly a few silvery whiskers poked out from her chin.

Maybe she was hard of hearing. He tried louder. "The sifter—have you seen her?"

The woman shifted her gaze to his pocket, then flicked it back up to him.

Scoundrel. He flipped her a coin.

She caught it midair. After a good once-over of the tuppence, she pocketed it and mumbled, "Dedfield's office, I expect."

Gooseflesh rose on his arms. Had Kit been found out? Made sense. Someone had tipped off those thugs who'd assaulted him.

He stalked to the stairway, then sucked in a breath. At the top landing, hillwoman stood in the doorway, a blade in her hand.

Jackson took the stairs two at a time. The woman turned just as he yanked out the weighted stocking.

And swung.

The weight cracked into her forearm. The knife flew. Hillwoman shrieked as he spun her around and cranked her other arm behind her, wrenching her hand between her shoulder blades. "Move, and I'll break it," he warned.

Not that he would—but she didn't need to know that. With his free hand, he yanked out a pair of darbies and locked one iron onto her wrist, the other onto the stair rail.

"I shoulda known you and the woman weren't no new hires," she snarled.

He ducked from a swipe of her fist. "Indeed, you should have."

Without a second look, he strode into the office. Kit stood to the side of a massive desk, an ugly red line across her neck. Blood smeared the cuff of her sleeve. Her skirt was torn and her hair hung wild about her shoulders. But she remained on her feet, God love her, unlike the man who lay on the floorboards. Clearly she'd been up to some hijinks.

In a trice, Jackson closed the distance between them, lifting her face and scanning for any further hurt. "Are you all right?"

"I am now." With half a smile, she sank onto the chair, tucking her blade in her boot. "Or more like I will be once you slap some darbies on Mr. Dedfield."

"Sorry. They're already in service."

"Hillwoman?"

He nodded as he circled back to the door and snatched a length of rope he'd spied on his way in, then returned to the belly-down dust yard owner and reached for a wrist. He cocked a brow at Kit. "How about you tell me what happened and why exactly I'm tying up Dedfield."

In one swift move, Kit swiped a heap of black fabric off the floor. "Because of this."

She shook out what appeared to be a clergyman's cassock and. . . He blinked. A pox veil?

Sudden understanding crawled like fire ants under his skin.

"What the devil!" he roared. "I can hardly believe it." He jerked the knot tighter than necessary, digging the rope into Dedfield's flesh. "But why? What could the man possibly have against me?"

Dropping the garment, Kit lightly pressed her fingers against her raw neck. "He thought Sackett gave you information on him, that it was only a matter of time before the law came trotting in through his front gates, especially when you doubled back to ask him more questions."

"Huh. I never even thought." He sank back on his haunches, studying the big man laid out like a beached halibut. "How did you manage to take down a man of his size?"

A smirk twisted her lips. "Old street trick. Feign a knife throw, and when the mark ducks aside, run full charge and thump the hilt right into the ol' noodle." Lifting her fist, she playacted a whack to her own head.

"Well, well." Jackson brushed his hands together. "This is quite a haul, but I've two more to tie up out in the yard before they come 'round."

Kit's brow wrinkled. "Is that why you weren't here to help me?"

"Did you really need my help?"

"Actually, yes. If you hadn't managed hillwoman, I couldn't have handled Dedfield at the same time."

This was new. Even to him, Kit rarely showed such vulnerability. More of the change she had spoken of? This could take some getting used to. He arched a brow at her. "I have no doubt you would have figured something out."

"No, the truth is I *did* need you." She pushed up from the chair, and in two steps, she stood close enough that her warm breath feathered against his skin.

Impossibly blue eyes stared into his own, heating him to the gut. He was falling again. Unwilling. Unbidden. Unstoppable.

"I *do* need you, Jackson," she whispered.

He brushed back a sweep of hair from her brow, the silkiness of it sending a charge up his arm. Smudge-faced and battle-worn, she was a beauty—and she was wrong. As surely as the sun rose each morning, she was entirely and completely mistaken.

For the real truth was he needed her.

Chapter Thirty-Three

Oddly enough, the sergeant's office felt like home in a way the chief's never would. Could be the lack of a parrot threatening to hang him up, or maybe it was just the familiar scent of gunpowder and old leather. More than likely, though, it was that the black-moustached man behind the desk had somehow come to be a second father to Jackson... a father who would hurt afresh when Jackson gave his report.

"I saw Mr. Harpenny leave the station." Graybone fiddled with a pen while he spoke, flipping it round and round between his thick fingers. "Which means I can only assume you are thoroughly satisfied he had nothing to do with Mrs. Mann's or Bella's murder?"

Now there was a prickly question. Jackson shifted on the chair, wooden legs creaking. "About that, sir..." He inhaled deeply, searching for the fortitude to tell the man in front of him that ultimately there was no one to lock up for the deaths of those women. "With Baggett's previous research and after my own extensive questioning of the Harpennys, there is no way to prove or disprove that Mrs. Mann's or Miss Dalton's death was indeed murder. In fact, with the burn on Mrs. Harpenny's leg to corroborate the story of an accidental fire, a judge would be hard-pressed to convict either her or her son for the act of arson."

The pen snapped between Graybone's fingers. "But they tossed my Bella into the river!"

"True, but she had already died, sir. Everything indicates that Miss Dalton did not long survive the delivery of Kit. Even the Manns' housekeeper affirms your Bella was sickly the few days she served."

Jackson laid the woman's locket on the desk.

Other than his gaze following the movement, the sergeant didn't move a muscle.

Jackson continued. "Mr. Harpenny told me he overheard a conversation shortly before your Bella died. Miss Dalton gave her locket to Mrs. Mann in hopes she would deliver the necklace to her father. She charged Mrs. Mann to explain her disappearance was owing to a pregnancy and that he was now a grandfather. It was her dying wish that despite the disgrace, perhaps her father could be persuaded to redeem Kit from the foundling hospital. But of course, he never knew."

"*I* never knew." Graybone pounded his beefy fist against the desk, rattling the broken bits of the pen carcass. "If I had known, I never would have set foot on that ship, God as my witness." An otherworldly blaze ignited in Graybone's eyes. He swiped the locket from off the desk, clutching it with white knuckles.

Jackson leaned forward, helpless to know how to soothe the sergeant other than by the softening of his voice. "I'm so sorry, sir."

The tick of the wall clock measured out time, ignoring the anguish of the big man who looked at its face a hundred times a day. At length, the sergeant scrubbed his hand over his face, a sad shake to his head. "As am I, Jackson," he mumbled. "Sorrier than anyone shall ever know."

Jackson gripped the chair arms, stunned that this grizzled, no-nonsense sergeant had deigned to use his Christian name. Some sort of barrier had been crossed. Maybe even torn down. Whichever, the timing was off for such a breakthrough.

He'd set sail tomorrow.

He rose, anxious to put distance between the sergeant's obvious angst and his own twisting heart. "That about wraps it up, then. Mrs. Harpenny will be convicted for the murder of the valet and as an accomplice to the abduction, Mrs. Mann's bones will finally fill that grave in Kensal Green, and you and Kit may rest in the fact that Miss Dalton neither committed suicide nor was murdered." He shoved out his hand for a parting shake. "It has been my greatest honour to have served with you, Sergeant Graybone. I hope to reconnect when I return in a year."

Scarlet crept up the man's neck. He wouldn't so much as look at the offered hand. He couldn't. He was too busy stabbing Jackson with a stare so sharp it could draw blood. "You're a fool if you make the same mistake I did."

Jackson shook his head. "It's not the same. Kit and I have reconciled and will wed soon upon my return."

"Not one of us is promised a tomorrow. All we have is now to love and appreciate those who are dear. Don't go. Begin your life today with the woman God has given you."

He rubbed the back of his neck, wishing to God that he could. "I've already given the earl my word and cannot back out at this late date. Nor will I marry Kit just to leave her."

Graybone skewered him with an even stare. "Then take her with you."

"The earl won't hear of it. I've tried just this morning again to persuade him, and he is adamant."

"That's never stopped either of you before. Why not simply smuggle her aboard? By the time the earl finds out she's along, it will be too late to turn back."

Did the by-the-book sergeant before him just suggest he break the rules and defy a peer of the realm? And with a plan that might actually work? Jackson's mind whirled at the possibilities, but then he shook his head. "Appealing as such a possibility might be, sir, personal desire doesn't warrant such a deception." And if the fiasco with Kit had taught him nothing else, it was that deception cracked the foundation of relationship faster than anything else.

A mighty grumble rattled around in Graybone's throat, but he did stand and clasp Jackson's hand. "You are far too much like me, young Forge. If you must go, then Godspeed." He stood fully at attention. "Until we meet again, Inspector."

Jackson clicked his own heels and snapped a crisp salute. "Until then, sir."

He strode out of the office, setting course to Mr. Mann's town house to return the pictures of his wives. As he hailed a hack just outside the station, the sergeant's admonitions overshadowed the fact that this was his last time here at Old Jewry. He wanted nothing more than to stay and continue to mend his relationship with Kit. Or better yet, to sweep her away on an adventure that she would no doubt thrive on, though it would likely drive him to distraction before returning home. He sighed. He could not see a good path for either option.

Climbing into the hackney, he sat and stared out the window at a world that would soon look very different. He had no choice but to trust Kit to show up at the dock tomorrow as promised—and to trust God to work out the rest.

∽

Sitting at her dressing table, Kit brushed her hair to a fine sheen, but the overall effect was no different than putting a primped wig on a sow. A beautiful coiffure only did so much to draw the eye away from the scrape on her chin and bruises on her cheek. She tipped her head one way then another before setting down the brush with a huge sigh. Her hair might look well groomed, but her face would still be rough tomorrow morning when she bid Jackson goodbye.

Goodbye.

Her heart squeezed. How on earth was one supposed to live with that word? To eat with it? Sleep with it? How could God possibly expect her to make peace with such a demon? Would that tomorrow might never come.

She shoved away from the small table and stomped to the wardrobe. As she reached for her nightgown, her fingertips brushed her old green romping gown—the one she'd been meaning to give to Jo. She laid it over the back of the chair, smoothing a few wrinkles with the palm of her hand. Jo hadn't been particularly overjoyed at the prospect of working in the milliner's shop on State Street. In fact, the girl had spewed a few unsavory oaths about it until Kit explained that with a steady income, she could afford to buy supplies for the orphans she'd come to care for and that she'd be allowed to take her noontime meal with them every Saturday.

Shoes clacked down the hallway. Kit turned just as Mistress Mayhew stopped on the threshold with a cloth-covered tray in her hands.

"You have missed your supper again, Miss Turner."

Kit's brows shot to the heavens. This was a regulation breach of the highest order. "But food is not allowed in our private quarters."

"Do not get too excited. It is only a bowl of broth and some tea." The mistress clipped in with precise steps and set the tray on the nightstand. "Frankly, Miss Turner, I am worried about you."

"Me?" Kit raised a hand to her chest. "Whatever for?"

"One does not have to look closely to see you have been engaged in some rather unsavory pursuits." Her gaze skimmed from bruise to cut to scrape. "Neither have you taken a bite to eat these past several days. Are you well?"

La. Just as she'd suspected. Glossy smooth hair did nothing to detract from the bang-ups on her face. Kit curved her mouth into a placid smile. "I am fine, mistress. Thank you for your concern."

The woman's posture tightened like a bowstring about to snap. "I suspect you are not being entirely forthright. There is a heaviness about you, a slump of the shoulder when you think no one is looking, a lag in your step that prior to this month was never there."

"Mistress Mayhew, I—"

"Tut-tut." She raised a palm, staving her off. "A lady never interrupts."

Kit swallowed a smirk.

"Now then, as I was saying." Mistress Mayhew circled, eyeing her like a lump of clay to be molded. "I have noticed a distinct change in your demeanor, which I can only attribute to your failed wedding attempt. In light of such, though I shall require your utmost confidence upon the matter"—she stopped in front of her—"I should like to share a tale with you."

Kit blinked. Evidently this was to be a night of irregularities. In the four years she'd resided here, never once had the woman divulged a personal anecdote.

"By all means." Kit swept her hand towards the two chairs near the hearth. "Please, will you sit?"

Mistress Mayhew's skirts billowed as she sank onto the seat. After a few quick flicks of her fingers against silk, the threat of any unwanted creases in her gown vanished. She folded her hands just so then began. "As a rule, I do not speak of this with anyone, but in your case, Miss Turner, I feel an exception is in order if you are to avoid the same error I made." She frowned. "Not that I assume your situation is a mirror image, mind. Rather, you may glean what might apply and discard the rest."

"Yes, mistress." Kit nodded. "Do go on."

But she didn't. The woman merely fixed her gaze on the handkerchief in her hands.

Kit dared a light touch to her knee. "Rest assured, Mistress Mayhew, that whatever you have to say will not leave this room."

The woman's chest heaved, and when she did finally speak, her voice carried a weight so heavy each word dragged. "Believe it or not, Miss Turner, like you, I was once a young lady, wooed by many, in love with only one."

Now there was a new image. She'd only ever thought of the woman as the pewter-haired matron she was now. Even more novel was the heightened colour staining her cheeks.

The mistress daintily dabbed her brow with a lacy handkerchief, wafting lemon verbena as she did so. "Mr. Davenport cut a fine figure in his captain's uniform, which I realize sounds scandalous—and truly it is—but as I said, I was young. And as it turns out, foolish as well." She refolded her handkerchief and tucked it up her sleeve. "In the midst of our courtship, Mr. Davenport received an unwelcome deployment to the southernmost region of Gibraltar. It was to be a permanent post. A career enhancement, as he claimed. The very day he found out, he proposed marriage." The woman's gaze lifted, sorrow swimming in the depths of her eyes. "To my everlasting regret, Miss Turner, I turned him down."

"Did you not love him?"

"Most emphatically, I did."

Kit reared back her head. "Then why on earth did you say no?"

"Fear. Oh, not as you may think." She fluttered her hand. "I had no misgivings in my ability to flourish in a foreign land, nor did I waver in constancy for Mr. Davenport. My hesitation was born of an insecurity over Mr. Davenport's love for me. He gave me no cause, but even so, I simply could not get over the thought of him changing his mind about me once we put to sea. Miss Turner, I tell you this only so you will take one important truth to heart. Good men are not light-tongued with their emotions." She folded her hands and rose, staring down like a preacher in a pulpit. "I have no idea what has passed between Mr.

Forge and yourself, but I do know this. . .if a man like that tells you he loves you, he means it. And with that, I bid you good night."

Kit followed her to the door, mulling on all the woman had said, barely managing to murmur a suitable "Good night." For a long while, she paced the room from wardrobe to window, over and over. Mistress Mayhew was wrong. Completely wrong. She knew now that Jackson loved her. He'd made that abundantly clear. No, the trouble lay in trust. But how to show him she truly—irrevocably—was committed to him?

She pressed her head against the window, the glass cool against her feverish thinking. How indeed to prove to the man she loved that she was committed to him for the rest of her life? An idea kindled slowly, and the more she thought on it, the hotter it flamed. Maybe if she—yes! This could work. *If* she could manage to pull it off in time.

Whirling, Kit grabbed her coat and dashed into the night.

Chapter Thirty-Four

Time always flew when you didn't wish it to. Jackson jammed his hands into his pockets, stretching tall to gawk one way then the other. Next to him, his brother mimicked the action. Life on the London docks scurried like a kicked-over anthill. Stevedores, travelers, fishermen in oilskin dusters—but no pert-nosed pixie shoved her way through the throng. If Kit didn't show up, the plan Jackson had hatched in the wee hours of the morning to smuggle her aboard ship and marry her at sea would be foiled.

And he was running out of time.

"You're doing it again." His father poked him in the arm.

He huffed a long sigh. "It cannot be helped. Where is she?"

"Lady coming?" James frowned at their father.

Pursing his lips, his father pulled out his pocket watch. After a long look, he snapped the lid shut. "I grant you that Kit is late, but traffic is notorious around the wharf. James and I would likely still not be here had I not tipped the driver excessively."

For the hundredth time, Jackson fingered the ring box in his pocket. Why was it plans birthed in the middle of the night always seemed good in the dark but by light of day weren't nearly as brilliant? Reluctantly, he withdrew his hand. Perhaps she wasn't coming after all, though she'd led him to believe otherwise. Was this a case of once a swindler, always a swindler?

"Don't do it, Son."

He angled his head at his father. "Do what?"

"Give in to despair. After all that you told me last night of Kit's background, how she was abandoned at such a tender age, I doubt very much she would purposely put you through the same thing. Love always protects, always trusts, always hopes, and always perseveres. So, steady on, my boy. Your Kit may be a bit unconventional, but deep down, she is a good woman." Father squeezed his shoulder.

James bobbed his head. "Lady *is* good."

Jackson's heart swelled for these two stalwart men. They were right. Kit had shown nothing but love for James and respect for his father. Were she truly a swindler, she wouldn't have kept up the charade for so long.

"Pardon, sir."

A tap on the back turned him around.

"I'm to stow the gangplank now." The information traveled on a sailor's waft of briny breath. By the looks of his ruddy skin and permanent squint, he was a seasoned seaman. He tipped his head back towards the ship. "Either you're on or you're off, sir."

Jackson's gut clenched. He'd wished to God this moment would never come and yet here it was. Again. But this time would be different. *He* would be different. There had to be some reason for Kit's absence, and with God's help, he would think the best of her. He could choose to withhold judgment until he knew the truth—the whole truth—of the reason for her absence. . .and he would.

With steely determination, he reset his hat then nodded at the man. "Thank you. I won't be a moment." He handed the ring to his father, wrapping the older man's fingers tightly around the small box. "Hold on to this for me, would you? And whenever you chance to be in London, would you look in on Kit? See if she's keeping herself out of trouble?"

Father grinned as he pocketed the ring. "I shall be happy to, and I suspect your brother will be equally overjoyed at the task, eh James?"

His brother bounced on his toes. "Find Lady?"

"Jackson! Thank God I made it in time."

Jackson wheeled about.

Running harum-scarum, Baggett shoved his way through the crowd. Hat askew, his friend stopped in front of him, planting his hands on his thighs while huffing for air.

Instant alarm stiffened every muscle in Jackson's body. "What's happened? Is Kit all right?"

"Kit?" Baggett puffed as he straightened. "No idea." After one more deep inhale, he pulled a small wooden container from inside his coat. "I came to give you this."

Jackson flipped open the lid. Inside, a carved pipe lay nestled in black velvet lining, a small canvas pouch near the stem. The rich scent of tobacco stung his nose. "Not that I don't appreciate the gesture, but you know I don't smoke."

"You'll want to start in Africa. Bloody killer mosquitoes." He tapped his finger on the pipe. "Keeping a wreath of smoke about your head wards them off. Graybone and I thought you could use all the help you can get."

Warmth flared in his chest. He'd been so preoccupied with Kit that he'd not given a smidgen of thought as to how much he'd miss his friend. The earl was a fine man to work for, but he doubted very much Gordon-Lennox would stoop to socializing with the likes of his bodyguard.

Jackson clasped Baggett's arm. "Thank you."

Behind him, the bell clanged longer and louder than before, over-shadowing the jingle of tackle and groan of ship hulls banging against the quay. The same sailor as before stepped up to them.

"Sorry, sir. Can't wait any longer. I'll be hefting that plank now."

Baggett pulled away, chin lifted high. "Off with you, then. I find I can no longer bear the sight of your hideous mug."

Jackson tucked the pipe box under his arm. "Goodbye, Baggett. It's been an honour to serve with you."

"You as well. And don't worry, I shall keep an eye on Kit." He winked.

"Goodbye Father, Brother." He hugged one after the other, and then with a final salute to Baggett, he stomped up the walkway, barely planting his feet on deck before the board was stowed.

Standing near the gunwale, the earl faced him. Though the October morning couldn't have been greyer beneath such a low cloud cover, Gordon-Lennox appeared resplendent in his sharply creased trousers and smart pinstripe dress coat.

"I was beginning to doubt your commitment, Mr. Forge."

Jackson squared his shoulders, standing at full attention. "My commitment was never in question, my lord."

A slow smile lightened the severe lines on the earl's face. "Good man." Without further ado, he pivoted precisely and strode away, leaving Jackson alone with the rush of sailors coiling ropes.

The deck canted slightly as the ship left its moorings. Jackson clutched the gunwale while water purled against the hull. A chasm slowly grew between him and the only land he'd ever known. . .the only woman he'd ever loved.

Oh Kit.

He closed his eyes, blocking out the black water. Was he doing the right thing by leaving without knowing what had kept her? Had she fallen into another hole? Had one of her many enemies from her swindling days finally caught up with her?

Voices carried from the dock. Loud. Angry. A shriek and several curses. The shrill whinny of a horse. Jackson popped open his eyes.

A blue skirt raced to the quay. Kit, hands clutching. . .no. He squinted.

It could not be!

"Make way. Make way!" Kit crashed through the throng of people like a woman on fire, unstoppable and burning with need. The cameo her father had given her bounced against her collarbone with each stride and the copy of *The Pickwick Papers* in her pocket ground into her thigh. Must every blessed Londoner be at the docks this morning? The very powers of hell seemed to be against her today, starting with the marriage certificate that'd fallen behind a desk and taken forever to find, then on to the traffic jam over at Pidgeon Lane. And now a clogged boardwalk.

"Miss Turner, you must slow down!"

"Not yet, Vicar." She tugged harder on his hand.

"Indeed. Move out of the way!" Her father bellowed and dodged past a burly stevedore, lugging her and the vicar along for the ride as he took the lead. Hopefully, there wasn't any special punishment reserved for the act of yanking a man of God's arm out of its socket.

Her feet tangled in her wedding gown, nearly taking her down, but she soldiered on. No way would she stop now. With a stitch in her side and a burning blister on her heel, Kit stopped at berth number two.

"Good heavens!" The vicar fanned his face.

Good heavens was right. Her heart plummeted like a lead weight to her belly. The slip was empty. Jackson was gone.

She was too late.

Again.

No. God, please, no!

Squinting, she scanned the big ship easing into the channel, gaze darting from man to man on deck, and. . .her breath hitched. Blue eyes stared back into her own, an unruly curl of dark hair nearly covering one of them. Jackson hung over the railing, mouth agape.

"Jackson!" She waved her hand over her head like a Bedlam inmate. "I'm here. I'm here!"

Slowly, his head wagged side to side, eerily resolute, as the ship edged farther out of her life. He was done, finished with her, and she couldn't blame him. She'd let him down for the last time.

And just like that she was gutted. Her legs trembled. Her knees gave.

An arm caught her. She curled into her father's embrace and wept freely onto his coat. Big ugly sobs burned her throat.

"There now, Daughter. Calm yourself." Her father patted his hand against her back.

Calm? How could she possibly compose herself when the only man she'd ever wanted was sailing into oblivion? No. She'd never be calm another day of her life.

"Don't cry, lady!"

Another big hand landed on her shoulder.

Sniffling, she looked up. "James?"

"Yes, child, we're both here." Jackson's father stepped near, worry creasing his brow. "And your father is right. There is no need for such a display. Jackson was disappointed, yes, but he is not angry with you. He believes in you, as do I."

Her stomach twisted. "I appreciate the thought, but I'm afraid we haven't been completely forthright about my past, and with my history, Jackson—"

"Jackson told me everything last night, and we all agree he couldn't have found a better woman. He loves you, my dear, as do James and I."

Jackson told him—and his father didn't care? She bit her lip, not sure which fact stunned her more. Her gaze drifted from James to Jackson's father to her own father. Without Jackson, these men would now have to be the solid beams in her life, and after nearly a lifetime of being on her own, how grateful she was to have them.

"God hears your cry!" the vicar shouted behind her. "Look. See!"

She frowned at the man. Now was not the time for some lofty sermon. "Thank you, but—"

"Brother!" James cried.

Kit's heart skipped a beat as she whirled around.

Cutting through the water with big, strong strokes, Jackson closed the distance between the ship and the dock.

She clapped her hand to her mouth, heart banging around in her chest. "Jackson," she whispered against her fingers.

He climbed the ladder, dripping wet, and heaved himself up onto the wharf. His hair hung like seaweed, and the second he straightened, she threw herself into his arms.

"You came!" Their words echoed in unison, voices entwined like their bodies right there on the dock.

Kit laughed into his wet coat, nuzzling her face against the sodden wool, and suddenly nothing mattered anymore, save for the strong beat of Jackson's heart against her ear.

"I should have known you'd make a grand entrance." Jackson's deep tone rumbled.

"I'm sorry, Jackson. I tried—I *really* tried to get here on time." She pulled back, catching sight of the ship sailing away over his shoulder. "Oh no—your ship. The earl. I didn't mean to—"

"Don't worry about that." An odd smile quirked his lips as if he were conniving something. Jackson—conniving! "In fact, this might work out even better than I originally planned. That is, if you think you're up for an adventure."

Intriguing. She cocked her head. "Now who's being reckless?"

"Not so reckless, when it includes bringing along my best backup." He brushed the pad of his thumb over her cheek, the look of love in his eyes so genuine she nearly buckled again. "But more importantly, you're here now. And not alone, I see." He arched a brow at the vicar and her father. "What sort of swindle did she run on you, gentlemen, to drag you to the wharf this morning?"

The vicar sniffed. "Marriage is many things, Mr. Forge, but it is never a swindle when God brings two people together. And for some reason I cannot fathom, I believe the Lord wishes the two of you together despite this unconventional setting." He gestured towards the melee around them.

Kit laced her fingers through Jackson's, grinning. "I think unconventional suits us best. Shall we marry here and now?"

"Only if you promise me one thing."

"What?"

"That you, my little thief, never again leave my side."

"I would ask the same of you, sir." She let go of his hands, spit in her palm, and held it out. "Deal?"

He chuckled, the warm sound of love and peace prevailing against the flurry of the docks. Then he spit in his own hand and shook hers, pulling her into his arms as he did so. "Never again, my love." He kissed the crown of her head.

His father tapped him on the shoulder. "You might be needing this." He handed over a small black box.

"Thank you, Father."

James planted a sloppy kiss atop her head just as he'd seen Jackson do. "Love you, lady."

She grinned and gave him a hug. "I love you as well, my new brother."

Her father cleared his throat. "This is a fine show of emotion, but ought we not save the warmer feelings for after the ceremony?"

Jackson arched a brow at him. "Always the stickler for detail—and this time I cannot agree with you more." He grabbed her hand and pressed his lips against her knuckles. "So, are you finally ready to marry me, my bride?"

She smiled into his face. "I was beginning to think, Mr. Forge, that you would never ask."

Chapter Thirty-Five

One Year Later

A wild rumpus of humanity bubbled and boiled on the London docks. Sullen clouds hung so low over the wharf all Kit need do was rise to her toes to punch a hole right through one of them. Yet this was not a day for fighting but for wide grins and loving embraces. At last, she was home. *Home.* The word wrapped around her like a cozy woolen jumper.

She gripped the gunwale, waiting impatiently for the gangplank to lower while scanning for faces dear to her heart. She'd missed them, those men, fiercely.

Footsteps drew close behind her, followed by the earl's commanding voice. "I suppose it is time for us to part, Mrs. Forge."

She dipped a final curtsy to the imposing Earl of March. . .though after traveling with the man for the past year, he wasn't nearly as daunting as that first day they'd met. He'd been quite the irritated ogre when Jackson had jumped overboard to marry her and then had the audacity to rent a dinghy for them to catch up to the earl's ship. But being the man really had no other choice at the time, he took Jackson back into his good graces along with her. Which turned out to be fortuitous. Even Tutsi warriors could be outsmarted with a street swindle—a simple bit of trickery that Kit had employed to save all their lives in the Congo rainforest.

"And so we are to part, my lord." She met his gaze, a directness that had at first offended the great man but one that he'd learned to accept. "It has been a pleasure serving you."

"The pleasure, Mrs. Forge, has surprisingly been all mine." Bowing, he kissed the back of her hand. "I hope you and your husband will be frequent guests at Goodwood House."

"I am certain we can find time between cases."

He angled his head, his derby not daring to move askew. "So, it is to be directly back to work for the two of you, then?"

"As soon as we are able to find care for our new addition."

"That could be a challenge. I've never seen such a feisty one. Yet I have no doubt that whatever the two of you set out to do, it shall be accomplished. Until we meet again, my dear." He gave a sharp nod of his head.

"Goodbye, my lord."

He spun on his heel as a resounding thud hit the wharf. Kit whirled to see the gangplank connecting the ship that had been her world to her new future. She glanced back at the hatch for her blue-eyed husband. No sign of him yet. Not to worry, though. He could catch up to her as easily on the dock as he could on deck.

Pressing her hat against her head with one hand, she grabbed the rope railing and descended—which was, perhaps, not one of her better ideas. Down here, it was harder to see through the great mass of bodies.

"Kit! Over here."

She lifted to her tiptoes, squinting over bowlers, bonnets, and a few kerchiefs. Sure enough, a beefy hand rose high over the crowd, arching in a big wave. Her pulse raced as fast as her feet as she dodged between two young men carrying caged chickens.

"Father!" She flung herself into his arms. The wool of his uniform tickled her nose as much as his scent of gunpowder and pork rinds.

"I have missed you, girl." He pressed a kiss to the crown of her head and released her.

"We have missed you too." Jackson's father and his brother edged sideways past a cart of gourds and pumpkins.

"Lady!" James jumped up and down, a toothy smile lighting his face.

Kit planted a kiss on each of their cheeks, her heart swelling. How good it was to belong to a family. "I am so happy to see you all." She grinned at each in turn. "And Jackson is practically beside himself to show you the new addition to our family."

Her father's jaw dropped, as did Mr. Forge's. James merely bounced back and forth from the ball of one foot to the other. Kit glanced over her shoulder to see her broad-shouldered husband trotting down the gangplank, their new little one in tow.

"Lord, have mercy," Jackson's father breathed.

Her father shook his head. "Oh, girl, what have you done?"

"Baby?" James clapped his hands. "Baby kitty!"

"And here I thought it would be a grandson," her father grumbled.

Kit frowned at both fathers. "You didn't expect. . .but of course you did." She laughed. "Honestly, can any of you truly see me as a mother of anything but a rescued tiger cub?"

"I can." Jackson stopped beside her, handing off the leash to James, who immediately dropped to his knees for some face licks. Jackson tucked her under his arm, his lips warm against her cheek as he whispered, "I think you'll make a fine mother."

Her brows rose. Never once during the past year had Jackson voiced such a thought, and though she hated to admit it, something deep inside her responded with a foreign desire. "This is the first you've mentioned it, Husband."

"It was neither seemly nor safe to think of such in the wilds of Africa, but we are home now. There is no better time." He winked.

She smirked. "It might be a girl. Think you can manage two of us?"

"Not at all." He looked down his nose at her. "But I'm willing to try, my love, and that is the best any of us can do."

Historical Notes

Mudlarking

When Mistress Mayhew tells Jackson that Kit "looked as if she were about to go mudlarking the Thames," here's what she meant. . .

A mudlark is someone who scavenges in the foreshore of a river for all manner of things that might wash up or be lodged in the silt. During the eighteenth and nineteenth centuries, *mudlark* specifically meant a person who operated on the London stretch of the Thames River. Any of the items found would be sold to make money. Mudlarking does continue today, so next time you're in London, slap on your muck boots and go snooping around for treasure.

Casual Wards

When Mr. Harpenny rescues Kit from the hole into which she'd fallen at Scampson's Warehouse, he offers to get her into a casual ward. A "casual" (or sometimes a "vagabond") is what Victorians called tramps or wayfarers. Workhouses were available for the homeless, but they were quite undesirable places to live. More like prisons, really. And a casual ward—which was part of a workhouse—was even more disagreeable. The Victorians did this on purpose so that vagrants would be motivated to find work and lodgings elsewhere. The ward generally consisted of a large room containing scant bedding (think a pile of straw with rags for blankets) and a sanitation bucket. An occupant would be required to work before leaving the following day, usually pointless jobs like breaking stones or picking oakum (old, tarred ropes and cordage salvaged from ships—it tore your fingers apart when working to separate it for reuse).

Omnibus

First appearing in 1829, the omnibus was a precursor to the trolley. These were large, enclosed, horse-drawn carriages with four windows, which traveled along a set route (like a bus route). At each stop, they picked up and dropped off passengers, who rode on benches lining each side or climbed up to sit on exposed seats up top. The driver rode at the front of the carriage with a conductor assisting and taking fares from passengers at the door at the rear. This form of transportation was popular among the middle class. Those with less funding couldn't afford the fare, and the upper classes either hired a hackney or owned their own carriage.

Hellfire Clubs

Gentlemen's clubs were all the rage in eighteenth-century London and are still in operation today. Whites, Brooks, Boodles, and many others were common places for gentlemen to gather. More notorious, though, were the hellfire clubs—which were kind of like *Fight Club* in that members did not talk about them publicly. Suffice it to say, then, that nobody really knew what went on in a hellfire club, but of course rumors abounded of all sorts of iniquity and revelry.

The first hellfire club was founded in 1719 by Philip, Duke of Wharton, and surprisingly accepted women as well. This gathering died out toward the mid-1700s, but other branches and incarnations continued well into the nineteenth century. It is said there are some branches meeting at historic educational institutions even today. . .but are they really? Who knows? No one talks about it.

Borough Market

Whenever I skip across the pond, I make it a point to stop at the Borough Market for some great meals. Believe it or not, this market has been in operation for the past thousand years. Yes, you read that correctly. It actually began as a bridge, constructed in 990. During the Victorian era, a railway viaduct was routed through the middle of the market, which brought in more people—but also more noise, soot, and disruption. This area was—and is—a popular place to shop for food.

The Elephant and Castle Gang

Lots of times I make up names, but this fun moniker truly was a criminal gang. Formed in 1820, this band of hoodlums was a collection of burglars, fences, smash-and-grab aficionados, and thugs. Their specialties ranged from hiring out muscle to bookmaking or bankrolling. A police detective of the era, George Cornish, once described them as well-educated and dapper aristocrats of crime. Often they were simply called the Elephant Boys, denoting they were all male members. Often, fathers discipled their sons into the organization.

Late Victorian Dynamite and Demolition

Dynamite was invented by Alfred Nobel (of Nobel Prize fame) in 1862. Six years later, the first full-blown (pardon the pun) factory was built to mass produce the new explosive matter. Twenty years after that, a Hungarian engineer used five blasts of dynamite to take down a two-hundred-foot chimney, which opened the door wide for the use of the explosive as a tool for demolition.

Bibliography

Bondeson, Jan. *Strange Victoriana: Tales of the Curious, the Weird and the Uncanny from Our Victorian Ancestors*. Gloucestershire: Amberley Publishing, 2018.

Emsley, Clive. *The Great British Bobby: A History of British Policing from the 18th Century to the Present*. London: Quercus, 2010.

Flanders, Judith. *The Victorian City: Everyday Life in Dickens' London*. New York: Thomas Dunne Books, 2012.

Goodman, Ruth. *How to Be a Victorian: A Dawn-to-Dusk Guide to Victorian Life*. New York: Liveright Publishing Corporation, 2014.

Haliday, Gaynor. *Victorian Policing*. South Yorkshire: Pen and Sword History, 2017.

Hawksley, Lucinda. *The Victorian Treasure: A Collection of Fascinating Facts and Insights about the Victorian Era*. London: Andre Deutsch Limited, 2015.

Long, David. *Bizarre London: Discover the Capital's Secrets & Surprises*. New York: Constable, an imprint of Little, Brown Book Group, 2019.

Paxman, Jeremy. *The Victorians*. BBC Books, 2010.

Redfern, Barry. *Victorian Villains: Prisoners from Newcastle Gaol 1871–1873*. Newcastle Upon Tyne: Tyne Bridge Publishing, 2006.

Smith, Phillip Thurmond. *Policing Victorian London: Political Policing, Public Order, and the London Metropolitan Police*. Westport, CT: Greenwood Press, 1985.

Wade, Stephen. *Plain Clothes & Sleuths: A History of Detectives in Britain*. Gloucestershire: Tempus Publishing Limited, 2007.

Acknowledgments

Another book is simply another reason to be grateful for the wonderful blessings in my life. I'll name a few, but rest assured, my friends, there are many, *many* more who hold my sweaty little palm on this writing journey.

Publishing Wizards
My books would not even be available if it weren't for Annie Tipton, my editor at Barbour. Wendy Lawton, my agent at Books & Such Literary Management, keeps me on track. Reagen Reed, my copy editor, catches all my bloopers. Ladies, I am forever in your debt.

Long-Suffering Critique Buddies
These are the women who dot my historical *i*'s and cross my plot-hole *t*'s: Tara Johnson, Julie Klassen, Lisa Ludwig, Shannon McNear, Ane Mulligan, Chawna Shroeder, Dani Snyder, MaryLu Tyndall, Erica Vetsch.

Readerly Rock Stars
So many of you read my books, but I always like to mention a few: Anita Tanc Capota, Sue Griep, Josanne Hatley, Laura "Weirick" Lecy, Michelle Pollock, and Cindy Ferreira Whitney. I've always said I have the best readers in the world, and I truly do.

My Cheerleading Friends
This is my squad, my peeps, the people in my life who put up with me and my crazy ideas and look doggone cute in a cheerleading costume: Linda Ahlmann, Stephanie Gustafson, Grant and Cheryl Higgins, Kelly Klepfer, Sal Morth, and Maria Nelson.
And last but not least, to my one and only, Mark. . .my steadfast hero.

About the Author

MICHELLE GRIEP's been writing since she first discovered blank wall space and Crayolas. She is the Christy Award–winning author of historical romances: *Lost in Darkness, The Thief of Blackfriars Lane, The House at the End of the Moor, The Noble Guardian, A Tale of Two Hearts, The Captured Bride, The Innkeeper's Daughter, 12 Days at Bleakly Manor, The Captive Heart, Brentwood's Ward, A Heart Deceived,* and *Gallimore,* but also leaped the historical fence into the realm of contemporary with the zany romantic mystery *Out of the Frying Pan.* If you'd like to keep up with her escapades, find her at www.michellegriep.com or stalk her on Facebook, Instagram, and Pinterest.

And guess what? She loves to hear from readers! Feel free to drop her a note at michellegriep@gmail.com.

Other Books by Michelle